Advance Praise for

BLOOD ENGINES

"A fast-paced, thoroughly fun, satisfying read."
—Kelley Armstrong, *New York Times* bestselling
author of *No Humans Involved*

"*Blood Engines* wastes no time: by page three I
knew I was reading an urban fantasy unlike any I'd
previously encountered—the characters and world
are real, immediate, and unapologetically in-your-
face, throwing you into a story that trusts you'll
keep up with the fast pace without flinching. It
charges along with crisp pacing, a fascinating range
of secondary characters, and a highly compelling
lead in Marla Mason. I genuinely look forward to
the next book!"
—C. E. Murphy, author of *Coyote Dreams*

"Pratt is a deft storyteller whose blend of suspense,
magic, and dry humor kept me entertained and
turning pages. *Blood Engines* is one of the most
absorbing reads I've enjoyed in a long time, gluing
me to the couch. I adore Marla, her done-at-all-
costs character is someone I can relate to and want
to cheer for. Best of all, I didn't figure the ending
out until I got there. It's a book widower, and I
can't wait for the sequel."
—Kim Harrison, *New York Times* bestselling author
of *For a Few Demons More*

BLOOD ENGINES

T. A. PRATT

BANTAM BOOKS

BLOOD ENGINES
A Bantam Spectra Book / October 2007

Published by Bantam Dell
A Division of Random House, Inc.
New York, New York

ISBN 978-0-553-58998-6

Printed in the United States of America
Published simultaneously in Canada

www.bantamdell.com

OPM   10 9 8 7 6 5 4 3 2 1

For Dawson,
my spiritual advisor and minister of war

"Stiffen the sinews, summon up the blood."
—William Shakespeare, *Henry V*

BLOOD
ENGINES

1

Marla Mason crouched in the alley beside the City Lights bookstore and threw her runes. The square of royal-purple velvet spread before her on the ground was covered by a scattering of objects—a garlic clove, a withered cigarette butt, a two-headed novelty quarter, fingernail clippings, and the stone from the head of a toad. She studied the pattern the objects made for a long time, then sighed. "It's no good. This alley isn't any better than the other two places I tried. I don't know where all the lines of force are in this city, so I can't interpret the scatter worth a damn. I thought I could triangulate, but even then it's too vague. There's something or someone of power over there"—she gestured vaguely eastward—"but I don't know if it's the guy we're looking for. I'll have to do a wet divination." The air smelled faintly of piss and coffee, but not even those familiar urban smells set Marla at ease.

Her companion, Rondeau, stood slurping rice noodles from a waxed-paper box. "I guess guts never lie," he said, prodding the noodles with his chopstick and plucking out a morsel of chicken. "What are you planning to eviscerate?"

Marla wrapped up her velvet cloth and divining tools and stowed them in a leather shoulder bag. She stretched her arms overhead until she felt her joints pop, then sighed. She'd missed her morning workout, then spent several hours cramped in cattle class during a cross-country flight, and her body was feeling uncooperative. "If I didn't have such high moral standards, I'd do a human, just because it's more accurate. Then again, this isn't *my* city, so it's not like I have a responsibility to protect these people." She was kidding, of course. Murder for mystical purposes incurred a nasty karmic debt, and it was wasteful besides. There were better uses for people. "I don't know. A cat, maybe. Or a chicken. Nothing too advanced. I doubt Lao Tsung is trying to hide from me."

"Why do we have to look for him anyway? Why didn't you let him know we were coming?" Rondeau wiggled his fingers around his left ear. "Ever hear of a telephone?"

Marla snorted. "He's not the kind of person who has a phone number. There are ways to get messages to him, but it would take a few days, and there wasn't time for that. I'm in a hurry."

"I gathered that," Rondeau said, wiping his mouth with a wad of napkins. "I think my first clue was when you busted into my place, told me to pack a bag, hauled ass to the airport, and hustled me onto a plane. You didn't even let me sit by the window." His tone was aggrieved. "My first time on a plane, and you stick me in the middle beside a fat guy with sweat stains. He was *smelly*."

"Oh, you noticed that, too? I think it's your keen powers of observation I value most."

"You know, I kept hoping you'd volunteer the information, but since you *aren't*—what are we doing in San Francisco? What's so important that you have to see this guy Lao Tsung right *now*? And why did you need *me* to come?"

Marla considered. She and Rondeau had saved each other's lives far more often than they'd threatened them. Keeping secrets was a useful habit, and deeply ingrained, but it paid to remember she did have a few allies she could count on. "It's Susan Wellstone," she said, and found herself reaching almost superstitiously for the comfort of the daggers up her sleeves.

Rondeau's eyes widened. "Really? Her? Of all the movers and shakers in Felport, I never thought she'd be the one to move on you. Gregor, maybe, or Viscarro..." He tossed his empty noodle carton in a garbage can.

Marla shook her head. "Gregor would stab me in the back if I ever gave him the chance, and Viscarro will be there to steal the jewels and gold fillings off whatever corpse falls first, but Susan's the only one willing to *make* an opportunity, instead of just waiting for one. She knows that if she loses, I'll destroy her. But she's a perfectionist. She doesn't intend to lose. She means to overthrow me."

Rondeau frowned. "So why isn't she hanging upside down in a vat of acid right now? What are we doing on the other side of the continent? You can't be running away."

"I better not have heard a little upward lilt at the

end of that last sentence, Rondeau," Marla said, crossing her arms. "I know you weren't *asking* if I'm running away."

Rondeau held up his hands. "I know better. I've seen you duck from the occasional social obligation, but never a fight."

"Yeah, well." Marla ran her hand through her short hair, bits of scalp flaking away. She'd never had dandruff in her twenties. Getting older had its advantages, but dandruff wasn't one of them. "This isn't a fight I can win, not head-on. Susan's planning to cast a spell to get rid of me, but she hasn't thought through all the implications, and her spell's going to wind up wrecking my city, too. I can respect her desire to kill me—she wants my position, and she knows I'm not about to retire anytime soon—but I can't forgive her for risking Felport."

"So Lao Tsung can help you stop Susan's spell?"

"Lao Tsung knows where to find something that *can* help me. The Cornerstone. But don't go throwing that around to the local sorcerers."

"Ah," Rondeau said. "An artifact? I hate artifacts. *Things* shouldn't look at you, and that old weird stuff always seems to be paying attention."

"I thought you liked attention."

Rondeau rolled his eyes. "We're under a time limit here?"

"One that gets shorter every minute we stand here talking. Have I satisfied your curiosity? Can I get on with saving my city and my life now?"

"You never told me why *I'm* here. You could've left me behind with Hamil to, like, muster the defenses or something. You might be the first one up against the wall when the revolution comes, but Hamil and I won't be far behind."

"It's . . . not like that," Marla said. Explaining the nature of Susan's spell would be too complicated, and it wasn't something she was comfortable thinking about, beyond taking the measures necessary to thwart it. "Besides, I need you here to lift heavy things, guard doorways, and deal with any other shit I'm too busy to bother with."

Rondeau grinned. "A man likes to feel useful. Lead on."

"Do you think we can find a live chicken around here?"

"Maybe if we search high and low." They set off toward the hanging paper lanterns, pagoda store-fronts, and crowded afternoon sidewalks of Chinatown.

"I don't know why Lao Tsung decided to live in this shithole quakemeat city," Marla said. "He came here to find the Cornerstone, but then he *stayed*."

Rondeau grunted. "We've only been in San Francisco for an hour. You hate it already?"

Marla spat on the street. "Pretty white city by the bay, my ass."

"Don't forget 'cool, gray city of love.' "

"Yeah, I feel the love," Marla said, stepping over a pile of dirty stuffed animals someone had left on the sidewalk.

"I think it's nice. You're just jealous because we don't have cable cars back home." He glanced up a side street. "Not that I've seen a cable car yet."

"It's January," Marla said. "There should be snow

in January. A little fog is no substitute. I feel out of place. Far from my center."

"Well, yeah. It was, what, your second time on an airplane? I thought you were going to strangle random strangers during the layover in Denver. Haven't you ever taken a vacation?"

Marla laughed, and Rondeau nodded. "Me neither. This is my first one."

"This isn't a vacation. It's a matter—"

"Of life, death, and destruction, I know. That doesn't mean I can't take in the sights, right? What's the point of staying alive if you don't live a little?" They entered the closely packed streets of Chinatown, where off-season tourists wandered among the food stalls and the stores, picking through wares spilling out onto the sidewalks. There were tanks full of tightly packed wriggling fish, and wooden crates filled with strange fruit. The street signs had both English names and Chinese characters, and there were lots of fanciful architectural touches—faux pagodas made of wood on top of buildings, gold-painted facades, bamboo fences. "I love this place," Rondeau said. "There's nothing like this back home."

"Because our city never had a ghetto for underpaid, persecuted immigrant Chinese laborers in the 19th century," Marla said.

"I suspect San Francisco won't be offering you a position as a tour guide anytime soon."

"I distrust, on principle, any city that encourages me to leave my heart behind when I go." Marla abruptly stopped walking, and Rondeau almost bumped into her. "Hmm, there it is again."

"What?"

She waved her hands. "Whatever the divination was indicating. A field, a hum, a vibration. Something. Not far from here."

"I don't hear any hum," Rondeau said.

"Come on, it's this way."

"Ah," Rondeau said, following her down the block. "Might I suggest that we, say, *ignore* whatever magical you-don't-know-what we're now moving toward? Why borrow trouble?"

"I cause trouble, I don't stumble into it." Not precisely true, but the plane flight—and the *necessity* of flight—had made her cranky, and she'd always had a curious streak anyway. "Besides, maybe this magical something-or-other is what I'm looking for, the Cornerstone, and I won't need to find Lao Tsung at all."

"Right," Rondeau said. "Because we're in a Charles Dickens novel, and coincidences like that actually happen."

After about a block of walking, Marla stopped. "There."

"What? It's just a booth selling bootleg Jackie Chan videos— Oh. You mean *that*."

There was a folded space there, between a tea shop and one of the area's many jewelry stores—Marla could just see the shimmer. If there was a shop inside that shimmer, it wasn't one meant for ordinary tourists. "Want to go in?"

"I thought you just wanted to buy a chicken and find a nice quiet alley to scoop out its guts. Why do you want to mess with the local mojo?"

"Lao Tsung is a sorcerer," Marla said reasonably. "Maybe another sorcerer will know where to find him."

"Sorcerers are all at least half crazy by definition," Rondeau said. "Present company excepted. So what if we get, like, *attacked*?"

Marla shrugged. Being attacked wouldn't be so bad. Right now, loath as she was to admit it, she was *afraid*. A fight would at least take her mind off Susan's plot, flood her with adrenaline, and give her a work-out—physical or metaphysical, either would be welcome. "If we're attacked, try not to get in the way."

"I bet this will be just like *Big Trouble in Little China*," Rondeau said. "Weird herbs everywhere, stuffed alligators hanging from the ceiling, and a guy shooting lightning bolts out of his eyes."

"I'm trying to decide if that was racist or not."

"What?" Rondeau said. "Me, or the movie?"

Marla ignored him, glancing around. There were people watching her, of course, or at least looking in her direction—it was a busy street. Ah, well. Fuck it. She grabbed Rondeau's wrist and slipped around a table of bootleg videos, into a folded place in the world. Into a sorcerer's den.

They emerged into a large room with a décor halfway between herb shop and high-tech. The floors, walls, and ceiling were pristine white, with subtle curves instead of hard-angled corners, and tall dark wood shelves butted up against one another at strange (and probably occultishly significant) angles, crammed with tins, bottles, jars, and plastic bags, most of which appeared to be filled with various kinds of dried vegetable matter. Marla wasn't interested in herbal magic—she'd never bothered overmuch with any herbs you couldn't grow in a container on a fire escape or find sprouting wild in a railroad yard. The air should have been a riot of odors, but there was a curious neutrality of odor instead, with just a hint of the antiseptic.

A long stainless-steel counter stretched the length of the back wall. A concealed door behind the counter swung open, and an elderly Asian gentleman in a dark robe emerged, followed by a far less graceful young man, presumably an apprentice. Marla caught a brief glimpse of the space behind the door, where someone lay naked on an examining table, red welts across his skin.

The door swung shut, and Marla turned her attention to the men behind the counter. The apprentice was actually a woman, dressed in boy-drag. She'd done an excellent job, but when Marla first moved to Felport, she'd found work waitressing at various bars in the less-than-respectable part of town, and still had a good eye for costume. She *was* in San Francisco, where drag was king, so she probably shouldn't be surprised. Odds were the old guy was the master, and the young girl was either apprentice or servant. The old man spoke to her in Chinese—Cantonese, probably, the prevailing dialect in Chinatown—but Marla shook her head.

"Nope, sorry. I can do English and I can get by in French, and my friend here can speak Spanish and knows a few swear words in a language that predates the fall of Babel, but neither of us can speak any kind of Chinese."

"What do you want?" the girl asked, in clear, unaccented English.

Marla looked at the master. He was expressionless,

but she suspected he could understand English as well as the girl could. "I need information."

The old man shook his head and bowed a fraction of a degree.

"We sell herbs, not information," the apprentice said. She was trying to watch both Marla and Rondeau, which was difficult, as Rondeau had begun absentmindedly wandering around the shop, prodding at things.

"I'm looking for a man named Lao Tsung," Marla said.

The old man sniffed. The apprentice sneered, no longer pretending to be polite. "And you think all Chinese people know one another?"

Marla rolled her eyes. "Look, where I'm from, we keep track of all the important sorcerers who come around. Lao Tsung's been living in the city for years, and he's got power. He's not actually Chinese anyway. He's a very long-lived Mesopotamian, if that makes you feel any better. I figured you might know where he is, that's all. If you can't help me . . ."

The old man looked meditatively at the ceiling. "One thousand dollars," he said, his English crisp and faintly British. "That is the price of the information you seek."

Marla frowned. "Look, I could cut open a chicken and stir around its guts and find Lao Tsung—I've got the gift of haruspexy. I just thought it would be less bloody to ask the locals. I don't want to step on any toes, I just want to do my business and leave."

"Haruspexy will not work. Try it if you want, but don't come back after. Already you waste our time. One thousand dollars."

Marla sighed and called Rondeau over.

He was holding half the money, which was perhaps a mistake, but he'd insisted. If Marla died in an earthquake, he'd said, how would he afford to get home? He gave the bills to Marla, and she passed them on to the apprentice, who examined them and nodded.

"Lao Tsung is dead," the old man said, without apparent pleasure.

"Bullshit," Marla said. "He's been alive for *centuries,* he came here specifically to get his cancer healed, and it worked. How can he be *dead*?"

"The answer to that question will cost one thousand dollars."

Marla was over the counter before the old man could even step back, pressing a dagger into his belly. He opened his mouth—presumably to loose some spell—and Marla shoved a wad of cash between his teeth, silencing him. "As you can see, it's not about the money. I just don't like having my time wasted. And Lao Tsung was a friend."

The apprentice was speaking quietly to herself, and Marla sighed. "Rondeau?"

"Yup," he said, and drew his butterfly knife, flipping it open with the ease bred of a lifetime on—and under—the streets. "Okay, so be quiet, or I'll have to cut your throat or something, and I just got this suit, so that would suck for both of us."

The apprentice stopped talking. "You are not sorcerers," she said. "You are thugs."

"There's a time and a place for magic," Marla said, "but it's a bad idea to get too dependent on the abracadabras." She returned her attention to the old man, who did not look terrified, or angry, or anything at all;

his expression was impossible to interpret. "I'm going to take this money out of your mouth, and give it to your apprentice, and then you'll consider yourself paid in full, and tell me everything I need to know about Lao Tsung, okay? And if you get itchy for revenge, let me tell you who I am—I'm Marla Mason. I run the city of Felport, and if you haven't heard of me before...well, I can make a name for myself on this coast by doing something incredibly nasty to you. But like I said, I just want to do my business and be on my way. Agreed?"

The old man nodded.

Marla took the wad of paper from his mouth and handed it to the assistant, who began straightening the cash on the counter, spreading the bills out, smoothing the wrinkles, making piles. The master must be a disciplinarian son of a bitch, Marla thought. "So," she said. "Lao Tsung."

The old man mumbled something in Chinese.

"As we told you, Lao Tsung is dead," the apprentice said, without looking up from the money, apparently unconcerned with Rondeau and his knife. "He was killed this morning by frogs."

Marla repeated those words to herself—"killed this morning by frogs"—considering the possibility that it was some idiom translating badly. "He was killed by French people?" she said at last, frowning.

The apprentice looked at her, bored. "No. By *frogs*. Hop, hop? Frogs. Lao Tsung lived in Golden Gate Park, and he was discovered this morning covered by small golden frogs. The frogs hopped away, and no one tried to stop them—we assume they are poisonous. There are frogs in the rain forests venomous enough to kill a hundred men."

"What, they bite? I didn't even know frogs had teeth."

"No, they are just filled with poison, and sometimes their bodies sweat poison. The natives use frog venom to poison their spears, and have done so for centuries. But to find so many frogs, so virulently poisonous, *here,* in this climate, where it is far too cold and dry for them to live long..." The apprentice shook her head. "It is a mystery." She finished counting the money, and swept all the cash into a single pile and put it under the counter. "My master is an expert on toxicology, among other things, and we have been commissioned by certain parties to determine the nature of Lao Tsung's death, and to discover if it was the work of another sorcerer or simply a strange happening."

"I want to see his body," Marla said. If Lao Tsung's body was here, haruspexy *wouldn't* have worked—places like this, in folded space, tended to scramble the effectiveness of divination. Which made her wonder what her divination *had* been pointing toward. There must be something else, or someone else, with big magic nearby.

The master spoke briefly in Chinese, and the apprentice nodded. "I will show you his body," she said.

Marla chewed her lip. The master seemed cowed, but he could still be dangerous. It couldn't hurt to separate him from his apprentice. "Rondeau, keep an eye on the old guy. And I *mean* it. Watch him."

Rondeau sighed and nodded. "Listen, sir, I don't want to hurt you, but I've got this knife, and if it comes down to it, I have other resources, too. But I'd rather we just chatted while they're in the back, you know? I've never been here before, so I want to know about good restaurants and sightseeing, stuff like that. And if you decide you don't want to speak English anymore, we can take turns making comical animal noises at each other."

The old man just stared, expressionless.

Marla let the apprentice lead the way into the back room, where the dead body that used to be her friend Lao Tsung lay on a table. He didn't look any older than forty, his black hair in a long ponytail, his body lean and sinewy. Killed by a swarm of frogs. Swarm? Herd? "What do you call a bunch of frogs?" Marla asked. "It's a murder of crows, a pod of whales, like that, so what are frogs?"

"A colony," the apprentice said. "Sometimes a knot. Sometimes an army. I think, in this case, an army. You may examine the body—you may do anything you wish, you've made that clear—but I would advise you not to touch it with your bare hands. We do not know the exact nature or the extent of the poison."

Marla nodded and stepped closer to Lao Tsung. What a way to die. At least it was unusual.

Then Lao Tsung's mouth opened.

A tiny golden frog, no more than an inch and a half long, hopped out of Lao Tsung's mouth, and sat on his chest. It was a beautiful little frog—black eyes, skin almost shiny. Lao Tsung's flesh began to turn red, until the place where the frog sat sported a welt as big as the others on his body.

Then the frog jumped.

* * *

After standing in silence for a while, and not hearing anything much from the back room, Rondeau said, "So is the Alcatraz tour worth doing? Marla says it's probably ghost-choked and psychically unsettling, but I think it'd be interesting. You ever been there? Or are you like those New Yorkers who've never been to the Statue of Liberty, you don't do the tourist thing?"

The master turned, slightly, and glanced toward the door to the back room. Rondeau waved his knife around a bit. "Hey, eyes front."

"Help me," the master whispered. "Please."

Rondeau narrowed his eyes. "There's no point in trying to mind-fuck me. I don't have any authority. I'm just here to carry stuff around, run errands, and keep Marla company."

"I am not the master," the master said. He trembled. "I am the apprentice. My master told me I would be his successor, heir to all his treasures, but it was a cruel joke. He stole my body, and trapped my mind in his own. In *this*." He raised his arms in disgust, then let them drop.

"Ah, shit," Rondeau said. "He pulled a Thing on the Doorstep trick on you, that's what you're telling me?"

Rondeau flipped his knife open and closed, thinking. If this was true, Marla was in the back with a real sorcerer, one who was skilled and nasty enough to switch bodies with someone. Something like that, a meta-rape, incurred a serious karmic debt, but sorcerers powerful and unscrupulous enough to achieve the trick usually had ways to avoid paying the price for such monstrous acts. But if Rondeau went rushing back there to warn Marla, then the *real* master might do something bad, which Marla wouldn't be prepared for. And if this old guy was *lying*, Rondeau would have turned his back on the sorcerer Marla had told him to watch. "Shit," he said. No course of action seemed like a good one. "Okay, I've got this knife ready to slip under your breastbone, so just start backing up. We're going to ease into the back room and you can tell your story to Marla."

The old man whimpered. "If my master finds out that I told you, he will kill this body. He has only left me alive to keep up appearances until he is ready to announce himself as his own successor. What he has done is a crime, and the council of sorcerers would not allow him to go unpunished."

Rondeau hesitated. But his loyalty had to be to Marla. "Sorry," he said. "If you're telling the truth, we'll try to help you." Maybe that was going too far, since Marla probably wouldn't give a shit about the hijacked apprentice, but Rondeau would help, if he could. "I have to protect Marla, and that means letting her know what she might be dealing with."

The master bowed his head and began to shuffle backwards toward the door.

The frog jumped straight for the apprentice, who threw up her hands and spoke a stream of slippery words. The frog stopped in midair, dangling at roughly shoulder-level, kicking its legs.

"Nice bug-in-amber spell," Marla said. "I don't know many apprentices who can do that to anything bigger than a mosquito."

"Thank you," the apprentice said. "Your compliment honors me." She went to a shelf and took down a small glass jar, then put on a pair of heavy rubber gloves. She slipped the jar over the hanging frog and screwed the top on.

"You'd better poke some air holes in the lid if you don't want the frog to die," Marla said.

"I do not object to the frog's death."

The tiny frog hopped around inside the jar, trying to scrabble up the sides of the glass. Marla peered in at the little poison beast. It was a golden, almost metallic, yellow, without any markings at all. "So that's what killed Lao Tsung, huh? With a little help from his friends. Do you have any idea who might have unleashed the frogs?"

The apprentice frowned. "Our investigation is ongoing—"

"Please. We're all friends. I'm not here to be a vigilante, or get revenge. I'm just . . . curious."

The apprentice nodded, curtly. "Lao Tsung was seen yesterday in a conversation with a man who is unknown to us, an . . . eccentric stranger. The conversation apparently became quite heated. The man appeared to be Central or South American, and was clothed only in his underwear and some sort of cape. It is possible that he was simply an insane person, shouting as the deranged sometimes do. There have always been mad people in this city, even before *you* arrived."

"Stop, you'll hurt my feelings," Marla said. Even if she had time for vigilantism, that description wasn't much to go on. She looked down at Lao Tsung's body. She might have touched his cheek with her fingers, but she couldn't, because of the poison. There was no time to deal with these emotions. Her life, and the safety of her city, were on the line now. Without Lao Tsung to tell her the location of the Cornerstone, she had no idea where to go from here. She didn't have any other contacts in this city. She sighed. "When in doubt, start at the top."

"I beg your pardon?" the apprentice said.

"I need to talk to the person who runs San Francisco."

The apprentice sniffed. "That is not the way we do things here. My master is the most senior sorcerer in Chinatown. North Beach is run by a strega named Umbaldo. Russian Hill, the Haight, the Financial District, the Mission, the Tenderloin, they all have their own leaders."

"No shit," Marla said. "Imagine that. You think the city I come from is one homogenous mass? I bet you guys have some sort of council, right, some way to resolve disputes?"

"Of course," the apprentice said.

"And that means *somebody* has supreme authority, right?"

The apprentice pinched her lips together. "Yes. But it is an *office,* not an individual. The strongest sorcerers pass the duties from one to another, each serving for a few years."

"What a fascinating civics lesson. Who's in charge *now*?" The apprentice frowned and didn't answer. "The sooner you tell me," Marla said, "the sooner I leave you alone, and get my business done, and get off this coast entirely. Okay?"

"His name is Finch," she said. "He runs the Castro."

"How do I find him?"

"He is . . . not so easy to find. But he has parties, every Friday. They begin at nine or ten, though he is not always there in the beginning. I am told he usually arrives by midnight, when things are at their busiest."

"That's tonight," Marla said. "Great. Show me where he lives." She grabbed a pen and folded map of San Francisco from her bag. The apprentice peered at the map for a moment, then said, "On this street." Marla wrote down the street name and the number.

"Will you be at the party?" Marla said.

The apprentice shook her head. "My master does not approve of such activities. They are beneath his dignity."

Marla nodded. "Listen, I'm not here to piss anyone off. I just want to do my business and get out of town. Let your master know that. Tell him he never has to see me again, and that I appreciate the help."

"My master respects strength," she said. "But, as you dislike being made to wait, he dislikes being bullied. It would be best for you to complete your business and leave the city as soon as possible, or my master may feel it necessary to take action against you."

"I always did have a knack for making enemies," Marla said. "I'll be leaving now."

The door opened, and the master backed in, Rondeau guiding him. "Hey, Marla," he said.

"You can let our gracious host go, Rondeau. We've got what we need."

Rondeau blinked. "Um, well, but—"

"Save it. We're going." She took his arm and

tugged him through the door after her. "Pull the door closed. I don't want to turn my back on them."

Rondeau did as she said, and then Marla ran for the exit, Rondeau following close behind.

When they got outside—almost knocking down a few pedestrians in their headlong rush out of thin air—Marla hurried along the street, putting distance between the shop and herself. She glanced back, feeling distinctly that she was being followed, but the apprentice and her master were nowhere to be seen. Probably just nerves. Who else besides those two would *want* to follow her here?

"Marla, I'm trying to *tell* you something," Rondeau said.

"Tell me over dinner," she said. "We've got a few hours to kill, and I think I saw an Italian restaurant earlier."

"Well. Yes. I imagine you did. We were in North Beach, after all. Don't you know *anything* about San Francisco?"

"Cable cars. Golden Gate Bridge. Fog. Hills. Gay pride. If you're coming here, wear some flowers in your hair. That's the gist, right?"

"You do have a way of stripping things down to their essentials," Rondeau said. "But, seriously—*listen*."

Across the bay, in Oakland, San Francisco's looked-down-upon stepsister, a former movie actor named Bradley Bowman—or just "B" to his friends, most of whom were dead or had conveniently lost touch with him—sat in a trash-strewn, weed-choked vacant lot, dropping Valiums into a sewer grate, one pill at a time. "I had one of *those* dreams," he said. "I was standing under an overpass. Frogs rained from the sky, and some of them hopped under the overpass with me. A man in an old-fashioned beaver hat stood half in shadow by a pillar, watching me, and when I waved at him, he nodded. There were hummingbirds flying around my head, moving almost too fast to see. A woman in a purple cloak came out of the shadows, stepping on frogs as she walked, and then she tried to kiss me. When her lips touched mine, I found myself wrapped up in a cocoon, and I didn't know what I was going to transform into. What does it mean?"

After a moment, something spoke from beneath the sewer grate. It talked for a long time, its voice lazy and relaxed.

"Shit," B said. "Is there anything I can do to prevent it?"

The voice spoke again, more briefly this time.

B sighed. "Guess I have to, then. Damn. I hate going into the city."

The voice from below murmured.

"Don't," B said. "Please. Coming here, talking to you . . . this is hard enough without stirring up all those old memories." He stood, slung his battered knapsack over his shoulder, and trudged toward home, lost in the fog of the past.

2

I'm impressed, Marla. I was sure you'd check us into some fleabag in the Tenderloin."

Marla glanced over. Rondeau stood on the balcony of their suite in a posh hotel near Union Square, beneath the darkening sky. He seemed happy and relaxed, and for an irrational instant, she was furious with him—didn't he understand how *serious* things were? But of course he didn't, not really. Because she hadn't told him. Marla's life was threatened on a regular basis, and he probably thought this was just more of the same, an ordinary assassination plot. She hadn't elaborated, because she was ashamed of the position she'd let Susan put her in. Marla had never thought the woman was a real threat, and was paying the price for her carelessness now. She forced herself to answer him calmly. "The Tenderloin? Is that the meatpacking district?" She emptied her capacious leather bag onto the bed and started spreading things out.

"I don't think San Francisco has a meatpacking district. But it's the seedy part of town, lots of strip clubs, bars, stuff like that. Seems like more of your kind of place."

"I don't like going into strange dark alleys any more than you do, Rondeau. Back home, I *know* the dark alleys, and I know I'm the most dangerous thing that's likely to be walking up and down in them. Now that I've pissed off one of the big local sorcerers—who's maybe a body-jumper, if what the old man told you is true—I plan to stay out of the shadows as much as possible. But you're right, I wouldn't have picked this hotel. I let Hamil make reservations for me. He thinks room service is humanity's greatest achievement."

Rondeau wandered in from the balcony. "Do you think Hamil can keep a lid on things back home, keep Susan from casting her spell right away?"

"I hope so. They used to be friends, though she doesn't completely trust him since he became my consiglieri. But I've got one advantage. Susan thinks she's still acting in secret. She doesn't know that *I* know her plans—I've got an informant on her staff—so maybe Hamil can stall her until I find the Cornerstone. I told him to do whatever's necessary to distract her."

Rondeau frowned. "What, you mean, like, sleep with her?"

"Conspire with her to overthrow me was more what I had in mind." She shrugged. "Everybody knows I'm tough to work for, so maybe she'll believe he's willing to betray me."

"Are you worried about her, Marla?" Rondeau said, pointedly not looking at her, riffling through a neighborhood dining guide that came with the room.

"Susan, I mean. How bad is this, on a scale of pretty bad to catastrophe?"

Marla thought about how to answer that. She was doing her best not to dwell on the threat that hung over her, just to *deal* with it, but the fact was, she was frightened. She couldn't remember the last time she'd been frightened when she wasn't in actual physical danger. "If I can't stop Susan from casting the spell she has planned, it's going to be beyond catastrophe. Her plans are dangerous enough that I'd just assassinate her, if I could, and you *know* I don't like messing with the balance of power that openly."

"So why *don't* you?" Rondeau said. "Maybe coming here and finding the Cornerstone seemed like an elegant solution this morning, but since it's turned out to be more complicated than expected, maybe we should fly back home and gear up for battle."

"I wish I could. Susan has defenses. At the first sign of danger, she'd go deep into the basement of that skyscraper she owns—and the basement goes down even farther than the building goes *up,* from what I've heard—and fill every doorway and passage with traps, mercenaries, and thugs. It would take *days* to break through, and by then, it'll be too late. I just found out this morning about the spell Susan has in mind, and she's going to cast it in a day or two. I can't kill her in time to stop it. She knows she can't take me out head-on, so she's spent the past year preparing a big magic to wipe me out for good. I can't combat her spell, not on such short notice, unless I find the Cornerstone—I can use its powers to protect myself. But after I find the Cornerstone, yeah, we'll go back home and wipe out Susan. She's gone too far this time. I have better things to do than engage in all-out war, but she's left me no choice."

Rondeau sat in the swivel office chair by the desk and began spinning around. "So now that Lao Tsung is dead, you're planning on asking San Francisco's big boss where to find the Cornerstone?"

"Sure. Might as well start at the top."

"If some hotshot out-of-towners came to *our* city, and came up to *you,* and started asking about some big magical artifact, would you help them?"

"Doubtful," Marla said. "I don't think they'd be as persuasive as I can be." She took a long, ornately carved teak box from the bottom of her bag and set it on the bed. She touched several particular places on the intricate carving, and the lid popped open, revealing the carefully folded piece of fabric resting inside. Marla removed it and shook out the wrinkles. It was a cloak, dazzlingly white on one side and bruise-dark purple on the other. A cloak pin in the shape of a stag beetle was attached to the collar.

"Damn," Rondeau said, reverently, his spinning stopped. "You haven't worn that in ages."

Marla held the cloak at arm's length, examining it, then shook her head. "It misses me. It misses being *used.* But I was never sure, wearing it, whether I was using *it* or it was using *me.* It's big magic, and that always comes with a price, or an agenda." The cloak made her into a formidable killing machine, and she'd used it often during her rise to power, but each use exacted a price in her own humanity. Not in some touchy-feely guilt-and-regret way, but literally—for a short time after she wore the cloak, Marla lost her human emotion, committing atrocities without hesitation if they advanced her goals. During that period of inhumanity, she felt as if she shared her body with a cold, alien intelligence that wanted to take over her life. Each time she wore the cloak, that alien intelligence lingered in her head a little longer, and became stronger. If she'd continued using the cloak regularly, she had no doubt that its intelligence would have eventually supplanted her own completely, forcing her mind and humanity down forever. She'd given up using the cloak, but she'd kept it, of course, because it was too valuable to let go. Marla had only brought the cloak here because her life was in danger, and she couldn't ignore any advantage that might save her. She prayed she wouldn't have to use the cloak, and hoped that its influence had waned in the years since she'd used it last. "Just holding it makes me want to put it on again," she said. "Even though I don't like what I become when I wear it."

Rondeau rubbed his jaw, and Marla looked away. There weren't many things in her life she was ashamed of—in her line of work, shame could be a fatal emotion—but a long time ago she'd done something terrible to Rondeau during the cold, inhuman time that followed the use of the cloak. When Rondeau was just a boy, Marla had ripped off his jawbone and kept it in a jar to use as an oracle. A few years ago, when Rondeau had more or less saved Marla's life, she'd returned the jaw to him. It was too small to be put back on his body, even by a magical surgeon, and he'd long since acquired a new jaw anyway, but having it back had comforted him. It had also secured him as an ally, and no matter how honest the gesture had been, Marla was always aware of the advantage to be had from her kindness. She never stopped figuring out the percentages. That was why, even though she had a reputation as a ruthlessly straightforward, point-A-to-point-B strategist, she'd maintained her position as the most capable chief of sorcerers her city had ever known.

Marla folded the cloak and put it on the bed. She took a long, straight-bladed dagger from the bottom of the box, the hilt wrapped with alternating bands of purple and white electrical tape. "And your dagger of office," Rondeau said. "You're planning on going in heavy, aren't you?"

Marla admired the knife for a moment, then slid it into a simple black leather boot-sheath. The dagger was quite sharp, a handy close-quarters weapon, but it could also cut through the immaterial. Marla could carve up ghosts with that knife, cut off astral travelers from their bodies, and make smoke-demons bleed. Hamil had told her that, according to legend, the blade had been made from a shard of the Angel of Death's sword. The cloak was Marla's personal property, but the dagger only belonged to her while she served as custodian of Felport—it was a weapon of office, passed from one chief sorcerer to another. Though it was seldom passed on willingly.

"You know I believe in choosing the right weapon for a particular job," she said. "But I wasn't quite sure what this job might entail, so I brought everything I thought might be useful. The only two bona-fide magical artifacts I own."

"The only two artifacts I've ever even *seen*," Rondeau said. "It's not like you can pick them up at garage sales."

Actually, sometimes you could—she'd found the cloak in a thrift store—but Marla didn't correct him. She sank down in an overstuffed armchair by the mini-bar and crossed her legs. "So now we wait."

Rondeau looked at her, then at the nonexistent watch on his wrist, then back at her. "Marla, it's only like seven at night, and this party doesn't start until ten. You just want to *sit* for three hours?"

She frowned. "There's a gym in the hotel, but it's all ... shiny." Marla normally worked out at a boxing club, all duct-tape-mended heavy bags and industrial gray paint, air dense with the smell of sweat. "I could use a workout, but I saw a woman in there wearing a leotard, and if she tried to talk to me about her body-fat percentage, I might do something I'd regret."

"I'm not suggesting you go work out, Marla."

"Then, what? We already ate. You can't be hungry again, but if you are, there's always room service." Marla disapproved of room service—the profit margin for the hotel was too high, and she always felt like a mark when she ordered—but it was better than hearing Rondeau bitch.

"No, I'm not hungry, either. But I've never been out of our city, do you realize that? I grew up in the streets, and then I took over the nightclub, and I've been working for you ever since. Today was my first time on an *airplane*. Now here we are, in the jewel of the West Coast, and I want to walk around, enjoy the evening, do some sightseeing, eat sourdough bread, and ride a cable car, you know?"

"So go."

"Come with me!"

She sighed. "I'm supposed to be here *working*."

Rondeau grinned. "So call it reconnaissance, if that makes you feel better. You told me when you first moved to our city, you spent two weeks doing nothing but walking around, getting a sense of the borders and the order, finding escape routes, putting a street-level map of the place in your head. Why not do the same thing here?"

"I'm not planning on *living* here. Or even staying here."

"But suppose things go spectacularly badly with Finch tonight, and we have to stay longer to work things out. It might be nice to have a sense of the place."

Marla tapped her foot. She was likely to go stir-crazy if she just sat here, it was true. "Fine, let's go."

Rondeau rubbed his hands together. "It's not *that* late yet. Too late to go to Alcatraz or take a cable car tour, probably, but we can maybe hit Fisherman's Wharf, or—"

"Let's just go downstairs, step out into the streets, and walk. See where that takes us."

Rondeau sighed. "As long as we don't wind up someplace that sucks." He put on a black linen suit with a black shirt and declared himself ready to go.

Out on the well-lit street, Marla set off confidently in a random direction, walking briskly along the sidewalk. "Hold up, Marla," Rondeau said. "You got somewhere to be?"

She slowed down, stopped, sighed. "I'm not good at sightseeing, Rondeau. Maybe we should try to find Finch right away. Beat it out of somebody." Every passing hour gnawed at her. She had at least a day before Susan's spell was ready, probably longer with

Hamil trying to contact her and interrupting her meditations, but who could be sure?

Rondeau rolled his eyes. "We *know* where to find Finch. It's only three hours, and that's hardly enough time to beat anybody, even if we knew who to beat. A little patience won't kill you. Tell you what, let *me* lead."

Marla shrugged, then nodded. Rondeau grinned. "All right, this way. Union Square is a prime shopping district, from what I hear. Maybe a little too yuppie for us, but hey, look at it like an anthropological expedition. And if—when—you totally hate that, we can go over to Yerba Buena Gardens, the Metreon, all kinds of good shit."

"How do you know so much about this place?" Marla said.

"Hamil gave me some guidebooks and maps before we got on the plane. I read them all while you were sleeping. Speaking of which, I was surprised that a control freak like you, no offense, managed to sleep on the plane."

She shrugged. "I knew I might not be able to sleep tonight, so it seemed prudent. And if the airplane crashes, I'm dead anyway, so why not relax? Besides, I did have my cloak in my carry-on. As long as I had a little bit of warning, I could have put it on and saved myself."

"Letting me go splat?"

Marla stopped outside Crate & Barrel and peered into the window. "What the hell?" she muttered. "Kitchen chairs? Wineglasses? I thought it was going to be a warehouse supply store."

"And so the disillusionment begins. But seriously—you would've saved yourself and let me die?"

She glared at him. Sometimes he was worse than a boyfriend. "Rondeau, in a situation where I could save both of us, I would. In a situation where I could save only one of us, it would be *me*. And before you get all dramatic on me, about how you'd sacrifice your life for me and all that shit, *you* wouldn't die under the same circumstances. If our plane crashed, the body you're wearing would die, and your mind would have to float around for a while until you found a new body, but that's all. If you tried to take over *my* body I'd spit you out like a watermelon seed, by the way."

Rondeau raised his hands, wincing. He didn't like to be reminded of his essential nature. He could pass for human, and his body *was* human, but the soul, spirit, ka, or *whatever* inside that body was something else again, something even Rondeau himself barely understood. "Okay. Point taken. Though we don't know for sure if that's what would happen. I took control of this body when it was, what, six years old? And I don't have any real memories before that. I don't *know* what I am. Even Hamil just says I'm a 'parasitic psychic entity.' Maybe when this body dies, I die with it."

Marla shrugged. "That's the same deal all the rest of us are stuck with. Even Lao Tsung died, and I thought he'd outlive the sun. Killed by *frogs*. He should never have stayed in this city. I can't wait to get out of here."

"Speaking of Lao Tsung...what do you think about the old Chinese guy and his apprentice? I know you don't want to do anything to help them, but let's say *I* did. Where would I start?"

"You want me to tell you how to oust one psyche and reinstate another? Like it's any of our business anyway! Come on, Rondeau—surely you have some sympathy for the old guy. You've done the Thing on the Doorstep trick yourself, and the poor kid whose body *you* took didn't even get a shitty old body to replace his young one."

Rondeau stopped walking. "Fuck you, Marla. I'm *nothing* like that old prick. I was floating around, disembodied, with no memories, no sense of self, nothing. I saw—and that's not even the right word, I didn't see like I'm seeing you right now—some little street kid in an alley, and I drifted down and settled over him like mist, or I slithered in through his nose, or I put him on like a suit, I don't *know,* I can't *describe* it. I didn't do it on *purpose,* Marla. Whatever I was, that was my nature, that's all, and I didn't mean any harm any more than a..., than a *virus* does. This old sorcerer, he stole her life *deliberately,* and I know that must have taken some serious prep work and planning. You're always telling me that the body *is* the mind, that mind-body duality is a fallacy and there is no ghost in the machine, just one combined ghost-machine. That's why real ghosts are so violent and repetitive and crazy, right? Because they're just a broken piece of a dead whole, a fragment left behind when the real self goes. But this old sorcerer made his mind a self-contained thing that still works, and he *stole* a body, with malice aforethought and all that. It's fucked-up. I'm not like that. I wouldn't do that."

Marla was surprised. Rondeau seldom got so worked up—he was loyal, amusing, and a bit unpredictable, but angst didn't suit him. Still, if he wanted to talk seriously, Marla could do that. "Yeah, okay. You didn't take that kid's body deliberately. But I don't recall you ever feeling bad about it before, or even expressing the least bit of interest in what might have become of that kid's consciousness when you ousted it or overwrote it or whatever. You're getting all worked up now, but you never felt *bad* about what you did before, accident or not."

Rondeau shoved his hands deep in his pockets and hunched his shoulders. "You don't know everything I think and feel, Marla. You're not the easiest person to share that kind of stuff with. Besides, thinking about that apprentice getting her body stolen made me think about this body, about what I did, and what I am. I *do* feel bad now. Which is probably why I want to help that apprentice get her body back, if I can. To make myself feel better. So, no, it's not altruism. But can you help me?"

Marla hesitated, then shook her head. "I'm sorry, Rondeau. It's too hard. You'd need the apprentice and the old sorcerer both, and you'd basically have to reproduce what the old guy did, which I doubt you could do if he was conscious, as he's unlikely to cooperate. And even then... it can be done, but minds aren't meant to be swapped, you know? They get worn down. You remember Todd Sweeney, how he jumped from body to body? His own homunculi in that case, but still, there was *wear*, he got increasingly amoral and crazy, and eventually, if he'd kept on jumping, he would have stopped being human entirely."

"But one more switch, Marla. Come on. Would it be so bad?"

"Probably not. But I have to get that Cornerstone,

Rondeau, and get back home. In a day, maybe two, Susan is going to do something very nasty. Hamil will try to stall her, but I've got a couple of days, tops, before I miss my chance. I'm not prepared to tangle with the guy who runs Chinatown here, not when I have so much going on. When this thing with Susan is over, if it's still important to you, I'll hook you up with someone who can teach you how to switch minds, and put you in touch with some freelancers who can help with the wet-work. Okay? But I have too much on my plate right now."

Rondeau nodded, not happy, but apparently satisfied for the moment. "I'll take you up on that, when this thing with Susan is done. I'm serious about this."

Marla put her hand on his shoulder for a moment. "It's a deal." Rondeau had never exhibited much interest in doing the right thing before—he was one of the most profoundly self-centered people she knew, though his loyalty to her was real—and Marla found the change intriguing. Seeing Rondeau develop a moral sense was like watching a primordial sea-creature climb out onto the land for the first time.

"Spare a quarter?" A scruffy young man smiled and held out a paper coffee cup with a few coins rattling around at the bottom. Marla and Rondeau went past without even a glance of acknowledgment.

"See? This place isn't so different from home. They've got panhandlers here, too."

Marla snorted. "He looked like a guy on spring break from college, begging for beer money. Back home, the street people have *gravitas*, you know? They look like they've hit *bottom*." She glanced back, once again feeling as if she was being followed, but the college-boy-bum hadn't trailed along after them, and she didn't see anyone else, either.

Rondeau shrugged. "Go to the Mission, or the Tenderloin, and you'll see plenty of people like that, I bet. This is the chichi part of town, a major tourist destination. The cops probably hustle off anybody who might make the tourons uncomfortable."

They turned off Stockton, onto Geary Street. Marla squinted at the buildings lining the sidewalk. "Not a Gucci or a Louis Vuitton in sight! It's all theaters and art galleries. *Those* have got to lose money, huh?"

Rondeau shrugged. "A lot of people come here for the culture. Maybe they do all right."

Marla put her hand on Rondeau's arm to stop him. "That gallery isn't doing so well." She pointed.

On the other side of the street, near the end of the block, a sawhorse barricade had been set up. Glass littered the sidewalk from the broken front window of the gallery, and a bored-looking cop in a uniform stood by the sawhorses, thumbs hooked in the loop of his belt.

Marla could never resist a crime scene. She crossed the street, Rondeau sighing behind her, and strode toward the breakage. Something yellow near the bottom of an adjoining building caught her eye, and Marla crouched to look at it.

Another tiny frog, lying on its back, unmoving. Marla reached into her bag for a pencil, and nudged the frog with the eraser end. The frog didn't move. Lying there dead, it looked improbable, like a rubber toy. Marla glanced around and tossed the pencil into a nearby sewer grate. She didn't want to absentmindedly chew on the end of the pencil and poison herself. Opening the flap on her bag, she fished around until she found a plastic bag with a few peyote buttons inside. She tossed those in the sewer, too. She could always get more hallucinogens, if an altered state of consciousness proved necessary. She spared a moment's thought for where the things she was throwing away would *go*—both poisoned pencil and peyote would drain away, probably to the bay, where their effects would be largely diluted. And if a few fish got poisoned or started tripping, well, that was small karma, nothing to worry about, not compared to the vast debit she'd already run up in the course of keeping her own skin intact for so many years.

Marla carefully scooped the frog into the plastic bag, not letting her skin touch its body. Rondeau, meanwhile, was looking into the window of the gallery she crouched beside. "There are sculptures made of old vacuum cleaners and ironing boards and shit in there," he said. "Dressed in housedresses and frilly aprons."

With the frog neatly rolled up in the bag—one amphibian was smaller than the three peyote buttons had been—Marla stashed it in a side pocket of her bag, where she wouldn't accidentally touch it while fumbling for something else. She stood and looked into the gallery. "Pretentious bullshit," she said.

"Hmm," Rondeau said. "Let me calibrate your taste in art. Is there a statue you can think of that *isn't* pretentious bullshit?"

"I always liked Michelangelo's *David*," she said. "And that one by Rodin, of the woman trying to hold up a stone and getting crushed?"

"So you're steeped in the classics."

"I'm old-fashioned." She continued down the sidewalk, and when she reached the sawhorses in front of the shattered gallery, she leaned over and looked inside.

Now, *this* was old-fashioned. The gallery was filled with pre-Columbian artifacts—bowls, tools, weapons, and statues. Marla didn't know a lot about art, but she knew about magical implements through the ages, and there were a few of those here, too. The items she recognized were Meso-American, but no more uniform than that—there were Aztec, Toltec, and Olmec objects here, among others.

"Can I help you?" the cop asked. Marla chalked up another strike against San Francisco—this cop sounded like he actually *wanted* to help, like he was the clerk in a hardware store or something, and he smiled, blandly attractive, like a movie extra in a frat-party scene. In Felport, if a cop asked you that question, it would be in an entirely different and far more threatening tone of voice. Cops weren't supposed to be like *ushers*. They were the teeth and claws of civic authority.

Still, she did need help. "Yeah. What was stolen from here?"

The cop looked her up and down, then looked at Rondeau, who'd chosen a bad moment to pick his nose. "How do you know anything was stolen?" the cop asked, forced-casual, and Marla could see him mentally flipping through the *Police Procedural Handbook* to the chapter about stupid criminals returning to the scenes of their crimes.

Marla shrugged. "It could have been an act of vandalism, I guess, but it looked like a smash-and-grab to me." Plus, of course, there was the dead yellow frog in the vicinity, which suggested to Marla that there was some connection between this mess and Lao Tsung's death. She wasn't here to investigate his murder, but she had a couple of hours to kill before Finch's party, and this was *interesting*.

The cop nodded, then reached for a notebook. "If I could have your name and address, I'd be happy to send you some information as soon as we have it."

As far as ruses to get names and addresses went, Marla had seen better. She sighed, shook her left arm slightly, and felt a stone fall out of the concealed pocket sewn into the cuff of her sleeve. The stone was small, smoothly polished, and heavier than it should have been. "Catch," she said, and tossed the rock at the cop, underhand. He caught it instinctively, and his eyes widened. Then he just stood, pupils dilated, mouth hanging open, stone cradled loosely in his palm.

In Marla's city, every cop took an oath that put them under her sway, and she could activate them with a hand gesture or a word. She almost never had to do that—the police chief was handpicked, he belonged to her, and she generally got her information through him—but it was reassuring, having an army at her disposal, the cops themselves unaware they were sleeper agents. This rock was just a temporary charm, a one-use compulsion that she'd spent a long night imbuing. She hoped she hadn't just wasted it, but the cop belonged to her now, and would for the next few days. "What was stolen?"

"A statue."

"Can you describe it?"

"I saw a picture."

"You have the picture?"

The cop nodded and fished in his pocket, then came up with a neatly folded piece of paper. Marla opened it up—it was a photocopy of a photograph—and squinted.

She grunted. "I can't even tell what the hell this is. I hate pre-Columbian art."

Rondeau, who had progressed from picking his nose to picking his teeth, leaned over to look. "I think it's a frog," he said.

Marla snorted. "That's just because we've got frogs on the brain."

"It's a frog," the cop said. "They told me. Some kind of frog-monster. It has mouths on its knees and elbows. And fangs."

"See?" Rondeau said smugly.

"I've never heard of a frog with fangs," Marla muttered.

"You've got a poisonous frog in your purse," Rondeau said. "It doesn't have fangs in *reality*, but it sort of does *metaphorically*."

"Give me your cell phone," Marla said, handing Rondeau the photocopy.

Rondeau took a tiny silver phone from his coat pocket and passed it to Marla. She speed-dialed, and the phone on the other end was picked up on the second ring. "This is Hamil," he said, voice oiled and urbane.

"Marla here. I need you to look up a frog-monster, with fangs, and mouths on its elbows and knees, maybe Mexican or Central American."

"I take it you don't yet have the Cornerstone, then," Hamil said.

"I'm working on it," she said, flipping the phone closed and putting it in her bag. "Okay, Officer—" she squinted at his nametag "—Whitney, thanks for your help. I'll keep the photocopy. You just lost it somewhere, okay? One other thing—was anyone hurt in this break-in?"

"No," he said.

Marla nodded. So apparently the frogs weren't always used as a weapon—sometimes they were just *around*. She supposed it was possible the dead frog was a coincidence, that the theft of the statue was unrelated to Lao Tsung's death, but it seemed unlikely; it was too many frogs in too short a time.

"Let's go," she said, and strode off, Rondeau following. The cop stood by the sawhorses for a long moment, his mind recovering from Marla's manhandling, before he shook himself and wandered back into the gallery.

"We're doing the detective thing now?" Rondeau said. "He's a smooth-talking con man with a past, she's a no-nonsense dame in a world she never made? They fight crime?"

"I just want to get the Cornerstone," Marla said. "If that takes detecting, so be it. But you know me—I'm an information magpie, always interested in shiny bits of intel. I've never gotten in trouble because of knowing too much."

"So this doesn't have anything to do with avenging Lao Tsung's murder, if it was murder? I know you two were close. . . ." Rondeau raised an eyebrow.

"Let's put it this way: I won't go out of my way to

avenge Lao Tsung. But if, in the course of doing my business, I happen to find the person who loosed those frogs on him... I've got a frog of my own now, and maybe I'd like to see how far I can shove it down the murderer's throat."

"While wearing rubber gloves, I assume."

"You know I always play safely." Marla looked around, then stopped walking. "Someone's watching me," she said, squinting toward an alleyway between two galleries. Was it the person she'd sensed following her? But, no, this guy was in *front* of her. "Hey!" she shouted. "Who's there? What are you looking at?"

A man walked slowly out of the alley, wearing a beige overcoat that hung below his knees and a black knit cap pulled down low on his forehead. He was shorter than Rondeau and Marla both, and several days' stubble darkened his chin and cheeks.

"Just some homeless guy," Marla said, and started to walk on.

"Holy shit," Rondeau said. "Are you Bradley Bowman?"

The man nodded, flashing a surprisingly bright smile. "Yeah. I used to be. You can call me B."

"Why do you want to call him anything?" Marla said, looking the man over more carefully. She didn't see much that she hadn't seen before—just that he was in pretty good shape, in a wiry way, something she'd overlooked in light of his slovenliness and slouching, and that his eyes were a startlingly crisp shade of blue. "Who is he?"

"He's a movie star," Rondeau said. "He was in *The Glass Harp*! I love that movie."

"Me, too," Bowman—B—said. "The residuals from *Glass Harp* pay my rent and buy my sedatives."

"But you don't work anymore, right?" Rondeau said. "Because you tried to strangle that director or whatever?"

"That's the story," B said, and he was definitely amused now. "I don't work in the movies anymore, but I keep busy."

"If you're a movie star, why are you dressed like that, hanging out in an alley?" Marla said, genuinely curious.

"I'm not in movies anymore. And I was never a *star,* exactly, though everybody tells me I could've been. As for how I'm dressed...this was a nice coat when I bought it. That was just a long time ago. Sometimes I forget to do laundry, take showers...." He rubbed his hand on his chin and winced. "Shave. I have a lot on my mind. If I'd known I was going to meet someone so attractive, I would've taken some extra time this morning."

"Why are you bothering to flatter me?" Marla said.

"Self-centered much?" Rondeau said. "Your pop-cultural ignorance is once again your undoing. My man B doesn't swing in your direction, Marla. It's well known. He was talking about *me*. I'm the attractive one."

B shook his head. "I never did get used to strangers knowing what kind of people I like to sleep with, but when your sexual preferences show up in tabloid headlines, I guess it's unavoidable. Most people don't recognize me anymore, though."

"Sure, you look different," Rondeau said, "but it's

your *eyes*. Can't mistake those. I always thought they were colored contacts."

"You should see them in the summer. They get bluer then."

"Are you two *flirting*?" Marla said. "Since when are you gay, Rondeau? I knew you had a thing for club-hopping college girls, but this is news to me."

Rondeau rolled his eyes. "Don't be so narrow-minded, Marla. You gotta leave your options open."

"Great. Get his number, then, and let's go. You can look him up when you come back here to do that thing with the Chinese guy. For now, we've got things to do."

"Ah," B said. "This wasn't a chance encounter, actually. I need to talk to you."

Marla cocked her head. "About?"

"Something's going to happen to you. Something bad."

"I don't think you're qualified to threaten me, Mr. Bowman."

He held up his hands. "That's not what I'm saying. Sometimes I have . . . visions. No, that's too mystical, they're just *dreams*, but there's true stuff in them. I can tell when it's not a normal dream, when it's one of *those* dreams."

"And you dreamed about me?"

"Yeah. You were wearing a purple cloak. You weren't the only thing in the dream, though. There were frogs, too—it was raining frogs. And there were hummingbirds. And some old dude in a beaver hat." He shrugged. "Anyway, I knew I had to come to the city, that I'd find you, and here I am. So what's the deal with the frogs?"

Marla tapped her foot for a moment. "I can't be certain, Mr. Bowman, but it sounds to me like you've got a psychic streak. Lots of people do, though yours must be pretty strong. You picked up something, and you followed it—not a good idea, I have to say. That kind of initiative can get you in trouble. You say you saw me in your dream, and I believe that, but it doesn't have anything to *do* with you, okay? You just picked it up, like a radio signal, like hearing a cell phone on a police scanner."

B shook his head. "Listen, I *know* things, I can help you—"

"You're not a sorcerer," Marla said bluntly. "You don't hold yourself like someone who uses power. I can see that. Maybe you've heard some things, seen some things, maybe you're a third-rate seer, even, but you can't be any help to me, and you're not a threat to me, either. I'm incredibly busy. I have to go. I'd suggest you stay away from me, no matter what your dreams say. The last thing I need is the additional complication of your presence. I am simply too busy to be interested in you. Come on, Rondeau." She walked away.

"Sorry, man," Rondeau said behind her. "She's a woman with a mission. I love your work, really."

Rondeau caught up with her farther down the block. "Bitch," he said amiably.

"Starfucker," she replied.

"I wonder if that psychic streak is what ruined his movie career?" Rondeau said.

"Probably. Poor bastard. Neither one thing nor the other. At least you and me, we're up to our foreheads in magic, it's our element, we can breathe in it. He's probably been having dreams and seeing shit his whole life, but not strongly enough for any sorcerer to bother seeking him out to mentor him, so he's not part of *our* world, but he's too weird for the ordinaries, too."

"Pretty eyes, though," Rondeau said.

Marla laughed.

After Marla left, B seriously considered taking a train back to the East Bay and going about the regular business of his life: reading history and mythology books, sleeping as much as possible, sifting through his dreams. What difference did it make to him what happened to Marla? But he knew his life was tangled up in hers for the next few days, that causes already past had led to effects that were as yet unnoticed. She didn't want to acknowledge that, didn't believe it— fair enough. Things would become clear to her later. He just wanted to get through these next days, and see Marla get through them. Because if she *didn't*, San Francisco would suffer a disaster that would make the 1906 earthquake and fire seem trivial. After all, those nested catastrophes had only destroyed a third of the city. Things were likely to be a lot worse this time, and these days there was a lot more city to be destroyed. B had no great affection for San Francisco, but that was mostly because it was the center of his old life, when he'd worked in the movies and lived with his lover, H. Now he lived across the bay, in Oakland, where H had died, where the ghost that B was most responsible for resided. Even so, he'd had one of *those* dreams, and he knew from past experience there was no getting out of it—even if he tried to run away, events would conspire to draw him in.

He had the feeling Marla could be difficult to find if she wanted to be, and B wasn't much good at tracking people down. Fortunately, he had other methods. It was never very difficult to find an oracle, or a minor spirit, or a cryptophyte that could provide him with information. After wandering through various alleys, he noticed a huge metal trash bin, dented and smeared with filth. Rapping his knuckles gently on the side of the bin, he said, "Hey. This is Bradley Bowman. Who's there?"

A voice replied, low, hollow: "Murmurus."

"It's a pleasure to meet you. I need some information."

"I once taught in the classrooms of Hell," the voice said, wistfully.

"Now's your chance to teach again," B said. "I need to know how to find a woman named Marla Mason. Where she'll be later. I think something big is going to happen soon...tonight, or tomorrow. Do you know anything?"

"There are whispers in the gutters, voices humming across the glass," Murmurus said. "Frogs, and birds, and monsters. Old things come around again. Sleepers awakening. Sorcerers rising up against one another. Bodies stolen and bodies lost. The woman seeks something ancient and powerful, but she is not the only one who seeks it."

"I just need a place," B said. "And a time wouldn't hurt."

"The hill in the lake," Murmurus said. "A sweet red hill, filling the lake. There is nowhere else she *can* be. But she will arrive too late. Tomorrow will be too late."

"How can I repay your help?" B said.

"Books," the voice replied.

B had to walk a long way to find a used bookstore. He bought a cardboard box full of old paperbacks, making sure none of the titles was duplicated, but otherwise not paying much attention to the types of books they were. A disembodied spirit that lived in a Dumpster probably wasn't that picky when it came to reading material. He walked back to the Dumpster and tossed the books inside. Murmurus didn't make a sound of acknowledgment, but B felt a soothing sense of neutrality, of balance reinstated, come over him as he walked away. He'd learned you *always* had to pay your debts, or the nightmares would shake your life apart.

So now B knew where Marla would be tomorrow—though that was still an awfully big window of time—and he knew it would be *too late,* though he didn't know what it would be too late for—not too late for *everything,* he hoped. In the meantime, he had a whole night to kill.

Well, why not go to the Castro, grab a bite to eat, hang around? He hadn't been there in ages, and it had once been his happiest home. There were lots of memories there, but not all memories were traps or poisons. Maybe he could find a good memory to keep him warm through the night.

3

Marla and Rondeau wound up strolling in Yerba Buena Gardens. They were in the middle of a city, but all she smelled was grass and cool air. Marla had to admit—to herself, if not to Rondeau—that she liked the gardens, and suspected that if they visited Golden Gate Park, she'd like that, too. In the heart of her own city, where she lived and worked, most of the parks were magnets for drug dealers and users, perpetually trash-strewn, thoroughly unpleasant. The parks on the outskirts and in the suburbs were nicer, of course, but when her city had first begun growing, little thought was given to creating public green spaces. She'd been told the parks at home were nicer in the daytime, less dangerous, but Marla was usually sleeping during the brightest part of the day. Her work was more closely aligned with the night. But here, in this park at least, the night held no particular terrors, and a crowd of people milled around the modern building that Rondeau called the Metreon. Sounded like the name of a minor angel to Marla, but whatever.

There were whimsical statues in Yerba Buena Gardens, including a giant-sized metal chair high enough to walk beneath, and while Marla generally had a low tolerance for whimsy, she found the sculpture almost charming in its straightforward silliness. San Francisco probably had other charms, but there was much about it that unsettled her, including her mental geological map of the place, which included the fault lines that streaked all around the city. There were magics that benefited from living in a place that always teetered on the edge of natural disaster, but Marla didn't think the benefits were worth the possibility of sliding into the sea. Her own city seldom faced anything worse than ice storms in the winter and summertime heat waves. She didn't think she could handle the local politics here, either—passing the power from sorcerer to sorcerer made sense as a way of keeping everyone happy, but she wasn't so sure it worked well when it came to getting things *accomplished* and keeping the city safe. Sorcerers were backstabbing, vicious beasts at worst, cautious allies at best; how many of these pro-tem chief sorcerers were giving full disclosure to the people who came to replace them, letting them know about all the current problems and opportunities? Probably none of them. Marla preferred her own form of mostly benign dictatorship.

It occurred to her that someone would probably try to kill her at Finch's party. She'd pissed off the biggest sorcerer in Chinatown (maybe—it was always possible that was self-aggrandizement), who now knew where Marla was going tonight. That gave the night a little extra sparkle, at least. At home, people were always trying to kill her. It helped her keep her edge.

Something fluttered in her peripheral vision. "What's that?" she said, and Rondeau said, "Hmm?"

Marla stepped closer to the giant metal chair, eyes scanning the dark. Something swift, flying, darting randomly up, down, and sideways in the air.

"Hummingbird," Rondeau said.

Marla nodded. The bird was ruby-throated, wings an invisible blur. Marla frowned. Hummingbirds in January? They never appeared until spring back home, but there was *snow* there—maybe the appearance of a hummingbird in January at night was perfectly seasonable here, in this strange land where the trees had green leaves in winter. Marla flapped her hand toward the bird, and it zoomed straight backwards, then zoomed toward her. Marla and Rondeau walked on. They crossed the street and headed in the direction of the closed Museum of Modern Art, but when Marla glanced back, the hummingbird was still hovering nearby. She took a long step sideways, and the bird shifted with her, long beak pointing unerringly toward her face. Marla stepped back the other way, and the bird followed.

"Fuck," she said thoughtfully.

"That's weird," Rondeau said. "Maybe it thinks you're a flower." A second hummingbird buzzed up and began hovering over Rondeau.

"You've got one, too, Rondeau."

Rondeau looked around. "Huh. Familiars, you think?"

"Seems likely," she said. "Birds are tricky, but not unheard of."

"That was Somerset's thing, right? Birds?"

Marla nodded, remembering. Somerset had been the chief sorcerer of her city once, a brutal, cheerfully vicious man, and even after his death he'd been reluctant to relinquish power. He'd come closer to killing Marla than anyone else ever had. Somerset favored pigeons for his familiars—a flock of pigeons trying to hurt someone could do real damage. But a flock—hell, a *swarm*—of hummingbirds wouldn't be much good in battle, would they? Too fragile. But they were certainly *fast*. Marla jumped and snatched for her bird, and it avoided her easily, hovering just out of reach. Watching.

"We have to get rid of them," Marla said, "and then get lost. These birds probably have to return to their master to deliver whatever intelligence they've gathered—I doubt they're telepathic, or that they're rigged with surveillance equipment. Even the smallest microphones and cameras would be a burden for birds this small, so it has to be a magical transference, and that's easier with physical contact."

"Who do you think they belong to?"

Marla shrugged. "The Chinese guy? Finch? Maybe he heard we were coming to his party. I don't trust the Chinese guy to keep a secret. It doesn't really matter. I don't like being watched. When I want to know something about someone, I go *ask*. Spying is low-class."

"You know, Hamil and I *do* keep our ears open for you, though."

"Well, sure. That's different."

"Why?"

"Because this time, someone's spying on *me*." She

looked around. "Let's find a parking garage. Someplace with low ceilings. Or, better yet, an elevator."

"There's a parking garage by that convention center," Rondeau said, pointing. Marla set off in that direction, trailed by Rondeau and the hummingbirds. "You know, 'Finch' is kind of a birdy name," Rondeau said.

Marla nodded. "Already crossed my mind. Could be coincidence, but it could be sympathetic magic, too, or a nickname he got for being a bird-man." Marla shook her head. "This is like when I was first learning back home, before I knew who everyone was, what the surface and secret allegiances were, before I even knew people's *names*. I thought I was through being ignorant and pushy—I like being well informed and pushy much better."

"Welcome to a whole new pond, little fish," Rondeau said.

She snorted. "I'm always a big fish. Sometimes I have to hang out in the shallows first for a while, is all."

Marla opened a metal door on the side of the parking garage, intending to hold it open gallantly for the hummingbirds, but they zipped down close to the smalls of her and Rondeau's backs so they could follow. She swatted at her back, fast, but the hummingbird buzzed out of reach.

"Little bastards can fly backward, you know that?" Rondeau said. "Everybody knows they're the only bird that can hover, but they can actually go in *reverse*."

"Such are the wonders of nature," Marla muttered, and went into the garage. She felt instantly at home, with the low ceilings and exposed pipes, the piss-stained corners, the oil spots. This was the essence of the home of her heart, dark and somehow fundamentally illicit—why else did so many secret meetings take place in parking garages? The parking garage smelled like car exhaust and cold concrete. She followed the signs to an elevator and pressed the "Up" button. The scarred steel doors slid open. Marla and Rondeau got in, and the hummingbirds followed.

The doors slid shut, and Marla grinned. The hummingbirds were hovering in the corners of the ceiling, but the elevator was only about seven and a half feet high, and they couldn't get *that* far away.

Marla opened her leather bag and rooted around inside for a moment, then pulled out a towel she'd stolen from the hotel. She put down her bag and twisted the towel, as if she were wringing it out, and tied a fat knot at one end. "Step back, Rondeau," she said, and he pressed himself against the elevator wall. Marla swung the towel in a short arc, experimentally.

The hummingbirds instantly moved to hover right in front of Rondeau's face.

Marla lowered the towel. "Huh," she said. "Smarter than your average bird, aren't they? I guess we need magic. What do you think, Rondeau—want to Curse at them?"

"In an *elevator*?" Rondeau said. "Isn't that sort of dangerous for *us*?"

"We're not moving, and we're on the ground floor. Even if the cables snapped or something, we aren't going anywhere, and if the doors get jammed, I can get them open."

Rondeau nodded, the birds still hovering before his

face. "Yeah, all right," he said. "They're right in front of me, so I guess the sound of the Curse will hit them first anyway." Rondeau spoke briefly, three guttural syllables, and the air in the elevator car suddenly grew very hot and uncomfortable, the walls around them and the cables above groaning.

The two hummingbirds burst brightly, whitely, into flame, and fell to the floor of the elevator, their furiously beating wings throwing off streamers of smoke and shedding sparks. Marla and Rondeau jumped away from the flames, and Marla hit the "Door Open" button on the elevator. The doors slid apart slowly, creaking—Rondeau's primordial Curse had twisted something in the mechanism out of true. They exited the elevator, stepping over the flash-charred bird bodies.

Rondeau spat onto the concrete. "Gah, I hate doing that, speaking that language always makes my mouth taste like cat shit."

"You know this from personal experience?"

"When I was young, and I'd just taken over this body, I didn't know what was good to eat and what wasn't. Let's not get into that." He looked around nervously. "I always expect some sort of cosmic retribution for Cursing in the language of the gods, too."

"Maybe that bad taste is the retribution," Marla said. Rondeau had the gift of tongues, but only in a limited way. Hamil believed that when Rondeau capital-"C"-Cursed, he was mispronouncing the first Word that had created the universe. The results were always unpredictably destructive, though Marla couldn't recall them ever involving white-hot fire before. Marla suspected there was no such divine association—she believed in gods, plural, or at least in supernatural beings with powers far beyond those of even magic-savvy humans like herself, but she didn't believe in one creator-god who'd made the universe by speaking a series of well-formed sentences. It seemed more likely to her that Rondeau had lucked into some set of primal incantations, the language of demons, perhaps the language of whatever kind of creature Rondeau really *was,* inside that stolen body. Either way, the Curses were handy, though often more trouble than they were worth, and occasionally prone to backfiring in unpleasant ways, though never on Rondeau himself—just on innocent bystanders. Marla had once suffered a minor concussion as a result of one of Rondeau's Curses.

"Maybe we should head over to Finch's party," Marla said. "It's getting to be that time."

"Yeah," Rondeau said. "Let's hope we don't run into any more birds along the way."

As they walked through the parking garage, Marla saw a shadow near one of the ramps to an upper level. She stopped, blinked, whispered a spell to turn on her night-eyes, and looked again. There was a man, not very tall, slim, holding a cane. He wore something like a top hat, but it was vaguely furry, and he was looking straight at her, probably thinking himself safely hidden in shadow. "Beaver hat," she muttered. "Who was it who said something about a beaver hat?"

"What are you talking about?" Rondeau said, stepping toward her, briefly passing between her and the man. When his next step carried him out of her line of sight, the man was gone. Marla cursed—though her profanities were less destructive than Rondeau's, they were more heartfelt.

"Somebody was watching us, a little guy with a cane, wearing a fur hat."

"Huh," Rondeau said. "Should we worry?"

"I don't have *time* to worry about crap like this," Marla said. "I've got enough problems already."

"Probably just another spy," Rondeau said. "If he gets close again, we grab him. Otherwise, as long as he just watches, who cares? It's not like you're planning to be stealthy, right?"

"Yeah. It just *irks* me, being followed."

"Every time a strange sorcerer passes through Felport, you have *them* followed," Rondeau pointed out.

Marla glared at him for a moment, then strode off, out of the parking garage.

As they were walking back across the park, Rondeau's phone rang. Marla took it out of her bag, flipped it open, and put it to her ear. "Speak."

"I found out about your frog-monster," Hamil said. "An Aztec deity, though 'primordial earth-monster' might be a better term, called Tlaltecuhtli."

"I won't be able to pronounce that without practice," Marla said. "I'll just call him Mr. Toad if I run into him."

"Let's hope you don't," Hamil said. "I hope it's just a monster from myth, without any basis in reality."

"Give me the vitals," Marla said, pausing in the shadow of the giant chair.

"Often described as female, though that's not entirely consistent, she was one of the first gods, a giant froglike creature with mouths on her elbows, knees, and—ominously—'other joints.' She had a taste for meat of all kinds. While the other gods were trying to create the world, Tlaltecuhtli was merrily devouring what they made, which finally drove Tezcatlipoca and Quetzalcoatl to kill her. They ripped her in two, and her upper body became the Earth, while her lower half became the heavens."

"Big girl," Marla said.

"Some of the myth is quite poetic," Hamil said. "Tlaltecuhtli's body became the basis for most geography and all plant life—trees and flowers come from her hair and skin, the contours of mountain ranges follow the shape of her face, her eyes are the source of wells and springs, while her mouth is the beginning of all the great rivers. All the deepest caverns of the world lead inside her body."

"Pretty," Marla said.

"Except for the part where she still craves meat and sacrificial blood, or else she withholds the fruits of the Earth, causes natural disasters, etc.," Hamil said. "You know how the Aztecs were—any excuse to spill blood. They used to offer Tlaltecuhtli fruit sprinkled with the stuff. She was the dark side of an Earth goddess—her image was usually carved on the bottom of statues, where the carving could make contact with soil. She has other qualities, more ambiguous. Her mouth is sometimes described as the gateway to the underworld, and I found one depiction of her disgorging the souls of dead warriors in the shape of butterflies and hummingbirds."

Everything went crystalline in Marla's mind. "Hummingbirds?"

"Yes. I don't know how much you know about Aztecs—"

"Just what I've read in bad horror novels," Marla said. That wasn't quite true—she knew a bit about some of their artifacts, and had a general impression of them as bloody-minded heart-eaters, at least among the ruling class—but their myths were more or less unfamiliar to her.

"Ah. Well, apart from the fact that they sacrificed something on the order of twenty thousand people a year, with the limbs and hearts of victims providing the main source of meat for the ruling class, they had quite a sophisticated theology. They believed that blood was the true source of life, and that only blood sacrifices could appease the gods and, thus, keep the universe running smoothly. They called the life force *teyolia,* and thought it most potent when extracted from those whose hearts were filled with fear."

"Get to the part about the hummingbirds," Marla said.

"It's almost whimsical, really, when contrasted with the amount of blood they spilled." Hamil said, "But the Aztecs believed that the souls of dead warriors could return to Earth in the form of hummingbirds, and occasionally butterflies."

"Shit," Marla said. "There were some hummingbirds spying on us earlier today."

Hamil grunted. "Do you really think there's a connection? It's more likely they're just someone's familiars, yes?"

"Of course," Marla said. "But . . . it's intriguing. Little yellow frogs, hummingbird spies, stolen statues . . ."

"Little yellow frogs?" Hamil said.

"Never mind. Or, rather, I'll tell you later."

"I did see something more about the humming-birds," Hamil said. There was the sound of flipping pages. "Yes. Hummingbirds are warriors for the sun god, whose name you would find even more unpronounceable than Tlaltecuhtli's."

"Huh," Marla said, and there was a world of interested speculation in that single syllable.

"Marla," Hamil said, "I'm sure you've stumbled into something fascinating, but remember—"

"I know. I'm not here to get mixed up in local politics, I'm just here to find that certain something we need. But somebody killed Lao Tsung, and I have good reason to think that same somebody also stole a statue of Ms. Toad."

"Oh, dear," Hamil said. "I should have known this wouldn't be a simple shopping trip."

"Yeah, well, I'm following a lead, and I might be able to get . . . that item we're looking for . . . tonight. If I can, I'll forget all this other stuff and come home right away."

"That's probably for the best," Hamil said. "Let the West Coast take care of itself, hmm? It's not like they don't have sorcerers of their own—silicon mages, geomancers, tidal shamans, jellyfish-witches, I'm sure they can handle whatever's going on. You just stumbled into someone else's fight."

"Sure," Marla said. "But it looks like Lao Tsung stumbled into it, too, and if I have the chance to stomp whoever killed him . . ."

"Understood," Hamil said.

"Where do things stand with Susan?"

"Ah," Hamil said. "Unchanged. I tried to arrange

a meeting with her, but she isn't taking any visitors, especially not any who are connected with you. I'm afraid she knows you're aware of her plans—the way you left town so quickly, it's a natural supposition for her to make. And our source in Susan's organization was found crawling in the street this afternoon with his hands and feet cut off and his tongue and eyes removed. We tried to put him out of his misery, but Susan had cast a protective spell on him, and we can't hurt him physically at all now. He'll live for another six months, at least. I think it's safe to assume that she discovered he was giving us information."

"Shit," Marla said. "Give the guy a lot of morphine, would you? If needles won't break his skin, pour laudanum down his throat. Keep him comfortable. You know, when I find out one of my employees has betrayed me, I just *kill* them. Simple, direct, effective. Why does Susan have to be so fucking dramatic?"

"I'm sure it points to a fundamental sense of insecurity on her part," Hamil said. "Be safe, and hurry back."

"Will do," Marla said, and flipped her phone shut. Frogs, hummingbirds, angry body-switching Chinese sorcerers, little guys in 19th-century hats, and now primordial earth-monsters. This trip was not going as smoothly as she'd hoped.

4

Marla hammered on the bathroom door. "Rondeau! It's time to go!" It was nine o'clock already, and even if Finch didn't show up until later, Marla wanted to get the lay of the land before she faced him. They'd stopped by the hotel so Rondeau could change, and then he'd insisted on taking a shower.

Rondeau yelled something unintelligible from the bathroom. He'd been in there for half an hour, enjoying the endless stream of hot water. Marla couldn't really blame him—she'd indulged in a long shower herself during the dull afternoon. She'd almost forgotten what real water pressure felt like. Taking a shower at her apartment was like being spat on by an irate camel.

A few minutes later Rondeau emerged, dressed in his usual vintage-store finery—a powder-blue '50s-prom-style tuxedo. He looked at Marla critically. "You're wearing that?"

Marla considered her outfit. Black cotton pants, loose, so she could run or kick easily. Black boots with reinforced steel toes. Gray long-sleeved T-shirt. Her cloak, white side showing, of course. She was nervous about wearing the cloak, but if Finch got nasty she might need it. As long as she didn't reverse the cloak and let the purple side show, there was no danger. It was a peculiarity of the cloak that it was not reversible in the usual sense—no matter how hard she tried, she would never be able to put it on with the white inside and the purple showing. The colors simply didn't cooperate, as if the cloak were made of moebius cloth. If the need arose, however, a simple mental command would reverse the cloak, and the purple would show...but she hoped it wouldn't come to that. Things would have to get pretty bad before such steps became necessary. Her dagger was tucked away safely in the magically protected teak box, under the bed. The cloak was enough for tonight, and it wasn't obviously a weapon, so it stood a better chance of getting through whatever security Finch might have set up. "Yeah, I'm wearing this. Why?"

"Because we're going to a party, right? A soiree? Don't you have anything more..." He waved his hands vaguely. "...festive?"

"No, Rondeau, I don't have anything more festive. I only brought one change of clothes. You brought a freaking suitcase. Besides, I'm not going to enjoy Finch's hospitality. I'm going to get information."

"Sure, but I just want us to fit in, so we don't draw undue attention to ourselves. See, I'm thinking of the *mission*."

"Nobody's going to look twice at me when I come in with you anyway. You wearing that tuxedo is all the camouflage I need. Besides, this is California, where casual is king, right?"

"I guess," Rondeau said. "It wouldn't kill you to wear a skirt occasionally, you know."

"No. But it might kill you to suggest it again," Marla said, showing her teeth.

They took a bus from Union Square to the Castro, Marla sniffing suspiciously. "Where're the piles of filth? The aggressive panhandlers? The guys at the bus stop who look like they're just waiting for the right moment to shove a yuppie under the tires? I don't trust a city that has a bus system this clean."

"They get a lot of tourists," Rondeau said, leaning back in a sideways-facing seat. Marla, too antsy to sit, was standing beside him, hanging on to an overhead rail. "They have to observe the proprieties a little more. Nobody comes to our city to visit, unless their relatives die or something. Besides, this is the middle of the city still—it's got to be nice. I'm sure there are places around here that are unpleasant enough to meet your low standards."

Marla frowned. "It's not that I like dirty stuff for the sake of dirt, Rondeau. It's just . . . I distrust all this cleanliness. It feels like I'm in Disneyland or something, someplace monitored and managed."

Rondeau reached up and pulled the cord, making the "Stop Ahead" sign by the driver light up. "Our stop," he said.

"Already?" Marla said.

"San Francisco doesn't sprawl as much as our own pockmarked metropolis," Rondeau said.

The bus stopped, and they got off. "Welcome to the Castro," Rondeau said as the bus chugged away from them. Marla looked up and down the street. Aside from the rainbow flags hanging from the windows of well-kept Victorians and over the doors of various businesses, it could have been any bustling, well-lit avenue in a prosperous city. Though there were more men holding hands here than Marla generally saw elsewhere, and there was a man wearing a leather vest over his otherwise bare chest. "I thought there'd be more guys in dog collars and buttless chaps," Marla said.

"We could come back later this year for the gay pride parade, or for Folsom Street Fair, and I bet you'd see more buttless chaps than you can shake a riding crop at."

"I'll keep it in mind for my next vacation," Marla said. There was no gay district as such in Marla's city, though of course there were bars and clubs geared toward such clientele, and Marla found herself wondering, in a municipal-management frame of mind, whether the incidences of domestic violence in this neighborhood were of greater or lesser frequency than that in straight neighborhoods with similar population and economic conditions. Probably not much different. People were people.

"This used to be a run-down neighborhood," Rondeau said—presumably sharing his hard-won tourist-guidebook wisdom. "Then in the '60s gay men started buying up the old Victorians and renovating them, and before long this was the unofficial gay capital of the world. Some people are afraid the Castro's going to go the way of Fisherman's Wharf, though, lose all its authenticity and become a kitschy tourist-trap. It's pretty popular with straight tourists, for some reason."

"Small-minded bastards want to see the modern homosexual in his natural habitat?" Marla said, drawing a glance from a middle-aged man and woman taking pictures of the rainbow flags. She grinned at them nastily and they shuffled off.

"Um," Rondeau said. "Dunno. There's supposed to be some great bars around here, though."

"What's the dyke presence like?" Marla said. Rondeau wasn't the only one with flexible sexuality. She'd had her share of affairs with women, though she'd never given up entirely on men; as far as that went, she'd had a fling with an incubus once, and a one-night stand with a woman she suspected of being a Rakosh dressed in a beautiful illusion. After you'd mated once or twice with the supernatural, mere differences in genitalia seemed irrelevant—humans were at least all built along the same lines, with the same basic nerve endings, just in different configurations. These days, she didn't have much time for romantic entanglements of any sort.

"Eh," Rondeau said. "They come out for the pride parade, and they're *around,* but I get the sense they're a minority in occupied territory."

"You 'get the sense,' oh bold explorer?"

"All right, fine. The guidebook *says* so, then. But I'm practically a native compared to you."

"Let's scout out Finch's place," Marla said. "Lead on, native guide."

After peering at the map for a while, Rondeau set off away from the bright thoroughfare, down a side street. "This area is still heavily residential," Rondeau said. "Tourist influx notwithstanding." Neat Victorians stood behind wrought-iron gates, and trees in iron cages lined the sidewalk. There were more rainbow flags, posters in windows bearing political slogans, and one black-and-blue S&M flag. A couple of the houses they passed had signs discreetly marking them as bed-and-breakfasts.

"I guess that's it," Rondeau said, "on the other side of the street." Finch's house, a dark blue three-story Victorian, was near the top of a hill. There were perhaps fifteen people standing in a ragged line in front of the house, which had a small porch blocked off by an elaborate wrought-iron gate. Marla and Rondeau stood in the shadows, watching as an attractive, dark-haired woman wearing a wine-red velvet cape opened the gate from the inside and spoke to the assembled crowd. She beckoned four people forward, who promptly disappeared through the front door, into the house. The apparent hostess chatted briefly with the others waiting, then went inside herself.

"Weird party," Marla said. "Making the guests wait."

"But I didn't see money change hands, and more important, nobody handed over invitations," Rondeau said. "So maybe we can get in without any fuss."

"Unless they all know one another," Marla said. "But we'll obliterate that obstacle if we come to it." She crossed the street, and Rondeau followed. They took a place at the back of the line. Most of the people waiting were youngish, and diversely dressed—some in leather jackets, some in ordinary street clothes, some in velvet and lace, all talking to one another comfortably.

A man with short black hair and Buddy Holly glasses glanced at Marla and smiled. "Have I seen you here before?"

"Maybe," Marla said.

He looked her up and down, openly appraising. "I think I'd remember you. Maybe I'll see you downstairs later?"

"Anything's possible." Her admirer was, quite obviously, not a sorcerer, and Marla's initial assumption that Finch's party would be a gathering place for the magically inclined was apparently mistaken. She hadn't yet come up with a new theory. Maybe Finch just liked to entertain. That wasn't unheard of, even among the sort of deeply self-centered people the magical arts attracted. Some people enjoyed seeing their radiance reflected in the eyes of others.

Rondeau was deep in conversation with a willowy, pale woman with white-blond hair. She was beautiful, Marla supposed, in a nearly-translucent, fragile way. Her eyes were rimmed with kohl, and she looked up at Rondeau with a mixture of childlike awe and sexual longing, but Marla suspected that was her default expression, an accessory as carefully chosen as the knee-high black boots and the black latex flip-skirt. The look certainly worked for her—it had captured Rondeau like a Venus flytrap snared flies.

The caped woman emerged from the house, and Marla stood on her tiptoes to get a glimpse of what lay beyond the door, but all she saw was a staircase leading up, blocked off with a velvet rope, and an open doorway to the right of the entrance, with the suggestion of movement beyond. The gatekeeper held up four fingers, opened the gate, and ushered four more people inside. The gate closed again, and Marla began to feel a slow burn of impatience start in her chest. She'd had to stand in line at the airport, too, just this morning, and that had nearly driven her insane. Marla hadn't had to wait in line for anything in a long time, and it didn't suit her.

"I hate this line," her erstwhile admirer commented to the short-haired, stocky woman in biker's leathers standing in front of him. "I remember in the old days, there was no waiting, even if you got here later than this. Now you have to come before nine to get even a crappy spot downstairs."

"According to you, *everything* was better in the 'old days,'" the biker muttered, without turning around. "Personally, I'm glad more people come these days. I was getting sick of seeing the same bunch every week."

The young man sighed theatrically. "Sure, I guess, but some of these new people have no manners."

"Some of the old ones didn't have manners, either," the biker replied. "Hell, even Mr. Finch can be a pushy bastard."

"It's his party—he can have all the party favors he wants, right? And if you don't like it, you don't have to come."

"I don't know why I hang around with you, Jared," the biker said. "You're some kind of a post-feminist misogynist, I think."

Marla was reassured to hear both that Finch lived here and that these people had been here before—that this wasn't some killing-ground she and Rondeau were being lured into. That would have been a pretty amusing way for the Chinese sorcerer to get his revenge—sending them into a sacrificial pit disguised as a party.

Rondeau wandered back to stand beside her. "That's Zara," he said, nodding toward the blond girl.

"Oh? Did you learn anything useful from her?"

"She likes drinking vodka and Red Bull and she shaves *everything*," Rondeau said. "She's one of the most forthcoming people I've ever met, actually, though she seemed disappointed to hear that I don't have anything pierced. Maybe I should look into it."

"You don't have much of a threshold for pain," Marla reminded him.

He shrugged. "No, but I think Zara could expand my threshold for pleasure."

"Nah," Marla said. "She's all image. People with real technique don't have to flaunt their kink like she does."

Rondeau looked at Marla speculatively, and she gave him another grin. There was a time when he'd been hopelessly in love with her, though he seemed to have gotten over it lately; probably the plain fact of spending so much time with her in a business capacity had worn down his romantic aspirations. Marla in person wasn't easy to idolize—she was too earthy, too cranky, and too prone to practicalities.

The velvet doorkeeper appeared, and let four more people in, including Zara. Now that Marla was closer to the wrought-iron gate that blocked the porch, she noticed that the metal wasn't curved in a sunburst or fleur-de-lis or any other standard design. The gate was clearly custom-made, the metal twisted in a sinuous and organic design that suggested flowers and snakes. She recognized the shape.

The design was a veve, a ritual symbol, used in a ceremony to call up a loa, an occupying spirit. This was not the well-known veve of Papa Legba (which Marla had even seen on the occasional T-shirt), not did it belong to any of the better-known gods of Voudon, like Baron Samedi or Maitre Carrefour or Damballah. This was the veve of a minor spirit, one of the Guede, a loa of sexual passion. When summoned, a loa would take over the body of one of its worshippers, using it to communicate and satisfy corporeal desires (many of the loas were gluttons for rum and candy); the loa signified by this particular design would push its adherents to acts of sexual excess and gratification, and gain power from the mass coupling (and tripling, and quadrupling, and so on). Having the design in a gate wouldn't actually call up the loa—the ceremony was more complicated than that—but as a design choice, it was certainly suggestive. Marla now had a pretty good idea what kind of sorcerer Finch was. Marla herself was a general practitioner when it came to magic; Hamil sometimes called her a brute-force-omancer. Many sorcerers chose to specialize to a greater or lesser degree, however, becoming necromancers, pyromancers, diviners, aviomancers, biomancers, technomancers—all with their own strengths and weaknesses, all with their signature obsessions.

From the design on the gate, Marla suspected Finch was—at least in part—a sexual magician. What Marla had always somewhat contemptuously referred to as a "pornomancer." Her own first teacher, Artie Mann, had been a pornomancer, though of an unconventional sort. It was actually a relief to discover this about Finch—pornomancers weren't known for their offensive capabilities, though it wouldn't do to underestimate Finch, and she *was* just making assumptions based on an odd home-design choice.

The woman in velvet emerged, opened the gate, and beckoned the next four people—including Marla and Rondeau—inside.

Sexual excess was not immediately apparent. Once inside the dim foyer, Marla and Rondeau joined the same people they'd been waiting in line with outside. By standing on tiptoe and looking over the heads of the people in front of her, Marla could see a woman standing at a counter as if tending a ticket booth. She was handing people clipboards, and retrieving clipboards from people who were finished filling out some kind of form.

"What, we have to sell our souls to get into this party?" Rondeau said.

"I guess so," Marla said.

"It'd better be a pretty good party, then. I like to get full value for my soul."

"Full value for your soul wouldn't get you a cup of coffee at a convenience store," Marla said, but her heart wasn't in the banter; she'd suddenly realized what kind of party this probably was. She had to admire the Chinatown sorcerer for sending her here with a straight face.

The line moved forward, and the people who were finished with their clipboards went down a short hallway and turned right into another room. Marla and Rondeau each took a clipboard, which contained a sheet of paper printed with a set of rules and disclaimers, with a place at the bottom for signature and date. Marla closed her eyes briefly and pressed her hand to the paper, feeling with a sense beyond touch until she was sure the paper wasn't magically prepared. This contract would be binding only in the legal sense. Some sorcerers could write a contract in such a way that the signers were bound by pain of death to obey, but Finch hadn't done that here. Marla scanned down the rules. Nothing unexpected. This *was* the kind of party she thought, which was likely to make the evening more complicated than she'd expected.

"No drinking, no drugs, no touching without permission," Rondeau said, bewildered. "Don't monopolize the equipment in the dungeon, safe scenes are good scenes, use gloves, dams, condoms.... Oh," he said, and Marla was not surprised to hear a smile in his voice. "You brought me to a sex party, Marla. You *are* letting me have a little fun on this trip."

Marla sighed, signed an indecipherable scrawl at the bottom of the paper, and handed the clipboard back to the smiling attendant. Rondeau did the same. "That'll be twenty dollars each," she said, and Marla nodded to Rondeau, who handed over two twenties.

"For twenty dollars each, there'd better be some decent food in there," Rondeau said. "Oysters wouldn't be amiss."

"We've had bad luck with oysters," the woman said, putting their money under the counter. "There's asparagus, though, and lots of sweets. You're here early enough that there's probably still plenty of food."

The pressure of people behind them was building up, so Marla and Rondeau went down the hallway, into the other room. The line outside was meant to keep this preparatory area from becoming hopelessly clogged, Marla realized, and possibly to keep the house from getting too crowded.

The next room was jammed with people in various stages of dress, undress, and dress-up. They wore corsets, spiked heels, leather collars, net body-stockings, baby-doll teddies, capes—every kind of lingerie and fetish gear, though some wore nothing but their skin, and some wore sarongs or boxer shorts. The majority were young and reasonably attractive, the sort of hip urban crowd Marla might expect to see at a dance club in Felport. A long table ran along one end of the room, staffed by volunteers who got to attend the party for free, Marla supposed, in exchange for helping support the infrastructure for an hour or two. The people behind the table were handing out brown paper grocery sacks with numbers written on the sides. "Remember your number!" they admonished, as the party guests put their street clothes and other personal items into the bags, which were in turn given back to the volunteers, who put the filled bags away on shelves made from scaffolding. A shelf along another wall held hundreds of neatly folded towels in faded primary colors, and once the guests had girded or ungirded their loins as desired and stowed their belongings, they took towels and went deeper into the house. Several of the guests still carried bags or cases with them—party supplies, Marla supposed.

"I've never been to a party like this before," Rondeau said. "But I always knew they must be out there somewhere. I *love* this city."

"We have parties like this in our city, too," Marla said, sliding closer to the wall in order to let the crowd ebb and flow around her. "My old mentor, Artie, used to throw them. He loved having people over, fucking on his living room floor, while he sat and smoked a cigar and ate a ham sandwich and watched."

"Some people have a strange sense of fun," Rondeau said.

Marla snorted. "He didn't do it for fun. He—"

But before she could finish, Zara appeared before them, smiling at Rondeau. Maybe her simpering look from earlier *had* been aimed at him in particular, then. She wore a wide leather collar, shiny black, with a silver ring in the front, and a black latex maid's apron. Silver bars pierced her nipples horizontally, and she had a ring in her belly button. In one hand she carried a battered leather backpack—not unlike Marla's—from which the handle of a whip protruded. The deeper contents of the bag clinked, metal on metal, when it shifted. To his credit, Rondeau didn't stammer or drool—he smiled and nodded to her. "You look wonderful."

She dropped an ironic little curtsy. "I'm going to walk around a bit and see who's here, then I'll be downstairs. You should look for me later." She glanced at Marla, then lowered her eyes demurely. "If that's all right with . . . everyone."

Marla laughed. "He doesn't belong to me, sweetheart. Don't worry."

"Yeah," Rondeau said. "I don't belong to anybody."

"I'll see you, then," Zara said, and slipped into the stream of people pouring deeper into the house.

"All is forgiven," Rondeau said. "The way you took the window seat on the plane, the sightseeing tour that culminated in a parking-garage elevator, all of it. I think I'm going to like it here."

Marla considered trying to restrain Rondeau, to

make him focus on the serious work at hand, but what harm was there in letting him run off and play? He wouldn't be much help in talking to Finch, and it might prove advantageous to have a secret ally in the house. "All right," Marla said. "But check in with me in an hour or so. I'll meet you in the kitchen. And if I'm not there, come *looking* for me, all right?"

"You're a princess among peasants, Marla," Rondeau said. He went to get a paper sack, then began to strip.

Marla sighed. It would be more conspicuous to walk around a party like this fully clothed, and she didn't want to start any buzz or commotion—she just wanted to find Finch. She'd thought her days of walking around mostly naked before crowds of strangers had ended a long time ago, when she gave up waitressing in favor of sorcery. At least she wasn't a novice at public nudity. She asked for a grocery sack and undressed, stripping down to boots, panties, and cloak. With the cloak closed around her, she looked as modest as a nun, though of course it slipped open with every step. Marla was a long way from prudish, but she had a chief sorcerer to parlay with tonight, and negotiation in the nude hardly seemed like bargaining from a position of strength.

She went deeper into the house, to look around, and to look for Finch.

Jared, the young man who'd leered at her in line outside, started following her right away, and no number of glares thrown over her shoulder seemed to discourage him.

5

B sat with a few people he didn't know in the hot tub behind Finch's house, pleased that so far no strangers had recognized him. He'd never been a superstar, but he'd had a certain flavor-of-the-month quality for a while, and had starred in one very high-profile, successful film; he thought of himself as the cinematic equivalent of a one-hit wonder. There had been a time when he'd craved attention, and loved being recognized, but these days he preferred obscurity and when he was recognized, it was sometimes all he could do to be graceful about it, especially since so many people started by saying "Didn't you used to be . . . ?" Though when cute guys like Rondeau knew who he was, and expressed appreciation, he wasn't above basking a little.

B hadn't intended to come to a sex party tonight, but when he'd gone to one of his old hangouts he'd run into Daniel, a friend from before B got into the movies. Daniel greeted him as if he'd seen B just last week instead of six years before, and suggested he come to the party.

"I'm not sure I'm in the mood to hook up tonight," B said.

Daniel clutched B's elbow in mock alarm. "You? B? Once the terror of the seven club scenes? Too bad, but who cares? It's fun even if you don't fuck. Though that's sort of like going to a casino, not gambling, and having a great time at the all-you-can-eat shrimp buffet. Still, there's a hot tub, and if you like to watch—and I seem to recall you do—then there's plenty to see. The guests are usually pretty hot, too, though you have to put up with the dykes and the hets. The guy who throws the parties, Finch, is a total bear, but he likes to mix things up at his parties."

"I know Finch," B said. "I used to go to his parties back in the day. But I don't know...."

"Or you could sit here and drink fizzy water and turn guys down all night," Daniel said. "It's *your* call. You can even come back to my place first, get a shower, I'll loan you something a little more fashionable than the street-people chic you're wearing now."

So B had come, and was spending the evening *sitting* in fizzy water and turning guys down. Women, too, for that matter. But everyone here was well mannered, and no one seemed more than a little put out by B's polite refusals. B remembered orgies where everyone was drunk and high and nobody remembered who or what they'd been fucking all night once morning came, but alcohol and drugs were absolute no-nos at Finch's parties. That made sense, at least when one considered the dungeon—there was stuff down there that no one should use while mentally impaired. B had never been heavily into S&M. A few props, a little leather, that stuff could spice things up, but he'd never gotten off on elaborate scenes and equipment. Still, he had to admire their unseen host's completism—there was stuff down there B had never seen before outside of a magazine or video.

He slipped out of the water and sat on the edge of the tub for a bit, cooling off. Someone had told him that the people who ran the party periodically turned up the heat in the hot tub to drive people out, so that the same few people wouldn't monopolize the tub all night. But B figured, since he wasn't fucking anyone or eating the snacks, his twenty dollars had bought him a permanent place in the tub.

When he saw Marla Mason emerge onto the back deck, B sank down into the tub up to his chin. He did *not* want her to think he was following her—who knew how she'd react? Of course, he'd planned to be where she was going tomorrow, so he'd have to deal with it then, but he was here to relax, to forget about oracles and monsters and sorcerers for a while. His stomach began to churn, acid sloshing, and he wondered if he was getting an ulcer again.

Some guy with the standard-issue San Francisco hacker-boy look—short hair and chunky glasses—was following Marla like an overeager dog. He was naked except for a nasty-looking steel choke-collar, but the leash wasn't in Marla's hand—it was dangling down his back. He was talking—pleading almost— and Marla was ignoring him, clearly annoyed, stalking across the deck with the precision of an irritated cat. B couldn't help but grin—Marla had found herself a willing submissive, and she wasn't willing to do anything about it. She did emanate a certain dominant quality, though B wasn't sure how that would translate to her bedroom preferences. She must be like catnip to the submissive het men here, though.

He thought about going to talk to her, to rescue her from the eager sub, but she probably wouldn't be happy to see him. Maybe he didn't have enough psychic ability for her to take seriously—what did he know about it, after all? Maybe he really was a midget among giants. But his dream had been clear: Marla Mason would die unless he did something to stop it, and if Marla Mason died, the whole city would be destroyed—worse than the exodus of busted dotcommers at the turn of this century, worse than gentrification, worse even than the 1906 earthquake and fire. B didn't know the details, but it had something to do with frogs. Which sounded silly, but the visions didn't lie, any more than the oracles and sibyls B so often found himself in contact with did.

Only the risk of a whole city getting more-or-less destroyed could bring B back across the bay, from the home of his current low-key equilibrium in Oakland, to this miserable place where he'd been so happy, once, back when he deserved such things.

Marla stood on the back deck for a long moment, then darted down the steps to the basement. Her self-appointed submissive followed.

B grinned. She'd just gone into the dungeon. Not a great escape route to choose when fleeing an overzealous submissive. *Good-bye, frying pan. Nice to meet you, fire.* He sat back in the bubbling water. Why worry about Marla? She wouldn't die tonight, the spirit in the Dumpster had assured him of that much. All his problems would still be waiting for him in the morning.

Someone slid into the water next to him, jostling a little—that was inevitable, given how packed the hot tub generally was—and then that someone said, "Hey, B. Didn't expect to see you here."

B opened his eyes. It was Marla's friend, or associate, or lackey, or whatever, Rondeau. "Um," B said. "It's a total coincidence, I just came here to—"

"It's cool," Rondeau said. "I'm not exactly here on business myself, though I can't speak for Marla."

A willowy, pale blonde slid into the hot tub, sat in Rondeau's lap, and began to nuzzle his ear. Rondeau winked at B. "I won't even mention to Marla that I saw you, 'kay?"

"Thanks," B said. "But it really is just a coincidence."

"Marla doesn't believe in coincidences. Events have gravity, she says, and when the same people and places and images and things keep popping up together, especially when you *know* something big is happening, that's not coincidence. It's confluence. It's *magic*. So you know. Maybe we'll be seeing you around."

"Magic," B repeated, but Rondeau didn't seem to hear him. The blonde in his lap was doing something with her hand under the water that had wholly captivated his attention.

B leaned his head back again. Confluence. Sure. He could appreciate the sense in that.

Marla didn't have a chance to look for Finch in peace, because she'd picked up something in the anteroom. "My name's Jared," he said. "I want you to whip me."

"As much as I'd like to see you whipped," Marla said, "I'm busy."

That turned out to be the wrong thing to say, because now the moron thought she *wanted* to whip him. She hadn't meant to encourage him, but with a masochist, it was hard to be discouraging. If she threatened to kick his ass, he'd goad her further in hopes of achieving that result. And if she *really* kicked his ass—not in some safe-sane-and-consensual way, but the way she increasingly *wanted* to—they'd throw her out of the party, and she'd blow her chance of seeing Finch.

Jared followed her down the hallway, and Marla kept hoping someone else would grab hold of his leash, or at the very least that it would snag on a doorknob, but no such luck. The house was nice, what Marla could see of it, though the decorations were a bit one-note—the pictures hanging on the walls were prints of Mapplethorpe's nudes and framed programs from all-male revues, stuff like that. Made sense, if Finch was a pornomancer, but dully predictable.

The hallway ended at a small living room decorated with lots of white wicker furniture and a big-screen television playing porn. People in various states of undress sat around, probably recuperating from or gearing up for heights of sexual excess. The doorkeeper in the velvet cape was there, sitting on a bar stool, watching the television. "Excuse me," Marla said.

The woman looked up and smiled. She was pretty, dark-eyed with full lips and a dark cast to her skin. "Mmm," the woman said. "I wouldn't mind licking *your* boots. But I'm working tonight—just taking a little break to rest my feet." She wiggled her ankle, and Marla glanced down to see spike heels, the clasps held closed with little golden padlocks. "Finch likes to keep me on my toes."

"You're, uh, close to Finch?" Marla asked. Her admirer was hovering impatiently behind her, but she chose to ignore him.

"Oh, he doesn't fuck me," she said, laughing. "Though he's told me my ass is as pretty as a boy's, which I take as a compliment. He's been helping to train me as a submissive."

"You seem pretty bold for a sub in training," Marla said.

The woman grinned and shrugged. "Like I said, I'm taking a break."

"Is Finch around?" Marla said. "I need to talk to him."

The woman looked at her again, more speculatively. "You don't strike me as someone who wants sub training, and you look like you know how to be a dom already."

Marla found herself strangely flattered. It was always nice to hear that she radiated confidence.

"No, that's not what I need to talk to him about," Marla said. "We have some mutual friends. I just want to chat with him."

"He'll be down later, probably," she said, shrugging. "Just have fun in the meantime, grab something to eat." She nodded to Jared. "You should probably beat your boy, too—he looks like he's about to wiggle out of his skin."

"He's not my boy," Marla muttered, drawing her cloak around her and stepping into the kitchen, which adjoined the living room. There was juice and bottled water on the counter, and a buffet of sorts laid out on a sideboard, with asparagus, bowls of M&M's, hummus, pita bread, artichoke dip—all finger food. Jared was still following her, and in the kitchen, Marla turned on him. "Look, aren't there rules about unwelcome advances?"

He looked wounded. "You *said* you wanted to see me whipped. There are rules about messing with someone's head, too, you know."

"I meant you *deserve* to be whipped, you annoying little shit," Marla said.

"You're right, mistress."

"Don't *call* me that," she snapped. "Gods, you're a fuckwit." He clearly enjoyed being scolded, so she clenched her teeth and went through the French doors onto the back deck.

It was a little slice of paradise back here, Marla thought, suddenly jarred from her irritation. This was a hidden garden courtyard in the midst of the city's streets. Marla took in all the amenities: a multilevel redwood deck with stairs leading up to the second floor; a hot tub big enough for ten; in the far corner, a majestic oak tree strung with electric fairy lights, branches spreading out as if administering a benediction; a pagoda-shaped fountain, furry with moss, standing on a mound of smoothly polished rocks in the adjacent corner; and a fourteen-foot privacy fence around the whole thing. Even the people in the hot tub, and the others standing in loose knots and talking, wearing sarongs or towels or nothing at all, seemed like a natural part of the garden. It was altogether beautiful.

That's how Marla knew there was a spell on the place. Though she could just barely believe in her own innate capacity to appreciate landscape and architecture, she knew she'd never like any landscape *better* with people in it. Marla sniffed the air, not trying to *smell,* exactly, but to sense at least the essential nature of the spell; sniffing helped her concentrate, because it seemed to somehow externalize the metaphysical process.

The spell was simple, not really powerful enough to qualify as mind-control—it was simply calming everyone down, instilling in them a fleeting sense of gestalt with the other partygoers. Sort of like a mild airborne dose of ecstasy. Marla's pet riot-cops back home used a much stronger version of the same spell for crowd control. There was an element of sexual enhancement here, too, a little nudge to the libido that Marla felt between her own thighs, but not as much as she might have expected, given that Finch probably drew his power from the sexual energy around him. She supposed that providing people with a fabulous house and a host of new partners to have sex with was enough to get everyone's urges ramped up, even without the help of magic.

Marla glanced back. Jared was still there, looking both eager and downcast, and Marla briefly considered giving him what he wanted—a few lashes, a boot to the ass, then an order to go fuck someone else. A spark of anger floated up through the top of her calm then—she *wanted* to be irritated, she got her *edge* from being irritated, and Finch's randy-sheep spell wasn't going to change her. She needed to find the host of this party and find out what he knew about the Cornerstone, and then she could *go*.

Both to get away from the tagalong submissive, and to see what else there was to see of the house, Marla went down the low stone stairs into the dark basement. Her vision adjusted instantly to the gloom, and it was light enough that she didn't need her night-eyes.

The basement—or dungeon, she supposed, though it wasn't a *real* dungeon, being dry, well insulated, and lacking vermin—could have served well as the set for porn movies, except for the low ceilings. Everything was black, even the carpet and the support pillars, and especially the equipment, which was of a better quality than Marla had expected. One could improvise a spanking horse from a sawhorse and some padding, after all, but Finch had invested in a black-leather number with chrome accents. Marla hoped the young man currently chained over it, receiving the attentions of his broad-shouldered companion, appreciated the luxury and the lack of splinters. A woman lay bound to a gyno table, which was suspended from the ceiling by heavy chains—the table was also black leather with chrome accents. That seemed to be Finch's motif. Not exactly original, but she supposed pinstripes or polka dots would have been out of place.

One group had dispensed with the need for bondage equipment entirely. They had a woman in pigtails bound tightly to a support pillar with cling wrap, and the two men fondled her roughly, slapped her face gently, and kissed her. There were a few doors along one wall, presumably with closet-sized spaces behind them, with oval holes cut in the door at crotch height—what sex party would be complete without a few glory holes? None of them was in use at the moment, though. There were cages of varying heights and sizes—one was the size of a jail cell, while another was almost too low to even crawl into; the occupant would have to slither in. Marla briefly considered the cages as a way of getting rid of her persistent admirer, but a quick glance showed her that none of them had real locks, just latches that could be lifted from the inside as easily as the outside. This *was* a public party, after all—longtime playmates could use locks, but it wasn't such a good idea when playing with strangers. In addition to the people playing, there were others with penlights, and bags filled with safe-sex supplies—gloves, dams, condoms, lube, and the like. Dungeon monitors were here to make sure everything was safe and consensual, and that no one was so caught up in the moment that they forgot to use protection.

Marla turned a corner, wondering how many rooms the basement had—she suspected the division into rooms was meant to make it seem more vast and labyrinthine than it actually was. A small crowd was gathered to watch a woman with an impressively large strap-on fuck her girlfriend, who was dangling in a full-body leather sling. Marla paused for a moment to watch—the couple had charisma, and a good sense of showmanship. People didn't just come to sex parties hoping to sleep with strangers, after all; those with exhibitionist tendencies came to show off their skills with current partners, too. The room beyond held a few alcoves with padded floors and mattresses, most of which were inhabited by people having more-or-less straight sex. One couple was unpacking a suitcase filled with whips—a ribbon flogger, a cat-o'-nine-tails, a quirt, even a long bullwhip. A varnished-wood X-frame with metal rings at the four points leaned against the back wall. Marla turned to her admirer. "Okay," she said. "You think you want a whipping?"

"Oh, yes."

Marla went to the couple on the mattress. "I'll give you a hundred dollars for that bullwhip."

"Actually, it cost about five hundred," the man said.

"Five hundred?" Marla said. "That's what you get for shopping at fetish stores—next time, go where the ranchers go. You'll get a better whip for a lot less money. It might not be shiny black, but it'll get the job done." She sighed. "But, okay, I'll give you six hundred for it."

"You know, it takes a lot of practice to use one of these correctly. If you don't know what you're doing, you can really hurt somebody—"

"Look, is it a deal, or not?" Marla interrupted. "I know how to use a bullwhip. Don't teach your grandma to suck eggs." She reached into her boot for her money clip and counted out six hundred dollars in twenty-dollar bills.

The man glanced at the woman he was with, shrugged, and said, "Sure. We mostly use it as a prop anyway."

Marla picked up the bullwhip, did a few swimmer's stretches, and lashed the whip through empty air with a resounding crack—the sound came from the end of the whip breaking the sound barrier. People crowded around the doorway, made curious by the whip-crack, most likely, and eager to see the show.

Marla set the coiled whip on the floor and led Jared to the X-frame. She tied his wrists and ankles in place with the loops of heavy cotton rope that protruded from the arms of the X. "You're sure you want me to do this?"

"Oh, yes," he said. His eyes were wide, and he kept licking his lips. No one could say he hadn't asked for it.

Marla turned her head and nodded to the crowd in the doorway. They'd all heard Jared ask for this—they shouldn't have an excuse to throw her out now.

She took the bullwhip to the far end of the room. Marla cracked her knuckles. "It's been a long time," she said, "but let's see if I can still write my name in somebody's ass." She let the whip fly.

When Jared cried, "Safe word! Red! Red!" Marla let the whip drop. The people watching burst into spontaneous applause.

"That's it?" she said. "You follow me around, asking me to beat you, and all I get is seven strokes?"

Jared didn't answer, just panted and leaned his forehead against the wall before him.

"Somebody should untie him," Marla said.

Block letters, each line a stroke of the whip that had just barely drawn blood, spelled out "MA" on Jared's left butt cheek. The lettering was so neat, it might have been written with a knife.

Jared, untied by one of the watchers, stepped off the X-frame and winced. "I thought we might play more," he said, not very hopefully. "Something less... stingy."

"No, thanks," Marla said. "I said I wanted to see you whipped, and I got what I wanted. I'm sure you won't lack for people who want to dominate you, walking around here with 'MA' written on your ass." She glanced around. "That bullwhip's up for grabs, if anyone wants it. Just clean the tip with some alcohol." Drawing her cloak around her, she slipped out of the room, and up out of the dungeon, people complimenting her on her whip-handling all the way. Marla even muttered acknowledgment to a few of the comments.

Whipping the idiot had been fun—she hadn't done anything nasty in *hours,* and she'd been feeling fidgety. But now she wanted to find Finch. After her performance with the bullwhip, other people were going to start following her around and asking for her attention, and she simply wasn't in the mood.

She spotted Rondeau in the hot tub, with Zara squirming in his lap, and walked in their direction.

Then she saw Bradley Bowman in the hot tub beside them, doing his best to be inconspicuous. "Well," she said, crouching by the tub, behind them, whispering into Bradley's ear. "I *know* you didn't simply follow us, because I would have noticed. Has someone been using their little twitch of psychic ability to find out where I'm going to be, hmm?"

"It's not what you think," B said. "When you blew me off this afternoon, I went looking for something to do to pass the time, and I ended up here."

"So you've been to these parties before?" Marla said, voice silky and dangerous.

"I think he's on the up-and-up, Marla," Rondeau said. "He nearly peed in the pool when he saw me. I don't think it has anything to do with us. This party is just the place to be, is all."

Zara yawned, pointedly, and Rondeau went back to nuzzling.

"There's no such thing as a coincidence, Rondeau," Marla said. "Not on a night like this. If B's here, he's almost certainly here for a reason, even if we don't know what it is."

"See?" Rondeau said to B. "I told you." Zara made a petulant noise at his inattention.

"Confluence," B said.

"That's right," Marla said. "Now, what do you know about Finch?"

B shrugged uncomfortably and glanced around at the other people—the ordinaries—in the hot tub. "Nothing much. Nothing more than anybody else knows."

Marla sighed. Discretion was all well and good, but she was tired of being patient. She'd wasted too much of today killing hummingbirds and whipping idiots, and she wanted some forward momentum. She dipped her finger into the hot tub and swirled it counterclockwise. After a moment, the ordinaries in the tub climbed out and wandered away. Even Zara climbed off Rondeau's lap and went into the house.

Rondeau sighed. "I only had sex with her once. We were sitting here so I could recuperate."

"Maybe you can hook up with her again later," B said, sliding out of the water.

"Yeah, sure," Rondeau said. "But do you think I really want to look underneath all those other people to find her?"

"You know," B said, "you could've asked me to

get out of the tub, and we could have gone to a private corner of the yard to talk."

"Marla prefers direct action," Rondeau said. "Which is why you'd better start telling her about Finch."

"I meant what I said, pretty much," B said. "Finch is a rich, horny, pushy, generous, no-nonsense bear of a guy. He throws parties and trains submissives. He also runs an independent press, publishes erotica and nonfiction about sex. I'm pretty sure he makes pornos, too, all kinds, though that's the shady side of his business, and I think on paper he doesn't have anything to do with movies at all." B glanced around. "I hear he does stuff for the, ah, specialty market. Really hardcore S&M, the kind that's only questionably legal in this country. I've heard rumors that he does snuff films, but I think that's bullshit, it's just the kind of thing people say when they hear about somebody making illicit movies."

Marla shook her head. "Bowman, we're not the vice cops. I don't care if Finch makes movies of dogs pissing on his mother. You've got a streak of extra-perception—what does *that* tell you about Finch?"

B shook his head. "I haven't actually seen him in person in years, not since before . . . I became this way. So I don't know."

Marla made a disgusted sound. "Maybe this is just coincidence, you being here. Wasting my time. I think I'm going to have to start beating people up until Finch comes around to deal with me personally."

"Wait, you just want to *see* him?" B said.

"Yes. That's why we're *here*. But I'm tired of waiting."

"Well, hell," B said. "I'll show you up to his room, if you like."

"Give it your best shot," Marla said. "If it were me, I'd make sure my room was really hard to find."

"Oh, I've been there before," B said. "Back when I was famous. Finch and me and a couple of other guys had some fun together one night."

"Lead on," she said.

"Should I come, too?" Rondeau said.

"No," Marla said. "No reason for us to look like a parade. Besides, if things get nasty, I'd like to have some backup Finch doesn't know about. If you hear a commotion, come running."

"I shudder to imagine a commotion that you couldn't handle but *I* could."

"Stranger things happen," Marla said, and followed Bradley Bowman up the stairs to the deck on the second floor. There were couples in various stages of undress and excess in all corners of the deck, and Marla and B wove around them. The second floor was all windows in back—and inside, the floor was covered with groups of sucking, groping, gasping people. Half a dozen men stood on either side of the walkway to the door, watching the people inside through the windows while they tugged on their cocks—walking past them would be like running a gauntlet, Marla thought. Fortunately, B kept leading her around the side of the house. "Finch is on the third floor, up these stairs," he said.

"What stairs?" Marla said, annoyed, and B took her hand. She gasped. There was a wooden stairway, right there, going up the side of the house, ending at a door. She hadn't seen it, or sensed its presence at all.

Marla almost *never* failed to notice a door. She looked at B with new respect. Maybe he was more than a half-assed seer.

"It's usually not so hard to find," B said. "I've been here for smaller parties, stuff like that, and it's not usually hidden at all. But I think Finch likes his privacy for these big gatherings."

"I'm sure he does," Marla said. "He's probably sitting up there, soaking in all the accumulated sexual energy, storing it up for use later."

"What do you mean?" B said.

"I think Finch is a sexual magician. All these people fucking produces a kind of energy, and a sorcerer can tap into that to power spells, to commit acts of magic. The people downstairs think they're just having a good time—and they are, maybe even a better time than they would have otherwise, since Finch has spells on the place to make people want to fuck more—but they're also giving Finch his strength."

"Are you a, uh, sexual magician, too?"

Marla laughed. "From anyone else, I'd think that was a come-on. No, I'm not a pornomancer, I'm a foul-rag-and-bone-shop sorcerer. I do a little bit of everything. Jill-of-all-trades. I know a lot about sex magic, though. My old mentor, Artie Mann, was a pornomancer."

"Did he throw parties like this?"

"Sometimes, but for a different reason. Artie didn't like to depend on anyone else for anything. He did a big spell to make himself impotent when he was in his twenties, at his sexual peak."

"He was a sex magician who couldn't have erections?" B said.

"It was kind of brilliant, actually," Marla said. "He owned a bunch of strip clubs, and he surrounded himself with young women, and I think he chose me as an apprentice as much because of my appearance as for any other reason. He wanted to fuck *constantly*, but he couldn't, he'd made it impossible for himself, and the frustration and tension built up in him to tremendous levels. He used the energy from that tension to power his magic. So while Finch needs all these dozens of people screwing to give him power, Artie just had to go to one of his strip clubs, and in a pinch, he could just watch some porn. He did sometimes have people over to his place for parties, though not on this scale. He didn't draw his power from the guests, though, like Finch does."

"Wow," B said. "Pretty smart. Except he couldn't *fuck*."

"I never said it was a flawless method," Marla said. She glanced up the stairs. "I should go up and introduce myself. You know Finch. Is he the type to listen to a reasonable request?"

B shrugged. "Sure, I guess. He doesn't take shit from anyone, but he's always struck me as a reasonable guy. I used to think he was great, super-nice, to throw these parties in his house, but I didn't realize he had ulterior motives . . . still, sure, he'll listen to a reasonable request."

"Good," Marla said. "That's good to hear." She cracked her knuckles. "We'll see how he handles *un*-reasonable requests, then." She went up the stairs to Finch's door, leaving B below.

6

Marla hesitated outside the door. She still had her boots on, and they were ensorcelled so that she could kick down just about any door that wasn't reinforced with iron, but did she really want to go in hard? Finch was the chief sorcerer of this city for the moment, and he was sitting on top of a geyser of sexual energy right now—maybe she shouldn't mess with him. He'd come down to the party eventually, after all.

She frowned and shook her head, then slapped herself hard on the cheek. Her head cleared. Finch had some sort of a self-confidence-deflation spell going on up here, probably to get rid of anyone who managed to wander up accidentally. Screw that. Maybe if he hadn't tried to cut her confidence out from under her, Marla would have simply knocked, but Finch's subtle little mood-altering spells pissed her off. She lifted her foot and kicked the door, just below the doorknob, and after a sharp snap the door swung open.

Finch was in the small bedroom beyond the door, standing up and fucking someone who leaned over the bed. Both Finch and his partner looked up when the door opened. Finch was a big, hairy guy—he could have been a lumberjack or a professional wrestler, though his brown beard was neatly trimmed, and the guy he was riding was...

Not human. His skin was grayish, his eyes mere depressions in his head, and as Marla stood watching he disappeared, shredding apart into wisps, leaving Finch standing empty-handed over a plastic-covered bed smeared with gray slime.

"Oh, *nasty*!" Marla cried. "You fuck *ghosts*?" She'd heard of ectoplasmophilia, though it was, to say the least, a rarefied taste—it took a lot of power to give a ghost enough substance to make penetration possible. Most of the sorcerers Marla knew, generally as morally relativistic a group as one could imagine, found the whole idea appalling, akin to bestiality, though personally Marla thought it was more like fucking *dead* animals. Ghosts couldn't technically consent, true, but they were only just barely conscious, just a psychic heat-signature left over from someone's death. Marla didn't think ectoplasmophilia was particularly immoral. She just thought it was gross.

Finch took a white hand towel from his bedside table and wiped gray goo off his cock. "Shut the door," he said quietly.

Marla kicked it shut behind her, and it actually closed, though it didn't exactly hang straight on the frame anymore.

Finch stretched his arms over his head, then cracked his neck. "I wish you'd come in ten minutes later," he said. "I would've been finished, and then I wouldn't be starting this conversation filled with quite so much rage."

Marla rolled her eyes. "Like I knew you were going to be shagging Casper. I thought you'd be sitting up here cross-legged in a mystic circle, collecting sexual energy."

Finch shrugged. "None of that energy is going to waste, I assure you. And you disapprove of my sexual practices, Ms. Mason?"

She wasn't surprised he knew her name. Since he hadn't tried to kill her yet, she'd assumed he must have some idea who she was. "I don't disapprove, exactly, any more than I disapprove of watching someone eat roadkill. To each his own. I just think it's disgusting."

Finch nodded thoughtfully, walking to a small closet. Marla tensed, but Finch just took out a thin red robe and put it on, tying the sash carefully. "Every sorcerer, apprentice, and low-class alley wizard in this city knows that if they betray me or hurt me, I'll bring them back from the dead and rape their ghosts. It's a surprisingly powerful deterrent. Even though most profess belief that the ghost is just a collection of metaphysical dead skin cells, not in any sense the soul of an actual *person*, they still don't want me to get my spirit hands on *their* ghosts."

Marla felt a grudging respect for Finch after he said that. Any sorcerer could make outlandish threats—it was practically their stock-in-trade—but Finch clearly followed through. He was also queer for ghosts, and got off on what he did, no question, but everyone had kinks—who was she to judge? "I can see why that might make people less inclined to fuck with you."

"And on that note, how can I help *you*, Ms. Mason?"

"Call me Marla," she said, and leaned back against the wall. "Did that Chinese guy call you and tell you I was coming?"

Finch shrugged. "Reporting on the presence of out-of-town sorcerers is one of his responsibilities while I'm in charge. He asked me not to kill you, by the way. He looks forward to that honor himself."

"Well, *that's* a relief," Marla said. "And here I was worried you were going to try fucking my ghost. Or do you only do that to boy ghosts?"

He waved a hand. "A ghost is a ghost is a ghost. They're malleable—I can shape them into nearly anything I want. You told my colleague in Chinatown that you were here to find something—something Lao Tsung had?—and that then you'd be on your way. How can I expedite matters, and get you out of my city?"

She crossed her arms. This was it. "I need access to a Cornerstone, and Lao Tsung told me there's one here."

Finch just stared at her. "A Cornerstone," he repeated.

Marla ignored him. Verbal delaying tactics didn't interest her.

"Hmm," he said. "It's true that there is one in San Francisco—I'm sure you know that much already—and it's true that Lao Tsung made use of it. In return for its use, he stayed here and acted as its guardian. But the stone itself . . . every use erodes it, Marla, and the making of such artifacts—if they were ever made at all, if they aren't the gallstones or coprolites of a primordial god or something else supernaturally occurring—is lost to us. I can't let you near the Cornerstone without a fantastically good reason."

The most fantastically good reason was that Marla *wanted* him to, and she'd pull his intestines out through his face if he didn't do as she asked, but there was no need to get nasty and physical right away. Especially since Finch might have tricks of his own. "Erosion? Be serious. You could cast spells with the Cornerstone every day and it would still last centuries."

"We take the long view," Finch said. "We want it to last millennia. It's a civic resource. What spell do *you* need to cast that requires the power of a Cornerstone behind it?"

"I need to cast a binding spell. An ironclad one that will last forever, and can't be undone. The Cornerstone is the only way."

Finch frowned. "That's rather vague. Aren't there other options for you? I understand there's a Cornerstone beneath the British Museum—"

"No, the old chief sorcerer of London, Ballard, got his hands on that one; he crushed it up and ate it last year. Ingested its energy as it dissipated. Don't you keep up with the international news? Now Ballard's an immortal statue in some protected monastery courtyard, set to wake up and become flesh again when the last rain forest is destroyed. Then he's going to summon the angry ghosts of all the devastated ecosystems and take over the world, or something, I forget what. Crazy idea, but it might work. I'll be irredeemably dead by then, though."

"He *ingested* a Cornerstone?" Finch said, and

from his voice, Marla couldn't tell if he was horrified or impressed.

Marla nodded. "Yeah, Ballard was a prick, but it's not like the Cornerstone was doing any good under the British Museum before he got hold of it."

"No, but it wasn't doing any *harm,* either, which is just as important. How do I know you don't want it for . . . something horrible? I had another visitor some weeks ago, who wanted to use the Cornerstone for his own ends, and I turned him down, too—don't take it personally. You aren't as clearly insane as that man was, but still, I'm hesitant. Why should I trust *you*?"

"This crazy guy," Marla said, sensing the edge of a hunch. "Was he an older man, carrying a cane and wearing an old-fashioned beaver hat?"

Finch frowned. "Very much no. He was young, and he wore snakeskin underwear."

Crap. So much for hunches. "Got him down to his underwear, did you?" She grinned.

"Hardly. He didn't wear anything else, except for an odd cape."

"Really." That sounded like the same person who'd been seen arguing with Lao Tsung. "What was his name?"

"It was something improbable. . . ." Finch looked up at the ceiling for a moment. "Mutex. He called himself Mutex."

"Sounds like the name of a third-string super-villain."

"I expressed a similar opinion. He assured me it was a very old family name. He's Central American, I think. Why do you care about him?"

"The guy in Chinatown told me Lao Tsung was

seen arguing with a guy in underwear and a cape, and if that same guy was here asking you about the Cornerstone, it's reasonable to assume he was asking Lao Tsung about the same thing—"

"I *am* aware of the connection, Marla, and we are investigating. This Mutex came to me first. When I rebuffed him, I suppose he somehow discovered Lao Tsung was the keeper of the Cornerstone, and went to him. It's possible he was somehow involved in Lao Tsung's death. As I said, we're looking into it. There's no need for you to involve yourself in our civic affairs. We've dealt with rogue sorcerers and inspired lunatics before. This Mutex, if he's more than a simple mad-man, will be dealt with as well."

Marla gritted her teeth. She didn't trust these people to wipe their own asses, let alone avenge her friend, but she knew that wasn't a rational reaction. She just liked taking care of things herself. She found delegation diffi-cult. "You're right. It's not my place, or my business, and I don't intend to get involved. I just want to protect my city—that's why I need the Cornerstone. I give you my word." Inspiration struck. "And if I give you my word in the presence of the Cornerstone, you'll know it's the truth." One of the peculiarities of a Cornerstone was that no one could lie if they stood within a few feet of it. In fact, Cornerstones reputedly led to a certain overly garrulous sincerity. Sorcerers weren't comfort-able around them for that very reason—when your en-tire life was built on keeping secrets and knowing things other people didn't, a stone of truth could be rather intimidating.

Finch began to crack his knuckles while gazing up at the ceiling. "I'm inclined to believe you," he said at last. "I made some calls when I heard there was a sorcerer in town claiming to be a chief from back east. You certainly sound like the Marla Mason I was told about, and as far as I can tell, you've always been honorable—as honorable as our kind ever can be, at least. My sources in your city told me you were blunt, impatient, prone to violence, indescribably lucky, honest, formidable, and well respected. I suspect you didn't bother to do any research about me."

Marla shrugged. "I figured I'd talk to Lao Tsung and be out of town by dinnertime. I didn't expect this much interaction with the locals. Will you take me to the Cornerstone?"

"I can take you in the morning," he said. "I will require certain promises and payments in return, of course, and I wouldn't mind having a formal ambassador in your city."

"What you're saying is, I'll owe you a favor."

"You'll owe me a *big* favor." He began to crack his toes, carefully, one at a time. "And not *me,* exactly. You'll owe the city of San Francisco a favor. The Cornerstone is a civic possession, and letting you take a bit of its power puts you in the city's debt."

"Fair enough," Marla said. She didn't like to be beholden to anyone, but without the Cornerstone, Susan would go ahead with her stupid, dangerous plan, and then Marla's whole city would likely fall to pieces, so it was worth a few promises on her part, even if they were promises she'd be forced to keep. "So can you keep your friend in Chinatown from trying to kill me in the meantime?"

"Oh, I doubt it," he said. "But I hear you can take care of yourself. They told me you killed Somerset."

Marla nodded. "Why do you think they respect me so much back home? Somerset almost took control of the city again, after he died, but I handled things."

"Then my friend in Chinatown shouldn't be a problem for you."

"What's his name anyway?" Marla said.

"He's never told any of us," Finch said. "He's the oldest sorcerer living in the city, though I don't think he was as old as Lao Tsung. Most call him the Celestial. He's of the old school—he believes names have power, you know."

"They do," Marla said. "But your true name isn't what's on your birth certificate, and anyone can use an alias."

"The Celestial believes that to name something is to limit it. He does not wish to limit himself. After you finish your business with the Cornerstone, and you officially owe the city a favor, he will be forbidden to harm you. In the meantime, though . . ." He spread his hands apologetically. "You're just a tourist who pissed him off. Shall we meet here, bright and early, say 7 A.M.? I'll take you to the Cornestone then, and you can be on your way by lunchtime."

"I'd rather go now."

Finch scowled. "You may not have noticed, but I'm soaking up the energy of several score romping bodies. I'm busy for the evening."

"Then just tell me where the Cornerstone is."

"No. I won't have you carrying off my city's major artifact."

Marla opened her mouth, started to protest, then stopped. "Yeah, okay. Fair enough. I'd do the same in your position." How could she possibly sleep tonight, wondering if Susan was going to cast her spell? Her source had told Marla she had a day or two, but her source had been *discovered*. Still, that didn't mean Susan could rush ahead and cast the spell early. It would require peace and meditation and preparation, after all, and Susan was probably a bit agitated after maiming Marla's informant. Marla wanted to get her protective spell over and done with, but tomorrow morning was probably soon enough. It would have to be. She didn't think she could beat the Cornerstone's location out of Finch, especially not with all the energy he had to draw on from downstairs. "I'll see you first thing tomorrow. I appreciate your help."

"I'm just doing what's in the best interest of the city," he said. "If I denied you, I doubt you'd go away quietly. I'm sure you'd do the same in my position."

"Probably I'd just kill me, if I were in your place," Marla said.

Finch nodded. "Oh, it crossed my mind to try, but I think I'd rather have you owe my city a debt. We can discuss more specific terms tomorrow. Go on downstairs, and enjoy the party." He stood up. "And never burst into my private rooms again, or we'll see which of us is *really* the better sorcerer."

Marla considered letting that go past, letting Finch get in the last word on his home turf, but it simply wasn't in her character. "I don't have to be the better sorcerer to turn you into a heap of meat and a bewildered ghost, Finch," she said. "You might be a half-decent pornomancer, but I could feed your balls to you in a fight."

"Oh, *please,*" he said, and suddenly Finch was gone, replaced by a shaggy grizzly bear with ragged claws and a powerful stench. The bear, towering over her, cocked its head and yawned.

Marla squinted at him. Illusions were easy, after all, if you knew what you were doing. Sight depended on the eye interpreting various wavelengths of light reflected from and absorbed by objects, and a talented sorcerer could make those wavelengths twist and bend in order to deceive the eye; sound was equally simple, requiring only minor variations in the vibrations of the air. Marla's eyes weren't like normal ones, though—with a bit of effort, she could see in the dark, and around metaphysical corners, and through illusions. She stepped up her vision, peering through to Finch's true form... and she saw a grizzly bear.

Finch had transformed himself into an actual (though certainly magically augmented) bear, and that was heavy-duty totemic magic. She whistled. "Wow," she said. "Not just a pornomancer, but a dancing bear, too. You've got range, Finch, I have to admit. I bet you're a lot older than you look, to have learned all that."

The bear was gone, and Finch was back, still yawning. "And you, Ms. Mason, are almost exactly the age you appear, I would wager. Don't try to outclass your elders and betters, especially when we've already reached an accommodation. I'm sure you're formidable, in your own little way—otherwise, you'd be of no use to my city—but I've been doing this a lot longer than you have."

Marla thought about reversing her cloak, but it would be criminally stupid to do so in this context, just to show off. She'd probably end up attacking him before she could flip the purple safely back to the inner lining. Besides, that wouldn't prove anything—the cloak was a powerful artifact, but it didn't have anything to do with Marla's power as a sorcerer. It was just a weapon, and while Marla could do more with the cloak than someone with no experience could, it didn't prove anything about her intrinsic abilities. She still thought she could probably beat Finch in a fight, but if she tried to prove that now, the whole house would likely as not come tumbling down, and with Finch crushed under a pile of rubble, how would she ever find the Cornerstone?

Letting go of her pride when it conflicted with the best interests of her city was one of the hardest things about being chief sorcerer. She simply couldn't engage in a pissing contest with this ghost-fucking bear. There was too much to lose.

"Take me to the Cornerstone tomorrow, and I'll get out of your pelt," Marla said. "I'll let you get back to ravishing the dead."

It was hardly an exit line for the centuries, but she'd had a long day, and it would have to do.

Marla found B and Rondeau, still alone in the hot tub. Marla crouched behind them. "I thought you'd be hip-deep in some fan of yours by now, Bowman," she said. "And you, Rondeau, why aren't I pulling you off Zara and dragging you out of this party against your will?"

"Zara was otherwise occupied already," Rondeau said, glaring down at the bubbling water in the hot tub. "She's an impatient woman with many strange and varied needs."

"Took off with another woman, huh?" Marla said, grinning.

"No comment," Rondeau said. He squinted at the house. "I note with interest that you aren't on fire, nor are you a purple flurry of killing rage, so may I assume that Mr. Finch wasn't home?"

"You underestimate my diplomatic skills, Rondeau. Finch and I *talked*. And, admittedly, indulged in some typical primate dominance behavior. He says he'll take us to . . ." She glanced at B, then back at Rondeau. "He'll take us where we need to go tomorrow morning."

"You trust him?"

"Rondeau, I'm surprised at you. Of course I don't trust him. But I think he'll do as he said. I'd cause him too much grief otherwise. Anyway, I expect to have my business done by tomorrow morning, and we'll be out of here by tomorrow afternoon."

"I don't think so, Marla," B said. "You really should listen, I have these *dreams*, and something terrible is going to—"

Marla sighed. "Listen, B-grade seer-boy, nobody ever taught you this, I guess, but there's no such thing as destiny. You guys who see as through a glass darkly and all that, you're just seeing *possibilities, likelihoods*, okay? You extrapolate beyond the limits of normal logic, or you get whispered at by various supernatural beings—and they *all* have agendas to promote and axes to grind, believe me, they don't report in an objective manner—but you don't *know* what's going to happen. Maybe last night in your dream the best-case scenario was pretty goddamn awful, but things have changed now, and if you get hit in the head by a vision tonight, I bet you'll see something different, like me and Rondeau getting on a plane and flying out of here, mission accomplished. Got it?"

"I hope you're right," B said. "But if not, if I need to find you—"

"You're a psychic," Marla said. "I guess you'll just have to predict where we'll be. Come on, Rondeau, let's get back to the hotel. We've got to get up early. See you, Bowman. I'll try to catch one of your movies on DVD when I get back home."

"Take it easy, B," Rondeau said. "And don't take it personally. Marla just does things her own way."

"Otherwise known as 'the right way,'" she said, and waved a hand to dispel the soft keep-away spell she'd cast on the hot tub. People started heading for the water right away. She stood up, and Rondeau clambered out of the tub. They headed for the door, leaving B behind.

7

Before Rondeau and Marla had walked a block from Finch's house, a man stepped out of an alleyway and blocked the sidewalk in front of them. He was broad-shouldered and short, a squat bulldog of a man, wearing what looked like a black karate gi. Marla and Rondeau moved to walk around him, and he slid over to block the way.

"I hope you're a mugger," Marla said, cracking her knuckles. "I've only whipped one ass so far tonight, and I could go for another."

"You should look for easier pickings," Rondeau said cheerfully. "She'll use your head for a punching bag."

"My master sends his greetings," the man said. His voice was formal, and he spoke with a faint Chinese accent.

"You work for the Celestial?" Marla said. "Have you come to drag us back to his lair, or just to kill us?" Rondeau was, prudently, stepping back, putting Marla between himself and the other man.

"My name is Ch'ang Hao. What is your name?"

"Your master didn't tell you that?"

"I prefer introductions to be made personally," he said, bowing slightly.

"Call me Marla."

"And your associate?"

"We're not at a cocktail party, Ch'ang Hao," she said. "State your business, throw a punch, or piss off, okay?"

He spoke past her, to Rondeau. "I regret the necessity of committing an act of violence against someone to whom I have not been introduced," he said, voice heavy with genuine regret. "It smacks of mere thuggery, a condition to which I never wish to sink. But, alas, circumstances are what they are. I—"

Marla threw a punch at his throat.

He blocked, knocking her hand aside, without even pausing in his speech. "—will do as I must." Bowing again, he slid his right foot back and brought up his hands, assuming a defensive stance.

"Get back, Rondeau," she said, and slid into a stance of her own. It had been a while since she'd used martial arts for real, and she hoped she hadn't lost the knack. Actually fighting someone was quite different from practicing at the gym or her friend Master Ward's dojo.

Ch'ang Hao moved sinuously—he was a snake stylist, or at least he was starting out in snake style. Of all the forms of five animals kung fu, snake was the most reactive, the most dependent on moving around your opponent. Fighting a snake stylist could be like fighting a pool of water, though there were plenty of whip-fast strikes for offense, and if you let a snake grapple with you, you'd quickly find yourself entangled. Not to mention the rumors about secret poisoning techniques if you got too close to a *real* snake master, which Marla suspected Ch'ang Hao probably was.

Marla's approach to martial arts was syncretic, like her approach to magic—she put together anything that seemed useful, and her own preferred style was hard to name precisely. If pressed, an educated observer would say she fought mainly with Jeet Kun Do, the style created by Bruce Lee—itself a combination of boxing and foil fencing with a core of wing chun. Jeet Kun Do was a style of brutal lunges, bone-snapping low kicks, and crippling grapples. Marla's sinewy strength was well suited to the style. The thing she liked about Jeet Kun Do was the fact that every attack was meant to be a fight-stopper. Long, drawn-out fights between martial arts masters were a cinematic invention, because a *real* fight didn't work well on a movie screen—a brief blur of action, too fast to follow with the eye, and it was over, usually in ten or fifteen seconds at the outside, excluding feints and moves meant to test your opponent's reactions. But Jeet Kun Do took that to its logical extreme. A Jeet Kun Do stylist meant every strike to be the last one.

Ch'ang Hao's hands rippled forward.

Marla struck back, intercepting his blows and trying to land her own at the same time. She liked Jeet Kun Do because there were no blocks, just counterstrikes that served as blocks. Ch'ang Hao hit hard, and he was fast, but Marla didn't have any trouble knocking his strikes aside. She knew he was just testing her at this point, seeing what she could do. She, in turn, winced when he hit, to make him think the blows hurt more than they had.

They could go on sparring like this, but she didn't care for games—she got enough of those with Master Ward at the dojo. She'd make Ch'ang Hao fight *her* fight. She went for his knees with a low kick, and when he stepped aside to avoid it, she got into grappling distance, grabbed him, twisted him against her hip, and bounced him onto the ground. Ch'ang Hao sprang up, lashing out at her—and snakes came out of his sleeves, little hissing asps, fangs bared, leaping straight for her face. Marla shouted a bug-in-amber spell, and the asps hung in the air, still hissing, as Marla stepped away from them.

Fucking snakes! First frogs, then hummingbirds, then Finch's bear trick, and now *snakes*?

"I've got it," Rondeau said, flipping out his butterfly knife and slicing the asps in two with a casual twist of his wrist. The severed snake-halves fell to the pavement.

Ch'ang Hao took advantage of Marla's distraction, striking at her head. Marla blocked with her arm—the blow numbed her from the wrist to the elbow—and jabbed her other fist into his throat. He dropped to one knee, then struggled to his feet, hissing inhumanly—and began to *grow*. Marla thought it was simply an illusion meant to intimidate her, at first, but no—he was actually gaining mass, getting taller, his shoulders broadening, the muscles in his arms and calves bulging. His clothes split at the seams and fell away, revealing a complex harness of brown leather straps with copper-colored studs he wore underneath. The straps cut visibly into his expanding flesh, and when a strange, yellowish blood began to run down his arms, legs, and chest, Marla realized the copper studs were actually the heads of nails—the harness was *nailed* to him, and as he expanded against the bonds, the nails dug in and wounded him. He gasped, standing eight feet tall now, but hunched over in the constricting harness. Marla didn't relax, but it was clear Ch'ang Hao wasn't about to attack anyone.

"That's some serious fucking bondage," Rondeau said.

"Hush," Marla said. But he was right—it was bondage, and not of the consensual, recreational sort they'd seen at the party.

Ch'ang Hao shrank down to his old size, wincing. "If I were in possession of my full powers, I would destroy you," he said solemnly.

"That's quite a trick, changing size while retaining your original shape," Marla said. "I've never known a sorcerer who could do that, not without getting cancer in the process. That kind of stuff plays hell with your cellular integrity." She was on edge, prepared to reverse her cloak at the slightest renewed threat from this man, consequences to her humanity be damned. She didn't understand what he was, and that made her nervous.

The man spat. "I am not a sorcerer. I am *older* than your kind. I lived with the serpents before man rose up on two legs."

Marla squinted, looking beyond the obvious. She was starting to get a headache, peering into the magical realm so often tonight. She could see the tiny silver threads now, like puppet strings, attached to Ch'ang's throat, shoulders, wrists, waist, and ankles. "But you got caught by a sorcerer," Marla said. "There's a serious thrall laid on you. And that harness keeps you from getting too big and dangerous, huh?"

"I am dangerous enough for most purposes at this size," he said. "I did not expect you to be so formidable. I confess, I did not recognize your fighting style."

"Jeet Kun Do, mostly," she said. "The style Bruce Lee invented."

"I do not know Mr. Lee," he said, as if it saddened him.

"You've never heard of Bruce *Lee*?" Rondeau said. "You're even more clueless about pop culture than Marla is."

"I don't imagine our friend in Chinatown lets Ch'ang out of his box very often," Marla said. "How big can you *get* anyway?"

Ch'ang Hao almost smiled. "When I am unencumbered, I can grow just large enough to defeat whatever enemy I face. No more, no less."

"And our friend in Chinatown is afraid of you getting big enough to defeat him, huh?"

"I see that you comprehend my situation fully."

Marla nodded. "Are you going to try to kill me again?"

"If you choose to let me go free, I will report to my master that you defeated me. He will be displeased. Perhaps he will send me after you again." Ch'ang Hao shrugged.

Marla nodded. "Look, if I could cut the ties that bind, set you loose from your master's thrall . . . would you do me a favor?"

Ch'ang Hao tensed. "This is not possible," he said at last.

"I've got a knife, nice and sharp, that cuts through the metaphysical as well as the actual. I used it to cut a ghost out of Rondeau once—he'd still be possessed if it weren't for me."

"It's true," Rondeau said. "She's a dab hand with the blade."

"I can cut the threads that tie you to your master," Marla said.

Ch'ang Hao looked into the sky for a moment. "If you do this thing, my master will be your enemy forever. He . . . values my service."

"He already tried to have me killed," Marla said. "I'm not especially worried about pissing him off worse."

"You will cut the harness away?"

"I didn't say that. I don't like the idea of you getting too big for me to fight, either. But I can sever the connection between you and your master, the thrall that keeps you from running away, the one that makes you keep going back to him, that makes you obey. I'll cut the leash, but I'll leave you muzzled."

"I see," Ch'ang Hao said, his face expressionless. "And what favor will you ask in return for this great service?"

She shrugged. "I like having ancient powerful beings owe me their freedom. I don't know what I want from you, yet. I won't ask for any service that would require your death, though. Maybe the *risk* of death, but not *certain* death."

The veins in Ch'ang Hao's arms began to bulge, and snakes came slithering out of his pores, tiny at first, but growing as they emerged, four long yellow-and-black serpents that fell from his arms to the ground and slithered around their feet. Something about Ch'ang Hao's bearing let her know this wasn't an attack. Each snake took the tail of another in its mouth, forming a circle with Marla and Ch'ang Hao inside. "Inside this circle, promises are binding," Ch'ang Hao said.

Marla nodded, feeling the power of his spell. "And a poisonous death for any promise-breakers, I assume."

Ch'ang Hao nodded. "If you free me from my master's thrall, I will owe you a favor in return, to be named at your convenience."

"Sounds good to me," Marla said.

The snakes began to devour one another, the circle constricting, and Ch'ang Hao and Marla stepped over them. The snakes somehow, impossibly, devoured one another completely, until no sign of them remained.

"My blade is back at the hotel," Marla said. "Come back with us?"

Ch'ang Hao frowned. "I am not properly attired for human company."

"What, because you're wearing a bloody harness of leather straps?" Marla said. She waved her hand. "Please. This is San Francisco."

"She's got a point," Rondeau said. "But I'll loan you my jacket, just in case."

Seeing Ch'ang Hao in the mundanity of a hotel room was oddly disconcerting. Marla had experienced the same sense of fundamental dislocation in the past, during her few brushes with non-human intelligent entities. It wasn't so bad talking to him outside, in the night, but having this ancient creature sit calmly on the edge of the bed while Marla sliced through the individual silver lines connecting him to his master . . . that was bizarre. She could *feel* Ch'ang Hao's age, radiating from him like the heat of a star. Most people would take him for human, as Marla had at first, but now that she *knew*, it was different. Standing beside him was like standing close to a lion—a mixture of awe, fear, and wonder. All that despite the fact that Ch'ang Hao was dressed in one of Rondeau's T-shirts and a pair of his flannel boxer-shorts.

Rondeau was unbothered, sitting up in bed watching a reality show about strippers on HBO. Maybe the fact that Rondeau was, at core, non-human himself made him more comfortable around beings like Ch'ang Hao. Or maybe he was just being Rondeau.

Marla's dagger of office cut cleanly through the last silvery thread, and the trailing ends that still touched Ch'ang Hao's back disintegrated into silver sparkles, then disappeared. The longer ends, trailing out through the walls back to their friend in Chinatown, turned black and melted away.

Ch'ang Hao stood up, turned slowly around, and bowed to Marla. "For the first time in decades, I do not feel the weight of the chain on me."

"I guess our friend in Chinatown knows you're not his lapdog anymore, right?"

"He, too, will feel that the connection has been severed."

"So is he going to try to kill us again?" Rondeau said. "Like, before morning? Because I could use some sleep. Watching Marla fight tires me out."

"My . . . former master . . . will be otherwise occupied for some time, I think," Ch'ang Hao said. "I may still be muzzled, as Marla says, but I am not without resources, and I may now turn those powers against my former master."

"Give him hell," Marla said. "But don't get yourself killed, all right? Not while you still owe me."

"I would not dream of dying and depriving you of a favor, Marla," Ch'ang Hao said.

"There is one more thing," Rondeau said. "It's possible that the guy you *think* is your former master isn't, and his apprentice is."

Ch'ang Hao appeared to mull that over, then shook his head. "This is not my first language," he said, apologetically.

Marla clarified. "What he means is, there's a chance that our friend in Chinatown has switched bodies with his young apprentice. We're not certain, but it's a distinct possibility."

"That is ugly magic," Ch'ang Hao said. "If it is true, he owes the world an even greater debt of suffering than I had imagined. It appeared to be the old master who gave me my orders, but I have seldom spoken to him, and cannot be sure. Though I owe no mercy to my former master's assistant, I shall proceed carefully, as I wish the fullness of my vengeance only upon him who imprisoned me. There are ways and means to tell which mind resides in each body." He bowed. "Good night, Marla. If you need me, simply find any snake, and tell it you require my service. The message will reach me."

Marla nodded.

Ch'ang Hao started to leave, then hesitated. "In

the interests of honesty, and so that you understand the nature of our relationship fully, I feel I must tell you something."

"Go on," Marla said.

"You and I are, from this time forward, mortal enemies," he said, almost sadly. "I regret that such a position must be taken, but I have no choice."

It was all Marla could do to keep herself from gaping. "What? Why would you want to be my enemy? I just cut your apron strings!"

Ch'ang Hao regarded her with his cold eyes, and it was obvious that the face he wore was merely a convenience; he was not human at all. "There are few things so terrible as being enslaved. But being only half free is little better. I wear a suit of spikes, Marla Mason, and I am tormented. It is in your power to set me free, and yet you do not. You choose to leave me bound, in agony."

"I don't know you," Marla said, striving to sound as cold as Ch'ang Hao did. "I can't risk cutting you loose. I don't know what you might do."

"I understand," Ch'ang Hao said. "Nevertheless, I do not forgive you for leaving me bound, and we must therefore be enemies. Had you chosen to set me entirely free, we might have been great friends. But you sought to make me another sort of slave, to your own will, and I will not forget that."

"You're like the genie in that story. He gets freed from his bottle, but he's been imprisoned so long that he hates people, and he kills the man who released him, instead of giving him a wish."

"You have extracted your wish from me," Ch'ang

Hao said. "And I will grant it when you call. Do not doubt that."

"Fine." She crossed her arms, trying not to let her discomfort show. Making an enemy of such a powerful being was probably one of the worst mistakes she'd ever made, but she dared not let him see how much it upset her. "Then here's my wish. I wish you'd change your mind about us being enemies."

"I am bound to perform a service for you," Ch'ang Hao said. "I am *not* bound to forsake my dignity or my honor, and I will not. Call me when you have a true request to make."

"And after that, you'll try to kill me?"

"I doubt I could kill you, so long as I wear this harness. But I do not expect to be wearing it forever." He turned to Rondeau. "It was a pleasure to meet you," he said, and then left the room. Marla sat on the edge of the bed and put her head in her hands.

"He was nice, for an ancient demon," Rondeau said. "Until he got to the part about killing you someday."

"I'm pretty sure he was a snake god," Marla said, staring down at the floor. "Or at least he used to be." She sighed. "Let's get some sleep. We have to meet Finch early tomorrow." Maybe there was no reason to worry. It was possible Susan would cast her spell tonight, and then Marla wouldn't have to worry about Ch'ang Hao anymore.

Rondeau went to his room next door, leaving Marla to undress, brush her teeth, and lay in bed, gazing up at the ceiling. She normally had no trouble falling asleep, but this business with Susan had shattered her calm, driven her across the continent, mixed her up in all manner of ugly business, and now, indirectly, made her an enemy of a snake god.

She'd had better days.

"Marla." A low voice, from the direction of the bathroom. Marla sat up and activated her night-eyes.

Susan Wellstone stood in the doorway to the bathroom. "Don't bother to get up," she said. A faint silvery sheen surrounded her, like an aura of translucent sparkles.

Marla leaned back against the headboard. "Why would I? You're here by astral projection. It's not like I could bash your head open anyway." Though there were *other* things she could do, if she could reach her dagger on the nightstand and then get to Susan. "What do you want?"

"Hamil has been calling me all day. I finally took his call, and he begged for your life." Susan smiled, and even in this attenuated astral form, it was a dazzling smile. She was tall and coltish, her features stark but beautiful. "We were friends, once, long ago. Lovers, actually."

"I've heard," Marla said, looking past her to the silver astral cord that stretched from Susan's back into the darkness, across psychic space, all the way to Susan's body in Felport. If Marla could get her dagger and sever that astral cord before Susan could recall her spirit, her soul would be loosed from her body forever, and she would be as good as dead. That would solve one of Marla's problems nicely.

"So for the sake of my past with Hamil, I've come to offer you a deal. I'm willing to let you live."

"Sure," Marla said. "I assume there's a catch."

"A small one, yes. Abdicate. Name me your successor. Swear you'll never return to Felport. That's all."

"How generous," Marla said.

"Actually, it is. I could dispose of you forever, and you *know* it—that's why you ran away, isn't it? Hoping that distance would weaken my spell? But it won't. That works for some magics, but not this one."

At least she didn't know about the Cornerstone. No one back home did, except Hamil, and he wouldn't have said anything—he'd been close to Susan once, but that was a long time ago, and these days he was scarcely more fond of her than Marla was.

"We'll see," Marla said. "I have no doubt that one of us will be dead before this thing between us is finished."

"Why not abdicate?" Susan said. She stepped forward, shimmering. "You know it's the sensible thing to do. You never deserved your position. I was the one training for it, rising through the ranks, making negotiations. But *you*—you short-circuited everything."

"I did it the old-fashioned way," Marla said. "Sauvage was in charge, until Somerset killed him, taking his position. Then *I* killed Somerset, so I got to run the city. I am, by definition, the strongest."

Susan laughed. "We'll soon find out, won't we? You never fought *me*."

"Please. It would hardly be a fight. This spell you're planning, it's craven, and you know it. You're afraid to face me head-on. I'll never abdicate to you. I love Felport. I live in its streets. I believe in protecting it. You never even come out of your climate-controlled skyscraper. Why do you deserve to run the city?"

"Felport is a shithole," Susan said. "Just another rapidly oxidizing chunk of the rust belt. But it's a stepping-stone to bigger and better things, more power, more control. That's all."

"And that's why you don't deserve to run the city," Marla said, throwing her blankets off and getting out of bed, letting her fury mask her true intention. "You can't even see why you're unfit. Being chief sorcerer is a *responsibility*. It's—"

"Consider my offer retracted," Susan said. "You're too stupid to live."

Marla snatched her dagger from the nightstand and leapt across the room, slashing out for Susan's astral cord, but by the time she landed and struck, Susan was gone, slipped entirely into psychic space, on the way back to her body.

"Bitch," Marla said, kneeling there in the dark, alone. But if Susan had come here, that meant she wasn't deep in her preparatory meditations, and *that* meant Marla had a little time yet before she cast the spell, after all.

She went back to bed, and this time she kept her dagger under her pillow.

8

Finch drove through the city in his silver Mercedes SUV, Marla sitting uncomfortably in the passenger seat. She had an irrational dislike for riding in cars. She'd inherited a vintage Bentley back home, but she only used it when she had no choice. Rondeau slid from one side of the backseat to the other, peering out the windows on either side, taking in the scenery, which was mostly hills, Victorians, and Asian eateries, as far as Marla could see. "So where are we going?" Rondeau said.

"Golden Gate Park," Finch said. "It's an interesting place, historically and in terms of magical opportunity, Marla." He had an armchair lecturer's voice, and Marla suspected he liked to hold forth.

"How interesting," she said, though she couldn't have cared less about any aspect of San Francisco's history. Rondeau, however, was leaning forward to hear.

Finch said, "In the late 1800s, when the area was dedicated as park land, it was nothing but sand dunes—that whole part of the peninsula was dunes, called the Outside Lands, well beyond the limits of the city proper at the time. In 1868 a surveyor named William Hammond Hall was given the job of turning that wasteland into a great urban park. The first step, of course, was to plant grasses to hold the sand in place and keep it from shifting constantly. After the grasses took root, they could plant bushes, trees, flowers, and so forth. Hall tried planting some of the sturdier native grasses, but none of them survived—they were utterly smothered by the sand. After many failed experiments with different grasses, Hall despaired. One day he was out camping near the Chain of Lakes—well, where the Chain of Lakes is now, the western part of the park. He had some barley to feed his horse, but the sand, which got in everywhere, wound up in the feed bag, and the horse wouldn't eat the grain when it was so mixed in with sand. Disgusted, Hammond threw the barley down on the ground. When he passed back that way a few days later, he saw that the barley had taken root. From that point, it was easy—first he planted barley, then grasses, and so on up to flowers, bushes, and trees."

"When does this become interesting?" Marla asked.

Finch sighed. "Do you know *why* the barley took root? Most people don't. It was the Cornerstone, Marla. Some sorcerer—we don't know which one for sure, but it was probably Sanford Cole, who later became the secret court magician to Emperor Joshua Norton—wanted the park to succeed, and he sank the Cornerstone down in the sand in the desert that would become the park. Then he spoke a simple binding spell—a spell made incredibly effective and permanent by the Cornerstone—and the next thing that got planted on the dunes took root. That just happened to be Hall's barley. Cole was an interesting fellow. You've heard of him?"

"Sure," Marla said. "He's the Ben Franklin of sorcerers. He's responsible for our foothold in America, according to some people."

"True enough. By all accounts, he was a good man. Can you imagine? A sorcerer that powerful, being described as *good*? That's not the way you or I will be remembered, I suspect. Perhaps it was a different time."

Marla kept silent, watching buildings slide past outside the window. People who thought things were fundamentally better or kinder in earlier times were clearly not true students of history.

"There's a legend that Cole will return in the hour of San Francisco's greatest need, you know," Finch said.

"Huh. Like Merlin, the way he's supposed to return to England?"

"In a few hundred years, Cole might be remembered the way Merlin is, at least among our people."

"You believe that story?" Marla said. "That he'll come back?"

Finch shrugged. "Not really. Some do, of course. Some of the techno-mages thought he would return when the dot-com bubble burst, but he failed to arrive, not surprisingly. I suspect Cole is gone forever. Though if he had constant access to the Cornerstone, I suppose anything's possible. Even returning from the dead."

"So this Cornerstone," Rondeau said, "it makes spells last forever?"

"Among other things," Finch said. "There are four known Cornerstones in the world—"

"Three, since Ballard ate one," Marla said.

"Yes, three in the world, and their origins are unknown. They're good for binding spells, for making things last, for making improbable things likely, for anchoring things. We've got the Golden Gate Bridge bound to the Cornerstone, so it won't fall down in the event of a catastrophic earthquake. Of course, the ordinaries don't know that, and they're still retrofitting the bridge to make it earthquake-proof by more mechanical means. But that's all right. It keeps people busy. Fortunately, most sorcerers only have a vague notion of what the Cornerstones are, and most of *those* don't know where to find them. The one under the British Museum was relatively common knowledge, and look what happened to it. I don't actually know where the other two are."

"Neither do I," Marla said. "I wouldn't know about the one here if not for Lao Tsung. But that other guy, Mutex, he heard about the Cornerstone in San Francisco somehow. Did he say why he wanted it?"

Finch waved his hand dismissively. "Mutex came to me raving about old gods, the universe running down like an unwound watch, blood sacrifices, and so forth. He said if people didn't start making offerings to his gods, the sun and stars and planetary bodies would stop moving in their appointed grooves." Finch shrugged. "I politely refused to help him, he became belligerent, and I had him escorted out. I sent out some inquiries about him following Lao Tsung's death, and heard back early this morning, though there wasn't much to tell. Mutex used to be a talented young man, apprenticed to a shaman west of the Andes in Colombia, but he abandoned his studies and spent some years traveling through the Americas, much of it in the jungle, doubtless licking the wrong sort of toad. The years of isolation seem to have affected his judgment."

"When you spend a long time away from people, sometimes you forget how to behave," Marla said.

"Persistent little bastard, though," Finch said. "I found out he'd secured appointments with most of the major sorcerers in the city—as I said, he used to be a promising sort, so most were willing to see him—and told them all the same thing, that he needed the Cornerstone, or the world would fall to pieces. Everyone turned him away. I imagine he slunk off to seek his fortune elsewhere."

"Huh," Marla said. She thought that sounded like either wishful thinking or stupidity. "After making appointments with a dozen sorcerers, putting up with all their bullshit, pressing his case, and then killing Lao Tsung, you think he just gave up and skipped town?"

After a moment of frosty silence, Finch said, "We are investigating Lao Tsung's death, as I said. He was a valued member of our community, and we will find out who, if anyone, is responsible for his death. There is no indication that a renegade jungle practitioner like Mutex could even hope to harm a sorcerer of Lao Tsung's caliber. He was your friend—surely you know how formidable he was."

Marla knew Lao Tsung was tough in a street fight, and he was no slouch at magical battles, either—but nobody expects to be killed by an army of frogs.

Marla sank down in the seat and put her feet on the dashboard, wrapping her arms under and around her legs. She felt very aggressive right now, and it might be best to present a meeker front—Finch was more than usually into dominance behavior, and while she'd enjoyed getting in his face last night, and while it had probably won her some measure of respect, she thought the present situation demanded a bit more finesse. "But Lao Tsung was the guardian of the Cornerstone. Don't you think Mutex might have found that out during all that time bothering the other sorcerers? Seems like a potential motive for murder to me."

"We are considering the possibility," Finch said. "Does that satisfy you? But I think you give Mutex too much credit. He is simply a madman, whatever his earlier promise."

"And madmen never kill anybody," Rondeau said from the backseat.

Finch glanced into the rearview mirror, his lips pressed into a thin line.

"Careful, Rondeau," Marla said. "He'll sodomize your ghost if you keep up that sass."

"Consider me chastised," Rondeau said.

"This is close enough," Finch said, and parked the SUV next to a fire hydrant.

Parking is probably easier in San Francisco when you don't have to worry about getting tickets, Marla thought.

"The entrance we want is just a couple of blocks north." They all got out of the car and walked down the sidewalk, Finch in the lead. The morning was cool, with a stiff breeze from the direction of the bay. "We'll reach the Cornerstone soon. You have the materials you need? You've made your preparations?"

Marla patted her leather shoulder bag. "It's all

here." The spell wasn't complicated—just a simple binding spell, but with the augmentation and permanence provided by the Cornerstone, it should be enough to thwart Susan's plan to take over Marla's city.

"And there's the park," Finch said, nodding, as if Marla wouldn't have noticed the expanse of trees and green ahead, as improbable a sight as any large park in the midst of a big city. They passed through the gates into a place of green trees and grass, the roofs of distant buildings poking up over the trees in the distance. "Strawberry Hill isn't far," Finch said, and strode off past people sprawled on blankets, young hippies playing hacky sack, and people reading.

"What kind of park is this?" Rondeau said. "Where are the garbage cans chained to concrete pylons? Where are the drug dealers? Why is there grass instead of asphalt? I don't see a broken merry-go-round anywhere."

"You should get out of your neighborhood more often, Rondeau," Marla said. "There are nice parks in our city, you know, too. Out in the suburbs anyway." Looking around, she grudgingly added, "Not so big as this, and they aren't safe after dark, mostly, but still."

After a while, Finch stopped walking, and pointed. "This is Strawberry Hill."

Marla looked. Strawberry Hill was a high, rounded lump of land in the middle of a small lake. "That's a lot of island for such a little pond," Marla said.

"Strawberry Hill has been described as a watermelon with a wet string tied around it," Finch said.

"But you know as well as I do that even a token moat can have a significant protective power."

"True," Marla said. "The Cornerstone is there?"

"Among the trees."

"How do we get to the island? I could probably leap over the water in a couple of the thinner places, but I assume you have another way?"

"There are two bridges," Finch said. "The rustic and the roman. But we're not going to take either of them. Because there's a *third* bridge." Finch glanced around, then waved his hand, casting a curtain of obscurement over the three of them—now the eyes of any observers would just...slide away from them. He made another gesture. "There."

A gently arcing footbridge was revealed, made of rough timbers tied with twine, and with handrails of gleaming copper, stretching from the bank before them to the slope of Strawberry Hill. "After you," Marla said, and Finch crossed the bridge, his feet not making any sound at all on the splintery wooden boards.

The island hill was heavily wooded at that point, though it appeared more sparse elsewhere, and Marla stayed close to Finch as he went into the trees. They trudged up the steep slope for what seemed to Marla a very long time, especially since it was such a small island. "Are you screwing around with Euclidean norms?" she asked, kicking a low branch out of her way, making it snap under her boot.

"There's a certain amount of topological crumpling going on, yes," Finch said. "We don't want people tripping over the Cornerstone by accident, so the hill is folded in on itself a bit, with the stone tucked away within."

"This is too much like really being in the woods," Marla said, gritting her teeth. Every brush of a leaf against the skin of her forearms felt like the skittering of insects, and didn't they have poison oak out here? She was an urban creature, and her years as chief sorcerer of Felport had intensified that intrinsic sympathy—in a way, she *was* her city, and she did not feel at home in even so circumscribed a piece of wilderness as this. She glanced behind her, where Rondeau was walking placidly along, hands in his pockets, knees going steadily up and down like he was on a StairMaster or something. Looking past him, Marla saw nothing but blue sky, no skyscrapers. The folded space had obscured any view of buildings. Marla clamped down on her rising panic, annoyed at her own reactions. She hadn't been in among the trees like this since she was a kid in Indiana, and she was distressed to find herself so discomforted by the experience—it seemed like a dangerous chink in her armor.

"The clearing is just up ahead," Finch said, puffing a little, and Marla felt a little glee over that, at least—she was in better shape than he was. She walked in her city every day, but she suspected that Finch did most of his business in the same aerie where he fucked the ghosts of his enemies.

Marla hurried forward, walking beside Finch, and they passed from the trees into the clearing together.

"What the living *fuck*," Finch said, and Marla stood speechless, taking in the scene before her with her typical threat-assessment glance, but unsure of *what* she was seeing, exactly, and certainly unsure of how to proceed.

First she saw the man, because men and monsters

were usually the most dangerous things in any given situation. He was dark-skinned and bare-chested, so thin that his ribs protruded, and he wore brief shorts that appeared to be made of green-and-red snakeskin. Heavy gold bracelets adorned his wrists, and his short cape, tied around his neck and hanging to just above the back of his knees, shimmered, strangely iridescent, like imperfect jewels transformed into cloth; prismatic, organic, and oddly disgusting. He held a large, round wicker basket tucked awkwardly under one arm. Marla sensed a strange power in him—spiritual gravity, heavy madness, something that tickled her well-tuned senses but did not fully reveal itself. Something new in her experience. He did not attack them—did not even look at them. He was looking at the other thing in the clearing. The far more improbable thing.

Marla recognized the Cornerstone instantly, a large chunk of blue-gray rock, easily two feet to a side, cut into a weathered cube, with a magical density so great that it actually warped the light within an inch of its surface, making its smooth faces seem slightly convex. The stone had been ripped from the earth at the center of the clearing, leaving a raw hole of black dirt behind, and soil still clung to the lower two-thirds of the stone.

The Cornerstone hung in the air a few feet above the ground, supported by a profusion of thin silver chains. The upper ends of the chains were attached to hundreds—perhaps thousands—of hummingbirds, individually tiny, but so massed that they formed a shimmering ruby-colored cloud.

"Hummingbirds again," Rondeau said, and Marla nodded, thinking of the same thing he probably was—

the birds that Rondeau had Cursed in the elevator. Cursing was too dangerous here—too many living things, too many trees, too many ways for a sudden, nasty shift in the fabric of creation to backfire and hurt something or someone valuable. They'd found their bird-wizard, though—Mutex, the freak in the shimmering cape, who apparently had designs on the Cornerstone, and was making off with it. Well, fuck *that*. Marla hadn't come this far to let some bird-watcher steal her artifact out from under her.

Before she could make a move, however, Finch was roaring. "Mutex!"

The caped man bowed, slightly. "I did not think you would remember my name, sir," he said. He didn't sound particularly crazy. "Not when you treated me so badly before. I did not expect to see you today. I had hoped to see you later, when I would have a better use for your blood. I am saddened that your *teyolia* will be wasted on this hidden ground."

"I'm going to eat you," Finch said, rage coupled with anticipation, "and then I'm going to ass-fuck your little spic ghost."

"Hey, watch the racial slurs," Rondeau said. "You fat bastard." That was the effect of the Cornerstone, Marla thought—people saying what they *meant*. She held her own tongue.

Mutex still didn't move. Neither did Marla. Finch was formidable—he could deal with the bird-man. Marla had her eyes on the Cornerstone, and the birds that were slowly carrying it away. She ran for the Cornerstone, leaping, her dagger of office in her hand, slashing out for the silver chains.

Hummingbirds swooped down to block her blow.

When her blade hit the birds there should have been blood, and feathers, and the sudden cessation of swiftly humming wings, but instead her dagger spun out of her grip as if she'd tried to stab some viciously whirling piece of heavy machinery. She looked at the birds, which looked back at her with a thousand pairs of tiny black eyes, then went for her blade, which was now lying in the dirt by the tree line.

"Shit," Rondeau said. "They're tough little mothers, aren't they?"

Finch, meanwhile, had transformed into a bear. He looked wholly natural among the trees, with Mutex as the obvious interloper—and obvious prey. Finch had two feet of height on the skinny magician as he stood upright and roaring, his fur bristling and matted. He dropped to all fours and advanced on Mutex, ready to maul him, or eat his entrails, or do whatever it was angry bears did to the objects of their anger. Marla had never observed a grizzly up close, only behind bars at the zoo, where they had a fat old one that mostly slept. She was curious to see what sort of damage Finch would do when he killed Mutex. Marla hoped that once the skinny sorcerer was dead, the hummingbirds would revert to more natural behavior, and either drop the Cornerstone or be dragged down by its weight—at the very least, whatever protective spell Mutex had cast on them would be broken, and she could dispose of the birds in a straightforward fashion.

Mutex smirked as he watched Finch approach. It was an expression Marla would be glad to see clawed off his face, though it worried her. Mutex clearly *thought* he had some trick in reserve, but Finch as a bear was more formidable than either a sorcerer or a wild animal. He had all his magical abilities—at least, those that didn't require good pronunciation—in addition to claws, teeth, and a physical constitution unmatched in nature. Bears were symbols of tremendous strength and ferocity, and Finch now embodied that symbol.

Mutex lifted the lid from his wicker basket and, in an almost casual gesture, tipped its contents out on the ground.

At first, Marla thought he was dumping out gold nuggets, a cascade of small, shining yellow objects, but then she saw them moving, and recognized them for what they were—tiny yellow frogs, like the one that had hopped out of Lao Tsung's mouth.

Well. *That* question was settled. Unless there was another sorcerer running a frog show in town, which seemed unlikely, Mutex was the one who'd killed Lao Tsung—doubtless after torturing him to find out the location of the Cornerstone. Hardly surprising, but it was nice to have confirmation.

The frogs did not attack Finch; they did not appear to take any notice of him at all. They simply spread out on the ground, hopping about randomly, bumping into one another, still disoriented by being dumped from the basket. The basket, Marla noted, was still full to the brim with squirming frogs, which meant there was some topological crumpling going on inside there, too; it was possible Mutex had a whole miniature ecosystem inside, filled with poisonous frogs.

Finch, still on four legs, tried to retreat from the frogs, clearly recognizing them for what they were—tiny hopping biohazards. Deadly poison with legs.

"Look out!" Rondeau called, but it was too late.

Finch's rear left leg came down on top of a frog, and he roared, lifting his paw and shaking it, stumbling in the process and brushing against several more of the frogs. He gave a nearly human scream, and did an ineffectual hop of his own, as if trying to jump clear of the widening pool of frogs, but he only landed on more of them.

Rondeau started forward, but Marla laid a restraining hand on his arm. The frogs were spreading out throughout the whole clearing now, scores of them, spotting the grass and churned dirt like yellow wildflowers, and Finch was surrounded. Rondeau and Marla couldn't help him. The frogs were like mobile land mines. Finch stumbled about, swiping at the frogs, but his strikes grew slower and slower, his movements more sluggish. Even his magically enhanced bear's constitution failed to stand up to the frogs for more than a few seconds, and Marla thought about the welts that had risen up on Lao Tsung's dead body—just how poisonous *were* these creatures? Marla felt a pang for Finch—he'd been a bastard, true, but she'd respected his power, and, ultimately, he'd acknowledged hers. That was as close to friendship as most sorcerers could afford to come.

Mutex watched Finch lurch about and die by degrees. The skinny sorcerer nodded thoughtfully, as if he were attending a lecture on fiscal policy or civic planning. Marla drew her non-magical, workaday dagger and held it by the blade between her thumb and forefinger. The knife wasn't weighted for throwing, but at this distance, with sufficient force, she could probably wound Mutex grievously in the throat. She drew back her arm and, in a smooth motion that would have pleased Lao Tsung, let the dagger fly.

Before the knife went a foot, it struck a hummingbird. The animal had intercepted the blade in a blur of ruby wings, moving faster than Marla's eyes could follow. The knife bounced back and gouged a divot in the ground at Marla's feet. The bird hovered for a moment, unharmed, and looked at her with tiny black eyes, then flashed away to rejoin the flock that was slowly but steadily carrying the Cornerstone away.

Marla looked to Mutex, who waved farewell and turned away. Finch was now an unmoving heap of brown fur, sprawled on his side among the frogs. The Cornerstone drifted after Mutex, into the trees.

"Want me to Curse?" Rondeau said, but Marla shook her head. It was too dangerous, too unpredictable, especially with so many lethal creatures nearby. The frogs still hopped, some of them jumping on Finch's dead bearbody. Marla looked after Mutex, but he'd vanished. The birds were gone, too, and the stone with them, all hidden by the folded space around the island. She couldn't follow them, either. The frogs made the clearing impassable, and if she went into the trees to skirt around them, she'd just be wrapped up in folded space herself, and might even wind up farther away from Mutex than she was now. When things got non-Euclidean, there was little hope of hot pursuit.

"We should leave," she said, but she stood still for a moment anyway. Because where would she go once she left this island? How would she track down Mutex and the Cornerstone? In her own city, she had access to innumerable contacts and wielded considerable influence. She had seers, sibyls, and oracles, and while their information might be obscure and cryptic, she could usually glean something useful from it, especially when she sought more than one reading, engaging in a sort of psychic triangulation. But *here* in San Francisco...the only person she could ask for help now was a snake god who hated her guts, and besides, *he* didn't know how this city worked, who the players were, or how to find the sort of people who were good at finding people. Sure, she could tell Ch'ang Hao to find and kill Mutex, and he'd do it *eventually*, but gods worked on their own timetable, and he wouldn't do it fast enough.

Marla would have to wander around, try to sniff out magic, try to find other sorcerers and tell them about Mutex, and convince them he was a real threat. But she didn't have *time*. Susan wouldn't wait. She was putting her spell together, making the proper arrangements, and preparing to loosen the couplings of reality and seize control of Felport. Marla *had* to find the Cornerstone, and soon.

"Um, frogs, Marla," Rondeau said, and, indeed, they were still there, still spreading, hopping incuriously in their direction.

"Shit," Marla said. Because, yes, the frogs—even if she did manage to track down Mutex, she had to contend with his toxic menagerie, didn't she? Tiny killer frogs were rather outside her realm of expertise. Still, Mutex didn't fear them, which meant there had to be some antidote, or antivenom, or charm—*something*. If she could find out how to protect herself from the frogs, she would at least stand a chance when she went up against him. Maybe if she wore her cloak with the white side out, its healing powers surrounding her, then the frogs wouldn't hurt her...but one look at Finch, turned into a feast for flies, convinced her otherwise. The cloak's healing powers wouldn't make her any tougher than a sorcerer with the totemic power of a bear, and Finch hadn't lasted long.

"Let's go," Marla said. She still had the frog she'd found by the gallery, safely wrapped in a plastic bag. The frogs probably couldn't survive for long outside the steamy, magically balanced environment inside Mutex's wicker basket. If she could just find someone knowledgeable, get some information... maybe she could get Langford to fly out here. Though without access to his lab and library, she wasn't sure the biomancer would be able to tell her anything. She couldn't think of anything else, though. She didn't know any San Francisco area frog-experts.

"That sucks about Finch," Rondeau said, subdued. "He should have climbed a tree or something."

"I think that's only black bears," Marla said, recalling a special she'd seen on television.

"Sucks," Rondeau repeated. They went down the hill in silence. "So I guess we have to go after this Mutex guy now," he said.

"Looks like it."

"I might have to invest in some of those rubber hip-waders, then. It didn't look like those frogs could jump very high."

"That's a good idea, until they get down in your boots and you can't get them out."

"You make a good point," Rondeau said.

The trip back through folded space was quicker than the trip in, as was often the case. She and

Rondeau passed over the bridge, which was flickering and fading from view, but still solid underfoot. They stepped out of the shimmer of obscurement, into ordinary air.

Bradley Bowman was there, sitting on a white-and-red checked blanket in the grass just ten feet away, reading a yellowed paperback with the cover torn off. He looked up, shaded his eyes, and nodded.

"Hi there," he said. "I hear you need to see a man about a frog."

Marla stared at him, this ignorant seer with his fuzzy dreams and annoying persistence, and then began to laugh. "Yes," she said, eventually, when she was done laughing. "I do."

Bradley stood up, bundling his blanket into a wad under one arm. "Come on, then," he said. "We have to go across the bay."

9

radley and Rondeau sat slumped in the train car, while Marla stood holding a handrail. "How did you know where to find us this morning?" she asked. "Another dream?"

B shook his head. "I consulted a—I think it was the ghost of a demon—that I found in a Dumpster, and it told me to find you at a sweet red hill in a lake—Strawberry Hill. I had another dream, too, but this time it was about you, looking at a dead frog through a magnifying glass, then smashing the glass in frustration. So I had some idea of what you needed help with." He shrugged. "I know where you can find out about frogs, so I thought I'd better come find you."

Marla nodded. "These dreams—you interpret them yourself?"

He shrugged, looking uncomfortable. "Not always. There's a . . . spirit I consult."

"The one in the Dumpster?"

"No, a different one. Lives in a sewer grate. Except it doesn't 'live' exactly. 'Haunts' might be a better term."

"I see." She considered her next question carefully. "Exactly how many ghosts, demons, and spirits do you know?"

B shrugged. "It's not like I'm friendly with them. But when I need to know something, I can usually find someone—some *thing*—to ask. So lots, I guess."

Marla crossed her legs at the ankle and leaned away from him, her arms still holding the grab-rail overhead. She looked at B, trying to activate her spirit eyes, but a headache blossomed just behind her forehead right away—she'd been peering too closely at too many improbable things lately. It was unlikely she'd see anything in him anyway. He really *was* just a low-grade seer . . . but maybe he was something more, too. It was possible that B had a kind of power she'd only heard about secondhand, something her spirit eyes wouldn't be able to discern anyway. If she was right, Bowman could be very useful to her. But that could wait. The first thing she needed to do was find out about the frogs.

After several stops, and a dark journey through the tunnel under the bay, B stood up and said, "This is it." They stepped off the train and took an escalator up a level, into a domed area, and then exited the train station. As always when Marla emerged from an underground place into the light, she felt a sense of new possibilities, as if she'd returned from the underworld and brought back secrets. There was power even in symbolic journeys.

B led them outside, to a paved parking lot bordered at the far end by a busy street. "Welcome to Berkeley."

"Huh," Rondeau said, making a great show of looking around. "Where are the hippies?"

"On Telegraph Avenue, up by the university," B said. "Nowhere near here. This is North Berkeley. And we're headed to West Berkeley, so I hope you like walking."

"I do," Marla said. "And Rondeau will do it anyway."

"Don't you people believe in *cabs*?" Rondeau said.

"*Anybody* could be driving a cab," Marla said, and Rondeau sighed; it was a very old argument between them. They walked in silence, Marla falling into pace with B's easy gait. He was a good walker. Marla decided to pry a little. "When did you start hearing things, seeing things, having dreams?"

"After I quit working in the movies." He laughed. "When I stopped making illusions, I started to see the truth. I thought I was crazy at first, but eventually I got tired of thinking I was crazy. It seemed like insanity should be more...volatile. Mostly I just wandered around, seeing stuff, talking to things. It freaked me out, but it's not like aliens were telling me to kill politicians or kidnap children, you know? The things I talked to just answered my questions. So I decided I wasn't crazy."

Marla grunted. Most seers *were* crazy, by any conventional standard, and B was something both more and less than a seer. "There wasn't any trauma that might have triggered your powers? Something physical, or emotional, some upheaval?"

In her short time with B, Marla had grown used to his natural warmth. His charisma had doubtless helped him in his career as an actor, and his descent into half-magical dereliction had not made him any less sympathetic and approachable. Now he closed up, his face becoming stony, a nearly physical wave of cold radiating from him.

"You should read the tabloids, Marla," Rondeau said. "Is . . . ah, B, do you mind if I . . . ?"

"Whatever," B said. "The whole world knows." He walked faster, putting some distance between them, enough that he didn't have to listen.

Marla fell into step beside Rondeau. "Well?"

"B had a lover," Rondeau said. "I forget his name. He wasn't an actor or anything, just some guy. Anyway, they used to party a lot together, get drunk, go out, do drugs. But one night, in some empty lot, B's lover overdosed on something and died right there in front of him, puking up blood and everything. That's when B's career went to hell. After a pretty serious binge, he went into rehab for a while, and when he came out, people thought his career would get back on track. Not long after that he tried to strangle the director on his new movie, and that was *it* for his career. That was six or seven years ago, I think."

"How do you know all this?"

Rondeau shrugged. "When you're a kid living on the streets, the sordid lives of celebrities have an unusual allure. And I sometimes read those shitty newspapers I used for bedding."

B slowed down and resumed walking with them. "I didn't try to strangle the director," he said, in a resigned tone. "He was hag-ridden. There was this monster clinging to his neck, like a lamprey, and it was sucking out his blood or his mental emanations or something and filling him with poison, making him mean, turning him into a monster himself. Nobody else could see the monster, but after H—that was my lover, I called him H—died, I could see all sorts of shit. H—or his ghost—told me how to kill the monster, so that's what I did, I soaked my hands in a potion of ditch water and belladonna that enabled me to touch insubstantial things, and I choked the monster to death. Everybody thought I was trying to kill the director. I didn't care, though. Nobody pressed charges—I think on some level the director knew I'd saved him, but it must have been deep in his subconscious, because he sure screamed when he fired me—and I didn't want to be an actor anymore anyway." He shrugged.

"So all this started after H died," Marla said.

B nodded.

"And you still talk to him? To H?"

B shook his head sharply. "Fuck, no. I talk to his *ghost,* an echo, an afterimage. It's not the real H."

"Good," Marla said, relieved. "I just wanted to make sure you understood the difference." Just as she now had a better understanding of what had happened to him. The shock of seeing his lover die had knocked something loose in B's head. It happened that way sometimes—when old worlds fell apart, new worlds opened up. But in B's case, it was possible that something more profound had happened. It wasn't just his perception that had changed. The way he affected the *world* changed. Now where Bradley Bowman went, wonders and terrors followed. Maybe.

And if "maybe" turned into "definitely," Marla was sure she could come up with some use for those powers.

They walked the rest of the way in silence, past houses crowded shoulder to shoulder, with tiny lawns and neat fences, until they reached a commercial district. "There," B said, and pointed to a sign that read "East Bay Vivarium."

"Ah," Marla said. "I see."

They went into a spacious, cluttered store. Glass terrariums on metal shelves lined the dark walls, and the sound of bubbling humidifiers registered faintly in Marla's hearing. B led them around several freestanding shelves, past tanks full of turtles, lazy snakes, huge scorpions, and lizards.

"God, this is like Langford's lab," Rondeau said. "Creepy-crawlies everywhere. Is this some kind of zoo annex?"

"It's a pet store," Marla said. She peered into a large tank inhabited by half a dozen water dragons, leaping from artificial tree branches to the walls of the tank and back again. Another held a huge iguana, the size of a small dog, resting on a rock, its tongue flicking slowly in and out. She moved on to an open-topped tank filled with water and rocks. Tiny pinkish lizards with slick skin sat on the rocks, staring up at her. Another tank held small frogs. Not like the one in her bag—these were green, with bulging eyes, and toes with round suckers on the ends, and they clung to a branch in the tank. Still, she supposed they'd come to the right place.

Rondeau wandered off to look at ball pythons, and Marla went in search of B. She found him at the counter in the back, talking to the clerk, a stocky man in his twenties, with close-cropped dark hair and what Marla guessed was a semipermanent scowl. "Marla, this is Ray," B said, and the clerk nodded to her. He wore a navy blue bowling shirt with the name "Butch" embroidered in curving white script over the right breast.

"I was just saying, I don't know much about frogs," Ray said. "Snakes are more my thing. But if you show me what you've got, I'll see what I can do."

Marla glanced at B, who nodded. "Ray's good people," he said.

She nodded. She couldn't see the harm in letting an ordinary see the frog. Opening the side flap of her bag, she removed the plastic bag, unrolling it so the little yellow frog was visible, but still covered in a thin layer of clear plastic. "I wouldn't recommend touching it," Marla said. "I don't know much, but I know it's poison."

Ray hunched over and peered at the frog, then grunted. "Turn it over. Let me see its underside." Marla did as he asked, and Ray nodded. "Damn. Hold on. Let me get a book." He headed for the back of the store.

Marla turned to B. "How do you know him?"

"He's a writer, actually, and he interviewed me back in the day, when I was just getting to be famous. We stayed friends after that, used to go out to bars together and stuff. We're even tighter now, though, since we both stopped drinking. He says the freelance writing market's shitty right now, so he has to work here." B shrugged. "He knows a lot about snakes."

"Hmm," Marla said. "So he's not . . . like you? Ah, like us?"

"You mean does he talk to dead people? No. Not that I know of. But he'll be discreet, mostly because he doesn't give a shit, and he's a friend, so it's okay to talk to him. I wouldn't have brought you here otherwise. My life sort of depends on you, I think. So don't worry."

"Half my job is worrying. And the other half is making sure I don't have anything to worry about."

Ray returned, holding a coffee-table book with a

bright-color cover. He set it on the counter and began flipping through the pages, past pictures of dozens of different frogs—dark green ones, tiny ones with bulging eyes, even a startlingly blue one.

Then he tapped a page with his forefinger and spun the book around so Marla could see it right-side-up. A golden yellow frog stared, black-eyed, straight at the camera. The image had caught the frog in motion, and it stood as if in a superhero's crouch, like Spider-Man right after sticking a difficult landing, one front foot resting on the ground, the other held up, toes splayed, wide mouth turned down as if in a frown of concentration. "This is one of only a few photographs in the world of, ah, let's see, *Phyllobates terribilis*," Ray said. "Golden poison dart frog. Mr. Terrible. All the vital stats are there."

Marla bent over the book. This was the animal, all right. Ranging in size from one-half to two inches long, uniform metallic yellow in color. Unlike other poison dart frogs, it had "teeth"—really a bony plate in its upper jaw. Marla didn't like the sound of that. The Aztec frog-monster in that stolen carving had teeth—fangs, in fact. That wasn't the only way Mr. Terrible differed from other frogs. Unlike most species, these were social animals, congregating with their own kind, and they were fearlessly diurnal, probably because they had little to fear from predators, being almost unbelievably poisonous. Each of these frogs had enough toxin in its skin to kill a hundred adult humans, and poison darts made from their venom remained potent for up to two years. Two-tenths of a microgram of their venom was lethal in the human bloodstream, and each frog contained a hundred micrograms. But even that level of toxicity didn't explain the instantaneously appearing welts Marla had witnessed on those touched by the frogs. Mutex had somehow magically hot-rodded these frogs, made them even more poisonous than they were in nature, which was a bit like loading an elephant gun with dynamite—just plain overkill. Mr. Terrible didn't exactly thrive in this environment, though, favoring the tropical rain forests, especially in Colombia, which was where Mutex had supposedly spent some time studying.

A subheading labeled "Beneficial Uses" caught Marla's eye. Apart from helping native hunters poison their prey—the tribespeople heated the frogs over fires, then wiped their darts on the frogs' sweating backs— Mr. Terrible had other useful qualities. Doctors were working with extracts of their poison, batrachotoxin, to make painkillers that were potentially ten times as effective as morphine, without the nasty, physically addictive side effects. Marla wondered if Mutex had used some sympathetic magic to tap into that quality, too. If so, he could be formidable in battle. People who didn't feel pain were difficult to fight.

She turned the page. And there it was: "Predators."

Mr. Terrible only had one natural predator. *Leimadopis epinephelus*. It was a snake, naturally immune to the frog's poison, and it chowed down on Mr. Terrible and all his brethren at will.

B and Ray were chatting, and Marla interrupted Ray in mid-sentence. "I want to buy a snake."

"Oh, yeah?" Ray said. "What did you have in mind?"

"I can't pronounce it," she said. "One of these." She tapped the name.

Ray frowned. "I think you're out of luck. Even if I

could get you one—which I can't—it'd be an illegal exotic pet. Not unlike that frog you've got in your plastic bag there, but since it's dead, that's probably less of a problem."

"Money isn't an issue," Marla said. "Neither is legality. Time, however, *is*. I need one of these snakes, and I need it before morning."

Ray looked at B for help, and B cleared his throat. "I don't think he's holding out on you, Marla. They don't have that snake here, and it's not something he can get."

"Truth," Ray said. "There might be one of these snakes in captivity somewhere in the state, but who knows? It's a relatively rare snake from the rain forest. I don't even know what they look like, and I know more about snakes than the average guy."

"I *need* one," Marla said. "You must have *some* idea where I can find one."

Ray lifted his hands in a gesture of helplessness. "Sorry. I'm sure there are dedicated reptile smugglers out there somewhere, but I don't know them. And even if I did, I doubt old *Leimadopis* would be a hot seller."

Marla swore, then ripped the relevant pages out of the book. Ray started to protest, and Rondeau was there as if by magic, handing him a suspiciously large bill. Ray's half scowl deepened, but he put the money in his shirt pocket. "Want me to try to reach Langford?" Rondeau said. "He's got sources. Maybe he could, I don't know, ship us a snake by special courier."

"It might come to that," Marla said, folding up the pages and walking away. Rondeau followed, as did B, after saying his apologetic farewell to Ray. "But I'm afraid it wouldn't happen fast enough. He'd have to *find* a snake first, after all, and that takes time, even for a biomancer."

"I guess this explains Mutex's ugly red-and-green snakeskin short-shorts," Rondeau said. "He probably didn't buy those out of a catalog, though."

"Probably not," Marla said.

"Why do you need that snake anyway?" B said.

"She needs a little sympathy," Rondeau said.

"Exactly," Marla said.

"And what does *that* mean?" B asked.

"The circumspect nature of the response indicates that sorcerers like to have a few secrets, B," Rondeau said, putting an arm around his shoulder. "We're only as good as our mysteries, after all."

They walked another dozen or so steps before Marla said "We're idiots, Rondeau."

"I know," Rondeau said. "It just hit me, too. But, ah, are you sure you want to use that tool for *this* job?"

"For now, this is the only job that matters. If I don't succeed at this one, there won't be any more jobs." Marla didn't like this, either—it seemed a trivial use of a powerful resource—but anything that might help keep her alive wasn't *truly* trivial.

"Yeah," Rondeau said. "I can see that. We need a snake."

"Ray already said he can't get you that snake—" B began.

"No, no," Rondeau said. "Not the poison-frog-eating snake. *Any* snake will do, for now."

"B," Marla said. "Go back and buy me a garter snake or something, would you? Something small."

B hesitated. He didn't like being jerked around. Marla could appreciate that. But she didn't want to get into the habit of explaining herself to him. If she did, B might expect an explanation when there wasn't time to give him one, and such a delay could prove fatal. Then again, if he *was* more than a half-assed seer, if he actually had the power she suspected, she needed him as an ally. She shouldn't push him too far. So when he hesitated, she said, almost gently, "Don't forget, your life depends on mine. And bringing me a garter snake right now will help us both."

B nodded, and headed back to the Vivarium.

Marla and Rondeau sat on a low concrete wall that marked the edge of a strip-mall parking lot. "So after we get one of those frog-eating snakes, what then?" Rondeau said.

"We find Mutex, and I rip his extremities off until I get the Cornerstone back."

"And how do we find Mutex?"

"Have you ever heard of that band '. . . And You Shall Know Us by the Trail of Dead'?"

"Ah," Rondeau said. "Got it. We follow the bodies."

"Maybe," Marla said. "That's the worst-case scenario. There's a small chance that we might be able to find a shortcut." That small chance was B, if he turned out to be what Marla barely dared hope he was.

"All hail the great god Shortcut," Rondeau said, a little glumly.

"Say hallelujah," Marla agreed.

10

B returned with the garter snake, a long, dark green curl of life in a small white cardboard box. "You're not going to sacrifice this or anything, are you?" B said, as Marla peered into the box.

"I don't think so," she said. "I can't imagine that sacrificing eight inches of snake would get me much in the way of favors anyway." She cleared her throat, put her face close to the box, and said, "Ch'ang Hao, this is Marla. I need to call in that favor now." She lifted her face away, and they all watched the snake, which lifted its head up above the sides of the box and swayed a little.

"Ah," Rondeau said. "So what now?"

"Apparently nothing instantaneous," Marla said.

The snake crawled over the edge of the box, flowing like living green water, and fell the short distance to the ground, where it continued slithering away, roughly westward.

"Think the little snake's going to deliver the message in person?" Rondeau said.

"Anything's possible." Marla sighed. "I'm not good

at being patient. I say we head back into the city, grab some food, and see what else we can find out about Mutex. I wish I knew where to find the other sorcerers in this city. If Mutex really did go around accosting all the big noises in the city, maybe he let something useful slip to *one* of them."

They went back to the commuter train station and boarded an empty car on a San Francisco–bound BART train. Rondeau and B talked about restaurants, while Marla thought about where to start in her search for other sorcerers in the city.

The door at the far end of the car opened, and two men entered. Marla looked at them, frowning. They were identical twins, in their twenties, with buzzed-short black hair and glasses with chunky black frames, and they wore matching clothing—red T-shirts, khaki cargo pants, black hiking boots. They each had mobile phones, PDAs, pagers, and other devices clipped to their belts, and carried matching black laptop bags over their shoulders. Marla figured they had more computational power hanging on their bodies than had existed in the entire world circa 1950. They stopped in the aisle beside Marla's seat, each gripping the overhead rail left-handed, leaning slightly toward her at precisely the same angle. "You're Marla," one of them said.

"You have to come with us," said the other. Their voices were exactly the same.

"We're all on the same train," Marla said. "Going the same way. So for the time being, I don't have any objection to that."

They looked at each other with eerie simultaneity, then back down at Marla. "We'll get off the train at

Civic Center," one said. "and you'll come with us. Someone wants to meet you."

Marla crossed her legs, bumping one of the men gently in the knee with her foot in the process. He stepped backwards, out of her way—and so did the other guy, though she hadn't touched him. She glanced at Rondeau, who raised an eyebrow, and Marla shook her head fractionally. B looked a little frightened, which just went to prove that he didn't know much about Marla at all, since these were clearly people of the henchman variety, and Marla had never met a henchman yet that she couldn't fillet one-handed if the need arose.

"Who wants to meet me?" Marla said.

"Mr. Dalton," one of them said.

"Let me guess," Marla said. "He's the new pro-tem chief sorcerer, since Finch's untimely demise?"

"You'll find out who he is when he decides to tell you," the other one said, clearly trying to be menacing.

Marla rolled her eyes. "Well, it's another twenty minutes before we get back to the city, so why don't you two sit down?"

"Don't give us any trouble," one said, as they both sat down on the seat opposite.

"Do I look like a troublemaker?" Marla said. "You two just saved me a lot of walking around and asking questions. Hell, I'm thankful. I want to meet your boss."

"How'd you find us, though?" Rondeau said. "When we didn't even know where we were going?"

The henchmen smirked. "We have our ways," one said.

Marla snorted. "Sure you do. There's a pair of you

on every train, and probably on every street in the city, right? They're homunculi, Rondeau, or heavy astral projections, or some shit like that. Just duplicates. Dupe One and Dupe Two here happened to be the ones who bumped into us."

They weren't smirking anymore. They were scowling instead.

"Ah," Rondeau said. "I thought they were twins with that whole psychic-linkage thing going on."

"That would explain the way they move in tandem, maybe, but it doesn't explain the identical oozing pimple they've each got just to the left of their noses." Marla tapped the side of her nose, and the henchmen reached up simultaneously and touched the spots on their own faces.

"This is the weirdest day of my life," B said. "And that's saying something."

The henchmen squinted at B. "Hey," one said. And the other continued, "Aren't you Bradley Bowman?"

"Um," he said. "Yeah."

"I read a rumor online that you might get cast as the lead in an American movie version of *Dr. Who*. Any truth to that?"

"It's news to me," B said.

"I knew it was bullshit," one said, taking out his laptop and opening it on his knees, presumably to spread the truth among the infidels online.

"Tell me about your boss," Marla said, to the henchman who wasn't tapping away at a keyboard.

He shrugged. "You'll find out all you need to know soon enough. I'll tell you, though—you should be more scared than you look. You're in deep shit, from what I hear. Mr. Dalton isn't the only one looking for you."

"I've always had a gift for making friends easily," Marla said. She had an idea of the accusations she was going to face soon, and tried to decide whether she should bother going through the tedium of explaining things, or just break Mr. Dalton's kneecaps and extract the information she needed. Ah, well. No need to decide now. She could play it by ear when they arrived.

They rode the escalator up to street level, one henchman in the lead, the other bringing up the rear. They were in the heart of downtown San Francisco (or, rather, *one* of the hearts), right on Market Street, with gleaming office buildings rising on all sides. Marla felt instantly more at ease here—it was almost as good as being home. A few rusting iron bridges and an oil refinery or two, and she would have felt completely at peace. They walked along Market to an apartment building, down a short flight of stone steps to a bare metal door, painted green, just below street level. Marla took note of the location. Some sorcerers liked to get high above the ground, in penthouses and aeries. Others preferred more subterranean dwellings. There were crucial differences between those two sorts. Those who lived underground were usually more willing to get their hands dirty and deal with things personally.

The henchmen ushered them into a low-ceilinged room with bare concrete floors. Rondeau, looking around, said, "Wow. Modern Geek Eclectic." There were three battered couches in various colors, a steel bookshelf overspilling with paperbacks, an enormous rear-projection television screen against one wall, huge speakers in the corners, a DJ booth with multiple turntables on a raised platform, and a bar along another wall, done up in full bamboo-and-fringe tiki-bar style. Various movie posters, mostly for vintage sci-fi and horror movies, were thumbtacked to the plaster walls. There were also five or six computers and monitors scattered around the room at untidy workstations, and miscellaneous piles of cable and computer components heaped here and there on the floor.

"Back here," a henchman said, and led them through a door into another low room, this one filled with several rows of lab tables, each with flat-screen monitors and humming computer hard drives. They passed through that room and into another, this one a sprawling office with dark blue carpeting, a foosball table, a pinball machine, and a huge oaken L-shaped desk with its own complement of oversized black flat-screen computer monitors. The back of a leather captain's chair faced them from behind the desk, and Marla rolled her eyes again. What a James-Bond-villain gesture *this* was going to be.

"Mr. Dalton," a henchman said. "Your guest is here." They stepped back, standing on either side of the door.

The chair swiveled. The man sitting in it (with his elbows on the armrests, and his forefingers steepled together, even) was identical to the henchman, though he wore a different T-shirt, ragged khaki shorts, and bulging red-tinted WWII-style aviator goggles. "Have a seat," he said. "I'm Dalton."

"I gathered that," Marla said, and sat in one of the mismatched chairs on her side of the desk. B sat down, too.

Rondeau wandered over to the pinball machine.

"Sweet!" he said. "It doesn't even need quarters!" He started to play.

Dalton frowned.

"Don't mind him," Marla said. "He's got the attention span of a canary. I'm Marla, by the way."

"I know who you are," he said. "An out-of-towner. Also the last person seen with Finch before he died."

"I do have that distinction. And you're the local technomancer. Can't say I ever saw the appeal of this stuff, but then, that's why I'm not a silicon mage."

"Silicon?" Dalton said. "Please. I've got nothing but diamond processors here. They run faster without overheating."

"I can't tell you how fascinating that is," Marla said. "But we've got better things to talk about."

"True," he said. "Like why you killed Finch, and what you did with the Cornerstone."

"How did someone as stupid as you get into a position of power?" Marla said, genuinely astonished. Beside her, B winced.

"Hey, B!" Rondeau said. "Come here! They've got the Area 51 arcade game! Let's shoot some aliens!"

"Go on," Marla said. "Have fun."

B muttered something gratefully and went to join Rondeau.

Dalton leaned forward. "I don't think you understand who you're dealing with. It's my job to find out what happened to Finch, and to mete out punishment."

"Listen, diamond-boy, I didn't kill Finch. We made an arrangement. He was going to do me a favor, and I was going to do *him* a favor. Before we could do anything, though, we got ambushed by a lunatic named

Mutex and his amazing dancing killing frogs. *He's* the one who killed Papa Bear and stole the Cornerstone."

Dalton tapped a few keys on one of the keyboards in front of him. "Oh-kay," he said after a moment. "You're on the level."

Marla glanced around. "I don't sense a truth-circle."

"What, with chalk and burning herbs?" Dalton snorted. "Please. This room is wired with sensors so delicate they'd make a CIA operative weep with envy, and I've developed a system that actually *works* as a lie detector, not like that polygraph bullshit that only really pegs stress. I know you're telling the truth. But I'm not happy to hear it. Mutex? I thought he was long gone. He tried to get a meeting with me, and I let one of my mirrors talk to him. It wasn't—"

"Mirrors?" Marla said, thinking of enchanted looking-glasses.

He gestured toward the door, where the henchmen still stood. "Them. My mirror-selves."

Marla twisted around and looked at them. Their clothes had changed, and now they wore what Dalton wore. "They're not homunculi?"

"Ha. Vat-grown clones, on a psychic link party-line with me? Please."

If he says, "What? Please" *one more time,* Marla thought, *I'm going to choke him with a computer cable.*

"I don't have time for retro technologies like that," Dalton went on. "My mirrors *are* me, duplicated, running on a thirty-minute refresh rate. Every half hour I get a ping from them, and they get updated to whatever my present state is—so their clothes change to match mine, they know what I know, everything."

"And this is done with computers?" Marla said.

"Sure. Computers and what we call, for want of a better word, sorcery. Everything in the world is information, Marla. Me, you, this desk." He thumped the desktop with his fist. "And information can be manipulated and reconfigured endlessly. When you break it down, everything's made of math and emptiness."

"Maybe there's something to technomancy, after all," Marla said thoughtfully. There'd only been one prominent silicon mage in her city, and Marla had flung him off a rooftop for interfering with her fiscal policies by trying to steal several million in city funds.

"Technomancy is the key to everything," Dalton said. "You're like a savage digging in the dirt with a stick compared to me. So was Finch, and so's every other sorcerer in this city. See, they don't *get* it." There was a certain light in his eyes now, an almost evangelical excitement. Marla had seen it in necromancers talking about bones, and in pyromancers talking about the cleansing power of flames. "Are you familiar with Nick Bostrom's simulation theory?"

"I'm afraid not," Marla said, sitting back more comfortably in her chair. She had a feeling this might take a little while.

"He's a philosophy professor at Oxford. He makes an argument that it's quite likely we're all actually simulations of long-dead people, running in an emulated environment created by our own technologically advanced descendants."

"Ah," Marla said.

He sighed. "I'm trying to tell you something *important*," he said.

"Is it about Mutex?" she asked.

"Potentially," he said. "Here's the core of Bostrom's argument. First, you have to begin from the premise that it will someday be possible to re-create a human mind in a nonorganic environment. That is, to make a computer that operates in a manner indistinguishable from a human mind, to create consciousness in a machine."

Marla had talked to her friend Langford, the biomancer, enough to know that such things were maybe theoretically possible, though the technology was a long way off, so she nodded. "All right."

"Then ask yourself whether humans are likely to ever achieve that technology. I think it's obvious that we will, unless we cause ourselves to become extinct first, which seems doubtful, frankly. The tenacity of cockroaches is *nothing* compared to that of humans."

Marla twirled her finger in a hurry-up motion.

"The final question is this: do you believe that such advanced people would *never, ever* run sophisticated computer simulations of their own ancestors?"

"I wouldn't say *never*," she said. "People dress up in Civil War uniforms and pretend to shoot one another in fields, so I guess running a computer simulation of our ancestors isn't so different."

"Then you must agree that, in all likelihood, we are actually simulations living inside a computer. We're completely unaware that we're simulations, truly sentient and conscious, but actually running on some unimaginably complex computer system sometime in our own subjective far future. It's simple probability. If our descendants *can* create such simulations, then there's no reason to assume they would do so on a small scale, or for only one era. There might even be multiple versions of the same 'world' being simulated in dozens or scores or hundreds of computers, with slight variations. The odds are good that there are far more simulated minds running on computers than there are organic consciousnesses running on their original brains—and, so, probability tells us that, in all likelihood, we are simulations. It's not a new idea—science fiction writers have played with it for decades—but Bostrom's paper was one of the first attempts to treat it rigorously and take it seriously. You'll have to give me your e-mail address, Marla, I'll send you a link to the preprint."

"I think Rondeau might have e-mail," she said.

"I've got an AOL account," Rondeau said, in a helpful tone, without looking up from his arcade game.

Dalton looked at them as if they were exotic insects.

"So we're all living in a computer," Marla said. "Who cares? If we'll never know, and we can't tell the difference, why does it matter? It's like the free-will debate—for practical purposes, it doesn't *matter*. You have to live as *if* you have free will anyway, or else you just sit around until you die of starvation."

"But it *does* matter," Dalton said. "Bostrom thinks it matters because of the philosophical and theological implications, but it matters to us, to people like you and me, Marla. Because we're *sorcerers*. We do things that violate the known laws of the universe all the time. And do you know *why*? Because we're not *in* nature. We're in a computer program, and the rules of the physical universe don't apply. That's why I can instantiate duplicates of myself, using something we choose to call sympathetic magic, with the help of some very fast computers."

"Huh," Marla said. "I've heard stupider theories for how magic works."

"But the *real* implications are even more vast. Because we're running on a computer, and I *know* computers." He cracked his knuckles. "There's not a box in the world that I can't take over, not a system on Earth or in Heaven that I can't crack and own. And one of these days, I'm going to figure out how to own the box we're all running on, and that's the day I become god."

Ah, Marla thought. *A new variation on the basic megalomaniacal sorcerer model.* "And what about the people who are running the simulation? Why won't they just unplug you when you start to misbehave?"

"I doubt they're unaware of my efforts. I wouldn't be, in their position. They're watching me. Maybe someday they'll choose to show themselves. It would be trivial for them to do so. If nothing else, I'm sure they'll want to talk to me directly once I wrest control of this simulation from them. Maybe they'll upload my consciousness out of the simulation, into their physical world. Maybe I'll figure out how to upload *myself*. The possibilities are pretty much endless."

"And this has *what* to do with Mutex?"

He looked at her blankly for a moment, and she suppressed the urge to crack him across the face and smash the lenses of those goggles. She was on a timetable here, and her problems were a hell of a lot more pressing than Dalton's plan to own the box of the universe.

"Oh, right," Dalton said. "Bostrom talks about the impact of the simulation theory on theology. If the person running this particular simulation is, say, a fundamentalist Christian, then it's very possible that, in the afterlife, evildoers *will* burn in Hell—Hell being, in this case, just another simulation. Heaven could be similar. If we're just digital emulations, then there's no reason to discount the notion of the afterlife. Now, personally, I tend to think that fundamentalists of *all* stripes are a dying breed, and that they won't be around in several subjective centuries, which is probably when our simulation got started."

Marla found *that* idea even more doubtful than his original premise—fundamentalism was here to stay, in one form or another—but she didn't object.

"Of course, it is possible that someone might run a simulation within a given religious framework for experimental purposes, or even just for fun. Put people in a world where fundamentalist Christianity *is* true, or Zoroastrianism, or Voudon, or Hinduism—"

"Or all that crazy Aztec shit," Marla said. "That's what you're getting at, in your incredibly long-winded way, isn't it?"

Dalton frowned. "Yeah. Basically. Mutex tried to make contact with all the sorcerers in the city, and he told all of us the same thing, when he got the chance. He said the universe is running down. The old gods are starting to get hungry again. The wheels and axles of the universe are greased with blood, and the tremendous stockpile of blood the Aztecs built up with their hundreds of thousands of human sacrifices is dwindling. He says that if we don't start up the old ways again, the universe is going to grind to a halt, the stars will stand still in their orbits, and everyone and everything will suffer and die. It seems pretty far-fetched to me, but it's not impossible that he's right, if those are the parameters the programmer of this simulation set down, you know? Maybe everything in this universe really does run on an engine of blood."

Marla found Mutex's philosophy marginally more believable than Dalton's, but that was mostly because of Dalton's smug assurance that he was right—he was, in a way, something of a religious fundamentalist himself. She had no doubt that Mutex's gods had once been real, perhaps sustained by the belief of their worshippers. The notion that gods were kept alive by their believers was a popular theory of theology in her circles, since it explained why exorcisms, Voudon, Kabalistic magic, and other mutually incompatible magical systems all more or less worked. Or, maybe, there had been powerful people or creatures or other sorts of beings that chose to be worshipped as gods by Mutex's forebears, or just fell into the godly gig as a matter of luck and stumble. At any rate, she thought his theory about the universe grinding to a halt for want of blood sacrifice was probably bullshit, and she'd continue to think that unless and until he converted a whole lot of people to his way of thinking, in which case she'd start to worry about it *becoming* true. But *Mutex* believed it. She said as much aloud: "Mutex thinks he's a hero. He's the only one who can save the universe. By doing . . . what, exactly?"

Dalton spread his hands. "I'm not sure. He wanted access to the Cornerstone—which he got, from what you've told me. He told the other sorcerers he met with that he wanted to use the Cornerstone to awaken the sleeping gods and give them their due in blood. That doesn't sound good, but as for what it means, specifically, I couldn't tell you."

She thought of the dead frog in her bag, and of the

stolen statue of Tlaltecuhtli, the primordial froglike earth-monster. It wasn't a big leap to imagine that Mutex was planning to awaken the sleeping spirit of Tlaltecuhtli. What would such a ritual require, apart from the Cornerstone?

"Anyway," Dalton said, "whatever he's planning, he wants to use the heart's blood of dead sorcerers to do it."

"What?" she said, suddenly interested again.

"I'm not Finch's direct successor," Dalton said. "The strega Umbaldo was. She was found a couple of hours ago, surrounded by poison dart frogs, with her heart cut out. After her death, the mantle passed to me. My mirror-selves investigated her body—frog poison doesn't do shit to them, of course—and they found flecks of obsidian in the wound. Mutex is taking hearts. I don't know if the heart's blood of a sorcerer is more potent, or if he's just killing us because he's pissed at us, or—"

"He's killing you because you're dangerous, probably," Marla said. "The sorcerers are the only ones who can possibly stop him, after all."

"And you're all full of fear," B said. "You're all *terrified,* and he wants hearts filled with fear. *Teyolia.* The life force that feeds the gods and controls the universe. It's stronger when you're afraid."

Marla turned around in her chair and looked at him. She had almost forgotten B was there. Rondeau was trying to shush him, but Marla said, "Did you have another dream last night?"

"Yeah," he said. "I found a sybil to interpret it. I had to give her my autograph as payment, but I didn't sign my real name. She said it didn't matter, but I think she was disappointed."

He'd found a sybil. Just happened to find one. Maybe he really *was* more than a second-rate seer. "What are the sorcerers afraid of?" she asked.

B didn't hesitate. "The same thing you are. They're afraid of losing control."

Marla didn't react. It was a fair cop, but she didn't need to let it show, especially not in front of Dalton.

"Hey," Dalton said. "Weren't you in that bad sci-fi movie with Dolph Lundgren? You played his surly teenage son?"

"That wasn't me," B said. "I think that was River Phoenix. But it's okay. I get that a lot."

"River Phoenix is dead," Dalton said, matter-of-factly. "He overdosed years and years ago."

"It's a nasty way to go," B said.

"Not as nasty as having your heart scooped out by a crazed Aztec warrior-priest, and that's true whether the world is real *or* a simulation." Marla laced her fingers together in front of her. Finally, they might be able to get down to business. "What's your plan of action, and how can I help? I'm a guest in your city, after all."

Dalton shook his head, as if astonished at her audacity. "I wouldn't call you a guest, Mason. In fact, it's probably best for everyone if you go back to your own city. Let us take care of things here. Mutex is more dangerous than we'd expected, but we'll track him down. You have bigger problems. I'm sure you know you've already made a rather significant enemy. The ruler of Chinatown has put a price on your head. I don't care—I'm as rich as I'll ever need to be—but there are other people who might want to collect that reward."

"You'll have to put me in touch with a good bookie," Rondeau called, still apparently engrossed in shotgunning video-game aliens. "I might be able to get decent odds betting on Marla, since nobody in this town knows her. You know, back home, they won't even take bets on the people who try to kill her? It's a bummer. That used to be easy money."

"What he means to say is, don't worry about me. I can protect my own head. It's Mutex I'm concerned with." And the Cornerstone. Mostly the Cornerstone. But Mutex had killed her friend, and for Lao Tsung's memory—and because it coincided with her other goals—Marla would make sure he was stopped.

"I can't make you leave," Dalton said. "Well, I *could,* but it's not worth the effort. As for Mutex, he'll be caught. We might have trouble finding the Cornerstone, but once we capture Mutex and dissolve whatever safeguards he's created, we should be able to find it by divination. There are lots of built-in safeguards against that, since the Cornerstone isn't something we want apprentices and cantrippers to find, but I know a few techniques that should work. Once we get the big rock back...well, I can't promise to honor whatever agreement you had with Finch, but we can discuss things, and maybe reach an agreement. We'll have to investigate first, and find out what, if anything, Mutex did with the stone, see if any damage was done, but after that, perhaps you can make use of it, under supervised conditions, for a suitable price. It might be a while, but I'll be serving out the rest of Finch's term, so I'll be in charge for a few years."

"Years," Marla said. "I see. What makes you think you'll be able to catch Mutex anytime soon?"

"My mirror-selves are out in force, Ms. Mason. Every half hour, I get an update on their status. On my last ping, which happened shortly after you arrived, I learned that Mutex is only a dozen or so blocks from here, being pursued by my mirrors. They coordinated on that ping, and now they're closing in on him en masse. He's just meat, and his little poison frogs can't do anything to help him. My mirror-selves don't get poisoned. They're *in* meatspace, but not *of* it. You can knock them down, maybe, but you can't do any real damage to them." He thumped his chest—a rather grotesque gesture, Marla thought, given the greater context of heart-stealing—and said, "As long as *I'm* still operational, so are they."

"You're bringing him here?" Marla said. "Are you sure that's wise?"

Dalton smirked. "Don't worry. He won't be conscious when he arrives. And my mirror-selves will make sure no biological contagions make it into the office."

Was Dalton exhibiting stupid overconfidence, or merely a healthy sense of his own capabilities? Time would tell. Probably a very short time.

Something on Dalton's desk buzzed. He frowned, leaned forward, and tapped a key. "Odd," he said finally. "That was the door alarm, but it's closed, and I don't see anyone on the monitors."

"Shit," Marla said. "Could it be someone invisible?"

Dalton rolled his eyes. "I've got up-to-date decryption applications running all over this place, so unless they're using an all-new spell, I don't think *that's* likely. I've got infrared sensors, too, of course. More likely it's just a false positive on the system. Let me run back the video.... Nope. The door didn't even open. See?"

He turned the monitor, which showed a startlingly high-resolution view of the front door. Marla was used to grainy low-res security camera footage, so this was a surprise, but it made sense that Dalton would have better tech than the average person. The door *didn't* open, but there was something—a brief flicker, almost too fast for the eye to see, but Marla caught it. "What's that—"

Blood welled up out of Dalton's mouth, then fountained, spattering the desk and computers. Marla leapt backward, putting distance between herself and whatever had attacked Dalton—but what *had* attacked him? There was nobody else in the room, unless there *was* someone invisible. "B, Rondeau, get *out*!" she shouted, and they complied with alacrity, Rondeau dragging B by the hand. Dalton's mirror-selves came forward and flanked her, but they seemed at an utter loss as to how to proceed.

Then Marla saw a hummingbird fluttering high in the corner of the room, and knew this was Mutex's doing. Something invisible flung Dalton's body—he was quite obviously no longer among the living—on the desk, knocking over the monitors, which crashed and sparked on the floor. Something tore Dalton's shirt open, shreds of cloth flying, and then bright red arterial heart's blood gushed as his rib cage was ripped open. Something flickered behind the desk, like the ruby flutter of hummingbird wings, moving faster than the eye could see.

"This is bullshit," Marla said. The time had come when nothing else would work, so Marla reversed her cloak.

The benevolent, healing qualities of the white side disappeared as the inner lining—the deep purple of a bruise—became the cloak's exterior, clothing Marla in a veil of imperial shadow. When the cloak reversed, Marla's rational mind receded to a distant corner of her consciousness. She could move with superhuman speed in this form, perform feats of strength that would normally break her bones, but it wasn't much good for planning, or even for following a plan. While clothed in the purple, Marla could only assess and dispose of threats.

With her heightened senses, she could just barely see Mutex. He was moving incredibly quickly, his body a blur of faintly red-tinged motion, wielding an obsidian knife to cut out Dalton's heart. He'd accelerated himself somehow, far beyond the normal human time-scale, so that relative to himself, everything else probably seemed to be standing completely still. That's what the flicker of motion on the video had been—the brief opening and closing of the front door as Mutex had entered. He'd either somehow cloaked his body heat, or else he was moving so quickly that Dalton's sensors hadn't been able to pick it up. Distantly, Marla wondered how he achieved this effect without destroying himself—most experiments in physical acceleration this extreme ended with the researchers dead. Marla could only accelerate herself to this extent because of her cloak, which was a magical artifact whose origins and mechanisms were unknown and highly resistant to analysis.

In the microseconds it took Marla to identify Mutex and bunch her muscles to leap at him, he finished taking Dalton's heart and ran from the room, holding it, dripping, in his hand. On his way out he looked at Marla—

a stare long enough for her to notice, which must have been quite a long look from his perspective—and she jumped for him anyway, but missed by yards. He was out of the building before she hit the ground, landing in a crouch by the door.

With an effort, she reversed her cloak, and the healing qualities of the white side began to immediately soothe her strained muscles—though she didn't hurt as much as she usually did after using the cloak, since she hadn't actually *done* anything this time. Normally, when she reversed the cloak, she tore people apart. The purplish shadow-tendrils withdrew into the lining now, leaving her with the taste of pomegranate seeds in her mouth.

The mirror-Daltons stared at her. "That was amazing," one of them said. "You looked like . . . like a panther made of smoke, or . . . or . . ."

"I looked like a goddess," Marla said. She felt marvelous, crystal-sharp and filled with piercing white light, able to do anything. All her problems were suddenly in focus, and the solutions were obvious. Why *not* abdicate control of Felport to Susan Wellstone? Then Marla could sit back here as Mutex killed off all the other sorcerers in San Francisco. When he was done, Marla could kill *him,* and take over this city. It was bigger and more important than Felport, and once Marla established herself out here, she could send her warriors to kill Susan as punishment for her insolence. It all made sense, now that she was wearing the cloak again. Why had she ever taken it off? The cloak made the imposition of her will as simple as—

"*Shit,*" Marla said, clutching her head in her hands, grinding her teeth, and squeezing her eyes shut. The alien intelligence that possessed her in the aftermath of using the cloak receded a little, and she mentally *pushed* until it withdrew completely. Her hope that the cloak's power over her had faded was unfounded—it still had its hooks deep in her. "Damn. Yeah, I was like a goddess, I know. Not that it did me much good. Mutex got away, and Dalton one-point-oh is dead."

The mirror-Daltons looked at the body of their originator. "Oh, we're fucked," one said.

"Oh?" Marla said. Rondeau and B came back into the room. B's face was milk-white, and he was shaking. Real life was nastier than any of his visions had led him to expect, Marla supposed.

The Daltons nodded. One said, "We've got . . . shit, ten minutes until the next ping. When the computer checks his—our—the *original's* current status, and finds him offline . . . we'll just disappear."

"There's no way you can, I don't know, break the connection?" Rondeau said. "Make it so the computer doesn't check, or thinks the original is still alive, or something?"

The Daltons looked at each other. "Sure there is," one said.

"But not in ten minutes," said the other. "It's a very secure system, designed to be impervious to tampering. This is a problem we didn't expect. When we refresh in nine minutes . . . ah, fuck, I don't want to die." The Dalton sat on the floor and held his head in his hands.

Marla turned her attention to the one still standing. "I need a list of the names and addresses of all the other sorcerers in town." The Dalton didn't react. Marla snapped her fingers in front of his face, and he blinked. She repeated herself.

"What?" he said. "I can't tell you that. You're an outsider."

"Don't be stupid," Marla said. "Mutex has killed three of you so far. Finch, Umbaldo, and now *you*. He's targeting sorcerers, at least all the ones who dismissed or laughed at him. Apparently he doesn't have any problem locating you—the Cornerstone probably makes his divination spells infallibly accurate. That's three dead in, what, six hours? At this rate, there aren't going to be any sorcerers *left* in San Francisco, except for me, the outsider. But if you give me the names and addresses of the remaining sorcerers, I can give them a little warning, maybe manage to save some of them. How does *that* sound?"

"It makes sense," the Dalton said.

"Then you'd better get a move on, because you've only got about seven minutes to live."

"I'd rather spend my last moments jerking off," the Dalton said, but he went to a desk in the corner and opened a sleek, thin laptop. He tapped at the keys for a few moments, entered several passwords in succession, and finally opened a file. A printer on the blood-spattered desk began to hum and spit out pages.

"That's just names and addresses," the Dalton said. "The detailed dossiers aren't on the network, they're on a local drive deep underground."

"Guess I'll have to be surprised by their sparkling personalities," Marla said. "It looks like Mutex is hitting you in order of succession. Who's next in line to be chief-of-chiefs?"

The Dalton tapped the first page of the printout.

Marla picked it up, read, and nodded. She turned to B. "We're going to the Tenderloin. Which Rondeau tells me is *not* the meatpacking district. We're going to meet somebody named Bethany. No last name. How very pop-star of her."

"Bethany," the Dalton said. "Fuck. I like her. *Liked* her. I hope she doesn't wind up the way I did. But she's good, so maybe she won't."

"Yeah? Is she good enough to avoid what just happened to your original?"

The Dalton shrugged. "I would've thought *I* was good enough to avoid that, but I wasn't. She'll put up a fight, though."

"Good. I'm going to help her out. I'm not sure what I can *do* to Mutex, but I'll do my best. We'd better get moving, though. Mutex hasn't been taking frequent rest breaks." She glanced back at the Daltons, one of whom was still crying, while the other sat at the desk in the corner, staring blankly across the room at his sire's heartless corpse. They were staring imminent nonexistence in the face, and Marla's heart softened toward them. "Or do you want us to stay?" she said. "Until ... it's over?"

The Dalton at the desk looked at her for a moment, then shook his head. "No. No need. We might as well go alone. You've got more important things to do than watch us refresh out of existence."

"Okay," Marla said. She paused before heading toward the door. "But, hey. Good luck outside the simulation. I'm sure it's amazing on the other side."

The Dalton at the desk nodded and gave them a wave. Marla left, with B and Rondeau following.

11

B hung back with Rondeau as they followed Marla out onto Market Street, his mind still well and truly reeling from the events in Dalton's office. Despite all the outlandish things he'd seen, the oddest thing—in a way—was the look of human feeling on Marla's face when she wished the Daltons a pleasant afterlife. "That was almost sweet of her," B said. "What she just said to them."

"Yeah," Rondeau said. "It was."

"If I hadn't just seen her transform into a vicious, golden-eyed monster draped in purple shadows, I'd almost call it tenderness."

"The thing about Marla is, you've got to embrace the contradictions," Rondeau said. "The job she has to do, you have to be tough. I'm not saying she's got a soft squishy center or anything, but there's more to her than ass-whipping and blunt-force trauma. If there wasn't, I wouldn't be working for her."

B nodded. In his dream, the first dream about Marla, he'd felt a sense of connection, a depth of feeling, even a degree of enchantment with her. Reality hadn't done much to reflect the dream, however. B had the definite sense that Marla was trying him out to see if he was the kind of tool she could use. And if he turned out to be useless, she'd toss him aside. He had to make sure that didn't happen. If he didn't stay with her, the city would be destroyed. She probably needed him in ways that hadn't even occurred to her yet. Unfortunately, they hadn't occurred to *him* yet, either. He didn't know what the hell he was supposed to do. "So we're going to the Tenderloin now?" he said, looking at Marla's back, her steady stride down Market Street.

Rondeau nodded.

"Ah," B said. "The fun just doesn't stop. Does she even know how to get there?"

Rondeau shrugged. "She's got a bus schedule. We're probably heading for a bus stop."

"I thought time was of the essence here? Shouldn't we take a cab?"

Rondeau waved his hand in a be-my-guest gesture. "Go. Convince her. She doesn't like taxis. Because the drivers could be taking you *anywhere.*"

"Like bus drivers can't steer you wrong?"

"I do not claim to endorse her logic," Rondeau said. "I am merely reporting it. She mostly travels on foot back home. We could have a limo driving us around here, but Marla likes to keep her feet on the ground."

B sighed, steeled himself, and lengthened his stride. He fell into step beside Marla and said, "Would you like me to flag down a cab? They're not too hard to get on Market."

"We can get a bus, can't we?" she said.

"It'll take longer," B said.

She frowned, then nodded. "Yeah, all right. But only since we're in a hurry."

B raised his hand to the next passing cab, which was, fortunately, dented, battered, and in need of a wash. He could tell Marla approved. B and Rondeau got in the backseat, and Marla rode in front. She told the driver the address, reading from the piece of paper.

He grunted and drove on without comment.

The three of them stood on a corner in front of a liquor store with barred windows, dirty newspaper pages and discarded ice-cream wrappers blowing around their feet, the sidewalk permanently mottled and discolored with spit, vomit, ground-out cigarette butts, and ancient blobs of chewing gum. Marla inhaled, deeply, taking in the scent of piss and spilled beer, and, yes, she could have been in Felport, in the darkest part of the urban core, where she lived alone in an apartment building that would have been condemned if not for her influence. This was the neighborhood of easily gratified baser appetites, where sex and booze and drugs were just a quick cash transaction away, where the distance between want and have and have-not could be cut down to nothing in a moment. Every city had places like this, though some cities took pains to hide them. Marla liked it here. She understood its logic and its brutal grace. This was a place of simple motivations. Marla suspected she would get along with the sorcerer who had taken this neighborhood as her own.

"Now, this is almost like home," Rondeau said, looking up at a sign advertising "Live Nude Girls."

"Except around here, some of the strip clubs are employee-owned co-ops," B said, slouching against a light pole. His eyes were shadowed, and Marla wondered if he'd slept at all the night before, or if he always looked this much on the edge of being used-up. She suspected he did. It must be difficult, being half ordinary, half magical. Chimeras had short life spans. The strain of being more than one thing at once could tear anyone apart.

"So where to now?" B asked. "Into the darkest, cankerous, pee-smelling heart of the Tenderloin, where the damned and the poor college students dwell?"

Marla pulled the printout she'd gotten from Dalton's mirror-self out of her pocket. "Looks like this sorceress, Bethany, lives in the Tenderloin Station."

"The what?" B said.

"Tenderloin Station," Marla repeated. "It says it's underground."

"Somebody's fucking with you," B said. "There's no such thing as the Tenderloin Station. No trains run here. There might be a bus station...."

"I've got an address," Marla said. "A corner, at least, so we'll find out." She took a step toward the intersection, paused, pivoted on her heel, paused again, and huffed an annoyed exhalation.

"Oh, right," Rondeau said, and began unfolding a map. "Marla doesn't like not having a map in her head," he said, in an aside to B, which was, of course, perfectly audible to Marla. "And I'm not always as psychic as I should be when it comes to providing some external directional guidance."

Marla leaned over the map Rondeau held, muttering, tracing streets with her fingertip.

"Why didn't you just ask the cabdriver to drop you off at the appropriate corner?" B said.

"Because discretion is an impulse in me that extends beyond habit into irresistible force," she said. "In my city, every cabdriver reports to *someone,* often without even being conscious of it. I can't imagine things are so different here. It probably doesn't matter if my movements are being tracked right now, but I find it's best to always act as if things are as bad as they could possibly get. That way, you can only be pleasantly surprised. So I gave the cabdriver a random address on one of the streets mentioned in the directions. Now I'm just trying to figure out which direction I should be walking in. And it's...this." She pointed, and set off, B following along with Rondeau, who was trying to fold the map back into some semblance of pocket-sized convenience.

They walked past liquor stores with iron grates covering the windows, past peep shows, bail bond emporiums, and pawnshops without number; past vagrants who didn't even bother panhandling, heaps of reeking trash, broken glass, and cigarette butts, and alleys that smelled of wine and urine. They reached the corner indicated in Dalton's directions, an intersection dominated by a burned-out building that had once been a residential hotel, to judge from the faded sign. The walls of the building were intact, but the first-floor windows and doors were boarded over, while the second-story windows were broken, and opened onto fire-blackened walls. There were bas-reliefs of mythological creatures on the walls above the highest windows—gryphons, unicorns, and other beasts so faded by weather and vandalism that they could no longer be identified.

"Nothing here," Rondeau said. "No train station anyway."

"Maybe she's in the hotel," Marla said doubtfully. "Maybe there's a basement?" Some sorcerers thrived on desolation, and pyromancers often favored sites of arson for their lairs. But that didn't explain the wording of Dalton's printout, the words in crisp laserjet Helvetica: "Bethany. Tenderloin Station. Underground."

"Or maybe the real entrance is down there," B said, pointing to a bit of the cracked sidewalk to the left of the boarded-over double doors.

Marla looked, and the opening revealed itself to her like an optical illusion resolving. B's gifts as a seer were proving more and more valuable. There was a stairway there, leading down into a recessed rectangular opening. The stairs and walls were the same color and texture as the surrounding sidewalk, which explained part of the illusion, but there was clearly a patina of magic laid over the scene to make it truly indistinguishable from the surrounding street. Marla peered down into the subterranean entryway to a concealed door whose outlines were only faintly visible, the delineation of its edges blurring into the form of sidewalk cracks.

"I think that's our great ingress," Rondeau said, and Marla nodded, stepping down the stairs carefully—even staring right at them, they seemed to blur and dissolve beneath her feet. The stairs went down about seven feet below street level.

"Freaky," Rondeau said. "It looks like you're sinking down through the concrete, even though I *know* the steps are there. As soon as I blink, though, it slips out of focus."

"I didn't even realize it was supposed to be concealed," B said. "It's clear as air to me. I wonder how many things I walk past every day that are supposed to be hidden?"

"There's no telling," Marla said, and thought again how hard it must be for B, a being of perpetual twilight, Mr. In-Between, uncomfortable among ordinaries and unknown among sorcerers.

Marla went to the door, placing her hand against it, cold rough stone against her palm and the equally rough pads of her fingertips. She felt around the outlines of the door, looking for a catch, and found nothing. She stepped back. "B," she said, "do you see a way into this?"

B came down the stairs, his brow furrowed, and brushed past her to examine the door. He smelled of damp grass and black tea, a strangely pleasant combination, and for a moment, looking at his face in profile, Marla saw beyond the weight of grief and recent years, past his padded armor of layered thrift-store clothes, to the magnetism he tried so hard to disguise, an attractive quality that had first made him into a minor movie star and that now drew ghosts and visions to him. Marla seldom had time for romance, and even more seldom lamented that fact, but seeing B's beautiful profile—the corona of his so-much-eclipsed sun—gave her a brief pang of longing.

And, of course, he was gay. It was just as well. The

last thing this trip needed was another complication, even an incidentally pleasant one.

"Huh," B said. "There's, like, a *habit* hanging in the air here."

"Like a nun's habit?" Rondeau said.

"No, no, I mean a *routine,* an action that's been repeated so often that it's left an impression in the air. I can feel it, like the memory of a movement, I think it's ... like ... *this.*" He kicked the lower right-hand corner of the door, and as his foot moved Marla noticed the discoloration on that portion of the door, a spot kicked a thousand times, and when B's foot connected, the door swung inward, revealing a rectangle of darkness that even Marla's better-than-ordinary eyes could barely penetrate.

"Stairs," B said. "Metal, spiraling down."

"Come on, Rondeau," Marla said. "I'll lead, B in the middle, Rondeau gets the rear guard." She sighed. "I wish there was an intercom or something. I don't mind barging into sorcerers' lairs, but I hope she doesn't think I'm coming in heavy for war or something."

"You could take her," Rondeau said loyally.

"I don't *want* to," Marla said. "I want her to help *me* take Mutex."

"Oh," Rondeau said. "Right. Lead on, fearless diplomat."

"*Fiat lux,*" Marla said, pausing to pass her hand over Rondeau's and B's eyes. Now she could see into the dark, though the view was grainy and oddly saturated, like a digital photograph given too much contrast. B and Rondeau could see better, too (though B probably didn't need it), but there was no external light source, no hovering ball of light to reveal their position or create deeper shadows around them. Marla's light spell only affected the vision of the chosen recipients, stepping up the receptivity of the light-sensing apparatus in the eye, tweaking the brain's ability to interpret visual information. Langford the biomancer had helped her devise this spell. Marla hated the tinkerbell lights, floating balls of fire, illuminated auras, and all the other conventional light-producing magics most sorcerers used. This was a bit like having night-vision goggles on inside her eyes, but without the greenish tinge.

"Wicked," Rondeau said, peering around.

"Huh," B said. "Very nice."

Marla started down the tight spiral stairs, which descended through a space the size of an elevator shaft. The stairs were metal—copper, actually—and had almost certainly been specially made, probably as a sort of magical nightingale floor, the metal conducting physical information about the intruders down into the sorcerer's lair below. So much for worrying about showing up unannounced. If Bethany was down there, she was probably aware that she had visitors. Marla admired the craftsmanship, the nautilus whorl of the stairs spiraling down, the railing of delicately curved copper pipe, the steps embossed with raised starburst shapes to provide a surer tread. Marla didn't know any details about Bethany, but she could infer a few things. Bethany's magic would likely be chthonic, aligned with dark places underground, and thus entangled with the treasures of the Earth, metals and jewels. Judging by the stairs, she was probably a hands-on practitioner, a fabricator or artificer.

Or maybe she just had a lot of money to *hire* fabricators, and liked underground housing because it was cheap. Marla couldn't be sure. Being a stranger in this city was a constant disadvantage. She needed some kind of scorecard to keep up with the prominent personalities, though there were fewer of them with each passing hour, it seemed.

The stairs went down a hundred yards, two hundred, the spiral tight enough to make her a little dizzy, which was also probably an intentional effect, making visitors more off balance. Marla finally sensed an opening in space, a widening of the elevator shaft into the contours of a larger room, though even her enhanced eyes didn't penetrate very far into the darkness.

When she stepped off the last stair and her foot touched the concrete floor, floodlights burst on, dazzling her painfully, overwhelming the enhanced light-receptors in her eyes. *"Nix lux!"* she shouted, canceling the light spell and restoring all their eyesight to normal. B and Rondeau were cursing and rubbing their eyes.

That's a drawback of the spell she'd never considered. Tinkerbell lights would have been better. She squinted, purple blots hanging in her vision as she scanned the area around them for threats. There were none, fortunately. The moment of visual overload had left them vulnerable to a surprise attack, but that didn't seem to be Bethany's intention.

"I don't believe it," B said, stepping off the stairs, still rubbing one of his eyes. "It's a BART station."

A blue-and-white sign on the white-tiled wall read "Tenderloin." They were, unmistakably, on a subway platform, a long stretch of concrete bordered by tracks. The wall beyond the tracks lacked the ubiqui-tous advertising Marla had seen at other stations, and there was no bright yellow-and-black stripe painted on the edge of the platform to warn the clueless or visu-ally impaired that there was a short trip to an electri-fied rail just beyond, but otherwise, it could have been any of the train stations Marla had seen since she got to the city.

"There's even a map of the train system," B said. "Just like the ones in all the other stations. Except this one includes Tenderloin Station."

Marla examined the map, which used color-coded lines to indicate the routes. Tenderloin Station was marked with a circle, but none of the usual lines touched it. It had its own short line, delineated in black, running a short distance and then looping in on itself. Marla ran her finger down the map, to the bot-tom, where the train schedules were usually posted, but that section was blank.

Rondeau stood on the edge of the platform, peer-ing one way and then the other. "Do we go in on foot?" he asked.

"Only if I get really impatient," Marla said. "Otherwise, I'd just as soon do without the risk of get-ting flattened. Assuming Bethany is home, she knows we're here, and if she's curious—which she must be, sorcerers are an inquisitive sort—she'll send a train. Or else she'll come here herself, though I doubt that. Making people come to you is the stronger position."

They waited, Marla doing a simple series of mar-tial arts exercises to keep her body occupied, nothing too advanced; if they were being observed, it wouldn't hurt to seem less skilled than she was. Rondeau sat on the floor, staring at the far wall, singing Beatles songs badly. B was jittery, sitting down for a few moments, then rising to pace the length of the platform, stopping occasionally to peer into the tunnel.

"What's on your mind, B?" Marla asked.

"Ah," he said, "I've had weird experiences with trains. Not in secret stations, but that doesn't exactly detract from the likelihood of weirdness."

"What's your train story?" Rondeau said. "I could use some entertainment. I've gone through the whole *White Album* already, and Marla gets pissed when I sing anything from *Sergeant Pepper's Lonely Hearts Club Band*."

"Do tell," Marla said.

"It happened about a year ago," B said. "I met this guy, Jay . . . his girlfriend had just died, and he had this idea that he could go to the land of the dead and bring her back. And I had to help him, I knew it, because I'd had this dream about him before I even met him—"

"The way you dreamed about me," Marla said.

"Yeah. One of *those* dreams. I knew there was no use trying to avoid him—I'd tried to get out of stuff like this in the past, and it never worked—so I agreed to help. We hid in a BART station until after they closed. Late that night, a train came. It wasn't a normal train. It looked like a thighbone with windows, and there were bone hooks on the ceiling for handrails. We got on, and it took us way down deep, to some place. . . ." He shook his head. "I don't know where exactly. Thinking back, it's fuzzy, misty, just images—trees, shapes in the shadows, bees, maybe lizards, and a cave, except it couldn't have been a cave, because there were stars overhead. I don't know what happened to us down there—it's like I'm forgetting it even more now that I'm trying to think about it. But whatever happened, I made my way back to the train, and I came back up, alone. I don't know if Jay found what he was looking for, or if he ever made it out...." B looked bewildered now, and maybe a little scared.

Marla found herself approximately a million times more impressed by B than she had been a moment before. "You touched something old and powerful," she said. "The stuff that myths are made of. Don't worry about the way your memories are wobbling on you— the numinous is like that, it resists accurate reportage. You could *embellish* it, make up details, throw in a love story or a little suspense, make yourself a hero— that's how myths get made—but giving a true and accurate accounting is just this side of impossible, even for someone who can see as clearly as you do." Marla was increasingly sure that B was something more, perhaps much more, than a man unfortunate enough to be born a seer. She couldn't be *sure* he had other powers—some people just happened to encounter the numinous, that was the nature of the truly unknowable. But other people, a few so rare as to be statistically nonexistent, *drew* the numinous to themselves, or, as some sorcerers speculated, actually *generated* such fundamentally unknowable Mysteries by their very acts and movements, the way you could build up a charge of static electricity by shuffling across a shag carpet in your stocking feet. If B was one of *those,* an oracle-generator, he was lucky to still be alive, and as relatively sane as he seemed. Big magic affected people, and B's relative ignorance could only protect him for so long.

"Yeah," B said. "That makes sense to me. If I just *think* about it, it's clear, but as soon as I try to put it into words, it goes all hazy. Anyway, I guess I'm just worried that I'm going to see that bone train again. I get the feeling I was only supposed to ride on it once, and if I got on board again, I don't know what would happen. Nothing good, I don't think."

Just then the unmistakable sound of an approaching train—the rumble, the whine, the sound of air in the tunnel being shoved along by the approaching mass—began. Rondeau stood by B, giving him some support just by his proximity. Marla took up a similar position on his other side.

"If it's your train, you don't have to get on," Marla said. "I wouldn't ask that of you. But I don't think it's going to be the bone train. If Bethany had a train to the underworld—*any* underworld—at her command, she wouldn't be waiting her turn to run San Francisco. If she had easy access to the Land of the Dead, she'd have *much* more power than that."

"Hope you're right," B said, almost inaudibly.

The train barreled out of the tunnel, and at a glance B visibly relaxed. This was no giant's thighbone, but a high-tech train worthy of a techno-fetishist's fantasy, gleaming black metal with accents of sterling silver and surgical steel, with an engine, and several passenger cars, of smoked glass and reflective gleam. Marla thought again that Bethany must be a fabricator. Marla herself had never given a damn about appearances, happy to live in a crumbling brownstone or ride on a filthy city bus so long as all her needs were served. But Bethany clearly reveled in the glamour of surfaces, and so might be good at illusions, and, of course, telling lies.

"All aboard," Rondeau said, as a shining black door in the first passenger car slid open with a whuff of compressed air. Marla got on the train first. The interior matched the outside, black leather seats, and silver handrails overhead, and Marla sat down and crossed her legs. B and Rondeau sat as well.

"This is a lot nicer than the train I took to Hell," B said.

"High praise," Rondeau said. "I wonder who's driving this thing?"

"Probably no one," Marla said. "It's probably automated. I bet there's a little model train in Bethany's lair, and a bit of sympathetic magic to make the big train follow the path of the little one."

"That would be one way to do it," said a voice from the far end of the car, closest to the engine. "But actually I just piggyback on the city's electrical system and run my train the old-fashioned way."

Marla stood and faced the woman who'd emerged from the engine car. "Bethany, I presume," she said.

"And you must be Marla Mason. Trouble follows you. And, lucky me, here you are."

12

Bethany slid the door shut behind her. She smiled, and made an odd clicking sound—after a moment Marla realized it was the sound of Bethany tapping her teeth against the ring in her lower lip. Bethany had no shortage of piercings, along with more extreme body modifications. She was pale, tall, and slender, with black hair pulled back tightly into a ponytail. Her eyes were yellow, and had horizontal slits, like a goat's—either she'd undergone a transplant to give herself permanent *bruja* eyes or she was wearing novelty contact lenses. Short horns emerged from her forehead, just above her eyes, wholly subcutaneous implants, probably metal, that added to her devilish appearance. A large silver ring hung from her nose, like a bull ring, and smaller rings adorned her eyebrows and lower lip. Her earlobes had stretchers in place, though the lobes weren't very big yet, merely the size of quarters. Light scarification decorated her cheeks—what looked like Maori designs, though Marla didn't know enough about such things to determine their significance, if any. Bethany had brands on her bare upper arms, and a choker of thorns was tattooed around her throat. Small metal implants—ball bearings, horseshoe shapes, and blunt spikes—dotted her forearms and the backs of her hands. She wore leather pants and a leather halter-top that, Marla assumed, covered other bodily embellishments. "Come into the engine car, and we'll talk," Bethany said, and Marla noticed that her tongue was split for part of its length, and that the underside was not connected to the bottom of her mouth, which created an illusion of extraordinary length that accentuated the forked tongue's serpentlike quality. Bethany turned to lead them into the engine car, revealing a crisscross of leather cords running up her back, threaded through hooks implanted into the skin on either side of her spine.

There were magical advantages to such extreme bodily modifications, Marla knew, especially in the realms of transformative magic. Bethany had altered her body's original definitions significantly, which would make it easier to shift into *other* forms. Based on the design of her train, however, Marla suspected that Bethany's principal motivations for her bodily ornamentation were cosmetic.

"Where's the train headed?" Marla asked, following Bethany into the engine car. This compartment was more like a comfortable living room than a train car, with lounge chairs, a couch, a flat-screen television, and ranks of humming black component electronics. A small control panel with sterling fixtures stood beneath the curving front window, but otherwise there was little to mark this as a functional rather than a living space. Bethany sat in a lounge chair—leather, of course, as was all the furniture—and gestured for Marla and the others to seat themselves.

"We're not going anywhere," Bethany said. "The journey *is* the destination. The train simply circles the track. This is where I live."

"Constant movement," Marla said. "Good for screwing up location spells."

"A girl has to be careful when she lives in such a bad part of town," Bethany said. "I'd love to have a train that *goes* somewhere, but there's not a lot of room for surreptitious subterranean expansion under here. I've always wanted to live on a train, so I built this little loop. It's just a toy train set writ large, I suppose. I like to play." Bethany flickered her tongue.

Something in the front window went zipping past, a flash of gleaming blue on the wall of the tunnel.

"A toy," Marla said. "Spinning in a loop past runes inscribed on the tunnel walls, generating kinetic energy, turning widdershins, keeping a magical field humming along. Right?" Finch got power from his sex parties, Dalton from his computers, the Celestial from ancient objects and an apothecary of rare herbs and potions, and Bethany had her train. Marla found it all intriguing, if a bit foreign, since in recent years she'd drawn her power from the bustling activity of the whole city she watched over.

"Good eye!" Bethany said. "Dalton rode this train a dozen times—well, his mirror-selves did, mostly, Dalton One didn't go out much—and he never noticed the runes on the walls. Of course, he usually had other things to occupy him."

"It's a clever system," Marla said. She had always admired fabricators and macro-magicians, people who *made* things. Marla had always been better at tearing things apart, at least on the physical level (though she liked to think she was good at building more theoretical things, like the complex structure of loyalty, fear, and obligation that kept things running back home). And while Marla had little patience for people who wore ostentatious piercings and tattoos, in Bethany's case she could believe that body-modification was just an extension of that urge to change the shape of the natural and make the world accord with her own desires. "But are you clever enough to stay alive? There's a sorcerer named Mutex picking off your associates, and he's good at what he does."

"Yes," Bethany said, tugging thoughtfully on the ring in her lower lip. "He's becoming more than an annoyance. I just got word about Dalton, a bit before you arrived."

Rondeau, who was clearly already beyond mere boredom and well into the realm of utter distraction, began humming and tapping his feet. He was on to *Sergeant Pepper's* now.

"Are your boys hungry?" Bethany said. "There's a dining car a couple of compartments back, with a well-stocked fridge. I'm sure there's cold meat and bread back there if they want to make sandwiches for themselves."

"Scamper, you two," Marla said. "And stay out of trouble. If you notice any frogs or hummingbirds, give a shout."

"Pleasure to meet you," Rondeau said, nodding at Bethany. B nodded and started to follow Rondeau out.

"Wait!" Bethany said. "Are you Bradley Bowman?"

"So they tell me."

"From Hollywood to the hidden world," she said. "I hope I get to hear the tale of *that* journey someday." She returned her attention to Marla, dismissing B and Rondeau from her attention. "I'm not clear about your interest in Mutex," Bethany said. "I've heard you're pursuing him, and that you were on hand to witness his murder of Finch *and* Dalton—which makes you seem like bad luck, so you're lucky I let you onto my train at all—but why, exactly, are you after him? And what are you doing in San Francisco anyway, besides making enemies?"

"Mutex killed my friend Lao Tsung."

"Right, Lao. We came to the city at about the same time, though beyond that we didn't have much in common. I envied his longevity."

"He wound up dead, just like everybody does," Marla said.

"So you're operating out of simple revenge?"

Marla considered. She didn't know how much Bethany already knew. Dalton had believed Marla was responsible for killing Finch, and he'd known about the Cornerstone disappearing, but how much had Bethany heard? Surface anomalies aside, Bethany reminded Marla of herself—competent, no-nonsense, straightforward, savvy, mostly businesslike, with none of Finch's power-games, or Dalton's monomaniacal boorishness, or the Celestial's rudeness or avarice. Marla didn't *trust* Bethany, but then, if by some quirk of space-time or magical mishap Marla happened to come face-to-face with her own identical double, she wouldn't trust *her,* either. Marla was too smart to go around trusting people promiscuously. "Revenge is as good a reason as any," Marla said. "Don't you think?

I owe Lao Tsung a lot. But you should be more concerned with your own life. Mutex is coming for you, to kill you for giving him the brush-off and, not coincidentally, to rip out your heart and offer it up to his gods. But instead, how about we capture him?"

"You mean kill him, surely," Bethany said. "Unless you want to keep him alive for a while, to torture him. But that's not a good idea with a sorcerer as adept as he's proven himself to be. Every moment alive is an opportunity for him to regain the upper hand, as I'm sure you know."

Marla didn't see an easy way to bluff past this, so she gave in. "I can't kill him right away. He has something I need, and I have to find out where he's hidden it."

"Mmm," Bethany said. "I didn't think you were the type to indulge in revenge for its own sake."

"Revenge *is* nice as a side dish, though," Marla said.

"I'm sure. Capturing him will be more difficult."

"I don't care how good he is. He *can't* be as good as the two of us working together." Marla would have said that with more confidence if Ch'ang Hao had ever answered her summons, and brought her the rare jungle snake she needed, but with Bethany's help, on Bethany's apparently well-protected turf, they probably did stand a chance against the mad Aztec.

"You're probably right," Bethany said. She went to the control panel and made some imperceptible adjustments, then returned to her chair. "I'm glad your interests coincide with my own need for self-preservation. All right. Let's take him. But you'll owe me—and my *city*—a favor, in exchange for not killing him outright, and letting you get the information you need. It's not in my best interests, after all, to keep Mutex alive for any length of time."

Marla could appreciate that. "A favor it is."

"Do you think he'll come here?"

"He seems to like house calls."

"How much time do you think we have?"

"No telling. Let's assume he'll be along any minute now."

"Fair enough," Bethany said. "I should get warning once he opens the main door or touches the stairs, just like I did with you."

"And then?"

"Oh, I have tricks. I like building things, and there are lots of nice traps secreted on the platform. I just hit you with the bright lights to let you know I was watching, but I've got nastier things at my disposal. We'll hit him with remote Tasers—I've got the wireless kind, where the current travels on a spray of fluid, which comes from nozzles in the walls. That should drop him for long enough that we can secure and interrogate him at our leisure. I owe him a little revenge, too. I used to fuck Dalton, sometimes, and I was fond of him. He wasn't much in bed alone, but when he brought along a couple of his mirror-selves, it could be pleasant."

"I don't doubt it," Marla said.

Rondeau burst into the compartment, B close behind. Rondeau had his butterfly knife open, and B was pale and wide-eyed.

Marla shot to her feet. "Mutex?"

"Uh-uh," Rondeau said, pointing at Bethany with his knife. "*Her.*"

13

er, what?" Marla said, looking sidelong at Bethany.

"She's got a freezer full of hearts back there," B said. "Rondeau says they're human."

"And we know someone else who likes to snack on hearts," Rondeau said. "So I'm wondering if maybe we haven't found ourselves one of Mutex's cohorts and co-conspirators."

Marla looked at Bethany.

"That chest was locked," Bethany said, scowling.

"Rondeau picks locks," Marla said. "It's like a nervous habit. He's also curious, intrusive, and has no concept of personal privacy. Those are some of the qualities I value in him. Explain yourself."

"Don't command me on my own train," Bethany said, rising to her feet. "But, since we were getting along so beautifully, I *will* explain, in the interests of continued friendliness. If you'd opened the other locked ice chests, you would have found other things—livers, kidneys, lots of things, each in its own place."

"What, are you an anatomist?" Marla said. "Or do you have a stake in the organ trade?"

"Both good explanations," Bethany said. "But, no, neither. I'm a cannibal."

"Jesus," B said.

"Jesus advocated a limited sort of cannibalism," Bethany said. "But he's not the subject under discussion right now."

"A cannibal," Marla said neutrally.

"Do you disapprove?" Bethany said.

"That depends. Don't get me wrong, people-eating isn't something I've ever been interested in personally, but I'm aware that it's, ah, a complex subject. There can be power in it, I know." In the sorcerous world, the pro-cannibal/anti-cannibal debate was as ferocious as the arguments about abortion in the ordinary world. Marla just tried to stay out of it, though she found cannibalism disgusting, on a visceral level, much as she'd been disgusted by Finch's predilection for ghost-fucking.

"You can get diseases from eating people," Rondeau said. He hadn't put away his knife. Marla hadn't told him to.

"You can get diseases from eating nearly anything," Bethany said. "I don't eat brains or spinal tissue, so I'm safe from nasty things like Creutzfeld-Jacob."

"Where do you get the meat?" Marla said.

"Ah. This is what your approval depends on, yes?"

"I frown on murdering people and eating their parts, yeah," Marla said. "It's a subject I'm extra-sensitive about lately, since Mutex wants a return to the bad old days of theocrats getting fat off the meat of unwilling sacrifices. So, what, do you have people in morgues and hospitals, harvesting for you?"

"No, I do the butchering myself," Bethany said, sitting back down. "With the help of a couple of apprentices."

"Shit," Marla said. "I'm as morally flexible as the next guy, but there are some things I have trouble bending my judgment around. You kill ordinaries? People from your own city? For *food*?"

"Yes," Bethany said. "But before you try—and I stress the word 'try'—to execute me for crimes against humanity, let me assure you that I only eat the willing. I have no shortage of volunteers. Sometimes they even stay alive while I amputate a limb or two, and dine with me on their own flesh."

"You expect us to believe that?" B said. The whole situation clearly outraged him.

"There's no reason you shouldn't," Bethany said.

Marla nodded to Rondeau, and he flipped his knife closed. "It's true," Rondeau told B. "There are people who want to be eaten. With all the billions of people on this planet, there's no shortage of people who are into weird shit. And Bethany probably offers incentives to the suicidal and the terminally ill—pleasure in their last moments, shit like that."

"Occasionally, yes," Bethany said. "More so in the old days. Now it's mostly people who just want to be prey. It's a kink for some people, a fetish, though an almost invariably terminal one. They come from all over the world. I pay their travel expenses. The Internet has helped immensely. There are whole online communities, anthropophage newsgroups and mailing lists, everything. It's made my life a lot simpler."

"I'm pretty grossed-out right now," Rondeau said. "I'm going to go away and think about unicorns and fluffy bunnies and other noncannibalistic things for a while."

"Go with him, B," Marla said.

"I'm still confused," B said. "Is she one of the *good* guys?"

"Oh, B," Marla said. "We're so far past questions of good and bad that I can't begin to answer that. But if we can define 'good' as 'willing to stop Mutex from bringing primordial monsters to life and instituting a theocracy based on ritual human sacrifice,' then, yeah, Bethany counts as a good guy."

Bethany grinned at him, flickering her forked tongue. "I'd have expected less outrage from one of the most notorious party-boys from the Hollywood scene."

"I did a lot of crazy stuff, but I never *ate* anybody," B said. He left the car.

"Sorry to make you uncomfortable," Bethany said as Marla sat back down. "I didn't expect the subject of my eating habits to come up."

"Right," Marla said. "But if you don't mind me asking, what's the benefit? If you're mostly eating people who want, in their deepest hearts, to be prey animals, then it can't be the usual contagious-magic thing where you devour the flesh of brave and noble adversaries in order to take their strength for your own."

"True," Bethany said. "It's complicated, magically, but the gist of it is that I'm now at the absolute pinnacle of the food chain. I am the uncontested apex predator of San Francisco. I can eat anyone, and *nothing* can eat me. I run the Tenderloin, the most dangerous part of the city, and being the best predator in a neighborhood full of human predators is essential. You see?"

"Yeah," Marla said thoughtfully. No mugger or killer or rapist would be able to take Bethany out in a dark alley or something, in part because she literally *did* eat people like them for breakfast.

"Plus, I like the taste," Bethany said. "So now we wait?"

"I guess. Do you have a deck of cards?"

Bethany inclined her head toward the television monitor and the humming black electronics. "I've got some good video games."

Marla's entire experience with video games began and ended with a brief period working as an enforcer, many years before, when she'd had to occasionally beat protection money out of a pimp who ran a video arcade on the side. "You mean like Pac-Man?" Marla said.

"I think I can do better than that," Bethany said. "Dalton made a game for me, set in San Francisco, where an avatar based on motion-captures of me goes on a rampage to kill off all the other bosses in the city—except Dalton, of course. It's pretty good, and there's a great chaos engine, so there's a lot of randomization every time I play. Dalton calls it my hostile-takeover tutorial, because he made the AIs that run the enemy sorcerers base their behavior as closely as possible on the real thing. He said in five or ten more years he'd have fully sentient in-game avatars who really believed they *were* Finch, Umbaldo, the Celestial, all of them. Once we got to that point, it would be trivial to magically link the avatars to their real-life counterparts, so I could hurt them at a distance—like versatile voodoo dolls that really work. Guess I'll never see that version of the game now."

Marla, who had pretty well followed the drift of that, said, "That's funny, since Dalton believed *this* world was just a computer simulation, with all of us being self-aware avatars."

"He had some strange ideas. But, to his credit, the irony didn't escape him. Care to play?"

"How about I just watch you—"

The lights flickered, and the train slowed noticeably. "What the fuck?" Bethany muttered, rising and going to the control panel, which had gone dark. She pressed a few buttons and tugged a steel lever, which didn't move. "Shit," she said. "The controls are dead, and all my surveillance is out." She jerked her head up, eyes widening, goat-slit pupils narrowing nearly to the point of vanishing. "And there's somebody on the stairs."

"That's our Mutex," Marla said, standing up. "Better get your Taser spray up and running."

"It's *offline*," Bethany said. "I control it from here!" She slammed her hand against the control panel. "Fucking Dalton! This all used to be practically fail-safe, gears and wheels, pistons and engines, parts that *moved,* and I knew them better than I know the articulation of my own skeleton, it was a perfect retro-scientific steampunk wet dream, with magic filling in for the places where engineering broke down, but Dalton convinced me to upgrade to something modern and digital, all run with computers, and now somebody else has cracked my security, and they own my train!"

"Take it easy," Marla said. "I'm surprised Mutex is so technologically savvy—I figured obsidian knives were about the pinnacle of his tool-using skills—but we'll deal with it. So we don't have aerosol-mist Tasers. We'll improvise. You're an apex predator, and I'm no defenseless bunny rabbit myself. We know he's coming. He moves fast—blurry-fast—and he's got a lot of poison frogs and surprisingly invincible hummingbirds, but we can beat him, if we get our shit together."

"That bastard took my *train* away," Bethany said, her face twisted in a silent snarl, the rings in her nose glistening. "He's not getting back into daylight alive."

"Anger is good. Keep being angry."

"I can get the emergency lights on anyway," Bethany said. "They're just battery-powered." She flipped open a panel on the wall and clicked a few switches. Faint red light emanated from recessed panels around the ceiling and floor of the train car. It was like being in a submarine in a movie.

Marla glanced around. "How many ways are there for him to get onto this train?"

"Not many, while it's moving."

As if Bethany's words were a signal, the train slowed. "Huh," Marla said. "I think we're about to be boarded, hon. Get yourself prepared. The guy's a *blur,* but I can slow him down. When he comes in, wherever he comes in, I'll hit him, and while he's distracted, work some mojo. I know this train must have a lot of power stored up in it, spinning like a prayer wheel all this time, and you're going to need to tap into that. Hold him like a bug in amber, put ice crystals in his muscle mass, break every bone in his body, blow off his kneecaps, I don't care, but *drop* him. And keep him alive."

"Not a problem," Bethany said.

Marla held herself at the ready as the train slowed to a halt. She was prepared to reverse her cloak—there was no other option, not if Mutex was still moving so fast—though she greatly feared the consequences of using the cloak twice in one day. A period of inhumanity was preferable to death, but only just.

The train stopped. The doors hissed open without any instruction from Bethany, which made her snarl. Marla tensed.

No one tried to enter the train. The platform beyond was dark. In the faint red light from the train, and with her night-eyes using every available speck of brightness, Marla could make out something covering the floor of the platform, a silent, undulant mass of—

"Frogs," she said. "Shit." The platform was inhabited by hundreds of tiny golden yellow poison dart frogs, though in the red light they glowed witch-light orange. Marla considered her options. She could probably generate a fireball or a sheet of flame to scour the frogs. She'd have to suck the energy for the fireball from Bethany, though, which would put her out of commission. Marla couldn't take the thermal energy from the frogs themselves. They were amphibians, only as warm as their environment, and down here, underground, it was cold, which might explain why they seemed less inclined to hop and caper than they had on the surface. It was just as well. Conjuring flames in a confined underground space wasn't a good idea, especially since magical fire didn't much care if there was no immediate source of fuel—it would burn anyway, for somewhat unpredictable amount of times, and that could make this place an oven. But she had to do something. If the frogs were here in their lethal hundreds, a whole army of them, then their general, Mutex, must be nearby, too.

Something alerted Marla—the distant hum of a generator, a static crackle, something—and she squinted her eyes an instant before the floodlights on the platform came on. As she squinted, she registered movement and twisted, throwing her leg up and out in a side-kick. Mutex, moving almost too fast for the eye to track—but far slower, Marla noted, than he'd moved at Dalton's, which was heartening—slammed his solar plexus into the bottom of her heavy boot. The shock of impact vibrated up her leg painfully, but her bones were laced with trace amounts of cold iron and almost unbreakable, and she'd cast an inertia-enhancing spell on her boots, so she didn't lose her footing or slide back. Mutex *bounced*, the inevitable result of an almost irresistible force hitting an even more immovable object. He landed flat on his back, scattering his near-torpid poison frogs beneath him, doubtless squishing a few. He still wore his cape—which Marla now realized was made of insect wings somehow intricately woven together. It was fitting raiment for the king of frogs, she supposed. His never-ending-frogs basket hung on a strap on his back. She wanted to attack him now, while he was down, but the frogs all around him were too dangerous. But if Bethany could wound him, or knock him unconscious, then the two of them together could probably levitate him up onto the train, safely away from the frogs. Mutex started to sit up, touching the spot beneath his rib cage, though his face betrayed no discomfort, which meant he probably *was* using the frogs' batrachotoxins to block pain. Marla hoped she'd cracked a few of his ribs.

"Bethany, hit him!" Marla shouted.

"Oh, I'll hit, all right," she said, and something in her voice made Marla turn, but it was too late. Bethany had a Taser-gun in her hand, a matte-black weapon whose shape reminded Marla of a fluke or a lamprey, something nasty that wriggled and struck in the dark. It was unlikely the weapon had the range necessary to hit Mutex, which meant Bethany intended to use it on *Marla,* as if that weren't obvious by the glee on her face, her slit eyes and flickering tongue, the blush of heat and excitement in her cheeks; she was intoxicated by her own treachery. There was no time for Marla to move, to strike, or even to reverse her cloak, and once she was shocked by the electric current, she would hit the ground, and once she hit the ground, she was meat.

A guttural voice filled the train car, sounds that made the small bones inside Marla's ears grind together, a language harsh as glacial ice cracking. She saw Rondeau entering from the next car, his mouth open, his face twisted, and she realized that he was Cursing, loosing a profanity fit to offend the ears of a god. The random wave of destruction triggered by his Curse made the flat-screen television implode in a crash and tinkle of glass, caused the reinforced windows in the train car to crack, and made the Taser-gun short out in Bethany's hand, breaking and sparking. Bethany gasped and dropped the Taser. Marla sensed movement behind her and turned to see Mutex rushing toward her at merely human speed. Rondeau

Cursed again, and the train platform cracked, one side rising as if in an earthquake, tilting Mutex off balance, sending him tumbling into the ground again. Bethany was still staring at her hand, which was scorched and smoking, when B slipped up behind her, armed with a heavy cast-iron skillet he must have taken from the dining car. He struck Bethany on the back of the head, and she fell, eyes rolling in her head. B stared down at her, then dropped the skillet and wiped his hand on the front of his shirt. He looked at Marla, his eyes wild. "She was trying to kill you," he said, and Marla just nodded, since there was no time for anything more in the way of thanks or reassurance.

Mutex was on his feet again, standing in the middle of a field of torpid frogs, his arms crossed, looking at Marla, his face impassive.

Marla crossed her own arms, mimicking his stance. Rondeau stood on her left, and B on her right. "So," Marla said. "Time for us to have a chat?"

"You have caused me problems," Mutex said. "I can no longer ignore you in the hopes that you will leave. Perhaps you will see reason, and cease to pry into my affairs. You are a stranger here, and have no stake in this place. I am offering you an opportunity to leave unmolested."

Marla snorted. "Yeah, sure. I'll give you a chance to convince me. Let's parlay. Bethany was helping you, huh?"

Mutex cocked his head. "Of course. When you first set foot on the stairs, she alerted me, and told me to come help her kill you. You are developing an unsavory reputation in this city, and we both felt it was best to dispose of you now."

"Yeah, that was a good idea," Marla said. "Shame you fucked it up so much on the follow-through. I guess she rigged the train to slow down, fixed it so the power would go out, and all that. I wondered what she was doing at the control panel. But I don't get why she was helping you. She seemed smarter than that."

"She understood the importance of heart's blood," Mutex said. "That there is strength to be gained from human sacrifice. Our motives were different, but our aims were the same. I merely wanted her to give me the Cornerstone, but she was no friend to Lao Tsung, and she convinced me that it would be better to kill him and take the stone myself."

"So Bethany just wanted power? She didn't believe that the universe is winding down like an old watch, and that it needs a little blood to grease the gears to keep it turning?"

"In time, she would have come to know and respect my gods," Mutex said, and the absolute faith in his voice was chilling. "My aims are not selfish ones. I only wish to prevent the universe from dying, and to return the gods of my ancestors to the position of glory and respect they deserve. When Bethany looked upon the majesty of the returned gods, she would have been filled with faith. But for the time being, though motivated by baser desires for power and flesh, she could still offer considerable assistance. She knew the other sorcerers would oppose her, so she could not help me openly. Once control of the city passed to her, she planned to help me bring back the old gods, and take control."

"Probably by calling an emergency meeting of all the surviving sorcerers, am I right?" Marla said. "Get them all in a room to talk about the Aztec menace, and then lock the doors and let you mow them down. Or else just hit them all with tasers, to keep the meat fresh."

Mutex shrugged. "It was an elegant plan, but it seems it shall not come to pass. It sometimes pleases the gods to confront us with adversity. It is not the first time things have not gone according to plan. Is Bethany dead?"

Marla didn't glance down at Bethany. She didn't think the sorceress was dead—B hadn't hit her that hard, and Bethany most likely had spells to protect her skull. "Why do you ask?"

"If she is dead, then I will summon her noble warrior's spirit back to this world when the gods return."

"What, as a hummingbird?" Rondeau said. "Pretty fucking stupid form for a noble warrior spirit, don't you think?"

Mutex frowned, and Marla cheered Rondeau silently. Zealots hated blasphemy, and Rondeau blasphemed as easily as most people blinked. "Hummingbirds are a fitting vessel for the returned souls of dead warriors. But no. Once I have brought the old gods back to life, I will be able to open the gates to the Land of the Dead, and welcome the warriors back in approximations of their mortal forms."

"Pretty good trick," Marla said. "This is after you raise Tlaltecuhtli, right? Her mouth opens to the Land of the Dead, and all that?"

"You should not even speak that name," Mutex said. "You dishonor it further by mispronouncing it."

"Aztec isn't my first language," she said, grinning. He was *not* happy that she knew this much about his plans. "Surprised I know about your plans to raise Kermit the Earth-Monster? You shouldn't leave so many clues lying around. Then again, I'm pretty perceptive, so there's probably nothing you could have done to keep it a secret."

"You seem marginally more aware than the fools who run this city," he said. "I suppose a worm such as you might reasonably feel superior to maggots such as they."

"Okay, frog-boy," Marla said. "Keep underestimating me. It's a recipe for hilarious results. So. You want me to leave the city? We can work something out. I have terms."

"I am prepared to listen," Mutex said.

"Marla!" B said. "You can't *negotiate* with him! If you don't stop him—"

"Quiet, B," Rondeau said, pulling him back. "You really don't want to get into the middle of this right now."

"But—" B said.

"*Really*," Rondeau said, and B must have believed him, he went quiet, which was good, since Marla owed him, and didn't want to have to silence him herself.

"I need the Cornerstone," Marla said.

"Impossible," Mutex said flatly.

"I don't need to take it away forever," she said. "I just need it to cast one spell, and then I'll leave."

"I will not let you near it," Mutex said. "It is already in use, already serving to anchor the ritual that will return my gods to power. Any spell you cast would disrupt that process. No. The only thing I am willing to offer in this negotiation is your life. Leave the city, and I will spare you, though your heart's blood would surely do well to fuel my magic."

Marla laughed. "Afraid not, Mutie. You need a fear-filled heart, and I'm definitely not afraid of you." She wasn't, not exactly, though she wasn't nearly confident enough to attack him head-on right now, not with all those frogs around him. They might be slowed by the low subterranean temperatures here—they were, after all, creatures from the rain forest, despite whatever enhancements Mutex had given them—but they were still lethal.

"Then we are at an impasse," Mutex said.

"Looks that way. Negotiations broke down. They have a way of doing that when I'm involved. I don't know why—I'm the most reasonable person I know. Guess you'd better kill me now, huh?"

She expected him to back down, to slink away and return to fight another day. But she'd forgotten the power of zealotry. He came forward again, his limbs blurring with speed. "Get *back*!" she shouted, and Rondeau and B rushed for the far end of the car while Marla retreated to the far wall opposite the door. The moment Mutex cleared the threshold and entered the train, with just a couple of the frogs sluggishly hopping along in his wake, Marla reversed her cloak.

At this higher level of consciousness, Mutex was visibly much slower than he had been at Dalton's, probably no faster than Marla herself. He was surrounded by an aura of strangely flickering ruby light, and the distantly articulate part of Marla's brain recognized flickering shapes like hummingbirds in his aura. That was it, the way this faster-than-the-eye magic of his worked. He had a coterie of the returned dead in the form of hummingbirds, and he'd tapped into their magics to give himself the same properties a hummingbird had, the ridiculous accelerated metabolism, the tremendous speed and maneuverability. But it probably took a lot out of him. A hummingbird had to eat, what, several times its own weight each day, just to fuel those metabolic processes? Mutex was running out of energy, slowing down, and while Marla wasn't certain she could take him, she was reasonably confident that *he* couldn't take *her*.

That was it for rational thought. After that, she gave in fully and became the beast, something that ripped, and tore, and slashed, and gutted. She attacked Mutex with claws of spectral form but formidable sharpness, and he dodged, and struck, but while he was as fast as she, he lacked her savagery, her utterly instinctual grasp of the best places to strike and the best methods to wound. Mutex fought too rationally, and he was simply no match for her under these circumstances, and he retreated.

Unfortunately, while clothed in the purple, Marla lacked anything resembling an instinct for self-preservation. This was a state akin to the berserker madness that Viking warriors had once invoked, and so when Mutex fled she pursued him from the relative safety of the train. Mutex scooped up handfuls of tiny frogs and flung them at her. She batted the frogs away, but the poison still burned her. The pain did not slow her, only enraged her further, and she continued rushing for Mutex, much to his surprise—clearly he'd expected her to fall, dead from the poison. The red aura around him intensified, deepening almost to the color of arterial blood, and he raced across the platform, up the stairs in a flash, doubtless emptying whatever reserves of energy he held in his desperate rush to escape.

With her prey gone, Marla raced back into the train, looking for more targets, and she saw Rondeau and B. Before she could attack them, the tiny coherent compartment of Marla's mind wrested control of the cloak and reversed it back to white—at which point she collapsed to the ground in horrendous pain. The alien intelligence asserted itself, but uselessly, because it could not move her body—her flesh felt as if it had been etched with acid. Then the soothing coolness of the cloak's beneficent white side spread through her, and it began the process of healing her wounds. She sweat profusely, and where the drops of sweat hit the carpet, they burned through the fabric to the metal below. Her teeth chattered, and she shivered, aware of Rondeau and B bending over her, but the awareness was distant, as the cloak sealed her off from the pain of the poison leaving her body. And this was from the barest touch of only a few of the frogs, just glancing contact as she brushed them aside. If Mutex had lured her farther onto the platform, into the midst of the frogs, the poison would surely have overwhelmed even her cloak's ability to cope with the pain and damage. As it was, she wondered if she would survive this much of the poison, but even that concern had a detached quality, as the alien intelligence maintained control, trying to hold on through the pain.

Finally she rolled over, and vomited weakly, and then B and Rondeau were helping her to her feet. Normally after the cloak healed her, Marla felt no ill effects at all, only a ferocious hunger, and while she was hungry now, she also ached, deep in her muscles.

She thought Bethany had a good idea when it came to eating people, and she considered the possibility of snapping B's neck and eating his flesh raw, perhaps taking in some of his seer's power in the process. She reached for B's throat to choke him and throttle him down, but her muscles trembled, and the best she could manage was a weak clutching at his shoulders.

Then Marla shuddered and pushed at the alien intelligence, and though it resisted her ferociously, it couldn't hold on against her steady mental pressure, and Marla was herself again, although weak and famished.

The frogs hadn't killed her, but it had been a near thing—which was fortunate, in a way, since if she'd been less damaged the cloak's alien intelligence would have succeeded in killing B and eating a fair bit of him before Marla could reassert control.

She couldn't face Mutex's frogs again, not without some protection—there was no reason to think she'd be this lucky twice. She'd known that before, recognized the threat the frogs posed, but now that their poison had scalded her, she understood it more deeply, and knew they weren't a problem she could simply improvise around.

Bethany moaned and opened her eyes. "What?" she said, blearily.

Marla shook off Rondeau and B, who were still holding her arms, as if afraid she would fall down again. Marla drew her dagger and knelt, shakily, beside Bethany. She felt around in her own mind as if probing at a loose tooth with her tongue, feeling for some shred of the alien intelligence, but it was gone—

she was choosing to do this on her own, with her humanity intact, for what that was worth. Marla tried to think of something to say. It took a moment, during which time Bethany's eyes struggled to focus. "I enjoyed talking with you," Marla said finally. "Under other circumstances, I think we might have been friends. I understand why you did what you did. I understand the lure of power. But you would have sacrificed your city, would have let Mutex wreck everything and kill everyone in this place you're supposed to protect, and though I don't give a shit what happens to San Francisco, you *should*. It's your city. I could forgive you for trying to kill me. I've forgiven people for worse. But you didn't just betray me, you betrayed your *city*, and that can never be forgiven."

"Marla..." Bethany said, comprehension returning to her face. It was hard to tell if she'd understood the things Marla just said, but it didn't matter, not really. In a moment, Bethany would never understand anything else again.

Marla struck with her dagger. She made it as quick and clean as possible, but, this being a murder, it wasn't really quick or clean at all.

14

If you don't mind me asking," Rondeau said, "how exactly are we going to get off this train?" He leaned against a locked stainless-steel icebox, and he was actually cleaning his fingernails with his butterfly knife, probably because he knew how cool it made him look. The lights and power were on again. Rondeau had found the main power switch on the control panel.

Marla was sitting at a booth, still wet from a shower in the bath car, gorging herself on a roasted turkey she'd found in the one refrigerator that didn't contain human parts. She chewed thoughtfully, swallowed, then said, "I'll think of something."

"It's just that there's this little yellow minefield," Rondeau said. "Hundreds of frogs hopping around out there between us and the stairs."

"Mmm," Marla said. "You know, I was actually aware of that." She glanced at B, who sat at another booth, his head in his hands. "Hey," she said. "B. Sorry you had to see that back there, with Bethany. I had to do it. If we'd left her alive, it would have caused us a lot of trouble later. She—"

"I know," B said. "It's not that. Don't get me wrong, seeing you cut her like that, seeing the blood spray, that wasn't nice, but I've seen ugly stuff before. I didn't like Bethany from the moment I found out she ate people."

"Then what is it? What's wrong?"

B looked up at her, and Marla was shocked to see hatred in his eyes. "*You're* what's wrong. I've been here, risking my life to help you, and you were prepared to make a deal with Mutex, to let him do whatever he wanted in exchange for a few minutes with the whatever-the-hell-you-call-it, the stone. I knew you had your own reasons for being involved in this, but I didn't think you'd make a deal with that monster. And after that fucking noble speech you gave Bethany about how some things are unforgivable, of all the hypocritical bullshit—"

"Take it easy, movie star," Rondeau said. He wasn't cleaning his fingernails with his knife anymore, but he was still holding it.

"It's okay," Marla said. "He's got every right to be pissed. Why don't you tell him why he's wrong, Rondeau."

"Marla wasn't really going to make a deal with Mutex," Rondeau said. "If he'd agreed to take her to the Cornerstone, so much the better, but she wouldn't have left town after that. See, you've made the mistake of thinking Marla tells the truth when she's dealing with crazy sorcerers who want to destroy the world."

"I'm not all that honorable at the best of times, to

be honest," Marla said. "And I'm certainly not above lying to my enemies if it helps me get what I want."

"I'm supposed to believe you?" B said.

"I think, if you really look at me, you'll be able to tell whether or not I'm lying, B," she said. "Look at me with those seer's eyes of yours, look *deep,* and tell me if I'm telling the truth."

B stared at her for a long moment, then nodded. "I believe you."

"Good. Because I like you, and you've been surprisingly useful, and I'd hate to break up our fellowship over a little misunderstanding like that."

"But, ah, I do have another question," B said.

"Shoot."

"How exactly are we supposed to get off this train?" B asked.

Marla rolled her eyes.

"Seriously," B said. "Last time I looked, there were frogs all around the foot of the stairs, like they were trying to figure out where Mutex went. If there were only a handful we could avoid them, but there are *lots* of them out there. And the way the poison you sweated out ate through the carpet, I don't think the jeans and sneakers I'm wearing are going to be sufficient armor against them."

"You two should have some faith in me," Marla said, taking a last hunk of meat off a turkey leg. "All right. Time to show you some honest-to-gods magic, the kind of shit there's almost never time for in the heat of battle, which is why it's good to learn how to kick people's teeth in without any magic at all, if you were wondering. Open up all these iceboxes."

Rondeau wrinkled his nose, sighed, and nodded.

"Give me a hand, B. Marla always makes me do the dirty work."

"You don't have to take any of the meat out," Marla said. "You just have to let out the cold."

They broke open the half-dozen iceboxes. Cold air wafted out, and the iceboxes began to hum strenuously as they struggled to refrigerate the entire car. "All right," Marla said, "now be quiet for a while." She closed her eyes. This was going to be tricky. She'd practiced a lot with fire, and had an affinity with it, but she'd never been as good at dealing with cold. She opened herself to the air around her, trying to make herself a vessel, and the cold flowed into her from the machines. The iceboxes hummed, then squealed, then shorted out, one after another, as Marla drew their cold into her. Her bones felt made of ice, and once she felt her core temperature lowering dangerously, she flung the coldness out of her body, away from the train, out onto the platform beyond.

The cold left her, but she kept shivering, her teeth chattering, because she hadn't distributed the cold as efficiently as she should have, and she was now freezing from the inside. Rondeau draped his jacket around her shoulders, which was a nice gesture, but useless, since clothing was only good at trapping a person's own body heat, and her heat was negligible. "St-st-stove," she said, and B rushed to the gas range (how had Bethany rigged a gas range on a *train*?—she really had been very good) and lit up all four burners. He turned on the oven, too, and opened the door. Marla sucked in the heat, getting her body temperature up, stopping before she drew in too much and had to toss off a fireball to cool down, which would have ruined all that effort she'd put in with the cold. "Enough," she said, blowing out a last exhalation of cold vapor. B turned off the stove. "Let's go," she said, and led them back to the engine car, where the doors were still open.

The platform was covered in a sheet of ice about two inches deep, and tiny golden frogs were suspended inside like bits of fruit in a gelatin mold. "Walk carefully, it's slick," Marla said, and they made their way across the ice, walking over the frozen frogs.

"They're kind of pretty," Rondeau said, looking down. "It's a shame they're instant hopping death."

"Mmm," Marla said.

"Do you think they're dead?" B asked.

"I don't know. I think you can freeze amphibians, and they come back to life when you thaw them. But I'm not sure. I don't think they can get out of here, though, and if they live, they'll starve. I don't think there's much in the way of flies down here."

"Maybe Mutex will come back for them," B said.

"Maybe," Marla said. "If he lives through the day." They reached the stairs, and climbed up out of the darkness.

"So what now?" Rondeau said when they reached the surface. "We go meet the next sorcerer in line for the throne?"

"Sure," Marla said. "Unless you have a better suggestion, yeah, I think we should get in touch with the next sorcerer in line. They can't *all* be collaborating with Mutex, and maybe the next one in charge will help us rally the troops. Sorcerers aren't usually very good at working together, but if things get dire enough, it's been known to happen."

"And if Mutex continues with his old modus operandi, and shows up to kill the next sorcerer?"

"Then we try to kill him first," Marla said. "Sort of like what we had in mind with Bethany, only preferably without the betrayal."

Rondeau shook his head. "We should have a plan. That's your line, I know, but it's true. We can't keep rushing in. Those frogs almost killed you last time."

"Didn't somebody say that the definition of insanity is doing the same thing in the same way over and over and expecting a different outcome?" B said.

"Yeah," Marla said. "It's a Chinese proverb. Which reminds me that I *do* have a plan, but it's rather dependent on my getting in touch with Ch'ang Hao, who doesn't seem to be answering his snake-o-gram. He struck me as an honorable guy—"

"God," Rondeau said.

"—honorable god, but I'm beginning to think he's skipped for parts unknown, and that the whole calling-him-with-a-snake thing was a load of crap. In which case . . . yeah, a new plan would be good. But it's worth noting that we're *not* doing the same thing, not exactly. I fought Mutex back there, and wounded him. He's lost a lot of steam. It wore me out, too, but I'm betting he's worse off. We've got a chance, especially if he crawls off somewhere to recuperate, and we find time to organize some resistance. So let's see who's next in line to rule the city and get their heart cut out." She took out the printout, opened it, read, and grimaced. "Naturally," she said. "Who else would it be? This . . . complicates matters. Mutex and I might actually have a common cause, here."

"Who is it?" Rondeau said.

"The Chinese guy," she said. "If he lost his heart, I wouldn't lose any sleep over it."

Rondeau took her arm and tugged her aside for a semblance of privacy. "You can't just let him die," he said.

Marla didn't answer. She *could* just let him die, of course. It would probably save her a little grief farther down the line.

"If the Chinese guy *did* steal his apprentice's body, then Mutex is going to kill the apprentice, not the sorcerer. She doesn't deserve to die, Marla."

"Death hasn't been limiting itself to those most deserving, in case you hadn't noticed," she said. She sighed. Clearly, this meant a lot to Rondeau, and maybe the Celestial would calm down when he realized they had a common enemy. It wasn't likely, but it was worth a try. "But, yeah, of course, I'll try to stop him. Come on, guys. Let's go into the house of my enemy."

"This is it," Marla said. The street outside the hidden magic shop was just as crowded now as it had been yesterday, but today she was a lot more worried about surveillance, so she wasn't willing to just dash into thin air. Marla muttered a brief diagnostic spell, which made the entry to the shop glow red in her vision, but revealed no magical traps. Of course, the Chinese sorcerer could have strewn bear traps on the floor beyond, and she wouldn't be able to sense those or any other mundane dangers, but since this was ostensibly a place of business, she doubted he'd set hazards that might catch paying customers. "You two, come close."

B and Rondeau flanked her, their shoulders almost touching hers, and she scooped a handful of yellowish powder from one of the side pockets of her bag. She rubbed her hands together, yellow dust puffing around them, and sang a brief snatch of pure melody. It wasn't much, just a look-away spell to keep anyone from seeing them disappear, but she had to get it just right to affect a street full of people without accidentally striking anyone blind. When she felt the spell take hold—it was a sensation of temporary but welcome stability, like finding a good handhold while scaling up the side of a building—she grabbed B's and Rondeau's hands and dragged them toward the door, into the shop, one of the many enemy territories she'd developed over the course of the past two days.

The neat shop, with its blend of modern and traditional elements, looked like the victim of a highly localized earthquake. Shelves were tumbled, glass shattered on the floor, herbs strewn everywhere, puddles of rare oils congealed on the floor. The long counter at the back of the shop was fire-blackened in places, part of its length bent and broken.

"I guess Mutex beat us here," B said. "Unless it's supposed to look like this?"

"No, it's not supposed to look like this," Marla said. "But I don't think Mutex beat us here, either, not after the pounding I gave him. This kind of destruction wasn't his MO at Dalton's, either—he was in and out, quick."

"A surgical strike," Rondeau said. In the silence that followed, he sighed. "Surgical. See? Because he cut out—"

"We get it, Rondeau," Marla said. "I'd better check

out the back room." She jumped over the counter and sidled up to the concealed door, sliding her hands along the wall to find the catch. She pressed on a lightly discolored section of the wall, tsking in her mind—that was sloppy of her nemesis, to let the frequent pressure of fingers lead to visible wear on a hidden switch.

She heard the click of some mechanism engaging overhead, and tucked herself into a forward roll just in time to avoid the arc of a slicing pendulum-blade that swooped down out of a concealed slot overhead, then back up into its place in the ceiling. "Shit," she said, angry with herself. She'd assumed the Chinese sorcerer was being sloppy, when he'd actually set a completely non-magical trap that depended on the victim's overconfidence. She wouldn't underestimate him again, and she began to think that maybe Rondeau was right about the Thing on the Doorstep trick. A sorcerer who liked hidden traps like this might like the ultimate hidden trap of residing in an unexpected body. She stood up and looked at Rondeau and B.

Rondeau was sniffing at a tin of what Marla could only hope was tea, while B was staring at the ceiling, his mouth slightly open. He still didn't quite have the hang of this new world he'd found himself in.

"The door's probably reinforced," Marla said, "so kicking it's unlikely to do much good, and I'd hate to shake any more nasty surprises loose. We'll have to figure something—"

The door swung open with a click. The lights in the back room were turned off. "Marla," said a doleful voice from beyond the door. "My enemy."

"Ch'ang Hao?" she said.

"Yes," said the voice. "I received your message. I am sorry I did not find you. Please come in."

"You want to turn a light on first?" she said. Voices could be impersonated, and she wasn't exactly confident in her safety even if this *was* the real Ch'ang Hao.

Ch'ang Hao laughed. "The electric lights are broken in here. But I'll do my best." Several faint glows appeared on the floor of the room, sinuous ropes of greenish light. Marla squinted, and saw that they were bioluminescent serpents, crawling steadily out from the center of the room. Some of the snakes climbed up the walls, and from there to the hanging overhead surgery lights, where they wound themselves. After a few moments the room was filled with green light, and she saw Ch'ang Hao sitting on the metal table that had, yesterday, held her friend Lao Tsung's body. Ch'ang Hao held the garter snake Marla had sent to him in his hand, where it wound around and around his fingers like a set of living rings.

"So what happened?" she said.

"I tried to kill the master, and the apprentice attacked me. I performed a simple spell, to see which mind lived in which body, but it failed. I believed I had done it incorrectly—such magics are not the focus of my skill, after all. I think now that my spell was blocked. At any rate, I lunged for the master, or the one I believed to be the master, and the apprentice cast a spell that made me stop in mid-leap, hanging paralyzed in air."

"A bug-in-amber spell," Marla said. "Go on."

"They would have done more, perhaps imprisoned me again, but I began to *grow*. I can still grow a bit despite the cruel bondage you have chosen to leave me in. As I grew larger, my hands and feet extended beyond whatever field paralyzed me, and I was able to grab for them."

"Not bad," Marla said. "How did anyone ever imprison you in the first place?"

"I grew drunk at a celebration, and woke in chains," he said. "But that was long ago, before my enemy the sorcerer was even born. He inherited me from his own master, who had inherited me in his turn. But this new master was still clever enough to escape me. Before I could grow large enough to reach for them, they fled. The paralysis faded soon after."

"Why didn't you go after them?"

Ch'ang Hao stared at her. "Ah," he said, after a moment. "You have not tried to leave yet, then."

Something went cold in Marla's chest. "Oh," she said. "We can't leave."

Ch'ang Hao nodded.

"It's a pitcher plant."

He nodded again. "I had assumed the shop was sealed off from the world entirely, but then the snake you sent arrived, and I realized it was still possible to enter. It is, alas, impossible to leave. The door is gone. I am no longer trapped in the dark box where the new master kept me, and I am no longer trapped by threads of compulsion, but I am still trapped, here, in this shop. That is why I could not heed your summons." He hung his head. "That is also why there is so much wreckage. In my wrath, I smashed the shop. I regret the outburst. It was unseemly."

"Well, fuck," Marla said after a moment. "Let me look into this." She went into the main part of the shop, where B and Rondeau were already standing by the place where the main door should have been. "Guess you overheard, huh?"

"Yep," Rondeau said. "It turns out that B doesn't know any special action-movie tricks for escaping a space-time pocket that's been cut off from its real-world umbilicus."

"I never did any of my own stunts," B said apologetically, and Marla thought with something like exasperated affection that Rondeau's sense of humor was rubbing off on him.

Marla stared at the wall of the shop, the blank wooden wall where a door should have been. "But we aren't cut off from the umbilicus," she said. "The Chinese guy didn't cut the cord entirely. After all, we got *in*. It's more like we're in a—"

"Humane mousetrap," Rondeau said.

"Exactly. Except no one's going to repatriate us to a distant grassy meadow."

"Can't you throw a fireball at the wall or something?" B said.

Marla raised an eyebrow. "I could, though to get the energy I'd have to suck away most of yours and Rondeau's body heat. If I did that, I wouldn't accomplish much more than setting this place on fire."

"No one wants to be trapped in a burning box," Rondeau said.

"So . . . we're fucked?" B said.

"Hey, it could be worse," Rondeau said. "There's plenty of stuff to eat here." He prodded a jar on a nearby shelf, then squinted at it. "Okay, this is dried sea-horses, bad example. But there's plenty of, ah, ginger and ginseng and mandrake and lots and lots of tea.

Think of this place like a bomb shelter. When Mutex raises a giant Aztec frog-monster and ravages the city, we'll be safe here."

"Except that stuff can still get *in*," Marla said. "And anything bad that comes in here can't get out again, and we'll be stuck with it. So it's not much of a bomb shelter, really."

"Hmm," Rondeau said. "Okay, point. How do we get out?"

"There might not be a way," she said. "Let me think." She sat cross-legged on the floor and put her chin in her hands, staring at the wall. What would the Chinese guy have done? He was a sneaky bastard, fond of traps and hidden things. Also, he was greedy as hell—she remembered the way the apprentice (who was, almost certainly, actually the master in the apprentice's body) had counted the cash, smoothing the bills out on the counter. This room was still full of magical objects, and probably lots of money, since it was more secure than any bank. The Chinese guy probably hadn't had time to get even half his valuables before fleeing Ch'ang Hao's ever-expanding fury. Would he really have cut himself off from this place, leaving his fortune behind?

Of course not. Which was further proven by the fact that he hadn't severed the ties between this place and the ordinary world entirely. He could still get back *in*. And he would want to, since so much of his wealth was here. There was no point in his being able to get in, though, if he couldn't get back *out*. Which meant there was some way to open this place from the inside. The Chinese guy would come back at some point, probably with some kind of serious magical firepower to subdue Ch'ang Hao. They *could* just wait for him to return. He probably wouldn't expect Marla and Rondeau to be here, and they might be able to get the drop on him, especially since they now knew for sure that the one they had to fear was the young Chinese woman in boy-drag. Marla was reasonably confident she could beat the Celestial into revealing the way out.

But that was the brute-force approach, and despite prevailing opinion, Marla *did* have strengths other than, well, simple strength. The Celestial had fled in a hurry, so he couldn't have done anything too complicated. The entrance was, in all likelihood, simply hidden. A briefly muttered spell showed her that there was no simple light-bending illusion hiding the entrance, the way there was on the other side. Which meant it was hidden somewhere *else*. "Okay," she said aloud. "The door is hidden here, somewhere. This isn't exactly a literal space—it's as magical as it is physical, and its physicality is entirely dependent on magic—so the door could be hidden in anything, disguised as anything."

"So it could be inside this jar of dried starfish," Rondeau said, picking up a wide-mouthed mason jar.

"Yes," Marla said. "So smash it open already."

Rondeau heaved the jar against a far wall. It broke open, and starfish arms showered out. "Nope," he said. "That's not it."

"Good start, though," Marla said, grinning. This was it, she was sure—pretty sure anyway. The Chinese guy had hidden the entrance, which was really just a spell that had previously been made to look like a door. Now it had been made to look like something else. Smashing whatever it looked like would have the same effect as kicking down the door. It would open the way out. Ch'ang Hao had actually been on the right track with his furious breakage. "Ch'ang Hao!" she called. "Get out here! We're going to bust out of this place!"

Ch'ang Hao lumbered out of the back room, and she briefly explained. He nodded, looking almost hopeful, and began methodically smashing jars and wrenching open tins. Rondeau was whistling and slicing up a dried alligator mummy with his butterfly knife, and B was gently pushing over long-necked jars of oil and letting them break on the floor. Marla found a jo staff propped in a corner, and though it was an inch too long to be the perfect size for her, it was good enough for her to assault some shelves and apothecary cabinets on the macro level, knocking them over and hammering them to splinters with the age-hardened wooden staff. After half an hour of continual smashing, Marla leaned on her staff and surveyed the wreckage. B was down to ripping open plastic bags of herbs and powders. Ch'ang Hao had thoroughly destroyed the back room, and was now in the process of removing the pendulum-blade from the ceiling and snapping it in half. Rondeau, whose attention had predictably wandered, sat in a corner, apparently reading a newspaper printed in Chinese. Maybe Marla was wrong. Maybe the door wasn't hidden, after all.

"What about that vase?" B said.

"What?" Marla said.

B pointed toward a corner by the back wall, where a pile of wreckage formed a little mountain. Everything had already been smashed to bits over there.

"What—" Marla repeated, irritated, and then she *saw* it, a beautiful blue-and-white porcelain vase with a fluted mouth, standing on an unobtrusive black-stone pedestal. "I didn't see that," she said.

"I still don't see anything," Rondeau said, and Ch'ang Hao shrugged and shook his head. "What're you going on about?"

"You're worth your weight in eye of newt, Bowman," she said, and picked her way through the smashed glass. She had to glance away from the vase to negotiate her way around a puddle of bubbling red sludge, and when she looked back, she didn't see the vase. Marla swore under her breath. The Chinese guy had put a seriously strong look-away on that vase, the kind of magic only a big-mojo sorcerer could throw, but B had seen right through it. He was a far better seer than she'd originally supposed. "You'd better break the vase, B. It keeps slipping out of my vision."

"Sure thing," B said. He picked up a chunk of rough black rock—probably a meteorite, Marla thought—and threw it overhand at the vase from across the room, a distance of some twenty feet. The vase shattered, and light poured out, forming into a ragged oval that showed the streets of Chinatown beyond.

"Good hit!" she crowed. "We're out!"

Despite the fact that the door was in the back wall now, it still opened onto the same place outside. Consistent spatial relationships were nothing more than a courtesy in this place. Someone familiar hurried past the oval opening on the street beyond, a slim man with a fur hat and a cane. Who *was* he, Marla wondered. Some henchman of the Celestial's, off to tell his master she'd escaped? How had he managed to follow her today, from Dalton's to Bethany's to Chinatown? Before she could point him out to the others, the old man was out of sight, and Rondeau and B were pressing past her to look through the opening. Based on the way the man had eluded her earlier, chasing him wouldn't do much good now, and she had other priorities.

"Damn, B, you're an action hero," Rondeau said.

"You did well," Ch'ang Hao said, and Marla wondered if B understood enough to be impressed at such praise from a being as old and powerful as Ch'ang Hao. Thinking of which...

"Ch'ang Hao," she said. "Now that we can get out of here, I need to ask you about that favor." She explained, briefly, about the frog-eating Colombian snake. "Can you give it to me?"

"I can bring you any snake that lives in the world," Ch'ang Hao said. "But it will take some time."

Marla frowned. "Time? You can't just...manifest one? The way you did with the asps, and those snakes that made the truth-circle, and the glowing ones in the back room?"

Ch'ang Hao shook his head. "I fear not. Those are mystical serpents. They do not eat, or breathe, or breed. You need a real, living, particular sort of snake. I can find it, unerringly, but it will take me...at least three days. One and a half to go to the jungle and find the snake, and as much again to come back."

Marla wondered if the city would even be standing in two days. "I guess that'll have to do," she said, though she suspected it would be too late.

"Wait," Rondeau said. "You can walk to a South American jungle and back in two days?"

"I have my own ways of traveling," Ch'ang Hao said. "Walking is part of it."

"Well, yeah," B said. "But is it faster than hopping on an airplane to get you most of the way? Say, from San Francisco to Bogotá?"

"What is an airplane?" Ch'ang Hao said.

"Ah," Marla said, rubbing her hands together. "This might work out after all. Rondeau, you're going to get Ch'ang Hao some proper traveling clothes, take him to the airport, explain to him how everything works, see him on his way, and all that."

"What is an airplane?" Ch'ang Hao repeated, patiently.

"A way of traveling great distances at relatively high speed and in considerable discomfort. All will be revealed," Rondeau said. "Just come with me." He turned to Marla. "Where do I meet you guys when I get back?"

"Just wait for us at the hotel room," she said. "B and I have some errands to run."

"We do?" B said.

"Yeah," Marla said. "We do. I'm tired of chasing Mutex around town, and now that Ch'ang Hao is going to get a snake for me, we've got other options. I'd rather get *ahead* of Mutex for once. It's time I found out just what, exactly, you can do, B."

15

Find me an oracle," Marla said, and crossed her arms.

B frowned. "Right now?" He looked around. They were just outside the limits of Chinatown, near the City Lights Bookstore, where Marla had cast her first divination to try to find Lao Tsung—yesterday afternoon, and a subjective hundred years ago. "Right here?"

"I need to know where to find Mutex," she said. "I need to know where he's going to be tomorrow." That would give Ch'ang Hao time to return with the snake. It might also give Mutex time to kill every sorcerer in the city, but that was a chance she had to take. More importantly, it might give Susan time to act against her, but there was nothing Marla could do about that, not now. The spell Susan planned to cast was complex, and Marla just had to hope it wouldn't be ready today. She knew Hamil was doing his best to stall things.

"Okay," B said. "I'll do my best." He went toward Jack Kerouac Alley, between Vesuvio and City Lights. He stopped near a pile of stacked pallets, and put the palm of his hand against the wall of Vesuvio. "Hey," he said. "Anyone here? I could use some help."

Marla had her spirit-eyes on, and she didn't see anything, not so much as a shade or a specter, let alone the concentrated power of an oracle.

Suddenly something rose from behind the pallets, a mist that took the shape of a man with ash-gray skin and monochrome clothing. Its skin—or its semblance of skin—was slack and wrinkled, and it mumbled something incomprehensible. B mumbled something back, then gestured to Marla. "Come on," he said. "Ask him what you need to know."

Marla nodded, and started forward calmly enough, but inside she was caught between shock and elation. B had conjured this oracle, drawn it up out of the stones and memory of the city. This being was, in truth, nothing but a semi-physical manifestation of B's own incredible perceptive powers. He was no mere seer, but something far more rare and valuable. Some of his visions were so powerful that he couldn't experience them via direct perception, and so he had to manifest outside sources to present the information. Marla had heard of such individuals, oracle-generating seers, but they were as legendary in their way as Merlin or Sanford Cole. Bowman thought he was summoning an oracle, and there was probably some sort of supernatural entity here—a ghost fragment of a dead Beat poet, perhaps—but that merely provided a focus and form for the expression of B's power. She turned toward the oracle. "I need to know where Mutex will be tomorrow afternoon," she said.

The oracle didn't look at her, but stared into space beyond her shoulder. Finally it mumbled, and B sighed. "He doesn't know," B said. "He says that is hidden from him."

Marla had expected Mutex to hide himself and his movements, but oracles were normally adept at penetrating such veils, and this *was* a true oracle, despite being generated by B's own psychic powers. If B's oracle couldn't find Mutex, then that meant...shit. It meant Mutex had cast his spell with the help of the Cornerstone, and it would take seriously big magic to peer into the future through a curtain that thick. Marla considered the unwelcome possibility that she might have to fall back on her other plan, seeking out the surviving sorcerers in the city and trying to find Mutex that way. She'd hoped for a more elegant, direct solution.

And maybe there was one. "All right," she said. "Then we need to find a better oracle. Where can we find the biggest, strongest, most powerful, all-seeing oracle in the vicinity?"

"Ah, shit," B said, clutching his head. "I got a headache all of a sudden."

But the monochrome oracle was mumbling, and gesturing with its paper-white hands, and B nodded, wincing as he did so. This question was taking something out of B to answer, even by projected proxy. Finally the oracle stopped talking, and sagged against the wall, like a half-deflated balloon version of itself. "Okay," B said. "I know. But we have to pay for this, first, before I can tell you."

Marla nodded. There was always a price to pay for help of this nature. The better the oracle, the bigger the price. It turned out that the price for this one was minimal. Marla went into Vesuvio and ordered a red eye to go. She carried the cup of espresso and coffee out into the alley, and gave it to B. He solemnly, almost ritually, poured it out at the oracle's feet. Steam rose up from the ground, and the oracle turned into steam itself, satisfied with a drink of hot life.

"We have to go to Alcatraz," B said. "That's where the big oracle is."

Marla nodded. This would be something different. Not a projection of B's psychic prowess, not one of his convenient oracles-on-demand, but an ancient, strange, inhuman thing. "Does it have a name?"

"The Portable Witch?" B said. "The Pebbled Witch? The Potable Witch? I'm not sure. Something like that. The oracle mumbled." B rubbed his temple. "My headache's going away, at least."

"That's good," Marla said. "So how do we get to Alcatraz? Steal a boat?"

"I hope not," B said. "But we might have to. The tours are usually sold out weeks in advance."

They made it to Pier 41 just in time to take the last ferry to Alcatraz, at 2:15. Marla would have just sneaked onto the ferry, but B went to try to buy tickets before she could stop him. The ticket sellers just laughed when B asked if there were any late cancellations. Marla couldn't cast a look-away spell, not while the ticket sellers were so conscious of their presence. So she cast a nasty but ultimately not debilitating nausea spell on a couple of tourists, who sold Marla their tickets at a generous markup; she felt they deserved a little extra money, since they'd be puking for most of the afternoon. Marla had to lean over the side of the ferry to vomit herself before long. The nausea spell was based on sympathetic magic, and she had to make herself at least a little sick in order for it to have any effect. Such were the sacrifices that sorcery demanded. At least Marla was willing to make the sacrifices herself. Mutex, by contrast, wanted everyone *else* to be sacrificed.

"So do we know what to expect when we get to the island?" Marla asked, sitting next to B on a bench. There was no one nearby, so Marla didn't bother to cast a quiet spell. And if anyone heard them talking, they'd just assume Marla and B were insane. No harm there.

"Not really," B said. "We're supposed to go to a particular cell—not one of the famous ones—and step inside, face the back wall, close our eyes, turn around three times, and walk forward, with our eyes still closed. Which, logically, would make us bump into the far wall, but I assume that won't happen. After that, we'll find the Parable Witch, or whatever her name is."

"If it's even a her. Or, rather, if it even *appears* to be a her. Because, honestly, it's going to be an 'it.'"

"This feels different," B said. "I talk to supernatural creatures all the time, but this . . ."

"This *is* different," Marla said. "Anyway, it had *better* be. Because the same-old same-olds won't help us find out where Mutex is going to be. He moves fast enough that chasing him is pretty much pointless. We need to get ahead of him and set an ambush." She glanced toward Alcatraz Island, a great rock in the bay topped with boxy buildings. "How long is this ride anyway?"

"Twenty minutes, maybe. I've been on the tour once, but it was a long time ago."

"We'll be there in ten minutes. Not much time for us to talk. I'll just say, you've been a help. A greater help than I expected. Don't let it go to your head, but thanks."

He nodded, then grinned. "So how do we fill the other nine minutes and forty-five seconds?"

"Casual conversation, I guess."

"Then tell me about Rondeau," B said.

"Hmm," Marla said. "Well, he owns a nightclub back home, likes big band music, hates dogs, and has stupid taste in clothes. Also, he's an inhuman psychic entity that long ago possessed the body of a little homeless boy, which he still inhabits. He's been living as a human, more or less successfully, though he does have the ability to Curse in the debased tongue of the lesser gods—that's one theory anyway—and cause localized, random destruction. He's been working for me for a few years, and we get along well despite the fact that I ripped his jaw off when he was a little kid. That is, the body he possessed was a little kid. At the time. There's no telling how long the real-true-essential Rondeau has been alive, if 'alive' is even the right term."

"Huh," B said. "I was going to ask if he ever dated men, but now I'm not so sure I want to know."

Marla waved her hand. "Rondeau's a good person, even if he's not exactly a person. And, while I've never inquired too deeply into his sexual orientation, I'd characterize him as primarily heterosexual but adventurous."

"Are you a real human being?" B asked.

Marla shrugged. "Born of man and woman, raised by man and woman. Woman anyway. The man was never around much. I grew up in the Midwest, dropped out of high school, and moved to the big city. I worked in strip clubs for a while, mostly as a waitress. That's where I met Artie Mann, a pretty big-time sorcerer back then. He saw something in me and took me on as his apprentice. I worked for him for a while, then went freelance. Got in good with a man named Sauvage, who ran the city in those days. Then he got murdered, and I tracked down and killed his murderer." Marla didn't like to remember that time. She'd almost died at the hands of Sauvage's killer, Somerset. "Almost by accident, I found myself taking Sauvage's place. I've been in charge of my city ever since."

"The way that guy Dalton was in charge of San Francisco?"

Marla shook her head. "It's a little different. Here there's a ruling council of sorcerers, and they pass the highest position around among themselves. Finch was the one in charge yesterday. After him there was a woman in North Beach, and after her, Dalton. After Dalton, Bethany, and after her, it's the Chinese guy, who's still alive and at large, and thus, technically, still in charge. Though, really, Mutex is the one running things now, for all intents and purposes."

"What does it mean, that you're in charge?"

"It's complicated," Marla said. "I work with civic authorities to some extent, as necessary, but I rarely take a hand in the city's mundane, day-to-day operations. I... protect my city, mostly, against outside sorcerers moving in, against magical dangers, against tyrants, monsters, shit like that."

"Does that sort of thing come up a lot? Monsters?"

Marla thought about Todd Sweeney, and the pale dog that had pursued him; about the not-quite-dead sorcerer Somerset and his flocks of pigeons; about the mad chaos magician Elsie Jarrow and her bloody smile; about a dozen other dangers that had appeared during her relatively brief tenure as chief-of-chiefs. "Sure. Monsters, and other things. Other things is why I'm in San Francisco now, actually. There's someone, another sorcerer, who wants to take my job. And in the pursuit of that goal, she's going to doom my city. I came here to get something I need to stop her."

"The Cornerstone."

"That's right," Marla said.

"And Mutex has it."

"Right again. It's a pretty useful thing to have."

"So you aren't really trying to save San Francisco."

"It's not my neighborhood, B," Marla said. "I mean your city no harm, but—"

He laughed. "I hate San Francisco. I live in the East Bay now. I haven't lived in the city for years, since I was in the movies. I have a lot of good memories of this place, but they're all bad memories, *too,* if you see what I mean. Because just thinking about those good days reminds me of bad things."

"I know what you mean."

"So neither one of us loves this place, but we're going to save it anyway."

"Well, sure," Marla said. "It's not like we have to go out of our way to do it. We'll save the city as a byproduct of killing Mutex." She looked at Alcatraz

again. It was looming. She could see the dock.
"Besides, the place has its charms."

"I guess I wouldn't want to see it fall into the
ocean."

"And it's not as if Tlaltecuhtli would just smash
San Francisco and then go into retirement. Mutex's
power would spread, and it would get to us eventually,
wherever we went."

The boat bumped gently up against the pier, and
the tourists began rising and milling about.

"Let's go see a witch about a frog," Marla said.

It was easy enough to slip away from the tour, though
Marla was somewhat interested in what the guide was
saying, about the brief American Indian occupation of
Alcatraz Island in the early '70s. She had more important things to do now, though, and she could always
get Rondeau to fill her in about the history of the place
later, since he'd absorbed everything in the guidebooks
like a sponge sucking up water. She cast a look-away
over herself and B, the effort of casting the spell making her ears ring a little. Maybe she should have
snatched some spell components from the Chinese
guy's shop. All these little magics were starting to take
something out of her, and it was harder to cast spells
this far from Felport and the center of her power.
Everything had a price, after all, and she was down to
paying with the substance of herself. She should keep
something in reserve for the bigger challenges still to
come.

The island was a desolate place, fit to be little more
than a roost for seabirds, but the views of the city and

the Golden Gate (both the bridge and the landform) were stunning, and must have been heartbreaking for the inmates when this was a working prison. B led her up the stairs from the dock to the gatehouse—he'd been here before, and had a sense of where they were supposed to go now. He took her into one of the damp, gray cell-blocks, past rows of windowless cells. "We're going to one of the solitary-confinement cells," he said, whispering, and Marla felt his whisper was appropriate. There was a presence here, or just *past* here, located a short distance away in a dimension she couldn't quite comprehend. In addition to that there were ghostly fragments of dead prisoners, and somewhere a wailing little-girl ghost that Marla assumed had been one of the Indian occupiers, or else one of the Native Americans from before the Europeans came, or possibly a tourist who'd had a tragic accident of some kind. She wondered if B could hear them, but upon reflection, she supposed he could sense them more clearly than she could herself. He'd shown his great acuity time and again, after all. She admired his calm and his attention to the task at hand all the more after realizing that.

He led her into a tiny cell with a toilet and a sink, the bunk long since gone. B took her hand, and they shut their eyes, then turned slowly together, three times, all the way around. They took a step forward in unison, then another, then another.

And another. And five more. The sound of the floor beneath Marla's boots changed from heavy stone to something creakier. "Can we look yet?" she said.

"I think so," B said. "We've walked past where the wall should be."

Marla opened her eyes. They were in a long, dim corridor with a wooden floor and wooden walls, extending forward into darkness. Marla glanced toward a narrow arrow-slit of a window, and the faint, silvery light that came through it, but she stopped herself from stepping closer and looking through the aperture. She didn't look behind her, either. It was better, in places like this, to keep your eyes on the path. "Forward?" she said.

"Onward," B said. He didn't let go of her hand as they continued. The corridor turned left at a sharp right angle, then extended forward again for another hundred yards or so. Then another sharp turn, this time to the right. Once, they passed a door, with a brass knob, heavily tarnished. B looked at the door, then shook his head, and led Marla on. She wondered what was behind the door, and realized, not for the first time, that there were mysteries piled upon mysteries, and that even an adept and initiate such as herself only saw a tiny fraction of the deeper world that existed behind and above the known world. The corridor eventually reached an ornate wrought-iron spiral staircase. "We're supposed to go up there," B said. The corridor continued on, leading to who-knew-what inner mysteries, but Marla only nodded and followed B up the spiral staircase, which passed through a rough-edged square hewn in the roof of the wooden corridor, into something like an elevator shaft. The walls of the shaft were still dark wood, though, and Marla was comforted that they weren't ascending through pure formless void.

The top of the staircase ended at a seemingly unsupported pier of wood, a walkway no more than an inch thick and barely two feet across, with darkness on all sides. B stepped onto it, and Marla followed. There was a doorway at the end of the walkway, standing open, and white light beyond.

B hesitated on the threshold. "I . . . I don't know where we are now, Marla, but if we step through this door, we'll be even farther away from the world we know. We may be miles and miles away now, or whatever the spiritual equivalent of miles are, but once we go into this room, we're *light years* away, you know?"

"Nothing ventured," Marla said. "I'm not about to turn back. Are you?"

"I guess not. I just wanted you to know what we're stepping into." He went through the door, and Marla followed.

The room was hexagonal, or so Marla thought at first. She quickly revised her opinion to octagonal, then decagonal, and then she simply gave up, because the walls were changing, too subtly for her to notice the transition. The walls of this faceted room were mirrored one moment, then opaque crystal, then obsidian. The ceiling was so far overhead that it vanished into darkness, and the light seemed to come from the air itself, the brightest portion falling on an empty wooden chair in the center of the room. The chair was as simple as it could be, made of the same dark wood as the corridor walls, with a straight back and narrow arms.

"There's no one here," Marla said.

"There will be," B said.

For an instant, something white flickered in the chair, a shape filling it, and then the chair was empty again. Marla heard a distant crackle, like static on a radio between stations.

Suddenly, in the kind of insightful flash that made her such a capable sorcerer, she understood. This wasn't the Portable Witch, or the Biddable Witch, or the Pebbled Witch. It was—

"The Possible Witch," B said. "That's what she is. She deals in the *possible*."

Marla nodded, impressed. He'd figured it out as quickly as she had.

Then the witch was there, dressed all in white, sitting in the chair. She—it, really, but for convenience, she—was immaterial at first, then gradually attained opacity and solidity.

"I'd expected three," she said irritably. The possible witch was an old woman, dressed in a white gown like a choral robe, and she sat stiffly (there wasn't really any other way to sit in such an uncomfortable chair, Marla supposed) with her fingers gripping the ends of the armrests hard, as if she were holding on to keep from flying away, which could be possible, for all Marla knew. Her face was pale, her hair mostly gray with streaks of black. Her eyes weren't human, and they weren't exactly insectile, though they were nearer the latter, faceted clusters of black glass with occasional flashes of pure crystal or mirrored silver. "Sometimes there are four of you, the fourth one a god, and on rare occasions there are five, the fifth a very old mortal man, but there are almost always three. Two of you narrows it down anyway, quite a lot, makes it easier, but it's not what I'd expected, not what was most likely."

"You know who we are, of course," Marla said.

"And I think we know what you are. The Possible Witch, yes?"

"I stand at the center of things," she said. "Though I don't just stand. I orbit, I oscillate, I vibrate. Every possible world passes through my sight. Some are more possible than others. Sometimes I'm dead. Mostly, these days, I'm dead. That's why it took me so long to find you. There are so many possible worlds, and locking in on one in particular is hard, when I exist in so few of them now. But here I am. And it's the two of you who've come, and it's now, at this particular time, that you've come. Which means you're not trying to undo damage, but prevent it."

Marla nodded. "We need to stop Mutex. We need to know where he'll be tomorrow, when I'll be in a position to stop him." Assuming Ch'ang Hao came through with the snake anyway. Ch'ang Hao was clearly the fourth one that the Possible Witch had mentioned, but she had no idea who the "very old mortal man" was. Probably a potential ally who'd died before Marla even met him.

"But you don't want to know *if* you'll stop him?" The witch's inhuman eyes glittered.

"Of course I do, if you know that," Marla said.

"Too close to call," she said promptly. "I see just as many paths one way as the other. Everything *branches*, you know. Every decision, every option. The universe doesn't make choices. It does *everything*, even very unlikely things, somewhere. There are some unlikely places in the universe. In this branch, in this world, it could go either way. You might win, you might lose. Doesn't much matter, really. Lose here, win somewhere else. So why worry? That's what I tell everyone who comes to see me, which is lots of people, when you take into account all the different worlds."

"It matters to me," Marla said firmly. Many-worlds theory was as irrelevant to her as Dalton's prattling about the world being a computer simulation. Maybe it was true—standing here, she had to believe that many-worlds theory was true, that a new universe budded for every decision that was made, from the atomic level on up. But she lived in *one* world, and that was what mattered. Anything else was irrelevant for any purpose apart from after-dinner philosophizing.

"Yes, I know. Narrow is the vision." The witch was grumpy, Marla thought, but that was reasonable, since she was mostly dead. "I can't tell you anything for *sure*. The present is finite-but-vast, the future finite-but-even-more-vast. The future is approaching the infinite, actually, almost, if that statement has any relevance, which is arguable. Still, I can narrow it down, narrow to the marrow, yes, I can. There are two of you. Finch is dead? Umbaldo? Dalton?"

Marla nodded.

"Narrowing down," the witch muttered. "Bethany?"

"Dead," Marla said.

"Your hand, or another's?"

"Mine."

"You killed the Celestial?"

"No," Marla said.

The Possible Witch whistled. "You've got more problems ahead than you know, then, but no matter, no matter. Hmm. Who won the World Series last year?"

Marla looked at her blankly, but B spoke up,

naming a team Marla had heard of, vaguely. She didn't follow sports.

"They win often," the witch said. "That's not a lot of help. I know who's president, more's the pity, lots of burned-out cinders in *those* futures. Moving on, let's see. Which Cliff House is standing now? The second or third?"

"Third," B said.

"Did the second fall in fire or earthquake?"

"Um . . . fire, I think," B said.

"Sutro baths are gone?"

"Yes," B said.

"Alcatraz is a tourist attraction? Treasure Island exists?"

"Yes, and yes."

"Beautiful City or grid?"

"I don't understand the question," B said.

"San Francisco!" the witch said, leaning forward in her chair, still clutching the arms. "After the fire of 1906, was the city rebuilt according to the Burnham Plan, with streets and avenues following the curves of the hills, the ridges topped with lovely towers, and neoclassical public buildings placed artfully throughout the peninsula? Or was it rebuilt hurriedly, with streets thrown down across the hills in a grid, just like before?"

"The latter, I'm sure," B said. "There's nothing graceful about the streets downtown."

"Are passenger pigeons entirely, or only mostly, extinct?"

"Entirely," Marla said.

"Only four possibilities now," the witch said. "And nothing much to distinguish among them, at least no differences you'd be likely to know about, down to the level of whether a particular dog in India is alive or dead, whether a priest in Romania has syphilis or not. But four is good, and two of them are close together for your purposes, so I can give you a *probably,* a good stiff probably, but that's the best you're going to get from me today, understand?"

"Yes," Marla said. "Where will Mutex be?"

"Golden Gate Park. The Japanese Tea Garden. Tomorrow, late afternoon, or evening. A difference of two or three hours, maybe, so go at the earliest, say three o'clock. You'll probably get there in time, though as for what you'll *do* with that time, well, it branches a hundred different ways, and there's too many maybes between today and tomorrow, too many minor and major variations, for me to say for sure."

"You said that's two of four possibilities. What are the others?"

"In one of them, you're too late. Mutex's spell is done in the middle of the night, and destruction reigns, and you can't stop it."

Marla nodded. She'd suspected as much. "And in the last possibility?"

The Possible Witch's eyes moved independently of her face, a few tiny lenses telescoping forward in a manner that seemed caught between the technology of a zoom lens and the biology of a snail's eyestalk. "In that possibility, you'll never get there at all, Marla. *You* know why. Your enemy in Felport, mumbling over her spell. It's a question of whether she gets indigestion or not. She *probably* doesn't, her spell *probably* isn't delayed, so you'll *probably* live. But if she eats the wrong bite of salmon, she'll heave over the toilet, and the spell *will* be delayed, and you will be doomed."

Marla frowned. "Wait, if the spell *is* delayed, I'm doomed? That doesn't make any sense! Delays are *good,* I'm desperate for her to be delayed!"

The witch waved her hand. "You'll understand soon enough. Just be prepared for the possibility of utter failure."

Marla nodded glumly.

"Mutex is like a bulldozer," the Possible Witch said. "He doesn't let himself be deflected, and his course is remarkably straight and true, he moves right along in many a world. He's got the dedication of true religion. I know where *he'll* be anyway."

"I don't suppose...is he right?" Marla asked. "About the old gods needing blood to keep the universe spinning?"

"If he succeeds in calling up his god, and growing it to full size, he'll be right," the witch said. "His faith and his magic will *make* him be right, and the other gods he believes in will follow the Frog, appearing as quickly as he can spill blood to kindle and feed them. Just be glad you're in a world where he's trying to call up the Frog, and not in a world where he called up the Jaguar, and that over a year ago. I'm dead in most of *those* worlds, and glad of it, because there's only so much ugliness I'm happy to look upon." She flickered, going translucent for a moment, then solidified. "Now, you should go. I'm being called to talk to *another* iteration of you, who didn't move fast enough, who failed. I've got to give those yous some bad news about your miserable, nearly nonexistent prospects."

"Okay," Marla said, and grabbed B's arm. When a power like this said go, you did it quickly.

"But what about your payment?" B said. "Don't we have to pay you something?"

"You'll pay," the Possible Witch said, flickering. "You'll pay with *time*, which is something you can scarcely spare. But that's the way it is, when you talk to a *real* oracle. The payment is a lot more dear than a box of books or a cup of coffee."

"Let's go," Marla said, and pulled B toward the door, and down the stairs.

As they made their way back along the corridor, B said, "What did she mean, we'll pay with time? Is it like Rip Van Winkle, we'll come out and it'll be a hundred years later?"

"I doubt it," Marla said. "Otherwise we wouldn't be able to get to Golden Gate Park by tomorrow, would we?"

"So what does it mean?"

"I'm sure we'll find out," Marla said. "No use worrying about it yet." At the end of the corridor, they came to a black velvet curtain.

"The cell is through there," B said. "Ladies first."

"You lead us in, I lead us out," she said agreeably, and pushed the curtain aside.

Beyond the curtain, back inside Alcatraz, there was a prison riot going on, inmates running through brightly lit cell-blocks, guards shouting, and fires made of mattresses and sheets burning in the corridors.

"Shit," Marla said. "I guess *that's* what the Possible Witch meant about lost time."

She stepped out into a world that wasn't her own, and B followed.

16

The look-away Marla had cast earlier was still working, so they managed to avoid notice by the rioting prisoners or the guards. The patches on the guards' shoulders read *"Republica del Norte California,"* and everyone around them was speaking Spanish. They slipped through the complex of gates by following close to guards, who were rushing in and out, trying to get the riot under control. She and B made their way outside, to the far side of a building, facing the Golden Gate Bridge. They sat together in the late-afternoon light, and watched sailboats ply the waters of the bay.

"Should we try to get off the island?" B said. "Get a boat, or something?"

"No," Marla said. "The look-away I cast wouldn't cover a whole boat anyway, so they'd probably shoot at us. Better to wait it out."

"This is the time the Possible Witch was talking about," B said. "Sitting here, in one of those other universes she mentioned, unable to do anything in *our* world. Right?"

"I assume so," Marla said. "I *hope* so. Otherwise, we're stranded in one of those other branch-universes, and I'd rather not face that possibility unless I have to."

"Why would the witch demand such payment? What's in it for her?"

"Eh. It's more complicated than that. I know the smaller oracles you're used to usually want things for personal gratification, but for bigger entities, it's not always like that. There are just...rules. Chains of cause and effect. There's always a price, but it's not necessarily like paying somebody off. We spent some time at the center of the universes, seeing things people don't normally get to see. And the cost is spending time stuck in another universe, seeing things we don't necessarily *want* to see."

The Golden Gate Bridge disappeared. Marla blinked, but it was no trick of the light, no flash of neurological discord. The bridge was gone. The noise of rioting was gone from behind them, too. "Let me revise that. The cost is spending time in a *succession* of other universes. I guess it's a good thing we didn't steal a boat. We'd be getting awfully wet right now, with the boat gone from underneath us. I bet this is a sort of, I don't know, contagious reaction we picked up from being in such close proximity to the witch. This must be something of what it's like for her, shuffling from world to world to world. Except she sees everything at once, and even remembers it all."

"Look at that," B said, pointing into the bay. "Is that a ferry?"

"It looks like a floating palace," Marla said. A boat the size of a large building floated out there in the

Golden Gate, making the passage from the Marin Headlands to San Francisco at a stately pace. It was a beautiful thing, studded with towers and rippling flags.

"I've read about this," B said. "When they were first talking about building the Golden Gate Bridge, a lot of people opposed it, because they thought the Golden Gate was one of the most beautiful views in the world, and they didn't want to see it spoiled with a big bridge. But people needed a way to get from Marin to the city, and one of the suggestions was for a palatial ferry, to make the journey in style and comfort without spoiling the view. I guess that's the choice they made here."

"It's a shame Rondeau can't be here," Marla said. "He read a bunch of books about San Francisco history. He'd probably recognize lots of might-have-beens."

A moment later the bridge was back, and they both fell backwards, since the wall they'd been leaning against had disappeared. They stood up and looked around, and there were no buildings here at all, just seabirds and guano-spattered rocks.

"What do we do if a building appears right where we're standing?" B said.

"Die, probably," Marla said. "So let's move a little closer to the edge of the island, where that's less likely, hmm?" They settled down on a relatively unstained stretch of rock, near the foaming edge of the island, the water slamming against the rocks a dozen feet below.

The bridge disappeared again, though the island didn't change noticeably.

"The city is gone," B said. Marla looked. He was right. There was nothing there but trees and sand dunes.

"Maybe there are no humans in this world," Marla said.

"Or else they never found gold and silver in California," B said.

Marla grunted. "Maybe they all blew themselves up in the '50s."

"Great. Now I have to worry about radiation."

"Could be worse," Marla said. "There could be giant atomic ants and preying mantises."

They sat for hours, watching the world change around them. For a while they were on an Alcatraz still peacefully occupied by American Indian activists, with a bustling Indian Studies center where the prison had been. They took the opportunity to steal cold drinks of an unfamiliar brand from a cooler, and drank most of them before the bottles disappeared from their hands. They walked around the edge of the island, B pointing out the differences he recognized. Sometimes Treasure Island, deeper in the bay, disappeared entirely, and B told her that it was man-made—clearly there were some worlds where it was never made at all. For a while, the remains of a World's Fair stood on Treasure Island, complete with a rusting Ferris wheel and faded towers. "They tore the fairgrounds down during one of the world wars," B said, "to make the island into a naval base. Guess they skipped that war here." Many of the changes were small, just variations in San Francisco's skyline. Strange monuments appeared, while familiar landmarks vanished.

Sometimes it was so foggy they couldn't see anything at all, and once, for a tense fifteen minutes, there was a raging naval battle in the bay, with warships flying unfamiliar colors blasting away at one another with big guns, while San Francisco burned. The smoke was almost as thick as the fog, and B and Marla sat huddled in the shelter of a fallen wall, knowing that a look-away spell wouldn't prevent a shell from killing them and leaving their corpses in a world they could barely comprehend. That world passed, replaced by one where the peninsula that held San Francisco was gone entirely, just water in its place. "Guess the big earthquake hit here," Marla said. "Glad it didn't take out the island."

B nodded. By then it was dark, and the nearly full moon and the stars in the sky were the only constants. City lights twinkled on, and off. The night went on, and they slept in shifts, through the changing of worlds. Once there were submarine periscopes rising from the waters in such profusion that it looked like a gray metal forest. Once there were sea-monsters, prehistoric creatures that still lived, their graceful necks rising from the waves, their football-shaped heads looking lazily about, mouths full of knife-blade teeth, opening and closing. Once passenger pigeons blackened the sky above. Once Marla could have sworn she saw the lights of a sprawling city on the moon, but B was asleep, so she couldn't ask him, and she wasn't sure, once that world slid into another. For a while a giant statue loomed on the Marin Headlands, depicting a smiling young man wearing a top hat and an early-20th-century-style suit with a watch chain. After a moment Marla recognized him from pictures in her inherited library of the secret history of magic—it was Sanford Cole, the presiding secret genius of early San Francisco, court magician to Emperor Norton, and, according to Finch, the one who'd made Golden Gate Park blossom. She recalled Finch's story about how Cole would return in the hour of the city's greatest need, and wondered where he was now, when his city most assuredly needed him. Apparently he'd done great things in *this* variation of the world, at least. If they were going to be here for more than five or ten minutes, she might have made the effort to track him down and ask for his advice.

Finally dawn came, in a world where great bonfires roared on every high hill within sight, and by the time the sun was visible in the eastern sky, they were shivering in the cold, and there was a glacier visible to the north. "When will this end?" B asked through chattering teeth.

"Soon," Marla said, and it was half a prayer, because they only had hours now, before Mutex would be in the park. They had to meet Ch'ang Hao, assuming he'd made it back from Colombia with the snake, and Marla had to cast a spell, and then she had to actually *deal* with Mutex. None of which was possible while they flipped through this selection of alternate realities.

The cold vanished, and the sudden shift in temperature made Marla shiver even harder. B, who was looking toward the city, gasped, and then whimpered. "Marla," he said.

Dreading what she would see, her intuition giving her some hint of what it would be, Marla turned her head.

The city was no different than the one they came from, with Coit Tower and the TransAmerica Pyramid the most obvious landmarks. But there was smoke rising, and something the rich green color of jungle leaves moving beyond the buildings, visible only in brief flashes. There was a smell in the air, too, of turned earth, and rotten vegetation, and warm blood. That green something was almost as high as the tallest skyscrapers, and with a shuddering crash an apartment building tumbled over in an avalanche of concrete and glass.

Tlaltecuhtli shouldered its way through the gap in the skyline. Marla's eyes could scarcely comprehend its immensity. Nothing so large should be able to move on land. It was like a dark green mountain, its eyes yards across, perfectly black. It stood up on its rear legs, rising above the nearest skyscraper, and Marla's mental sense of scale gave way; it was as if she were looking at a model of the city that some child had dropped his pet frog into. Then Tlaltecuhtli opened its vast mouth, revealing fangs the size of buildings, and in the endless darkness of its maw there were red flutterings. Tlaltecuhtli vomited forth a torrent of hummingbirds. A flock of them—no, a *hover* of them, a *charm* of them, a *troubling*. The hummingbirds settled over the buildings like a ruby-red mist of blood, and in the fluttering they transformed into men, warriors wearing bright feathers and golden jewels, armed with swords. The warriors poured down into the streets, on their way to harvest hearts for their gods.

"Her mouth opens on the Land of the Dead," Marla whispered, and knew they were too late, that they'd come back home, to the world of the third possibility.

Mutex had succeeded, and his monstrous god was risen. The world was lost. She'd be better off throwing herself into the sea now, probably, because the alternative was to give up her heart on an altar of Mutex's devising, in the Palace of Fine Arts, perhaps, or on the steps of City Hall, or atop Strawberry Hill. Whatever place he'd chosen for his temple. But Marla wouldn't throw herself into the sea. She'd *fight,* and gather the surviving sorcerers, even if they were only apprentices and alley wizards and cantrippers, and make them fight in unison, though that was easier to say than to do. It didn't matter. Mutex wouldn't beat her. Not without suffering some himself in the process.

B was weeping.

Tlaltecuhtli turned its vast head, and looked upon them, and *saw* them, though they were mere specks on a small island. The great monster of the Earth crouched low, and then *leapt,* up and out toward them, and Marla looked into the sky, where doom was falling toward them like a great green stone.

And then the world flickered, and the sky was only blue. She looked toward the city, and there was no smoke, no monsters. B stood up, shakily, and Marla did as well. "It . . . that wasn't home," he said.

"No," Marla said. "I guess it wasn't. But it's what *could* happen. If we don't move fast enough. If we fail."

"Do you think this is it?" B said. "Are we back?"

"It looks like the world we left," she said. "Let's try to find a ferry."

There were tourists on the island, and a boat preparing to leave. Marla and B slipped into the back of the ferry, and sat huddled together. It wasn't as cold here as it had been in the glacial other world, but a San Francisco morning on the bay in January was still far from balmy. They were both miserable, cold, hungry, and shaken from their experience. They didn't speak on the trip back across the bay. When they arrived at the pier, Marla actually asked B to get a cab. They rode to the hotel, and Marla's hunger fought for space with her worry. They went into the hotel restaurant, where brunch was being served, and gorged themselves. When they were done eating, they took the elevator upstairs.

Rondeau wasn't in the room. There was no note.

"Maybe he went out for breakfast," B said doubtfully.

"He's flaky, but he knows better than that," she said. "Besides, his bed's made, and it's too early for the maids to have come in. Rondeau doesn't make his own bed, so that means he didn't sleep here." Maybe he *was* flaking out—maybe he'd run into Zara and slept with her. But Marla had told him to come back to the room, told him and *meant* it, and she didn't believe he would have disobeyed her if it had been in his power to comply.

She checked the voice mail on the cell phone, but there were no messages. The fact that she and the phone had been in other universes all night might have had something to do with that, she supposed. She noticed a light blinking on the phone beside the bed. "I guess there's voice mail for the room," she said, and pushed the button.

The first message had come in that morning, just a couple of hours before. It was the Chinese sorcerer, speaking in the sweet stolen voice of his apprentice.

"Meet me at my shop, today, at three o'clock. Bring me Ch'ang Hao, properly restrained, and I will return your lickspittle Rondeau to you. And then we will discuss restitution for the damage you have caused my reputation and my shop."

Marla swore. Then the next message began. It was her consiglieri, Hamil.

"Marla," he said. "I've been trying to reach you for hours. I just got word from another one of my spies. Susan is going to cast the spell tonight. If you don't find the Cornerstone now, soon, it's going to be too late."

That was bad news, but it could have been worse. Marla was going to confront Mutex this afternoon, and one way or another, things were going to end. She would get the Cornerstone, or she would die. If she got the stone, Susan's spell tonight wouldn't be a problem. If she died, well, Susan's spell still wouldn't be a problem.

Then the automated voice of the machine told Marla the date and time of Hamil's call. His message was older than the Chinese sorcerer's. Hamil had called the day before, in the afternoon, while she was in another world with B.

Which meant Susan had cast her spell to take over Marla's city the night before, while Marla was trapped in another universe.

Marla began to laugh.

17

"So what's the news?" B said.

Marla didn't hesitate. B had proven himself, as much as anyone could in two days. "The bad news is, the Chinese guy has Rondeau. I'm supposed to meet him at three o'clock today to negotiate his safe return, or, more likely, to walk into his ambush."

"Three o'clock. The same time you're supposed to lie in wait to ambush Mutex."

"I see you've been taking notes."

"So what's the good news? Or is this a bad-news/worse-news sort of situation?"

"Temporarily good news. I've been granted a stay of execution." Marla was marginally cheered, just thinking about the kind of day Susan must be having, checking her spells, finding them sound, checking her components, finding them flawless; and then falling into a depressed contemplation of the great intangible quality that drove all magic, from the merest cantrip needed to light a cigarette to the great spells that could cause earthquakes and raise leviathans: the sorcerer's *will*. Susan would have no choice but to assume her will was the weak point in her spell, that her attempt to destroy Marla had failed because Susan didn't need, want, *deserve* it enough.

But Susan would try again. Because, in truth, Susan's will was not a weak thing, and once the inevitable bout of self-doubt had passed, she could gather her strength and cast the spell against Marla again. Marla had another day, perhaps, to secure the Cornerstone, her only hope to thwart Susan permanently.

"My rival, Susan, tried to cast a spell last night," Marla said.

"The spell to depose you, which will lead to the downfall of your city? That spell?"

"Ah, right, I told you about that on the ferry yesterday."

"True. Though Rondeau told me most of it before then, actually, while we were on Bethany's train, before we found the freezer full of hearts."

"I can't leave that boy alone for five minutes," she said, and then came a pang, because Rondeau was probably being tortured right now, and she couldn't save him. She *couldn't*. Like she'd told him before, if it were within her power to save both Rondeau and herself, she would. But if she had to choose between them, she would choose to save herself. Killing Mutex and retrieving the Cornerstone were the only ways to do that. Saving Rondeau from the Celestial instead would only be putting off his death anyway, since once Mutex raised Tlaltecuhtli, they would all die. Gods, this city. It had killed Lao Tsung, and now it threatened to kill Rondeau. She would destroy the Celestial when this was done, make him suffer a thousand times whatever he inflicted on Rondeau, but that thought was no comfort at all; it was just what she owed Rondeau for his friendship and service, and it wouldn't bring him back to her.

"So Susan's spell didn't work?" B said.

Marla blinked. "No. I doubt the spell failed. Susan is a craftsman, and anal-retentive as hell. She wouldn't try to cast a spell without making a list and checking it twice, dotting her i's and crossing her t's and other such metaphors. She's a perfectionist, in the truest sense of that word—she does things *perfectly.* No, the spell worked, only it *didn't* work, because I wasn't here for it to work *on.*" Marla began to do a simple knife kata with her dagger, working out the kinks from a night of sleeping rough in a score of different worlds.

B's eyes widened, even as he stepped back, well away from her flashing knife. "She cast the spell while we were in another *universe,*" B said. "So it didn't affect you!"

"Oh, it gets better," Marla said, producing another dagger (this one was simple steel and wood, but weighted to match her dagger of office) and beginning a more complex two-knife kata, weaving a net of glittering steel. "Did Rondeau mention what Susan's spell was supposed to *do* to me?"

"No."

"Because he didn't know. I keep secrets. It's a habit. Sorcerers need secrets the way fishmongers need fish. But there's no good reason not to tell you, and it's funny, so: Susan's spell is supposed to delete me from this universe." That phrase—"delete me"—was the one her consiglieri, Hamil, had used when warning Marla of Susan's plot, but now it reminded Marla of mad Dalton's notion of the world as computer simulation. Maybe the other worlds they'd traveled to were other simulations, running on vastly powerful networked computers. After a moment, Marla decided that the idea wasn't really all that interesting. Whether the universe was a computer simulation or not, it was still a world of concrete, sewage, and unexpected moments of grace—debating the nature of reality didn't change the fact that she had to live in it.

"Delete you?" B said.

"*Erase* me," Marla said, tossing her knives up and catching them before starting another routine. "Snip me out of the tapestry of reality like a snagged thread. See, even if she killed me—assuming she could, which she couldn't—that wouldn't necessarily help her take over the city, even though she's the strongest sorcerer there, apart from me. She'd have to deal with my vengeful associates, and possibly my very psychotic ghost, so instead she wants to cast a spell to cut me out of the world entirely. It's big bad magic, subtle and strange. First, the real, physical me will vanish, poof. Then, slowly, the other proofs of my existence will fade away. Within two weeks my friends will forget about me; within three weeks my enemies will. The things I've done in my life won't be undone, but every record and memory of who *did* those things will grow vague and eventually disappear. Soon I'll even drift out of people's dreams. And I won't even have a ghost, because I won't die, I'll just stop being *alive*. And if, gods forbid, there's an afterlife, I won't see it. I'll just be gone."

B stared at her as she spoke. "Marla," he said. "You really deal with hard people, don't you?"

"Yeah," she said, thinking, *And I'm the hardest one of all.* "So Susan tried to wipe me away, break my ties to the world, but since I'd *already* left this world, there was nothing for the spell to work on, so it just . . . fizzled."

"Has anyone ever done this spell before? No, never mind—you don't know, right? How could you know?" He laughed, harshly. "That's the whole point."

Marla wondered what would happen to B's movies if someone cast an erasure on him. Would they be unchanged? Would he be replaced in all footage by a star of a similar age, or some forgettable character actor?

More pointless mental meandering. She usually kept her thoughts in better order than that, especially in times of crisis, but she supposed she was just trying to avoid thinking about Rondeau being tied up somewhere—though not at the sorcerer's shop, not yet. Nowhere Marla would be able to find him. She returned her attention to B. "We assume the spell has been done before. It's tough to perform, but no harder than half a dozen other spells of such magnitude. It takes about a year of steady prep work—I'm talking hours of meditation every day—which is why my spies had time to discover that Susan was planning it. Even so, I cut it close."

"Will it be another year before Susan can try again?"

Marla flipped a dagger in the air and caught it. "I wish. No, she can do it again in a day or so, once she replaces the spell components that were consumed in

the casting, and gives herself over to more meditation." So that was what the Possible Witch had meant.
If Susan had eaten a bit of bad fish, spent the night
puking, and delayed her spell until this morning,
Marla would have been back in *this* world, and the
spell would have worked on her. "So I've got to move
fast to get the Cornerstone."

"And the Cornerstone is useful because . . . ?"

"Good to see Rondeau exercised some discretion.
The stone is an artifact, a sort of . . . magnifying glass
and industrial-strength fixative for spells. It makes
magic stronger, and it's especially useful for binding
spells, and making things last forever. It's also handy
for overcoming the inertia of reality."

B looked at her blankly.

Marla made a vague hand motion. "Reality is
pretty resilient. You can bend it, but it always snaps
back into shape. That's why magical gold turns back
into leaves and cow patties after a while—magic bends
the rules of the world, but it can't break them. With
the Cornerstone, you can bend reality to the breaking
point, and do all sorts of things. Like make yourself
live forever. *Really* forever, not just a long time, like
my friend Lao Tsung lived. Fortunately, most people
who are powerful enough to brew up magic like that
are smart enough not to try it. The ones who do go for
eternal life usually get about a century past their normal life span and then go bat-shit crazy. They'll still be
floating around in space when all the stars have
burned out, poor bastards. You can do other things
with a Cornerstone, in theory."

"Like bring a god back to life?"

Marla nodded. "Unfortunately. You have to bend

reality a *lot* to get it to accept a giant frog-monster whose mouth opens onto the Land of the Dead. But Mutex can push things that far, with the Cornerstone."

"So what are you planning to do with it?"

"I'm going to use the Cornerstone to bind myself to this world, and I mean *bind*. Hell, after I cast the binding, I doubt even a visit to the Possible Witch would be able to shift me. I probably couldn't even get to her temple, since it's outside of this reality—so yeah, there are drawbacks. It's a hell of a sacrifice, actually. I won't be able to enter folded space anymore, like the Chinese guy's shop. But I'll be erasure-proof, so it'll be worth it. And *then* I'll deal with Susan."

"Wait," B said. "Didn't you say that if Susan succeeded in casting her spell, it would doom your city to destruction? But it sounds like it would only doom you."

Marla tucked her daggers away. She was sweating now, and her head felt clearer. "It *would* bring doom down on Felport. Because I'm the only one qualified to look after my city. All the other sorcerers, those bitches and sons of same, are incompetent or power-hungry or paranoid to one degree or another, and if any one of them—Susan included—took over, the whole damn place would fall apart. No one else can strike the perfect balance of fear, loyalty, obligations, and threats that I do to keep business and magic running smoothly. Most other chief sorcerers can't even leave their cities without risking a coup, but look at me—I can go away for a few days, and the only thing I have to worry about is being edited out of existence. Most of the other sorcerers hate me, but they know I'm the one who keeps things running smoothly, and they accept it. Except for Susan. She was always too ambitious for her own good."

"Ah," B said. "So it's more of an *indirect* sort of certain doom that faces your city in your absence."

Marla shrugged. "Destruction is destruction. Believe me, I know." She sat on the bed, stretching, working the last of the knots out of her shoulders and neck.

After a few moments of silence, B said, "You're not going to rescue Rondeau, are you?"

"I can't. If I do, Mutex gets away, and I don't get the Cornerstone, and I disappear. Which will be lucky for me, what with a raging frog-monster and resurrected warriors destroying everything in my absence."

"Rondeau is your friend."

"Best one I've ever had," she said. "My brother in arms." *I'm the hardest one of all.*

"I'm going to save him, then," B said.

Marla considered possible responses to that. "Oh, good," she said at last. "That way two of my friends will die."

"I'm your friend?"

"Yeah. For what it's worth. Which, as you know now, isn't much, at least not under these circumstances."

"It's a lot better than being your enemy," B said. "I have to go save him."

"I'll bring flowers to your funeral." B didn't answer. "*Why* do you have to save him? I admire your— I don't know, your pluck—but why do you *have* to?"

"Because I saw Rondeau in a dream, too," B said quietly. "And if he dies, you fail, and Mutex succeeds, and this city, and then the rest of the world, falls."

"Oh," Marla said. "You might have mentioned this before."

He shrugged. "It was just last night. It was one of *those* dreams, and I haven't found a ghost to interpret it, but it was pretty clear. Rondeau dying, and then *you* dying, and me, and everybody."

"So the fate of the world depends on *Rondeau*? It just seems so . . . unlikely." And maybe it was a lie. B was an actor, and they were, by nature, convincing liars. Maybe B was just trying to convince her to save Rondeau. Then again, he hadn't given her cause to mistrust him yet, and it wasn't hard to envision a situation when a quick Curse or a knife-thrust from Rondeau could affect things significantly.

But how could she save him? Who could she bring in? There was no time to fly anyone into the city, not even time to find local talent, assuming Mutex hadn't killed or frightened off all the sorcerers in the Bay Area. B was willing to try to save Rondeau, but he was a seer, not a soldier. How could he possibly—

Marla thought of a way. A dangerous, stupid, terrible way. The only way.

She unclipped the silver stag beetle pin from her throat, and removed her white-and-purple cloak. "Put this on," she said. "You won't be able to use it very well, no more than you could use a katana properly if a samurai handed the sword over to you, but I can teach you enough to keep you from chopping off your feet. And, in truth, it's more like a machine gun than a katana. If you aim it with a little care, the weapon will do most of the work."

B didn't move to touch the cloak. "I saw what you became when you wore that," he said. "You became a...thing. Like a jaguar made of darkness. Like a bruise with teeth."

"Only while the purple is showing," Marla said. "The white makes you an angel, heals you, keeps you strong. The purple..." She shrugged. "Darkness. Teeth. Yes. All the ugly things you have to be, sometimes, to defeat things that are even uglier. Like I said on Bethany's train, we're past simple things like good and bad, and into the realm of the practical. There's more to it than that. After you use the cloak, a little bit of what makes you human is pushed down, suppressed—it might even wear a little bit of your humanity away permanently. I've used the cloak dozens of times over the years, often enough to be frightened of using it more, but if you use it once or twice, it shouldn't damage you forever." *At least, I don't think so.*

B took the cloak and let it drape over his arm, the white showing, the purple lining only visible in glimpses. "Teach me," he said.

"Okay," Marla said. "Only we'd better do this on the roof. I don't want to have to pay for damage to the room."

On the roof of the hotel, B was magnificent, except he wasn't; the cloak was magnificent. Anyone wearing the purple would become a minor god of death and movement, a flitting dark shadow with the sinuous lines of a jungle cat, blurred by a soft-focus nimbus of shadow, and so it was with B, attacking the light-ghosts Marla conjured for him to practice against, dancing figures that resembled Marla herself, but drawn with strokes of lemony light. Marla had only once seen another wear the cloak, when the undying bird-mage Somerset took it from her briefly, but now that she wasn't in particular fear for her life, she could admire the artifact's terrible beauty.

B learned the rudiments of control easily, how to reverse the cloak from white to purple with a single focused thought. Marla could clothe herself in the purple without the intervention of her conscious mind, as an instantaneous reaction to dangers ascertained by the workings of her subconscious alone, but B would not wear the cloak long enough to develop such an affinity, nor would he learn the many subtle techniques for directing the ruthless, murderous efficiency of the cloak's effects. Marla had practiced long enough, grown into the cloak thoroughly enough, that while wearing the purple she could actually stop herself from killing someone who had threatened her life. B would have no such control—whatever enemy crossed his path while he wore the purple would be shredded beyond repair, and B's body would be used roughly in the process, his joints twisting, muscles twanging under incredible pressure, tissue ripping. The first time Marla had used the cloak, she'd dislocated both shoulders and one kneecap, and cracked her collarbone, experiencing several long moments of nauseating agony before the healing properties of the cloak's white side took effect, soothing her pains and straightening her disarranged limbs.

That was the cloak's perfection—to transform its wearer into a killing machine, using the body's resources up nearly to the point of the wearer's death, and then, in the aftermath, healing the wearer. The power was awesome, the loss of self-will terrifying, and that combination of awe and terror had led Marla to gradually give up using the cloak, though she'd found its use both intoxicating and comforting for many years, and she had some sense of the thrill B must be feeling now, as he leapt about on the hotel's black roof, shredding Marla's barely material doppelgangers into wisps of dissipating light. When B landed (on all fours, scarcely recognizable as a human, more a twilight-colored catlike thing with golden eyes), no longer confronted with obvious enemies, he caught a glimpse of Marla, and turned toward her, tensing to leap.

Marla prepared herself, whispering an opening invocation, preparatory to a nasty spell that she hoped she wouldn't have to use. She could stop him from hurting her if he tried, but it would take an effort, and it would probably be noisy, and might even leave them both unconscious for an hour or so. But she had to test this—to see whether, in the full heat of frenzy, B could recognize her as an ally, and prevent himself from attacking her. Marla herself had occasionally had trouble with that distinction, but she suspected the tendency to attack her friends while wearing the cloak had something to do with her own deep and fundamental mistrust of everything outside herself. B was a more trusting person—oddly, since he saw more clearly than most—and she had reason to hope that he would make the adjustment more quickly than she had.

B didn't attack her. Instead, the purple shimmered, becoming opalescent, then fading to the soft snowbank whiteness of the cloak's benevolent side. B lay sprawled on the rooftop, wrapped up in white, his hair mussed. He grunted, and Marla saw his twisted shoulder move back into place seemingly of its own volition. He looked up at her, and it wasn't B behind those startling blue eyes, not now—it was something cold and inhuman, sizing her up, perhaps wondering how she would taste, wondering if there was any advantage in killing her. He started to get up, and Marla pressed down on his shoulders. "Shh," she said, and after a moment he stopped pushing against her, and the coldness in his eyes receded.

"Holy shit," he said. "That was like being some kind of psychotic superhero. I felt like Spider-Man on angel dust."

Marla crouched beside him so they could talk more easily—he wouldn't be able to stand up for another few minutes, probably. She understood his enjoyment—there were few things more intoxicating than physical power. Because she knew the thrill he was feeling, and because she knew he was a good listener and would understand the importance of this without having the words shouted into him, she spoke gently: "Yes, but Spider-Man just ties up the bad guys and leaves them for the police. You're not going to do that, B. Mercy and restraint won't even be an option. Do you understand?"

There was a pop as his elbow straightened itself, but he didn't wince, only nodded. "Right," he said, subdued. "I'm going to kill someone, aren't I?"

"Yes," Marla said. "It's you that's doing the killing, too. Not the cloak, though the cloak will make the killing possible, and even enjoyable, in a way. The cloak isn't the killer, though, any more than a sword is a killer. The weapon isn't responsible. The one wielding the weapon *is*." *And you are my weapon, Bowman.* She hated turning him into this, but it was necessary.

B looked at her, his tropical eyes full of understanding, almost more understanding than Marla could bear. "Don't worry," he said gently. "I'm not your weapon. You're not the one wielding me. I'm making this choice myself."

Marla nodded, though she didn't believe it—she was setting B on this path, and the killings he did on her behalf would weigh on her even more than the lives she'd taken personally. She could stomach the killing she'd done herself. She never did so without good reason, not anymore, and as she grew older she found fewer and fewer reasons to kill, because there were almost always other options. But she was far less comfortable with making B—affable, solid B—into a murderer. "I just want you to understand," she said.

"I guess this is a big thing," he said. "The decision to kill somebody. This isn't a heat-of-the-moment thing. I'm going in there with this as my goal. It's not quite as big a step as actually *doing* the deed, but deciding to do it . . ." He shook his head.

Marla nodded. She knew what he meant. The first time she'd consciously killed someone, it had changed her entire understanding of the world. There was no act more monstrous than the taking of a human life; all the worse acts were merely matters of scale. The only real justification for such an act was to prevent greater bloodshed. And even then, it was philosophically uneasy ground, even for someone as relentlessly practical as Marla. She tried not to think about the killing much, which was, she knew, one of the few ways in which she was truly cowardly.

"It's going to be ugly, B. Go in heavy. Reverse the cloak as soon as you see the Celestial. You won't attack Rondeau—you'll recognize him as an ally, the same way you recognized me." That last was as much a hope as a declaration. "Go for the sorcerer. And if they're both there, go for the young one, because that's the real enemy, in the apprentice's body." That would spoil Rondeau's wish to restore the apprentice to her own form, but he'd get over it, if the end result was the preservation of his own life.

B sat up, his injuries healed. He stretched his arms over his head, testing his flexibility. "What about, ah, magic? Won't the sorcerer try to fight me?"

"Don't worry. Spells slide off the purple like water slides off a duck. You won't have a problem. It's . . . going to be messy, B. It's best you don't look back at the mess you'll make of them when you're done. Just take Rondeau, and come back to the hotel. Then wish me luck, because I'll be tussling with Mutex by then, if all goes well." She wanted to tell him to resist the moment of inhuman coldness that would come over him after he reversed the cloak, but why bother? Even *she* couldn't resist it. She would just have to hope it wouldn't last long.

B frowned. "Shit, Marla, I just realized—if I've got the cloak, you *don't*. You're going to face Mutex without your best weapon."

"*I'm* my best weapon, B. Don't worry about me. If I can get past Mutex's frogs, and his hummingbirds, and deal with his tendency to move at mind-blurringly high speeds, I shouldn't have any trouble taking him out, even without my cloak."

"That's a lot of ifs," B said.

"This is an iffy business. Come downstairs. We'll order room service. I know we ate already, but using that cloak burns calories like you wouldn't believe."

Marla felt ridiculously like a mother sending her son off to his first day of kindergarten, but in this case, she was sending a seer and oracle-generator into mortal danger. She wanted to pat his cheek and tell him to be careful. Instead, she said, as gruffly as she could, "Bring my cloak back in one piece. And you'd better be in one piece inside it."

"How about Rondeau?" B said, smiling, still pumped from his first experience using the cloak. "How many pieces do you want him in?"

"No more than two," Marla said. "As for the Chinese guy, you can break him into as many pieces as you want." She hesitated, then decided to give in, a little, to the protective impulses she was feeling toward this man, her newest brother-in-arms, who had so recently been a stranger. "I appreciate your doing this. You don't have to."

"I know," he said.

"Don't die."

"Yes, ma'am." He sketched a salute, kissed her cheek—impulsively, and she accepted the kiss gladly—and opened the door. He walked out, the cloak looking strangely right on his shoulders, absurd yet regal. The door swung closed after him, and Marla turned back to the bedroom to meditate a bit, and prepare for her own confrontation—with Mutex, what would be their last meeting, unless things went improbably wrong for both of them.

Someone knocked on the door.

"B?" Marla said, thinking he might have returned, thinking better of his mission, or to ask for advice, or to take this last opportunity to go to the bathroom. But when she peered through the peephole, it was not B, but an old man with a long face, wearing a beaver hat.

Her mystery follower, here. Was it an attack, then, or something else? She'd never seen his face before, not this close, and there was something oddly familiar about it.

Marla eased the door open, keeping her foot braced against the door so she could slam it and hold it closed if the old fellow tried to shove his way inside. "Can I help you?" she said, looking at him through the crack between the door and the frame. He was short and slim, but held himself with tremendous dignity.

He looked at her, his face blank, then nodded. "I think so," he said, his voice scratchy and attenuated, as if he had not used it in a long time. "You are the most powerful sorcerer in this city, except for two others, who are both palpably mad, and therefore made weak by their own faltering minds."

"I know you," Marla said. "You've been following me since I got to the city."

"I have been following *lots* of people. I have been trying to figure out a great many things."

"But there's something else…you're familiar. Where have I seen your face?"

"I can't imagine," he said, as if the question

amused him. "Unless you are much older than you seem—and I don't smell that kind of age on you—you were not born the last time I walked in this city. It is an impossibility that we have met. But I do need your help, I think. There are two mad sorcerers at large in this city, and now that I am here, there are two who are sane, which rather improves the odds, I think."

Marla stared at him, trying to place his face, and then she found it—she'd seen his face only yesterday. But not in the flesh—in stone. In a statue of his younger self, in another universe, where his exploits were known in the world at large—as opposed to this world, where his history was known only to initiates of certain Mysteries. "I know your name," she said.

"I'm flattered." He took off his hat. "But allow me to introduce myself all the same, for I would hate for you to think me impolite. My name is Sanford Cole."

"You were the court magician for Joshua Norton, the nutcase who declared himself emperor of America and protector of Mexico," Marla said. "In the 1800s."

"The 1870s, mostly," Cole said. "It's not as if we dominated that entire century. But, yes, I knew Joshua, and helped him, as he helped me. It is a curious thing, but when a land has a monarch, even one of such peculiar pedigree as His Majesty, that land gives up certain secrets, and allows itself to be molded in a way wild lands and places governed by more enlightened forms of government do not. As the court magician to a reigning emperor, one at least humored if not exactly obeyed by the public and the government, I was able to shape things in this city that might have otherwise been beyond my power to change." He frowned. "When I decided to . . . rest . . . I thought things were in fair shape. The city had survived an earthquake and a fire, and risen like a phoenix from the wreckage to enter a new century. But now, in the *next* century, I find that things are very dire indeed, with all but one of the city's protectors murdered or fled—so many of the cowards fled!—with the surviving protector mad with vengefulness and neglecting his duties, and with a madman set to open the mouth of Hell. This pending disaster woke me, and I had been *comfortable* in my slumber. And here you are, a stranger, doing what you can to stave off the destruction of the place I hold most dear."

"I didn't come here to interfere in this city's business," Marla said, still holding the door. She couldn't tell if Cole was pissed or not, and if this *was* him, returned—and she suspected it was—she didn't want to face his anger. "But I've been swept up in things."

"I understand," Cole said. "Your help is most welcome. This has always been a city of immigrants, after all. A place where people come to make a new life."

Marla snorted. "I'm happy with my old life, thanks. I'm here to keep my old life from ending, actually."

Cole nodded, though he looked a trifle hurt. "This is also a city that admires a healthy self-interest, and so long as the needs of San Francisco are congruent with your own, I would appreciate your assistance. And, in return, I will do what I can to help you achieve your own goals."

Marla thought about that. It didn't take much thought. She stepped aside, and Sanford Cole, the closest thing to Merlin this age had ever seen, came inside.

18

Marla didn't have anything to offer Cole, except crappy coffee brewed in the little four-cup coffeemaker the hotel provided. Sipping from a Styrofoam cup, Cole made a face. "I can say in all honesty that this is the best cup of coffee I've had in decades."

"Right," Marla said. "Suspended-animation humor. If I survive the rest of the day, I'll buy you a grande latte. Coffee's come a long way since your day. But we've got other things to do first."

"You seem to have a plan of action in mind already," Cole said. "Which is more than I'd hoped for. What can you tell me?"

"Mutex is making his move today, this afternoon or evening."

"And what *is* his move? Remember, I slept through all the rising action. All I know of this Mutex is that he is a powerful sorcerer—I have a talent for sensing that much, which is how I found you—and that he's killed or driven away all the sorcerers who are meant to be protecting this city. What is Mutex's goal?"

Marla was a bit surprised, having thought of Sanford Cole as a near-omniscient being, but upon reflection, it made sense—even the greatest sorcerers were just people. When they stopped being people, they stopped being sorcerers, and became monsters. Marla filled him in on Mutex's religious notions, and his plan to raise Tlaltecuhtli. While she spoke, she had a hard time ignoring the digital alarm clock on the bedside table, every minute eroding the little time she had left to act.

"Mutex must not succeed," Cole said. "And you say he intends to complete the ritual today? How can you be sure?"

"Have you ever heard of the Possible Witch?"

"I have *heard*," Cole said. "But the path to reach her has been closed since the days when the Ohlone Indians fished the waters of the bay."

"I had some help getting to her," Marla said. "I know an oracle-generator. An opener of the way."

"Astonishing! Emperor Norton had similar powers, but they drove him mad."

Marla filed that tidbit of information away. As far as she knew, no one knew that Norton had possessed such powers, and she liked to impress Hamil and Langford with such esoteric trivia. The thought made her painfully homesick, and she turned her attention back to the matter at hand. "My guy isn't insane. He's a little weird, but that's normal for a seer. We went to see the Possible Witch, and she gave us the best likelihoods about Mutex. He's going to be at the Japanese Tea Garden today—possibly soon—and if I don't stop him then, it's going to be too late for *anyone* to stop him."

"What is your strategy?" Cole asked.

"Strategy. Right. I can handle Mutex, pretty much, except for his poison frogs. I had a way to get around that—I sent a . . . ah, an associate of mine to find me a snake that's immune to the frogs' toxins—"

"And you planned to use sympathetic magic to make yourself immune as well, of course. But . . . ?"

"But my friend hasn't shown up yet, and I'm running out of time to wait for him."

Cole frowned. "Is your friend, by any chance, shall we say, a non-human?"

"I think he's an ancient Chinese snake god," Marla said. "And he's not my friend. He owes me a favor, but he considers me an enemy, and wants to kill me."

"Your enemy? I'm sorry to hear that. You should have said you were waiting for a god. I've been sensing a god within the city's borders for nearly an hour now. He appeared rather suddenly, but then, gods do that. He's south of here. It may be—"

"*South* of here?" Marla slapped her forehead. "Shit. I bet he's at the airport. Rondeau was supposed to pick him up. Damn it. Cole, come with me. I've got to do something I swore I'd never do again."

"What?"

"I can't believe it's come to this," Marla said. "But there's no other way. I'm going to have to *drive*."

Cole looked appropriately horrified by the notion.

B took a bus to Chinatown, feeling self-conscious in his cloak, though he didn't draw more than the usual number of stares—only this time it wasn't people looking at him because he seemed vaguely familiar, but because he was wearing something outlandish. He kept thinking of Sam Raimi's *Spider-Man* movie (there had been a rumor in certain circles that B was being considered in the lead role for that back when it was being cast, but it had been groundless, as all such rumors were since he'd left the business). In B's opinion, the best scenes in the film were those where Peter Parker was exploring his newfound abilities as Spider-Man, the simple glee he'd demonstrated as he leapt and spun and deadlifted tremendous weights. How many kids hadn't imagined having just such powers? B certainly had. And, unlike most kids, he'd grown into a person who did, apparently, have powers of a sort, though B would trade all the second-sight and oracle-finding prowess in the world for, say, invisibility or the power of flight, straightforward powers that didn't necessarily create more questions than they answered. Now B did have such powers, though they were borrowed from the cloak—speed, strength, and a will to violence. He wanted to feel that Spider-Man kind of joy, and he had, while he was up on the rooftop, trying out his moves. But now he was on his way to *use* those moves, to commit an act of violence against a living person, and he didn't feel joyful. He'd seen Marla in action, watched her fight while wearing the cloak (though he hadn't been able to follow the action in any useful way; Mutex and Marla had both been blurs during the battle on the train), and watched her kill without using the cloak at all. B didn't know if he was capable of killing someone that way. The advantage of the cloak was that it removed such conscious concerns from the mind—once B reversed it, his logical, coherent mind would recede, and he would attack whomever he perceived as an enemy. That was liberating, but B didn't think it would ultimately provide much comfort. He had put on a brave face for Marla, but he was terrified both of failing *and* of succeeding. Still, he had to save Rondeau. B lived a mostly lonely existence, because he suffered visions and afflictions that normal people couldn't understand and that he didn't dare share, and he'd found a friend in Rondeau. If it was in his power to help a friend, he would.

B got off the bus near Chinatown, and walked to the street that hid the Celestial's shop.

"I don't know when I've been more terrified," Cole said, as Marla slipped into a narrow space between a bus and a taxi.

"I hate driving," she said, and changed lanes again to get around the cab, which wasn't going fast enough for her taste. "I'm not very good at it." She reached for the gearshift, which wasn't there, because the minivan she'd stolen was an automatic. She nearly threw it into reverse before she noticed. "Shit," she said. "I wish *you* could drive."

"Automobiles were essentially novelty items when I last had occasion to travel," Cole said. "I have never been inside one before, and I can say with assurance that I have never moved at such speeds when I was not actually flying. Even if you were a good driver, I would be terrified." He gripped the edges of his seat with both hands, but otherwise didn't *seem* particularly frightened.

"We're safe," Marla said. "I cast a strong repulsion on the car, to keep the police from bothering me for speeding, and also to help prevent accidents. See?" She swerved left, dangerously close to a silver SUV, which braked suddenly and jigged away from her. "It's literally impossible for another car to hit us. Though I could still conceivably slam into a wall or something— you know, hit stuff that can't move out of the way."

"I am quite relieved," Cole said. Marla saw a sign for the airport and zoomed across two lanes to take the exit. Cole looked out at the system of overpasses and shook his head in wonder. "It's amazing. I haven't really looked at the city in almost forty years. Half my time walking around was just spent gazing at the changes, as much as looking in on you and the other sorcerers. Things have been built up tremendously."

"I thought you went to sleep in 1910 or some-thing."

"Around then," Cole said. "But I have, from time to time, opened my eyes and looked around to make sure the city was still standing."

"What made you choose hibernation?"

"This city is my legacy, the only worthwhile thing I ever helped create. I wanted to see it flourish through the ages." He looked at her sidelong. "Surely you can relate. You have a city of your own, don't you?"

"Yeah, Felport, back east," Marla said. "It was pretty much built before I got there, but I've been try-ing to help it along the way to becoming something better. Which is why I don't appreciate Susan trying to cut me out of existence." She'd explained the particu-lars of her mission to Cole earlier in the drive, and he'd assured her that the Cornerstone could help pro-tect her in the way she'd hoped. Marla hadn't really doubted that, but it was nice to have confirmation.

"I hope she doesn't try to cast the spell again while you're driving," Cole said. "If you disappear, I don't think I'd have much hope of getting this vehicle under control."

Marla nodded. "I hope she doesn't try to cast it again, too, but for somewhat different reasons."

"Mother of God," Cole said, staring out the windshield.

Marla looked. A jetliner was rising into the sky at a steep angle. "Oh, right," she said. "No commercial air travel when you were last up and about, huh?"

"Those things are common?" Cole said, craning his neck to watch the plane ascend.

"Oh, yeah. Hundreds of flights every day. Maybe thousands."

"Is it safe?"

"Safer than driving, from what I understand," Marla said, and whipped the car over into the lane marked "Arrivals," forcing a BMW into scraping the guardrails in the process.

"Indeed," Cole said. "Do we know where we're going?"

"Right there," Marla said, spotting Ch'ang Hao at the curb. He was dressed in a shapeless brown overcoat, and he sat on what appeared to be an antique steamer trunk, his elbows on his knees, his chin in his hands.

Marla parked the stolen minivan at the curb and climbed out. "Ch'ang Hao!" she said. "Sorry you had to wait. Rondeau got kidnapped, and I was in another universe."

Ch'ang Hao stood up and nodded. "Normally I would doubt such excuses, but I trust you would not lie to me. There need be no lies between us. I would have made my way to you on foot, but . . ." He looked around, at the parking garage, the spiraling concrete ramps, and shrugged. "I could not get my bearings. I do not like being surrounded by so much concrete. And I did *not* enjoy flying."

"I don't blame you," Marla said. "Still, better than centuries of bondage at the hands of the Celestial, right?"

"Ultimately," Ch'ang Hao said. "Though there were moments, jammed into the tiny seats, when I thought back fondly on the spaciousness of my prison. The spell you cast enabled me to pass through security unmolested, though I had none of these passports they desired, and their machines beeped at the nails on my harness."

"Did you . . . have any trouble? Once you arrived?"

"I found the serpent," Ch'ang Hao said. He shook his head. "The jungles are being cut and burned. It is shameful." He looked her in the eye. "It makes me look forward to the extinction of man."

"I don't blame you. And you brought the snake back?"

"I did. It is in this trunk, sleeping, dreaming of food and warmth. I did not wish it to be afraid in its last hours of life."

"Thank you, Ch'ang Hao," she said. "Your debt to me is fulfilled."

"I am aware of that. I do not need you to tell me the nature of my obligations. May I trouble you for transport away from this place?"

"Sure thing, if you promise not to kill me while I'm driving. Let's get this trunk into the van."

Ch'ang Hao helped her lift the steamer trunk in, and then he climbed into the backseat. Marla got into the driver's seat in time to hear Cole introduce himself. Ch'ang Hao introduced himself with his customary courtesy.

"Are you going after the Chinese guy again?" Marla asked, pulling away from the curb and driving toward the freeway.

"I owe him a debt of pain," Ch'ang Hao said. "A far greater one than I owe you."

"I should tell you," Marla said, "your former master is the one who kidnapped Rondeau. He demanded that I bring you back to him in exchange for Rondeau's life."

Ch'ang Hao considered that. "Do you intend to do as he asks?"

"No. I doubt I could take you against your will even if I wanted to. I just wanted you to know, your old master might be dead. I had to come get you, and now I've got to go deal with Mutex posthaste, so I sent a friend to rescue Rondeau. Assuming things went well, he probably had to kill the Chinese guy."

"No," Ch'ang Hao said. "My old captor still lives. I would know if he died."

Marla drove in silence for a while. "Shit," she said at last. "Shit. That means B failed. Which means both he and Rondeau are most likely dead."

"I am sorry for your loss, Marla," Cole said.

"Rondeau seemed an honorable man," Ch'ang Hao murmured.

"Yeah," Marla said. This was more than a personal loss, though. B had told her that Rondeau was crucial to her success, and that without him, defeat was assured. If there was ever a time to give up, this was it.

But no. The future wasn't fixed. There were strong possibilities, yes, and maybe the odds were astronomically against her without Rondeau, but that didn't mean she should give up. When there was only one game in town, that was the game you played, even if the odds were against you. "I'm sorry, too. But you know who's going to be *really* sorry? Mutex. If I hadn't had to deal with him, *I* could have gone to save Rondeau. And once I turn Mutex into a splatter on the ground, I'm going to help you out, Ch'ang Hao, and we're going to kill the Chinese guy together. If that's all right with you."

"I respect your wish for vengeance," Ch'ang Hao said, "and you are welcome to join me. He is our common enemy. Any outstanding business between us will be dealt with later. I have many things to attend to before I settle my business with you. I wish to visit the jungles to the south, where my children die with the forests. I hope I can remedy that situation. I may be gone for years, and perhaps you will die while I am otherwise occupied. But if you live . . . I will not forget about you. We will meet again, when all this is over."

"I'll count the days," Marla said. "But right now, I've got to stop Mutex. I don't have time to drop you off anywhere, Ch'ang Hao, so you'll have to come along. I don't expect you to fight with me, though if you want to work off some frustration doing so, you're welcome."

"Perhaps," Ch'ang Hao said. "Where are we going?"

"For a walk in the park," Cole said.

*   *   *

B found the entrance to the Celestial's shop easily, and also saw the golden threads shimmering at chest-height across the doorway. He figured they were meant to be invisible. But B could see through things like that, more and more—apparently his spirit-eyes bene-fited from all the exercise he'd been giving them, as they seemed to grow more acute with each passing hour. It was disconcerting; the corners and shadows of the world increasingly teemed with potential and present spirits, and B could see them all, beating their ragged wings against the membrane that separated this reality from whatever strange lands lay beyond. He could blind himself to the creatures to an extent, let them fade into the background of his awareness, but they never went away completely. His whole life was beginning to resemble one of *those* dreams, full of just-glimpsed mysteries and portentous commonplaces. In a way, it was a relief to be so fully immersed in this un-canny world—he no longer felt on the verge of having a nervous breakdown. He almost felt as if he belonged. None of which made him more comfortable about the prospect of entering a sorcerer's workshop with mur-der in mind.

Ducking beneath the golden threads to avoid set-ting off any traps or tattletales, he crept into the shop as quietly as possible. The wreckage from earlier re-mained, but there were no people inside, at least not in the front room. B stepped carefully through the broken bottles, crushed canisters, and scattered herbs, striving for the stealth and grace he'd often playacted in his movies.

Voices emanated from beyond the twisted, blackened metal counter at the rear of the shop. The concealed door was slightly ajar. B couldn't make out the words coming from behind the door—his extraordinary senses didn't extend into the auditory realm, apparently—but he thought the language might be some sort of Chinese. B crept forward and pushed open the door to the back room a bare quarter of an inch more and peered inside. The room was lit by lanterns with red shades, reminding him uncomfortably of the emergency lights on Bethany's train. In the flickering light, the shadows seemed to squirm. Rondeau was there, past the surgical table, bound to a chair with duct tape, his mouth sealed over. He looked incredibly bored. The Celestial was there, too, along with the apprentice, and seeing how fiercely the younger one gesticulated and spoke, and how submissively the older one nodded and stared down, B had no doubt that Rondeau was right about the older sorcerer stealing the younger one's body. The younger one was really the Celestial, so she was the one B had to destroy. That meant the apprentice would never get her real body back, and that was sad, but B didn't have much choice.

B took a slow breath, preparing himself to reverse the cloak. In that moment, he saw something glimmering in the room beyond, tiny filaments like the ones spread across the door, but while those had been golden, these were red. In the red light they were nearly invisible, even to his eyes, which meant anyone else would have likely walked straight into them. The filaments crisscrossed the front half of the room thoroughly, from wall to wall and ceiling to floor, forming a somewhat messy grid that cut B off from Rondeau and the others as surely as a wire fence would have. He didn't know what they did, but he suspected it was nothing good. If the golden wires at the front door had been meant merely to notify the Celestial of Marla's arrival, then these red wires were likely meant for uglier purposes.

What was B supposed to do *now*? The cloak gave him great power, but of a strictly physical nature. If he couldn't get to the sorcerer, he couldn't hurt him, and that meant he didn't have any edge at all.

"Marla!" the Celestial shouted. "I hear you breathing, you sneaking creeping bitch. You've come early. Enter, and bring Ch'ang Hao so that I may leash him."

There wasn't much point in trying to run away, and B at least had the element of surprise—or, at least, bewildering inexplicability—on his side. He pushed open the door and stepped in, careful to keep far back from the red filaments.

"You are not Marla," the Celestial said. "But you are wearing her clothes. Don't tell me she sent an apprentice to deal with me."

"Why not?" B said. "You're talking to me through your apprentice, aren't you?" He looked toward the old man. There was no reason to let the Celestial know that B was aware of his body-swapping tendencies. Marla hadn't told him much about the ways of sorcerers, but she had made it clear that a secret was something to be held and valued.

"My master does not wish to sully his lips by speaking the foul bitch's name," the Celestial said smoothly. "Come closer, apprentice, so that I may give you a message to take to your bitch mistress."

"I'm okay standing here, thanks," B said. It occurred to him, distantly, that he was terrified. His stomach fluttered with something like stage fright, which he hadn't experienced on an actual stage in many years. But he kept his posture relaxed, his voice clear and firm, using the tools of acting that he'd put away but never forgotten. Rondeau's eyes were wide, doubtless trying to convey to B that there was a trap here, don't come any closer, but B had already figured that out, so he nodded to Rondeau in a friendly way. "Anyway," B said. "Marla had some business to take care of, so she sent me to chat with you."

"I will bear no further insults," the Celestial said, eyes narrowing, small pale hands curled into fists. B wondered if the old sorcerer had always been so prone to rages, or if switching bodies had made his mind fracture. When Rondeau had told B about the Thing on the Doorstep trick, he said that could happen, that the trauma of moving the psyche to a new body could create anything from hairline fractures to great gaping chasms in the mental landscape. "She cannot trifle with me. She *will* come, she *will* bring back Ch'ang Hao, whom she stole from me, she will come *now.*"

B's eyes were adjusted to the dimness now, but the shadows continued their squirming, and he frowned, because the shadowy movements didn't seem related to the flickering of the lamplight. He squinted, and suddenly the movements took on sense. There were spirits here, dozens of them, possibly more, twisting and writhing. There were creatures with fangs and night-blue faces, sinuous dragon-shapes, coiled serpents, a one-legged bird, a stag with a huge rack of antlers, a grotesque toad—but the majority were human, wearing robes, faces twisted in a range of expressions that seemed to run from disappointment to fury.

And every one of them was turned toward the Celestial, who was still shouting about Marla's injustices. A crackling field of energy was forming around the Celestial, especially the hands and forearms, and B realized with surprise that he could actually *see* the sorcerer gathering energy. He'd seen something similar with Marla on Bethany's train, a whitish mist forming around her as she'd prepared to freeze the poison frogs solid, but he hadn't really understood. The Celestial was about to do something, cast some spell, and B had to stop him.

"Hey!" he shouted, speaking not to Rondeau, or the Celestial, or the elderly apprentice, but to the spirits who churned just beneath the skin of existence. Every one of them snapped to attention and looked at B, most of them exhibiting shock, a few smiling bitterly. "You can come out," B said. "I'll help you."

"Who are you talking to, lickspittle?" the Celestial said, and the crackling black energy hid his hands completely now.

"Them," B said, and spread his arms in a gesture of welcome. He reached out to these ghosts and fragments, the way he reached for spirits and oracles, and he felt them respond.

The spirits burst into greater visibility, and though they were still insubstantial, still flickering on the edges, everyone could see them now. They strode out of the corners toward the Celestial, and where their bodies touched the red filaments the wires snapped harmlessly and disappeared. The Celestial backed away, his gathered magic forgotten and dissipating, his eyes wide. "Ancestors," he said. "Honored ancestors, you misunderstand, these things I've done, I had no choice, I meant no harm to you or your memories. . . ."

The spirits didn't speak. They just *pressed in,* squeezing in a tight knot around the Celestial, who shrank away, hunching onto the ground and covering his head. They did not strike him—B doubted that they could—but they hissed, barely audible, and they *looked,* and they *whispered,* and whatever they said made the Celestial shake his head and moan. The apprentice in the old man's body stood back, looking at the creature, expression completely unreadable.

B wondered what the spirits were. The Celestial's actual ancestors? Or phantasms of guilt or madness that B had given a sort of temporary life? Whatever they were, they seemed to have the Celestial occupied, and so B hurried to Rondeau and began stripping the tape away. When he tore off the duct tape from Rondeau's mouth, Rondeau said, "Is Marla dead?"

"Not last time I saw her," B said, unbinding Rondeau's ankles. "She wanted to come herself, but we got the word from an oracle about when Mutex was going to make his move, and it's *soon,* so she had to go deal with that."

"She gave you her cloak?" Rondeau said, stunned. "So you could come save *me?*"

"Yeah. Not that the cloak turned out to do much good."

"I think you did all right on your own," Rondeau said, looking toward the Celestial, who was dimly visible through the translucent mass of angry ancestors berating him for his crimes. "But we need to find her and give her back this cloak. She's a badass even without it, and normally she doesn't wear it, but this is some serious high-stakes shit we're in." He shook his head. "I can't believe she gave you her cloak."

"Well, I told her I'd had a vision about you, and that if you died, we wouldn't possibly be able to defeat Mutex."

"Damn it," Rondeau said. "I wish you hadn't told me that, B. I don't need that kind of pressure. I got kidnapped last night, and it's been a long-ass day."

"Don't worry," B said. "I didn't have a vision about you. I lied. I just wanted Marla to send me to rescue you."

"B," Rondeau said, with real admiration. "You must be one stone-cold liar, to fool Marla."

"I *did* used to be an actor," he said.

"And here I thought you got all your roles because of your good looks."

"The good looks didn't hurt," B said. "But I'm a man of many talents."

"Right. Speaking of your many talents...Are those ghosts and ghost-monsters and whatnot going to kill the Chinese guy?"

"I think they'd like to, but I don't think they can." In fact, the spirits were fading away, though the Celestial was still curled on the floor, apparently frightened into catatonia. Without his conscious attention, the spirits seemed to have difficulty holding their shape, even with B's help.

"In that case," Rondeau said. "Hey, apprentice!"

The apprentice looked at Rondeau.

"You've got every herb known to man and a few that aren't in this place, right?" Rondeau said.

The apprentice nodded.

"Then go, quick, and mix up something that'll put your master to sleep for a good long while. I don't trust him to stay curled up for long." The apprentice nodded again and hurried toward the front room, as well as she could in the old man's body.

Rondeau stood up and stretched, the bones in his spine cracking audibly. "I've been tied to this chair for fucking *hours*," Rondeau said, glaring at the prone Celestial. "If I weren't afraid of waking him up, I'd go give that bastard a kick." He grinned. "Assuming we don't get killed by Mutex and the golden frog all-stars, I'm going to *make* Marla help me, and we're going to do the Thing on the Doorstep trick again, and put things right. We're going to give the apprentice her body back."

B clapped Rondeau on the shoulder. "I think that's a good idea. But, ah...isn't there a chance it'll drive her insane?"

Rondeau nodded. "Yeah. There is. She knows that. But she wants us to do it. I think being in that dried-up old body is driving her crazy anyway."

The apprentice returned with a steaming cup of something, and paused long enough to look at Rondeau. He nodded at her. "Yeah," he said. "We're going to get you your body back."

The apprentice smiled. It was the first recognizable expression she'd made since B arrived. He went to help her tip the sleeping potion down her former master's throat.

19

Marla parked the van just inside one of the southern entrances to Golden Gate Park. "Snake time," she said, and climbed into the backseat next to Ch'ang Hao, then clambered over that seat into the rear compartment, where the steamer trunk rested. Marla flipped open the latches and opened the lid. The trunk was filled with green leaves, and smelled strongly of humidity and black earth. A long snake lay atop the leaves, green banded with red, a color scheme Marla recognized from Mutex's shorts. She'd settle for something a little less tailored. She glanced at Ch'ang Hao, who was pointedly not looking at her. She muttered a brief, nonspecific prayer of thanks, and then snapped the snake's spine. It didn't even wake up. She drew her dagger of office and slit the snake open along its belly, then peeled off its skin as deftly as she would peel a banana. "Hand me my bag, would you, Ch'ang Hao?"

Without turning, he passed her leather bag back. Marla opened a side pocket and retrieved a bone needle and black thread. She folded the snakeskin along its length, so that the moist inside didn't show at all, and quickly sewed it up. Then she sewed the ends together, making a loop like a snakeskin belt. She pressed the snakeskin against her face, letting the scales touch her open eyes, and whispered an incantation. Then she tasted the snakeskin with the tip of her tongue, leaving a generous dollop of saliva on the skin. She slipped the loop of snakeskin over her arms and her head, twisting awkwardly in the low space at the back of the van, until it rested around her waist like a belt. Marla pulled up her shirt and let the snakeskin touch the skin of her belly and hips, then put her shirt back down over it. "There," she said. "Now I've got nothing to fear from frogs."

"Not little poison ones anyway," Cole said from the front seat. "Giant monstrous frogs from Aztec mythology might still prove difficult."

"I'm not worried," Marla said, climbing back to the driver's seat, feeling the snakeskin shift against her body as she moved. "I've got a lot of rage I need to work off, and I've got the help of the greatest sorcerer since Merlin, right?"

"Hmm," Cole said. "As to that, I *have* been sleeping for the better part of a century, Marla. And while I am not wholly defenseless, do not expect much from me in the way of offensive capability. I have always been a cautious sorcerer, and while I will admit without false modesty that I have achieved great things, those feats always required careful preparations. I have never been much good in the heat of battle—at least, not unless I had ample time to lay a suitably ingenious ambush first. I am at your service, but there is a good reason that I sought you out, rather than going to dispose of Mutex myself."

"Oh," Marla said, feeling her furious courage abate slightly. She'd expected this to be an easy op, with Cole giving her support, but if he didn't have much to offer in the way of firepower . . . She looked at Ch'ang Hao. "So, big guy. Any chance you'd be willing to help me in the havoc to come?"

"I do not shy away from battle," Ch'ang Hao said, "but I have had my fill of fighting for others. My former masters often used me so."

"And let's not forget who *liberated* you from your former masters," Marla said. She regretted it as soon as the words were spoken. It was a stupid, insulting thing to say, and she never would have slipped like that if she'd been well rested, if she'd been back home, if she wasn't thinking about B and Rondeau dead at the Celestial's hands, if . . .

"That debt has been discharged," Ch'ang Hao said coldly. "I fulfilled my duty. Do not think to—"

"You're right, I'm sorry, it was a shitty thing to say," Marla said, holding up her hands. "Mea culpa. Look, if I cut your harness now . . . will you forget about killing me? Call it even?"

"You would cut me free now only to save yourself. I am disgusted by the suggestion, and I am finished making bargains with you. I reject your offer." He looked briefly upward, then back down at her. "Nevertheless, I will fight by your side."

"Why?"

"I will try to keep you alive, so that when I have fulfilled my other responsibilities, I may return, and take your life myself."

"How do I know you won't try to kill me while I'm distracted with Mutex?"

"You have my word that I will not attempt to take your life on this day," he said solemnly. "On another day, yes. But not this one."

"I'd hoped we could get past this," Marla said. "That I could make you understand why I've done the things I've done. That we could be . . . friends."

"The moment you used me as a tool, you closed off any possibility of the two of us becoming friends. Did you never think that, had you set me free out of kindness, I would have counted you a friend, and helped you out of kindness in return? Instead, you *bought* me. And now you've killed one of my children, and ornamented yourself with his skin. Imagine if I had killed Rondeau before your eyes, and dressed myself in the torn remnants of his flesh. That is what I have just watched *you* do. I know you had your reasons, but that does not change my response. No, Marla. We will not be friends." He shifted his huge bulk on the seat. "This space is confining. I will be outside." He opened the van door and stepped out, into the afternoon sun.

Marla looked out the windshield. "This is no kind of January," she said. "There should be wind, snow, ice. Look how clear it is."

"I grew up in the woods of Canada," Cole said. "I cannot say I mind the lack of snow here." He glanced out the passenger-side window, to where Ch'ang Hao stood impassively near some bushes, on the edge of the vastness that was Golden Gate Park. "You are a brave woman, to make a god your enemy."

"I didn't mean to make him my enemy. But I guess

I didn't come close to doing enough to make him my friend."

"Regret is a heavy burden," Cole said.

"If I feel regret, that means I'm still alive, so I'm all for it. We should get going. The Tea Garden's that way, according to the map." Rondeau had circled the Tea Garden on the map—it was one of the places he'd wanted to visit. *I should have let him come*, Marla thought. *I shouldn't have given him such a hard time.* And that was the closest she would let herself come to mourning for now.

"And you're just going to . . . rush in?"

"You know another way to get where we're going?"

"It might be worthwhile to observe our enemy's position from a distance, don't you think?"

Marla shook her head. "I wish. Mutex has hidden himself well. That's part of why he kept getting the drop on the other sorcerers—they couldn't tell *when* he was coming or *where* he was coming from. Once he got the Cornerstone, he made it so clairvoyance, divination, clairaudience, everything fails when it comes to him."

"Ah, but we know where he is now," Cole said. "The Japanese Tea Garden, yes?"

"So?" Marla said. "How does that help it?"

"This is *my city*, Marla," Cole said mildly, and Marla felt a sudden fierce kinship with him—this *was* his city, just as Marla's city was *her* own. Those other sorcerers, with their ruling council, had just been acting as Cole's regents, though they hadn't realized it. "Nothing can be hidden from me here," Cole said. "I can look upon any part of my city, and no power on this Earth or under it can prevent me from doing so. Do you have a mirror?"

Marla opened her bag and lifted out a wad of Styrofoam, bubble wrap, and clear packaging tape. Some sorcerers—Susan, for instance—had ornate hand-mirrors with mother-of-pearl backs inlaid with jewels, but Marla's scrying mirror was just a shard from a shaving mirror that had belonged to Sauvage, the sorcerer who'd ruled her city before Marla's tenure. She unwrapped the packaging and revealed the long, triangular sliver of reflective glass.

"This has passed through powerful hands," Cole said approvingly, lifting the glass gently and letting it rest on the upturned palms of his hands. He looked into the glass. "See," he said, and Marla looked.

The glass showed the walled Japanese Tea Garden from above, an image that grew larger when Cole murmured over it, the view zooming past pagodas, stone bridges, paths, and trees. There were bodies, too—dead tourists, dead staff, all with their chests cut open and their hearts removed. The blood still glistened. They'd died recently.

Then Mutex appeared in the glass. He held a heart in each hand and squeezed them, blood running out of his fists and spattering the earth around the base of a bigger-than-life-sized bronze Buddha. A pile of blood-speckled fruit—peaches, oranges, strawberries, lemons, and more—lay near the statue. Mutex's wicker basket was on the ground, open, and yellow frogs carpeted the ground around him, hopping from place to place. A gauzy charm of hummingbirds hovered above him like the roof of a ruby-colored tent.

"That statue of the Buddha was not here the last

time I saw the park," Cole said. "What is that near its feet?"

The image enlarged, revealing a hole at the Buddha's feet, a hole that was filling with blood. "There's something buried in the hole," Cole said.

"A statue," Marla said, remembering the statue of Tlaltecuhtli that had been stolen from the gallery. "It's the image of the god he's trying to raise. He's feeding it blood."

"He's dripping blood over the Buddha, too," Cole said. They both looked into the glass, captivated, as Mutex smeared handfuls of blood and soil over the bronze Buddha's belly.

"Most of the Buddhists I know are fairly easygoing people," Marla said. "But I think this level of blasphemy would annoy even them."

"The small statue is an offering," Cole said. "Perhaps a remembrance—something to awaken the spirit of Tlaltecuhtli and help it recall its true form. But the Buddha is the seed crystal. You see? The god can't appear without a body, it needs some physical form at its center. It's the same way an oyster needs a bit of grit inside it to form the center of a pearl. The Buddha is made of forged metal, a substance drawn up from the treasury of the Earth, which is appropriate for the god Mutex hopes to raise."

"And from a distance, if the light isn't good, a Buddha in the lotus position is shaped sort of like a sitting frog," Marla said.

"It takes a certain amount of imagination to see *that*," Cole said, "but I suspect you're right. We're looking at the inner core of a god."

"But where's the *Cornerstone*?" Marla said. "I don't see it."

"There," Cole said, and the view moved beneath a long bridge. The Cornerstone sat beneath the bridge, warping the light around it, surrounded by a ruby mist of hummingbirds.

Ch'ang Hao knocked on the passenger window, startling both of them. "Will we be going soon?" he asked.

Cole looked at Marla. She nodded, and they both got out of the van.

"You took the *bus* here?" Rondeau said, standing outside the Celestial's shop, still looking around for the car that didn't exist.

"I don't own a car," B said.

Rondeau shook his head. "I'm sitting there being tortured—well, I wasn't, but I *could* have been—and you don't even steal a car?"

"I could maybe just manage to steal a car if it still had the keys in it," B said. "But unless the door was unlocked, I'd probably hurt my elbow busting in the window. I'm not actually skilled in the criminal arts."

"Fine, sure," Rondeau said. "Let's find a car. That one'll do." He hurried over to a blue two-door coupe. B followed, wondering if Rondeau was really about to rip off a car in broad daylight.

Rondeau grabbed the driver's-side handle and tugged. The door popped open, and Rondeau grinned. He slipped in and unlocked the passenger door for B, who got in with him. "I don't know much magic," Rondeau said. "Just the Cursing, which is more a natural talent, like being able to burp the alphabet or turn your eyelids inside out. But I do know how to open shit. I learned how to do it with picks and jimmys and everything first, because Marla's a big believer in self-sufficiency without spells, but once I had that down, she taught me the shortcuts." As he spoke, he pulled out the ashtray and tossed it in the backseat, then reached into the cavity revealed and did something with the wires inside. The engine roared to life. Rondeau sat up, threw the car into gear, and drove.

"Don't you feel guilty about stealing a car?" B said.

"Nah," Rondeau said. "Especially not when it's a rental." He tapped a sheaf of papers clipped to the visor. "And *especially* especially not when I'm on a mission to help save the world. Even if I'm not actually crucial to that mission."

"I didn't have a vision about you," B said. "But that doesn't mean you don't have a role to play. We can both help Marla."

"Doomed to be a best supporting actor," Rondeau said. "It's a hell of a life. Where are we going?"

"Oh, right, the Japanese Tea Garden, in the park. I don't drive much, but I think I can figure it out—"

"I got it," Rondeau said, expertly piloting the car through the maze of one-way streets and double-parked obstacles that filled this part of the city. "I was excited about coming to San Francisco. I memorized all the maps."

"*All* the maps?"

"You're not the only one with natural talents," said Rondeau.

* * *

Marla and Cole crept toward the closed gates of the
Japanese Tea Garden, and Ch'ang Hao walked softly a
short distance behind them. A painted sign hanging on
the gate read "Closed for Maintenance," probably
something Mutex had found tucked in a shed somewhere. Marla closed her eyes, trying to visualize the
layout of the garden as she'd seen it from above in the
glass. "Mutex is toward the northwest, near the center
of the gardens. We can go northeast and slip around
past the actual tea house—there's lots of cover there,
hedges, and the gift shop—and get pretty close to him
without being seen, I bet."

"It's as good a plan as any," Cole said.

"Watch out for frogs," she said.

"I shall."

"Are the frogs going to be a problem for you,
Ch'ang Hao?" she asked.

Hao sniffed. "Frogs. No. I have nothing to fear
from frogs. My kind eat them."

Marla pushed on the gate. It was locked. She
pressed her hand against the wood, concentrated, and
was rewarded a moment later with the snap of a lock
and latch giving way on the other side. She pushed
open the gate, just wide enough to admit her, and
looked inside.

The Tea Garden was beautiful, and cultivated
enough that it didn't discomfort Marla the way nature
usually did. There were pebbled paths, graceful
bridges, running water, creeks, and statuary, all visible from where Marla stood. There was also a dead
tourist in khaki shorts lying in one of the pathways,

but that only detracted slightly from the beauty. She beckoned Cole and Ch'ang Hao, then slipped inside.

The atmosphere inside the gate struck her instantly—heavy, electric, crackling, roiling. There was deep magic happening here, or *about* to happen. Cole sensed it, too. "There's more to this than raising a god," he said. "That's the weight in the air, but I *smell* something else, another spell. Mutex is trying to do something more."

Before he could elaborate, the hummingbirds came. Perhaps Mutex had seen them and sent the birds, or perhaps the birds acted autonomously. They descended from the sky and hung before Marla and her allies, forming a ruby fence eight feet high, their bodies and invisibly thrumming wings fitted as neatly together as if they were an Escher print of interlocking birds. Marla tried to move around them, but the birds moved with her, staying in front of her, keeping her from moving forward. "Flank them," she said, and Cole and Ch'ang Hao moved off to either side.

More hummingbirds descended, and now they arrayed themselves in a semicircle, hemming in Marla, Cole, and Ch'ang Hao.

"Birds," Hao said contemptuously, and struck them with his fist.

He gasped and pulled his hand back, eyes wide. His knuckles were torn, leaking a yellowish substance. Snake god's blood.

"They're not just birds," Marla said. "They're the spirits of dead warriors, and they're the next best thing to indestructible. Rondeau managed to kill some, by Cursing at them, but I don't know how we can." She shook her head. "We've got to get around them." The birds hung before her, a multitude of tiny black eyes fixed on her face.

"Marla," Cole said, and when she looked at him, she was deeply unnerved to see naked fear in his expression. "I've figured out what the other spell is. I know what else Mutex is trying to do."

Beyond the nearly opaque wall of hummingbirds, something gave a throaty roar.

"Hold up," Rondeau said. "Gas station. Give me a minute." He pulled into the lot and parked the car at an inconsiderate angle across two spaces, and ran into the convenience store before B could protest. He returned a moment later carrying two cans of hairspray and a handful of cheap, translucent lighters.

"Planning to do your hair and smoke some cigarettes?" B said when Rondeau jumped back in.

"Nah," he said. "I've been thinking about Mutex and his menagerie. He's got frogs, yeah, they get all the hype, but he's also got hummingbirds, and those little bastards are all but unkillable. I Cursed a couple of them, and that killed them, but I was thinking about what *happened* when I Cursed them—they burst into flame. And Hamil told us that the hummingbirds were warriors for the sun god. So I'm thinking, blades don't kill them, beating the shit out of them doesn't kill them, but *maybe . . .*"

"Fire," B said. "Got it. And the hairspray and lighters are the classic ingredients for a homemade B-movie flamethrower that's as likely to explode in your face as anything else."

"You see?" Rondeau said. "Maybe I'm going to be indispensable to the fate of the world after all."

Moments later they reached the park. Rondeau double-parked just inside the gate—it was easy to do that, B reflected, when you didn't have to worry about getting a parking ticket—and started running flat-out in the direction of the Tea Garden.

B hurried after him. Rondeau didn't strike him as the running type. He seemed better suited to sauntering, strolling, or possibly swaggering. Since he was running, B figured it was a good idea for him to run, too, even if he did feel a little ridiculous with Marla's cloak flapping out behind him.

"Marlita!"

Marla turned, and there beyond the half-open gate was Rondeau, grinning, running, and carrying (rather improbably) a couple of aerosol cans. B was behind him, puffing as he ran.

"Rondeau," she said. "Rondeau! Why aren't you dead?"

"B played the cavalry," he said, and winked. "Because I'm so crucial to the fate of the world, you know."

"Don't let it go to your head," she said. "Is the Celestial dead?"

"No," Ch'ang Hao and Rondeau said, simultaneously.

B approached Marla, looking sidelong at the wall of birds. He unhooked her cloak and handed it over. "I didn't even get blood on it," he said. "I, ah, dealt with things another way."

"You'll have to tell me about that, if we survive the afternoon," she said, wrapping the cloak around her shoulders. "Right now we've got a wall of birds between us and our target, Tlaltecuhtli is stirring, and I think Cole was just about to tell me some *more* bad news."

"Cole?" Rondeau said. "I wondered who the old guy was. Nice to meet you. You're shit at following people discreetly, though, I gotta say."

"Yes," Cole said, "I suppose so. Formal introductions can wait. Listen to me. Mutex is raising the frog-monster, yes, but he's prepared *another* spell as well. He's going to cast a spell of psychic transposition."

B and Rondeau looked at him blankly, and Ch'ang Hao looked at him with the disinterest of a snake watching the strange capering of mammals it wasn't quite ready to eat. But Marla understood. "The Thing on the Doorstep trick."

"What?" Rondeau said. "Who's he going to switch brains with?"

"Tlaltecuhtli," Marla said, coldness spreading inside her, making her feel like a sort of animate statue of herself. "Mutex isn't just raising the god. He's going to *become* the god. He's going to take control of the god's body, and leave the god's mind in his human one."

"And because he's using the Cornerstone, he won't go insane, and the switch will be permanent," Cole said.

"Fuck," Rondeau said. "We can't have *that*." He handed an aerosol can to B, and holding the other in his left hand, marched up to the wall of humming-birds. He flicked on the lighter and depressed the button on the can, moving the flame into the spray. A modest gout of fire shot forth from the can, but the effect was dramatic—the birds touched by the flame fell, smoking and flapping, and while other birds moved in to fill the vacant positions, Rondeau kept sweeping the flame over them, and the fence grew thin. B stepped up at a different place on the fence and lit his own homemade flamethrower, turning his face away and wincing—sensibly, Marla thought, since there was a good chance that the flame would travel back up the spray and the can would explode in his hand.

"Rondeau, that's perfect!" B was right—Rondeau *was* crucial here. Fire had killed the birds before, and it would kill them again. "But I can do better than white-trash flamethrowers." Marla had just done this spell yesterday, so it was easier to do it now, with the mental patterns fresh in her memory. She sucked the remaining heat from the dead bodies inside the garden, but that wasn't enough to do anything noticeable with—and then she thought to steal heat directly from the hummingbirds. They were small, but there were lots of them, so maybe there'd be enough heat.

Once she tapped into the hummingbirds, she gasped. It was like she'd tried to draw heat from a campfire and found a volcano instead—the birds contained astonishing amounts of energy, heat bound up in their ruby breasts. She felt her temperature rapidly rising into the danger zone, and she flung heat back at the birds.

Rondeau and B shouted and dove out of the way as the hummingbirds all burst simultaneously into flame, showering onto the ground in smoking ruin.

Marla nudged one of the hummingbirds with her foot. She looked around at her companions, and showed her teeth. This was it. This was the kind of shit she lived for, what she got out of bed in the morning hoping for and went to bed at night dreaming of. "Onward and inward," she said. "And keep clear of the frogs, if you're not a snake god like Ch'ang Hao or wearing a magical snake-belt like me."

Since they'd already blown the element of surprise, Marla went straight up the path that led to Mutex. In seconds the Buddha was in sight, but it was no longer even remotely Buddha-like. It had grown to twice its former size and now towered nearly twenty feet high. Its features had softened and run, and it was no longer recognizably anything, just a squat, bulging bronze shape, vaguely froglike in its proportions. It *did* have a mouth, though, gaping big enough to swallow a bread box, with darkness inside. Mutex stood before it, surrounded by yellow frogs, his body streaked with blood. His back was arched, his head thrown back in an ecstasy of worship, his arms raised high. A flock of hummingbirds floated over the changing statue. They now carried the Cornerstone suspended from silver chains, just as they had on Strawberry Hill, but they hovered above the newborn frog god.

The smell of rotting vegetation was overwhelming.

Still running, Marla cried, "Mutex! This is for Lao Tsung!"

Mutex made no indication that he'd heard her, but he did sweep his arms down in a grand, maestrolike gesture.

When he did, the hovering hummingbirds flew off in a dozen different directions at once, severing the ties that held the Cornerstone. The stone—Marla's one hope for survival, the reason she'd gotten mixed up in all this madness anyway, the ultimate goal of this entire ordeal—fell straight into the ur-Tlaltecuhtli's vast, moaning mouth.

The frog-statue closed its mouth, and visibly swallowed.

The Cornerstone was gone.

Without breaking stride, Marla reversed her cloak.

With his superior vision, B could see right away that it wasn't Mutex anymore, that his *genius* had left his *loci* and successfully switched bodies with the ever-expanding Tlaltecuhtli at the exact moment that the Cornerstone fell into the monster's open mouth. But Marla didn't notice. She transformed into a beast, a jaguar of deep purple shadows, and in half a bound she'd crushed a dozen frogs underfoot, and in another leap she was on top of what *had* been Mutex.

B tried to imagine what Tlaltecuhtli must be experiencing—to have returned to consciousness after so long, to have felt burgeoning strength, and then to suddenly be confined in a small body, and, mere seconds later, to be torn to pieces by an enraged woman who'd just watched her only hope for ongoing life fall into a monster's mouth.

The purple shadow-beast abruptly disappeared, replaced by Marla cloaked in white, crouching amid the remains of Mutex's body. Small golden frogs jumped all around her, but she paid them no mind. Marla looked up at Tlaltecuhtli, who was now close to thirty feet high and spreading in every direction, crushing bushes and bridges and statues as he expanded. The bronze of the Buddha had changed to something closer to green flesh, and distinct limbs were forming, expanding out from the central mass. There was no sign yet of Mutex's consciousness, but he was in there, B knew, and once the monster was fully formed, he would strike with zeal and calculation, as Mutex had in his smaller form. B could already see the vague outlines of the gargantuan monster he and Marla had seen after their visit to the Possible Witch. Marla backed away, staring up at the frog-monster, her face empty of emotion, but B could see that she knew, that she understood that Mutex's mind still lived on. But he didn't know what, if anything, she could do about it.

"I wish..." Cole said, looking down at the golden frogs that covered the ground between them and Marla. He clenched his hands into fists. "I wish I could *do* something."

Rondeau gazed up at the frog-monster, and for once, he didn't look bored at all. He looked terrified.

Ch'ang Hao was methodically stomping on the poison dart frogs and kicking their remains aside. He went to stand beside Marla, and the two of them studied the swelling frog-monster like surveyors looking over a bit of rocky landscape. Marla spoke to Ch'ang Hao—B couldn't hear the words—and the snake god shook his head, grinding another frog under his foot as he did so.

After the alien intelligence receded, and Marla was no longer occupied by trying to figure out the best way to kill Ch'ang Hao for his earlier threats, she said, "I'm fucked." She had to shout over the sounds coming from Tlaltecuhtli, the occasional moans and the constant low sounds of meat stretching.

"I see toes," Ch'ang Hao said, his deep voice carrying easily over the noise. "And the beginning of fingers. There are mouths appearing on the elbows and knees. Once this creature assumes its form, it will begin killing. And once it kills, it will grow larger. That is the way of such gods." He sounded completely indifferent, and she supposed he was—he didn't care if humankind and all its works were destroyed. He likely hoped they would be.

"I can't fight this thing," Marla said. "I can't attack it any more than I could attack the Golden Gate Bridge, any more than I could kill the *moon*. In a few more minutes, we're going to get crushed just from the way this motherfucker is expanding. It's Mutex in there, too. I just ripped apart the *real* Tlaltecuhtli. I saw it in its eyes. Poor thing was confused—didn't understand what the hell was going on. I actually felt sorry for it." She did now anyway—she hadn't felt much of anything when she'd killed it, or for a little while afterward, until the cloak's effect wore off.

"There are few humans who can claim to have killed a god," Ch'ang Hao said. "Even by accident. You continue to accumulate distinctions." The flatness of his tone did more to advertise his hatred for her than any amount of anger would have.

"I know your opinion of me isn't as high as it could be," Marla said. "I wish I could do something about that." She backed away from the creature's expanding girth, and Ch'ang Hao moved with her.

"I comprehend fully what you are, Marla. I understand the reasons behind your actions. But they earn you no love from me, and I *will* kill you, if I can. I am saddened at the prospect of this frog-monster killing you first."

Marla nodded. She considered her options. There was really only one.

The weapon is not responsible for the action of its wielder, Marla thought. Like she'd told B on the hotel roof earlier—it is not the sword that kills, but the wielder.

And now Ch'ang Hao was her only sword, albeit a sword that would try to cut its wielder, in time. Even if she managed to stop Susan from deleting her from reality—and with the Cornerstone swallowed up like an after-dinner mint, how could she ever do *that*?— she'd have to contend with Ch'ang Hao's eventual attack. If she used him as a weapon now, he would not love her for it, and he would be a far more formidable foe later, too.

"Ah, well," Marla said. "Dead now or dead later, the only difference is the fate of the whole goddamned world. Fuck it." She drew her dagger of office and slid the blade between Ch'ang Hao's shoulder blade and the nail-studded harness the Celestial had bound him in. With a flick of her wrist, Marla cut the strap, and then repeated the motion at the other shoulder.

Ch'ang Hao looked down at her. "I hope you do not expect thanks."

"I think we both know why I just did that," Marla said.

"I could kill you now," he said. "You could not stand against me."

"But you gave me your word you wouldn't kill me

today. And you won't. Because you're honorable. And even though I'm *not* honorable in your eyes, you'll keep your word. And while I certainly can't *compel* you to fight this giant monster, I will point out that if you don't kill Tlaltecuhtli, he'll kill me, and then you won't get the opportunity."

"Your words are, as always, true and perceptive." Ch'ang Hao tore off the harness, copper nails popping out of his flesh, yellowish blood briefly welling from dozens of small punctures before they healed over. And then, finally unbound, Ch'ang Hao did what he had not done for centuries. He began to grow.

"My God," Cole said, when Marla reached him. "He—he—he's a *giant*."

"It's his thing," Rondeau said. "He gets bigger. He says he can grow just big enough to defeat whoever he's fighting."

"I suggest we retreat," Marla said. "Because to beat Mutex, aka Mr. Toad, Ch'ang Hao will have to get *plenty* big. Let's go." She began running for the gate, and the others followed after her.

Marla had just dealt Mutex his death blow. It was all over now but the drama. She'd fired the gun; Ch'ang Hao was nothing but the bullet. Normally, this moment would have filled Marla with the exhilaration of watching a victory unfold, but her joy was tempered by the fact that, in a day or two at most, Susan was going to edit her right out of existence.

Still. As she'd said to Ch'ang Hao—fuck it. Even if she was going to disappear in a few hours, it felt good to run *now*.

*　*　*

Marla, B, Cole, and Rondeau sat beneath a tree and watched Ch'ang Hao battle Mutex in the light of the afternoon sun. Rondeau had acquired an apple from somewhere, and he sliced off pieces with his butterfly knife. "It's like the best Godzilla movie ever," Rondeau said. "Hey, B, you must still know people in Hollywood, you've got to get this turned into a movie."

Ch'ang Hao, who stood quite a bit taller than the trees around him, pummeled Mutex, who was still not fully formed. His halo of hummingbirds tried to strike Ch'ang Hao, but the snake god threw mystical asps at them. Ch'ang Hao ripped off one of Mutex's arms and flung it onto the ground, where it transformed into a pile of mud and moss.

"I wonder how the civic authorities are going to explain this?" B said. "It looks like most of the people in the park have taken off, but I'm sure there are still dozens of people watching this."

"Beings such as these cannot be photographed," Cole said. "And most of the ordinaries won't remember this very well. Those that do won't be able to report it accurately, and all their stories will conflict with one another. The dead in the Tea Garden will be put down to mass murder. Some of the watchers will go mad." He shrugged. "It is a steep price, but better than the alternative."

Ch'ang Hao flung the one-armed Mutex to the ground, and the Earth shook.

"Earthquake," B said. "Only a little one, though."

"Ch'ang *is* fighting a primordial earth-monster," Marla said. "Even if it's only a baby one."

"Mr. Toad is kind of a shitty fighter," Rondeau said.

"That's the problem with taking over someone else's body," Marla said. "People are used to their *own* bodies. It's tough adjusting to a new one, I bet. Especially when your old body was human and your new body is a rapidly growing frog with too many mouths. I'm surprised he can control the body well enough to stumble around at all."

"Mutex could have been immortal," Cole said. "If he'd been allowed to take on his full size, he would have been unimaginably formidable. Mutex's plan was a good one. An evil one, of course, yes, but a *good* one."

"He shouldn't have taken something I needed," Marla said. "I would have left him alone if he hadn't taken the Cornerstone. Until he tried to expand his theocracy too far east anyway."

Ch'ang Hao twisted off Mutex's head and flung it to the ground, where it exploded in a geyser of vegetation, creeping vines and big, waxy, white flowers. The frog-body shuddered, slumped, and became a mound of dirt. Ch'ang Hao looked at the remains of his vanquished foe for a moment, then began shrinking. He was soon out of sight below the tree line.

"Think the collapsing god managed to smother all the poison dart frogs?" Marla asked.

"I will find out," Cole said. "Perhaps I can enlist Ch'ang Hao to crush any that remain. And I will find that odd basket Mutex had as well. It may simply be enchanted, but it could also be an artifact, and those are always useful."

Marla took off the snakeskin belt and laid it on the

grass. "Cole, could you give this to Ch'ang Hao? So he can, I don't know, give it a proper burial or whatever?"

"I don't think the gesture will make him forgive you," Cole said.

"Yeah," Marla said. "I don't expect it to. How many mortal enemies does this make now, Rondeau?"

Rondeau hummed and counted off on his fingers. "Do we count the Rummage twins as one mortal enemy or two?"

"Two, I guess. They've got separate issues with me."

"I count thirty-five, then," Rondeau said. "But most of them are shit. Not like Ch'ang Hao. And he's a god; gods are patient. So you probably don't have to worry about him for a while."

Marla didn't answer. The Cornerstone was gone. She didn't have to worry about any of her enemies, really, except for Susan. Soon enough, Susan would cast her spell, and that would be the end of Marla. At least when she was erased from the world she would have no regrets. There wouldn't be anything left of Marla to do the regretting, not even a ghost.

"Those two pretty much wrecked the Tea Garden," B said after a while. "That's too bad. It was a really nice place."

"They'll rebuild it," Cole said. "That's the nature of San Francisco. Earthquake, fire, economic depression, titanic battles between gods, no matter what, it rises from the wreckage and lives on."

"Maybe it's not such a shithole quakemeat city, after all," Marla said.

20

Marla sat in one of the comfortable chairs in her hotel room, looking out at the night skyline, her feet propped up on the windowsill. She was smoking a clove cigarette for the first time in years, because for the first time in years she wasn't worried about cancer or diminishing her lung capacity.

The door opened, and she didn't bother to turn around, because even if it was an assassin, what did it matter?

"Marla," Cole said. He sat down on the edge of the bed behind her.

"Hey," she said. "How'd it go?"

"It went well. I performed the psychic transposition—what do you call it? The Doorstep trick?"

"The Thing on the Doorstep," Marla said. "A guy named H. P. Lovecraft wrote a story with that title, about a bad wizard who stole a girl's body. You should read it. The prose gets a little purple, but the story's a good one."

"Mmm," Cole said. "I'll look for it. At any rate, I put the apprentice's mind back in her own body.

Nearly all the necessary components were available in the Celestial's shop. He was still unconscious, deeply traumatized by seeing the spirits of his ancestors. Or the things he *thought* were the spirits of his ancestors. That friend of yours, B—he's powerful. I don't think he has any idea how powerful."

"What did you do with the Celestial?"

"We gave him to Ch'ang Hao to dispose of, though he didn't seem to relish the task, as his enemy was catatonic. Ch'ang Hao asked me to tell you that he looks forward to seeing you again."

"Not if I see him first," Marla muttered. But soon, no one would ever see her again, so it was a moot point. "Do me a favor. Teach B, would you? Unless you're going back to sleep."

"No. Not for a while. I want to enjoy being awake for a bit first. I suppose I can stay awake for a few years, and teach B what I can."

"Good," Marla said. "He's a good kid. I'd hate to see him go crazy or anything." Cole was as fine a seer as had ever lived, and his ways were not particularly violent, unlike Marla's. She was still troubled by the way she'd tried to turn B into a weapon to kill the Celestial, and proud of him for finding another solution. Cole would continue to lead him down the seer's path. "Even if I were going to be around to teach him, I wouldn't want to. The way I do things... that's not right for B."

"I understand," Cole said.

Marla gestured toward the window. "So who's going to run things in San Francisco now?"

"That's an open question. I do intend to go back to sleep in a few years, and I have no taste for leadership anyway. Several sorcerers fled, and they'll be coming back soon, I imagine . . . but they'll be a bit surprised when they do."

"Oh?"

"I've cast a spell so that they can't come back into the city at all. They'll reach the border and find themselves repelled. If they try to push their way in, they'll get sick, and if they become truly insistent, they will die. Let Oakland have them. They deserted San Francisco in her hour of need, and they will not be allowed back into her good graces."

"I approve," Marla said. She crossed her feet on the windowsill. "Where's Rondeau?"

"Ah." Cole squirmed. "I cannot say for sure, but I believe he is making love to the Celestial's apprentice, now that she is back in her proper form and feeling grateful for his assistance. He said something about giving Mr. Bowman a try after he finished with the apprentice."

Marla laughed. "Same old Rondeau. He didn't help the apprentice for the sex, but he's happy enough to take advantage of it." She sucked on her cigarette, tasted the smoke, exhaled. "So, Cole. You know lots of the old lore. I've been meaning to ask you, since the apocalyptic showdown this afternoon—is there some other way I can protect myself from Susan, now that the Cornerstone is gone?" She had to ask, but she knew the answer.

"Is there a way to keep the erasure spell from working on you? No, I don't think so. Not unless you can find one of the two remaining Cornerstones, which seems unlikely, given that your time is limited."

"That's what I figured," Marla said. She wondered

if she'd be able to get back to her own city before Susan made her disappear. It would be nice, if her last sight was of her own city. It might be heartbreaking, too, but there were some things so sad and wrong that it was only right to let your heart break over them. "I didn't think there was any other way."

"There's not a *magical* way, no," Cole said. "Though there is one thing you might try...."

"What?" Marla said, hearing the note of desperate hope in her own voice, and knowing it was justified; she was, perhaps, just a few hours away from ceasing to be, and if there was a better time to be desperately hopeful, she didn't know what it was.

"You might consider diplomacy. It has often worked for me, when all else failed."

Marla shook her head. "I don't think Susan's going to be willing to negotiate with me. She wants my job, and she knows she'll never get it as long as I'm alive."

"Do you think she would still refuse to negotiate if I offered my services as a mediator?" Cole said.

Marla turned her gaze from the window to look at Cole. "You'd do that?"

"Oh, yes. Though it will be a true negotiation— I'm not offering to settle this for you by making threats or taking action against her. But, given time, I could cast a spell on her that would make her plans to erase you seem a paltry thing." His voice was grim, and Marla appreciated it—she'd made a friend of him.

"What can I possibly offer Susan?" Marla said. "She wants my city. That's one thing I can never give her."

"Oh, I appreciate that. But if Susan is as formidable, smart, and capable as you say, then I believe there *is* something you can offer that she might accept." Cole turned, pointedly, and looked out the window, at the city glittering below and beyond on the hills. Marla looked with him.

"Cole," she said. "You're a genius."

"It's been said before, yet I never grow tired of hearing it. I was not much help in the fight, I know— battle has never been my forte—but I pride myself on finding elegant solutions to difficult problems."

"You're sure you don't mind?"

"The way you describe this Susan, I think she might be a tool suited to the task."

"The only drawback is that I don't get to kill her when it's all over," Marla said. This could actually work. Susan was pigheaded and proud, so it *might not* work, but there was a chance.

Marla reached out and touched Cole's hand. "You're the strangest sorcerer I've ever met. I don't know if it's because of the time you come from, or if it's just *you*, but...you're different. I've always thought being the best sorcerer meant being able to utterly overwhelm your enemies, being the toughest thug, but that's not the way you approach things at all, is it?"

"There are many reasons to become a sorcerer," Cole said. "Many, perhaps most, do it for the thrill of power, or to strike back at a world that made them feel powerless. But some become sorcerers because it's the best way in the world to protect the things you love." He shrugged. "If you have to give up the things you love to increase your power, then what's the point of having the power at all?"

Marla nodded. She thought about which kind of

sorcerer she was. The answer was not as clear to her as she might have hoped, but at least she'd finally thought to ask the question.

Susan entered the hotel's conference room in her usual elegant fashion. She was tall, lean, blond, perfectly attired. Sitting down with the grace of a cat, she inclined her head toward Sanford Cole. "It's a pleasure to meet you," she said. She looked at Marla, but pointedly said nothing.

Marla stared straight into Susan's eyes—the left one was green; the right one, blue—and smiled. "Good to see you, Sue. Thanks for coming all the way out west."

"Neutral ground seemed appropriate," Susan said. "I wouldn't have come, but Hamil assured me you were telling the truth, and that Sanford Cole did indeed wish to speak to me on your behalf."

Marla had to bite back a dozen responses. She wanted to accuse Susan of treason, betrayal, idiocy, low morals, and pretentiousness, but she forced herself to keep smiling. Susan really was good at what she did. Marla's city simply wasn't big enough for the both of them, any more than one anthill could have two queens.

"This is Bradley Bowman, Cole's apprentice," Marla said.

"A pleasure," B said, beaming. He was no longer an in-between creature, an ordinary plagued by visions; now he was an initiate, learning from the best. It wasn't an easy path, but it *was* a path.

And it probably didn't hurt his mood that he'd had

sex with Rondeau the night before, and probably this morning, if the sounds coming from the hotel room adjoining Marla's own were any indication.

"I enjoyed your films," Susan said to B, cool as cut glass.

"Susan," Cole said, getting to business. "You wish to erase Marla from reality in order take control of her city, yes?"

"That's right. I would run Felport far better, and since I know Marla will never step aside, I have no choice but to stage a coup. The fact that she could not prevent me from banishing her into nothingness without your intervention should serve to prove my qualifications, I think."

"The spell didn't work when you tried it yesterday," Marla said.

"Then you shouldn't mind if I try it again," Susan said. "I'll just go and do it now, shall I?"

"I don't think such a banishing will be necessary," Cole said. "I believe we may be able to reach an accommodation."

"Oh? Marla is willing to name me her successor and go into voluntary exile?"

"Hell, no," Marla said. "But how would you like to move out west and run San Francisco?"

Susan stared at her for a moment, then said, "That is not in your power to give."

Marla snorted. "Ever hear of right of conquest? Besides, Cole supports my claim."

"There have been major upheavals in the past few days," Cole said. "All the powerful sorcerers who used to live here are either dead—"

"I killed a couple of them myself," Marla said.

Cole went on as if she hadn't spoken. "—or have otherwise departed forever. The . . . precipitating situation has been contained, but a power vacuum has developed in the aftermath. I owe Marla greatly for her part in saving this city, and she has asked that I offer you the stewardship of San Francisco."

Susan frowned. "I have no wish to be your puppet, Cole."

Cole waved his hand vaguely. "I'm going to the Marin Headlands, across the Golden Gate, to train B, away from the distractions of the city. Once he has a better grasp of his powers, I'm going back to sleep for a few more decades. I have no interest in running San Francisco, and I will swear to the same under the auspices of any spell you choose. I may walk its streets and eat its food, and I will always admire its beauty and vibrance, but I will not try to control it. But *you* will swear to protect this city to the best of your ability, under the auspices of a spell of *my* choosing."

"Come on, Susan," Marla said. "Why would you want our dirty, industrial, blizzard-prone city when you could have the jewel of the West Coast? This isn't a lateral move, either. I think most people would agree that San Francisco is a step up from Felport. You said yourself, my city's a shithole."

"But *you* would rather rule Felport," Susan said.

"I love that city. It's where I've made my life. You've always said that if you took over Felport, you'd run out the heavy industry, gentrify downtown, try to bring in high-tech companies. Why go to all that trouble, when you can come here? Not that this place doesn't have its problems—I've never seen such shitty traffic, or so many homeless people, and the Mission is like an open-air latrine—but it's got all that world-class theater and art and music you're always going on about, too."

"This is the proposal on the table," Cole said. "Leave Marla alone, and you may take over San Francisco. The offer will, of course, be withdrawn if anything happens to Marla during our negotiations."

"All my contacts and associates are in Felport," Susan said, but she sounded uncertain, and Marla could taste the win.

"So bring 'em. Hell, you can be like a medieval queen, and give out lands to your worthy knights. Let your lieutenants run the different neighborhoods. It's a totally clean slate out here. Organize it any way you like."

"I will need time to consider your offer," Susan said.

Marla sat back and nodded. Susan always made a big deal of thinking things through, being careful, not rushing in, but she wanted this, Marla could tell. Susan had never liked Felport, had certainly never loved it, not the way Marla did. Circumstance and opportunity had brought her there, when she'd started out as the sorcerer Gregor's apprentice, before she'd surpassed him with her own skills. Control was the important thing for Susan, and the chance to control a major city would be too great a temptation for her—it would even overcome her animosity toward Marla.

"We'll meet again this evening, then," Cole said.

"I wish we hadn't had to give Susan anything," Rondeau said as he packed his bag that night, after the negotiations were finished, the bindings sworn, and power over San Francisco given to Susan. "She doesn't deserve this place. She'll be a better ruler than Mutex would have been, but that's about all I can say in her favor."

"Watch your mouth," Marla said. "You're talking about Her Highness, Queen of San Francisco. I hope she doesn't get swallowed by an earthquake. In the meantime, I had Hamil send over some guys to rob Susan's apartments and make it look like the Chupacabra boys did it."

"Sweet," Rondeau said. "She's got some great furniture." He glanced at her. "Of course, now that you aren't going to disappear, you've got Ch'ang Hao to worry about."

"I remember. But I'm used to worrying. It's my job."

Rondeau went to the window and looked out at the city. "I enjoyed this place," he said after a while. "I'm glad we came."

"Yeah," Marla said. "Me, too." She closed her suitcase. "Now let's get the hell out of here, and go back home where we belong."

"I get the window seat this time," Rondeau said.

ACKNOWLEDGMENTS

I suppose it's possible to write a novel in isolation, but it doesn't sound like much fun. For this book I got help from a lot of people. Thanks to Cameron "Dawson" Panee and Jenn Reese, for giving me advice on martial arts—any cool moves in the book are thanks to them, and anything incomprehensible or dumb is my fault. My regular writing group—Darrend Brown, David Ira Cleary, Lisa Goldstein, Susan Lee, and Lori Ann White—critiqued the early chapters and helped me adjust my approach and get a better start. Other kind first readers who gave me valuable suggestions include Christopher Barzak, Susan Marie Groppi, Michael J. Jasper, and Jay Lake. I also thank the attendees of the 2006 Blue Heaven writing workshop—William Shunn, Sandra McDonald, Paul Melko, Mary Turzillo, Tobias S. Buckell, Brenda Cooper, Greg van Eekhout, Catherine Morrison, Sarah Prineas, and Charles Coleman Finlay—who helped me celebrate and whoop it up when I got the news I'd sold this novel. Scott Seagroves and Lynne Raschke have my eternal gratitude for letting me visit them in Santa Cruz whenever I need to get away and recharge myself. My agent, Ginger Clark, as always, provided wonderful insight, especially in regard to character issues. My editor, Juliet Ulman, is a joy and a wonder to work with, and her editing makes me look good.

I'd also like to thank the city of San Francisco—which I like rather more than my protagonist, Marla, does—and to point you toward Tom Cole's *A Short History of San Francisco,* which provided me with many fine historical tidbits, some of which I even managed to use in the book. .

And, of course, the greatest credit goes to my spouse, H. L. Shaw, who makes my life worthwhile, and who is the greatest fan in the world of my Marla Mason stories.

ABOUT THE AUTHOR

T. A. Pratt lives in Oakland, California, with partner
H. L. Shaw, and works as a senior editor for a trade
publishing magazine.

Learn more about your favorite slightly wicked sorceress at www.MarlaMason.net.

CAN'T WAIT FOR MORE MARLA?

Read on for an exciting
excerpt of the next
Marla Mason adventure...

POISON SLEEP

Coming March 25, 2008 from
Bantam Spectra!

Poison Sleep
on sale March 25, 2008

Do not move. My name is Julian Kardec. I am a slow assassin."

Marla exhaled. No point trying to surprise this guy. If he was telling the truth, she was dead already. Slow assassins didn't fail. But... the whole point of a slow assassin was to create dread in the victim, and make her last days—or months or years—haunted and miserable. If the victim didn't know there was a slow assassin after her, she wouldn't be looking over her shoulder constantly, wondering when the inevitable strike would come, trying fruitlessly to escape her fate. Nobody had ever let Marla know she was marked. "You aren't here for me," she said. "What, then, for Rondeau? Are you shitting me? I can't believe he's ever pissed off anyone who could afford to hire *you*."

Kardec chuckled. "I am not here for either of you. We have received...inquiries...about you, Ms. Mason, but the price we set has so far been too extravagant for anyone to accept. There is some concern among the upper echelons of my organization that, if threatened, you might lead a foolhardy attack on us directly. We would not expect you to succeed, but you might make things uncomfortable for us. The price we set for you is accordingly quite high."

Marla didn't know whether to be flattered that the most accomplished group of hired killers in the world had such respect for her, or annoyed that more than one person had contacted them about putting a hit out on her. Actually, that was kind of flattering, too. "So if you aren't here for murder most foul, what do you want?"

The knife withdrew. He'd made his point, she supposed. She turned in her seat to face him. He was a mild-looking man of middle years, with thinning hair, dressed all in black. She expected the residue of a lookaway spell to sparkle around his edges, but there was nothing. He'd avoided being seen just by sitting very still and being one with the shadows. Any doubt Marla had about his identity dissolved. You had to be pretty badass to do a trick like that without magic, and it was the kind of thing the slow assassins taught. "I am the outreach coordinator for my organization," Kardec said. "I've come to you, in your capacity as a civic leader, to inform you of some activity in your city. I am here with a few of my colleagues to apprehend a criminal."

"Since when do you guys do law enforcement?"

He smiled, showing small perfect teeth. "We enforce the laws of our organization, of course."

The light dawned. "Ohhh. You've got a deserter, huh?" She'd heard about them—men and women who went into the slow assassins, learned some tricks of the trade, and then slipped away to freelance. The slow assassins didn't like that. Once you were in, you didn't leave alive. Marla had never heard of a deserter living more than a few months. The assassins weren't slow when it came to dealing with things like *that*.

"Yes. He calls himself Mr. Zealand."

Marla frowned. "I've heard of him. He's been working as a freelance hitter for a long time, Mr. Kardec. He's one of yours?"

"Oh, yes," Kardec said. "He is not some initiate who broke under the stress of the patience we require.

He completed our whole course with great aplomb, and took a twenty-year contract as his first."

Marla whistled. The slow assassins would stalk their victims for as long as the customer wanted, though of course the victims never knew how long they had. Six-month contracts weren't too expensive—more than a normal contract killing, but nothing mortgaging a nice house wouldn't cover—but the longer the term, the pricier it got. She couldn't imagine how much money it would take to hire a slow assassin to stalk a victim for twenty *years*. Even she probably couldn't afford it.

"At first," Kardec went on, "we thought he was engaged in his duty. He introduced himself to his victim, and pursued at a reasonable pace as the victim attempted to flee. But at some point...Mr. Zealand got bored. He began taking other contracts, secretly. Simple murders and assassinations. We don't approve of such moonlighting. Eventually his actions came to light, and we sent a crew to apprehend him." He frowned. "They were all killed. At that point, some dozen years ago, Mr. Zealand went completely rogue, abandoning his first target." Kardec shook his head. "Perhaps if we'd started him on something easier, a two-year contract, maybe...but who knows. Mr. Zealand likes killing, and has made a nice living doing so. We've been after him for years, but he is a hard man to catch, and, of course, he is very familiar with our techniques. But we finally had some good fortune. He was seen here in Felport by one of our operatives, an assassin who studied with him years ago. We don't know what he's doing, who his target is, or who has employed him, but we'll find out."

"You want me to get in touch if I hear anything?"

Kardec produced a business card and handed it over. "My cell number. Please do. But don't spread the word too far—we don't want to spook Mr. Zealand. I was more concerned with you...overreacting...if you noticed the presence of several dangerous individuals in your city." He smiled thinly. "We slow assassins have a reputation for disregarding local politics, and it's true that we fulfill our contracts above all other considerations, but we don't wish to cause any unnecessary trouble."

"Understood," Marla said. "Thanks for the heads-up. And next time you try to touch me, with a knife or anything else, you'll have a spurting stump where your hand used to be. And I'm not speaking metaphorically."

Kardec slipped out of the Bentley, walking swiftly away to disappear among the derelict train cars.

"This has been a crappy morning," Rondeau said, starting the car. "It's not fair that I've got a clogged toilet in my future, and you've got a beautiful man in yours."

Marla snorted. "I'm not going to see Joshua because he's pretty, Rondeau."

"Oh? I thought being pretty was the only thing he had to offer?"

Marla considered. "Touché," she said.

Snow flurries began as Marla strolled along the salted sidewalks. It was February, and winter wasn't through with Felport yet, not by a long way. Marla turned a corner, three blocks from Hamil's building, and saw a woman sprawled out in the snow near the base of an apartment house. The woman's thick caramel-colored hair obscured her face. She wasn't dressed for the weather, wearing jeans and a pale yellow blouse with only a black wool scarf as a concession to the elements. Her cheeks were rosy, and her dingy white tennis shoes had no laces. The woman's arms were extended in a Y over her head, and her legs were spread apart, as if she'd passed out in the midst of making a snow angel. But there was no snow around her body, just dead grass, as if all the snow had melted around her.

Marla knelt and touched the ground. Warm, but not hot. She studied the woman, watching her chest rise and fall and her eyelids flicker. Not dead, only dreaming. Could a fever be hot enough to melt snow and ice? If so, Marla should have felt the heat radiating from the woman, and she didn't. Was she some kind of pyromancer, then? Or hag-ridden by a now-hibernating fire demon? Marla consulted her mental clock and chewed her lip. She should look into this, have the woman checked out, but she didn't have time to do it herself. No one else in town knew about Joshua Kindler and his valuable power, but the longer he spent in town unrecruited, the greater the chance Gregor or Ernesto or some other sorcerer would discover his presence and make him an offer. She'd send Hamil to check out the woman after she got to his apartment.

"Sleep well," she said, rising. And then stopped. "Holy shit," she said. This woman was *sleeping*. Marla tried to remember what the woman in the photograph at the Blackwing Institute had looked like. It had been a shitty picture, blurry, but this woman was petite, she had that mass of hair, it *might* be her. "Hey," Marla said. "Is your name Genevieve Kelley? Are you . . . lost, hon?"

The woman moaned, a sound of deep distress, and Marla knelt again. "You okay?" she said, and touched the woman's cheek.

The street tilted around, and the sides of the surrounding buildings bulged out like the bodies of huge creatures taking deep breaths. Marla ducked her head and tried to grab the pavement, vertigo upending her sense of gravity. This was like falling through space, but the only movement was inside her head.

The woman opened her eyes—they were violet, the color of crushed flowers—and clenched Marla's hand. "His mouth," she said, her breath a hot wind on Marla's face. "His reeking mouth."

Marla fell backward, breaking contact with the woman and sitting hard in the snow. She looked around, bewildered, head pounding.

What happened? Why was she on the ground? Had she fainted? *That* had never happened before. She looked at the homeless woman lying on the grass. *I didn't even see her,* Marla thought. *Did I trip over her?* She stood and brushed snow from her coat. The woman before her shifted a little, her fingers fluttering as if grasping for something. Marla felt a twinge of pity mixed with disgust. A thin layer of snow had started to form on the woman's face. She'd be buried within an hour if she didn't move. Marla nudged her in the side with her booted foot, but the woman didn't respond. Sleeping off a drunk, probably. Marla sighed, took off her long coat, and put it over the woman's sleeping form. That would keep her from freezing to death, at least, and Marla had other ways of dealing with the cold. She'd walk back this way when she left Hamil's place, and if the woman was still there, Marla would call someone from a shelter to pick her up. She stepped around the woman and went on her way.

Z watched as she knelt to examine a woman sprawled in the snow. Quite the humanitarian. Suddenly, Marla fell backward in the snow, landing hard on her ass. She sat still, chin on her chest, eyes closed, for almost a full minute. Z inhaled and exhaled seven times while Marla sat unmoving. Very interesting. Was she narcoleptic? No one had mentioned that. A woman who fell unconscious on the street would not be difficult to kill, he thought.

Then she jerked, lifted her head, and looked around, confused. Z didn't breathe, because the puffs of his exhalations made small clouds of mist, and she might see them when she looked his way. Marla rose to her feet, draped her coat over the still-unconscious woman, and then walked on purposefully.

When Marla turned a corner, the assassin slipped out of the doorway silently and padded after her. As he passed, the sleeping woman stirred and sat up. She yawned and stretched, as if waking in her own warm bed, Marla's coat sliding down her body to puddle in her lap. She looked at him, frowned, and said, "You remind me of someone. No. Wait. I remind *you* of someone."

Hamil greeted Marla at the door of his vast apartment, his bulk filling the entire entryway as he beamed at her. Beads of perspiration glistened on the dark skin of his shaved head. He smiled broadly. Hamil was her consiglieri, her chief advisor and closest ally among

Felport's secret magical elite. Without his support, she would have been assassinated during her first year as chief sorcerer, though since then, she'd solidified her position by saving the city from destruction once or twice. He still helped smooth over the inevitable interpersonal conflicts, though. The powerful sorcerers in Felport were used to deference and respect, and Marla was lousy at faking such things. "You're sweating," Marla said as he stepped aside to let her in. She gasped as the heat of the apartment hit her. "It's sweltering in here, Hamil! God, doesn't all the fat on you keep you warm enough?"

"It's only eighty degrees here," Hamil said, shutting the door. "You just feel hotter because you've been outside in the cold."

Marla shook her head. "Eighty degrees? Why so warm?"

He shrugged. "I'm growing orchids. They like it hot during the day." He led her across the gleaming tile floor toward a long low table that took up most of a wall, with about twenty evenly spaced pots, each bearing a single flower, all different colors and shapes.

"I guess they're pretty enough," Marla said. "But I don't quite get the point of making a flower comfortable at the expense of your own comfort." She squinted. "But . . . ah. Sympathetic magic, right?"

Hamil nodded, gesturing for Marla to sit. She settled herself on his black leather couch and he lowered himself into a big club chair, specially made to accommodate his weight. His apartment was sleek, modern, and spare, everything her own place was *not*, which was why Marla preferred to take her meetings here.

"Growing orchids is very delicate, but the result is a beautiful flowering. I am involved in some, ah, other delicate negotiations, as you know, and by caring for the flowers, I've created a field of sympathetic resonance. As the flowers prosper, so will my other endeavors."

Marla laughed. Hamil looked like a giant bruiser, a movie version of gangsta street muscle, but in reality he was a master of delicate sympathetic magics. Marla could work a few sympathetic magic spells—burning effigies to create bad luck for her enemies, that sort of thing—but Hamil was an artist of the technique. Specialization had its benefits, though Marla preferred her own hodgepodge approach to magic, using a little bit of everything. She'd been called a brute-force-o-mancer, and a foul-rag-and-bone-shop sorceress, and though both terms were usually meant as insults, she supposed they were accurate enough. She preferred broad adaptability to niche expertise.

"You can meet with Mr. Kindler in my office, if you like," Hamil said. "The heat there is less oppressive. He should be along shortly. He called to say he was running late."

Marla grunted. "He'd better learn to be punctual if he wants to work for me."

"Oh, yes, I'm sure you'll be very stern with him," Hamil said. "It's not as if he has some supernatural power that makes people fall in love with him—oh, wait, he *does*. He's a Ganconer, Marla. I doubt even *you* would find it possible to speak sharply to a lovetalker."

"Whatever. You'll see. Besides, he's not a Ganconer, a Ganconer's a kind of *fairy*, and I'm not even convinced those things are real, despite what your crazy-ass friend Tom O'Bedbug says. Joshua Kindler was born of man and woman. He's no elf."

Hamil rolled his eyes. "Yes, yes. But we call his

kind lovetalkers and Ganconers for convenience, even though they can do more than seduce. Once upon a time we called his sort Charismatics, did you know that? A good name, but since the 1950s that word has acquired so many religious associations, it's mostly been abandoned." He glanced at his watch. "I hear from one of my street urchins that you rushed out to the countryside this morning. Any problems?"

Marla grunted. "Your little orphans have eyes everywhere, huh? Yeah, I went out to Blackwing. Dr. Husch has a runaway."

Hamil's eyes widened. "Not Jarrow? No, of course not, you wouldn't be sitting here so calmly if that were the case. Who, then?"

"Genevieve Kelley. She's a psychic, *maybe* a reweaver. She's been catatonic for a long time, but Jarrow woke her up while *trying* to escape, and Genevieve's gone wandering. I'm going to track her down before she gets hurt, or hurts anyone else."

"Do we have a description? I can put the word out."

Marla shrugged. "White lady, dark hair, petite. Wearing a yellow blouse and a black scarf...Wait." She frowned. "Strike that last. We don't know what she's wearing. Probably a nightgown. I don't know why I thought...huh. Funny. I have like this mental picture of her in yellow and black." She shook her head. "I'll have Rondeau send the picture over."

"I'll expect it to arrive in six to eight weeks then," Hamil said dryly. Marla grinned. Rondeau was not the most reliable courier. She really needed to hire a personal assistant. She groaned. "*And* I met a slow assassin this morning. There are a bunch of them in town looking for one of their wayward brothers."

She recounted her conversation with Kardec, and

Hamil clucked his tongue. "An eventful morning. I hope this Mr. Zealand isn't in town to eliminate anyone we know. Well, unless it's Gregor, that insufferable prig. I wouldn't shed any tears over him." His phone rang, and Hamil flipped it open and said, "Yes? Ah, yes Mr. Kindler, I'll buzz you in." He closed the phone. "Your beautiful boy is downstairs. Don't be too rough on him. I'm sure he's very delicate."

"Yeah, a precious flower who's always gotten his own way. A little jolt will do him good." She cracked her knuckles.

A few moments later the doorbell rang, and Hamil opened the door. "Do come in," he said, and Joshua Kindler entered.

Once she saw him, Marla couldn't stop looking. His slim hips, his pale eyes, his dark long eyelashes, his sweet lips, his copper-colored tousled hair, his beautiful hands, the entirety of him. Looking at him was like sipping brandy, like snuggling into down comforters, like soaking in a warm bath. Just the sight of him was sensual. The thought of touching him—it was enough to make her a little dizzy.

Fucking pheromones, she thought. *Or aura manipulation, or empathic projection, or however the hell it works.* She didn't usually *like* having her senses hijacked, which was why she avoided most drugs and only indulged sparingly in alcohol. "Mr. Kindler," she said, putting a lot of steel and razorwire into her voice. "If you're going to work for me, you're going to have to learn to be on *time.*"

He still stood in the open doorway. He looked shocked, and in his shock, he was beautiful. Marla wondered if she was the first person to ever see that expression on his face, or even the first to cause it.

"I haven't agreed to work for you yet," he said cautiously, "Ms. Mason. I've just come to hear you out."

Marla shrugged. "So come into Hamil's office, and we'll talk."

"If you don't mind, Marla, I'm going to make a few calls," Hamil said. He couldn't take his eyes off Joshua, either.

Marla gave her assent, and beckoned for Joshua to follow her. He moved like a cloud, and for the first time she noticed his clothes, perfectly white coat over an immaculate shirt and slacks. Most lovetalkers didn't bother to make themselves look good, trusting their magical attractiveness to win over anyone they encountered. Marla had met a few who were disgusting slobs, who took pleasure in their ability to seduce people even while picking their noses or sucking on foul cheap cigars. Joshua was different, special, more wonderful than the rest—

Ah, shit. His power was *strong*. She shut the door to the study and pointed to a chair in front of Hamil's desk. She plopped down in Hamil's huge executive chair, grateful to have the desk between them. She squelched the mental voice that lamented her choice of clothes, that wished she'd worn something more feminine than loose pants and a baggy shirt, after all her breasts were still pretty good, she'd been a topless waitress once upon a time, early thirties wasn't too old for him—a whole annoying line of insecure bullshit.

Joshua sat down, gentle as fog settling over the city.

"Let me get right to the point," Marla said.

"Please," he murmured, looking at her from beneath his long lashes, eyes fixed on hers. Marla thought of pictures she'd seen of Persian harem boys, bronze-skinned and slim with girlish lips, and thought *I'd like to kiss him all over*.

She leaned forward in her chair, counteracting her urge to lean back and stretch, catlike. "Occasionally I require certain services." He raised an eyebrow and smiled, and Marla blushed, much to her irritation. "Not the kind of services dried-up rich women cruising in Cadillacs ask you for, Joshua. I think you know that."

"I would never suggest such a thing," he said, quirking an amused smile. The look didn't even piss her off, and her failure to get angry *made* her angry. That whole emotional tangle only served to fluster her further.

She gritted her teeth for a moment, then spoke. "You're charming. Unusually so. People like you, *everybody* likes you, even I like you and I don't like anybody. I've been told that I can be a little abrasive, and I don't have a lot of patience for bullshit. My job sometimes requires a lot of diplomacy, and frankly, I don't have the skills for it. You do, and your skills could be very useful to me."

"I'm sure." He looked into her eyes. Marla wanted to pour wine down his chest and lick it off. "But I have to ask...why should I work for you when I can get anything I want just by asking for it?"

"Because if you're not bored with that kind of life already, you will be soon. I think you're too smart to enjoy drifting through life, getting everything handed to you on a silver platter. You came here to meet with me because it seemed like it could be interesting, right? I can promise you interesting times, Joshua."

He chewed thoughtfully on his thumbnail, a gesture Marla found unspeakably endearing. "I'm intrigued," he said. "All this is new to me, understand, sorcerers, mysterious societies, underworlds within underworlds...I used to think I was just very lucky, and likable. I believed no more in magic than anyone does. Your associate, Mr. Hamil, has shown me things I can't explain, and so I have no choice but to believe there is a whole secret side to the world I never imagined before. He tells me you are the most able guide to that world I am likely to encounter."

"So that's a yes?"

"Yes," Joshua said. "I think this could all be very interesting."

"Great," Marla said. She wanted to take him in her arms and welcome him into her family. "Come to the nightclub tomorrow morning, ten o'clock sharp, and we'll talk about your compensation, that sort of thing. Hamil will give you directions."

He rose and extended his hand. Marla hesitated. Could she take his hand without dropping to her knees and sucking his fingers? Fuck, yes she could. She'd once kicked a hound from the underworld across a room. She'd killed Somerset, one of the most infamous sorcerers of all time. She'd apprehended the Belly Killer, and outsmarted *both* Roger Vaughs. She could control herself around a pretty boy.

Marla shook his hand, firmly. "Remember, ten o'clock. And don't be late, or the deal's off the table. You're not the only beautiful boy in the world." She came around the desk and left the room without giving him another glance.

Hamil sat reading in his chair, and looked up when she emerged. "That was quick," he said. "Did you charm him?"

"He's in," she said. "Tell him how to get to the club."